The Light in the Mirror

The Light in the Mirror

a novel

DAVID LANE

RESOURCE *Publications* • Eugene, Oregon

THE LIGHT IN THE MIRROR

Resource Publications
An Imprint of Wipf and Stock Publishers
199 W. 8th Ave., Suite 3
Eugene, OR 97401

www.wipfandstock.com

ISBN 13: 978-1-61097-275-8

Manufactured in the U.S.A.

ACKNOWLEDGMENTS

M Y GRATITUDE TO DOREEN Button, who went through the manuscript line by line, suggesting changes and enhancing style carefully and skillfully.

Thanks to Carla Aydelott for her help in typing various drafts of the manuscript, with excellent attention to accuracy.

I'm grateful to my mother, Janis K. Lane, who encouraged me and made helpful observations about the 1960s and 1970s.

Thanks also to my father, Dr. LeRoy L. Lane, for suggestions on revising several chapters, and for giving me a loving push when I needed it.

My brother, Jeff Lane, shared useful memories of the 1960s and 1970s and cheered me on in my writing.

Special thanks to Detective Sergeant Terry Fitzpatric, who advised me on police procedures in investigating a crime.

My thanks to former mayor, Jeff Miller. He provided information on mayoral candidacy and duties of a mayor.

I'm grateful to Dr. Thomas K. Wuest, orthopedic center administrator and orthopedic surgeon, for reading chapters dealing with medical procedures and providing helpful comments.

Thanks to Dr. George Knox for providing information on Scottish pronunciation, language, and culture, based on his travels in Scotland.

Thanks also to Tim Aho for information on Scottish vocabulary and accent, learned while living in England.

The following Passage inspired this story.

For we know in part, and
we prophesy in part; but
when the perfect comes,
the partial will be done away.
When I was a child, I used
to speak as a child, think as
a child, reason as a child;
when I became a man,
I did away with childish
things. For now we see
in a mirror dimly, but
then face to face; now
I know in part, but then
I shall know fully just as
I also have been fully known.
       I Corinthians 13:9–12

1

A Near Tragedy

"Yow!" Richard Hawkins let loose a yelp from the abrupt change in water temperature.

"Uncle Mac must be working in the kitchen. Well, that woke me up. Guess I'll forego my morning solo."

After showering, he toweled vigorously, put on shorts and slippers, and headed down the hall to his bedroom. He surveyed the image in his full-length mirror. Richard's high forehead, hazel eyes, and strong jaw reflected his naturally serious attitude toward life.

He gave his mustache a couple of strokes with the comb, then moved to the chest of drawers. Slapping a generous amount of shaving lotion on his face, he mused, "Even if I don't look like I've shaved, I might as well smell like I have."

Downstairs, Richard found his uncle in the kitchen preparing their breakfast of Quaker Oats. Richard helped by making toast and pouring orange juice. There was little conversation. Uncle Mac had raised Richard; their relationship was as secure in silence as it was in speech.

When Richard finished eating, he sat back, sipped his coffee, and gave his uncle an affectionate glance. Uncle Mac was busy at his morning ritual, working the daily crossword puzzle.

"Finished in 14 minutes." Uncle Mac's voice conveyed his satisfaction.

Richard responded teasingly, "Considering your years as a top librarian, a newspaper crossword puzzle is as challenging as high school algebra is for Einstein."

Uncle Mac chuckled, pleased with the comparison. Changing the subject, the Glasgow native said, 'If ye don't want Quaker Oats for dinner too, ye'll have to go to the store and get a few things.'

"Just a few? In that case, I'll walk. What do we need?"

Uncle Mac handed him a short list.

"I'm on my way."

Richard liked puzzling over something when he walked. Today, as he walked the five blocks to the grocery store, he thought about how long it would take him and a friend to paint his Uncle Mac's house.

Now, how could I convince Uncle Mac to give the old place some color? He'll insist on painting the house gray again. He smiled as he recalled how his uncle defended the color gray. "You see, laddie, the color matches Oregon's climate."

At that moment, Richard looked up to see a squirrel, frightened by his approach, dart across his path and into the street.

"Stupid squired!" he exclaimed, as a car came within inches of hitting the animal.

Maybe, I could get Uncle Mac to at least change the trim from boring white. But, no, he's stubborn like me.

As if to prove his own stubbornness, his mind flashed back to an incident that, years later, still made him feel ashamed. Often during his teenage years, his uncle would press him to take up golf. The theme of his insistence was always the same: Golf was good exercise and it would enable him to meet people who could help him land a job some day. "No, that's not my thing," Richard would reply.

He slowed his pace and kicked a pine cone off the sidewalk, reluctant to remember what happened on his sixteenth birthday. The memories intruded nevertheless.

Uncle Mac had bought him an expensive set of clubs. Weeks went by while he stubbornly refused to try the clubs out at the local golf course. Then one day, he traded the clubs to a friend for an old pair of skis. He rationalized that he should have what he wanted on his birthday and he didn't want golf clubs.

When he told his uncle about the trade he realized that it hurt his feelings, but his uncle only said, "Your friend got a gude bargain." Uncle Mac never mentioned golf again. Though Richard knew his uncle had forgiven him, he still felt guilty.

Trying to shake off the mood his memory had created, his mind quickly turned to the task at hand as the grocery store came into view.

The sky had gone from sunny to overcast in the time that Richard Hawkins took to finish shopping. As he stepped out of the store, he felt the early-warning drops of a spring shower. He had lived long enough in Verity, Oregon—all of his life—not to be surprised at sudden changes in the weather. The old-timers in his church had told him that 1999 would be a rainy year, and so far their prediction had been correct. Lines from Lowell's *The Vision of Sir Launfal* came to mind: *What is so rare as a day in June?/ Then, if ever, come perfect days.*

Ducking his head against the drizzle, he glanced up when he came to a street corner. As he was about to cross, he saw a young woman coming toward him on the sidewalk, about 150 feet away. Dressed in shorts and a T-shirt, she was jogging in the rain. *Someone else caught in this drizzle.* He looked more closely at the attractive runner. Her shapely, athletic body and her blond ponytail flying behind her presented a captivating picture.

When a white van pulled up alongside the woman, a man on the passenger side yelled something out his window at her. She stopped running and walked over to talk with him; she pointed down the street as if giving directions. As she spoke, the side door of the van unexpectedly slid open. Another man grabbed her, attempting to pull her into the van. The young woman resisted, striking him. As the two struggled, the woman kicked her attacker. He released his grip, but before she could get away the other man grabbed her. She screamed for help.

Richard dropped his grocery sack and sprinted to the van just as the men had nearly pulled the woman inside. He planted his fist against the face of the man, who was leaning out the door. The sudden crunch of knuckles to nose elicited a pain-filled expletive. Richard pulled the woman back out of the van at the same time that she planted her knee in the chest of the man who still had her in his grip. Their combined efforts freed her. The abduction thwarted, one of the men slammed the van door closed and they drove away with such reckless speed, they nearly hit an oncoming car.

"Are you alright? Did they hurt you?" Richard asked the young woman. She shook her head, but didn't speak. She leaned heavily on Richard's arm. One sleeve of her T-shirt, torn in the struggle, hung down her arm by a thread. He led her to a nearby bus-stop bench and watched her for a moment to be sure he could leave her to retrieve his damp grocery sack. As he started back toward the young woman, a police car pulled up to the curb with another right behind it.

"Did you see what happened?" the officer asked him.

"Yes, I did. I saw the whole thing. Two men in a white van tried to kidnap that girl on the bench over there." He pointed. "I think she's in a state of shock. She hasn't said anything since it happened."

"I'll be careful when I talk to her. The other officer will want to speak with you, sir. Just remain here." She walked toward the young woman.

Richard put down the grocery sack again. As he straightened, he saw the other officer approaching. Though slightly shorter than Richard's six-foot frame, he had the same slender, muscular build.

"A man in a house across the street saw what seemed to be an altercation and called us. The caller first assumed it to be a domestic argument. Can you describe what happened, sir?"

Richard repeated what he had told the other officer, but he could not give the make, model, or year of the van. "It all happened so fast," he explained. When asked if he noticed anything unusual about the van, he replied, "Well, it had a couple of bumper stickers. One said: 'Question Authority'. Is that helpful?"

"It might be, sir. I need your name, address, phone number, and date of birth."

"My 'date of birth'?" Richard questioned. "Why do you need that?"

"It's not that we plan to send you a birthday card," said the officer with a smile, "but you may not be the only Richard Hawkins in this part of Oregon."

"Oh, I see," Richard responded grinning, and gave the officer the requested information.

"Mr. Hawkins, I take it you'd be willing to help us try to identify these men, in the event we bring in suspects."

"Sure. Of course."

"The young woman can be grateful that you acted as fast as you did, Mr. Hawkins. You may have saved her life."

Since Richard was only a couple of blocks from his house, he declined the officer's offer of a ride home. He noticed with satisfaction that the young runner was talking, as the policewoman helped her into the squad car.

Richard picked up his pace as he headed for home, glad the rain hadn't spoiled any of his groceries. A sprinkling of drops promised another shower.

He ran up the steps of the two-story house's wide front porch.

When Richard entered the front door, he saw his uncle watching a newscast in the living room. Richard believed that most news programs made a special effort to create as gloomy a picture of events as possible. He was suddenly reminded of Eeyore in the Winnie-the-Pooh stories, who always saw the negative side of things. *An Eeyore Award could be given to the most depressing newscaster of the year.*

Mac got up from his chair to greet his nephew.

"It's gey dreich the day!" he said, pouring on the Scottish accent.

"Yes," Richard replied. "The day *is* dreary."

"I was beginin' to worry aboot ye. Ye were gone so long at the store."

"I'm sorry I worried you, Uncle. Would you believe that I had to help a damsel in distress?" he asked.

"I don't doubt ye cured some damsel's loneliness by your attention."

"Have it your own way, Uncle." Richard smiled to himself.

"Let's see what ye brought home, laddie."

"Oh, ye bought pickles too!"

"I thought you might like to have some," said Richard with a twinkle in his eyes, knowing this to be an understatement.

"Ye thought right, my boy!"

"I suppose you'll want to sample the pickles at dinner tonight, Uncle. I'll open the jar for you."

2

Recalling the Dead

THAT EVENING, THE TWO men sat down to dinner in their little dining room. It was Mac's turn to cook, and he had selected a menu
of tossed green salad, and spaghetti with meatballs. Complimenting his
own culinary skill, Mac said, "It's a really tasty salad, so it is."

"Yes, Uncle, it's very good." Richard's mind, however, was not on
the food. While he was eating salad, something was eating *him*. He was
waiting for the right time to bring up a subject that he'd been thinking
about for some time. Finally, when Mac served the dessert of fresh-baked
scones, Richard summoned the courage to say, "Uncle Mac, I've wanted
to ask you something for a long time."

"Yes, Richard?" Mac answered between bites. Richard's manner indicated the lad had something serious on his mind. Mac stopped eating,
and lowered his fork.

After a slight pause, Richard replied, "All the years I've known you
Uncle . . . you've never said much about my parents or my brother and
sister."

Mac looked uneasy for a moment in response to Richard's interest,
then let out a sigh and appeared to relax.

"I know they died in a car accident," Richard continued, "but you
never told me how it happened. I wish you'd tell me more about my
mother and father and my sister and brother—I mean . . . the kind of
people they were. And I thought . . . that uh, well, you could . . ."

"Aye, my boy," interrupted Mac sympathetically. "I understand. It's
natural that ye should want to hear aboot your mither and father—how

6

they lived and died. I suppose I should have told ye sooner. It's a wee bit hard to talk about, so I've been puttin' it off," Mac explained.

Richard nodded. He looked intently at his uncle, his keen interest obvious.

"Your mom was a virtuous woman. She was always lookin' for ways to see ithers awright."

"You mean, my mother was always ready to help others get what they needed?"

"My very words, Richard. Some women collect teapots, dolls, or jewelry. Your mom collected people in trouble. She was truly one o' God's helpers. Your mom was a gude Christian—I think I told ye that."

Richard nodded.

"God rest her soul, your mom had wisdom and wit beyond her years. Mary's way with words was all her own. One time she said, 'God gave us children so we adults would grow up.' Once newlyweds asked her why married couples had so many fights. She replied, 'It's not so many fights if ye don't keep count.'"

Richard chuckled at his mother's wit and wisdom.

"Mary dinna have a college education like ye have Richard, but she was always a reader. It made her thoughtful. I remember she told me once, 'When we leave God out o' our plans, we plan only for today. But with God in mind, we see beyond today.' I've tried to keep that in mind over the years. One time in a conversation with your dad and me, she said, 'Character is what we are, when no one's lookin'.' Mary liked talkin' with people who needed to do somethin' with their lives."

"It sounds like my mom had a lot of good qualities."

"That she did, laddie; that she did. She was one o' a kind. And so was your dad."

"You told me that my father was a college professor, who taught communication," said Richard.

"That's right. And like your mither, he was a gude Christian, who lived his faith—as your mom would say—'even when nobody was lookin'."

"What else do you remember about my father?"

"Well," began Mac, "he was very particular aboot how his classes were taught, so he was. Your dad always was glad to make the extra effort for the slow student. So while he expected a lot, he also gave a lot. He dinna lower his standards. He raised students to meet them."

"Hmmm," said Richard thoughtfully. He was remembering classes that he'd taken that needed an extra effort he didn't give. He resolved to give it in future classes, if he should decide to work on another degree.

"That's really how your dad and I got to be gude friends, and not just brothers-in-law. Bein' a teacher, he needed to have new information regularly. Since I was a relative and a librarian it was only natural that he'd come to me for help. He needed to do research from time to time, and I assisted him. Sometimes it was for a lecture and sometimes for a book he was writin'. As a matter o' fact, he and I were writin' a book together. I valued your father's friendship very much. We were workin' on the book when . . . when the accident happened. In those days, your family lived several miles outside o' Portland, where your father taught. And I lived only aboot a mile from them. One night, they invited me over for a small family party—I canna remember the occasion. Everyone was laughin' and havin' a gude time when suddenly your mom said that she needed to lie doon—she wis nearly nine months pregnant with ye. The next thing I knew your dad came rushin' out o' the bedroom, sayin' that he had to take your mom to the hospital. She thought the baby was comin' early. So, your parents and brother and sister hurried into the car and pulled out o' . . . the driveway."

"Why did my brother and sister go?"

"Because it was summer; Kathy dinna have school and Roger was between jobs. They planned to stay with friends in Portland, while your mither was in the hospital."

Mac's voice dropped. "That was the last time I saw them alive."

"Your dad had called your mom's doctor to meet them at the hospital. That stretch o' road in those days dinna have much traffic and so your dad could have driven top speed. As he moved into an intersection just outside Portland, a big tractor-trailer rig hit them broadside . . . the driver was speedin' . . . he was drunk. A woman in a nearby farmhouse heard the crash and went to investigate. By the time she arrived on the scene, a young man in a sports car had stopped. She ran back to the house to call for an ambulance and the police. While she was gone, the young man managed to get the car door open on your dad's side and found your dad was dead. Your brother, sittin' next to him, lived just long enough to ask aboot your sister. Your sister died in the ambulance on the way to the hospital; she never recovered consciousness. Your mither died a few hours after the doctor took ye by Caesarean section. Her last words were, 'Is my baby awright?' The nurse thought your mither heard her answer that ye were fine."

"What about the drunken truck driver?" asked Richard, his voice tinged with anger.

"*He* wasn't hurt very badly—a broken arm and some bruises," Mac answered somewhat bitterly. "He didn't even go to jail for what he'd done."

"He killed my *whole* family," Richard said, both rage and sadness in his voice.

"Yes, Richard, I understand how ye feel, my boy."

"I hope every day of his life he thinks about how he killed four people, because he didn't care that he wasn't fit to drive. I hope he can never drink enough to forget."

"I don't know if I said this before, but I *did* have an uneasy feelin' when they went rushin' out o' the house to take your mom to the hospital. I've thought many times since then I should have stopped them and told them to be careful. If I'd delayed them just a *few* minutes, the truck would have passed through the intersection before your parents' car got there. And then there wouldn't have been the accident, and your family would . . . still be alive."

Richard never realized before that his uncle felt guilty about the accident—that he felt he could have done something to prevent the deaths of his parents and siblings. Taking God's sovereignty onto his own shoulders was a heavy burden his uncle didn't need to bear.

"Uncle, it sounds like it would have been impossible to slow my parents down, even if you'd tried. After all, they had to get to the hospital many miles away, as soon as they could."

"Thank ye laddie, for your comfortin' words . . . that terrible night was twenty-four years ago. Hardly a day goes by that I don't think on it. And I've been takin' care o' ye ever since; in your early years with the help o' a housekeeper. Ye remember how Mrs. Tolliver took care o' ye 'til ye were fourteen years old."

"Oh yes, Uncle, Mrs. Tolliver was very kind to me." Thinking again about his lost siblings, Richard asked, "What were my brother and sister like?"

"Well," answered Mac, your sister was a darlin' lady with bright red hair. She was a gentle soul, like your mom. I remember she liked to tease a lot. Cathy was devout in her Christian beliefs. She taught Sunday

School, and served as a volunteer, helpin' disabled children. She was just startin' her senior year o' high school, and she was smart. She planned to go to college and major in English. As I recall, she had this dream o' one day becomin' a writer. Her favorite authors, she used to say, were Jane Austen and Madeleine L'Engle." Mac's voice dropped. Almost as if he were talking to himself, he said, "Sadly . . . she never got the chance to fulfill her dream."

Richard interrupted the silence that followed his uncle's words. "What about my *brother*?"

"Yes, your brother Roger," replied Mac, nodding and smiling. "Even though he struggled a wee bit here and there, he was a gude lad. I can still hear your dad braggin' aboot how well he played basketball. This was when he was in high school. He loved sports and was gude in all o' them, as I recall."

"Was Roger a good student in school?" Richard asked.

"Roger dinna take to studies very well," Mac responded. "He had some trouble findin' himself after he graduated. He would stay with a job a couple o' months and, when he'd start to get somewhere, he'd up and quit. Your mom and dad worried aboot him."

"I bet mom and dad worried a lot about him when the Vietnam War came along."

"Yes. Roger was eighteen, the right age—or the wrong age, however ye want to look at it—to be drafted. He went into the Army and after his trainin', was sent to Vietnam—into the thick o' the fightin'."

"Did you notice if the war changed him very much?"

"I never really heard how the war affected his outlook on life. As ye know, Richard, he came back after aboot a year with one leg gone."

Mac stood up from the table and pointed below the knee of his left leg. "He wore an artificial leg from here doon," Mac said softly.

Richard looked down at his left leg and patted it. "I don't know how I would have taken the loss of my leg. I hope I would have been as brave as Roger."

"I never heard him complain or indulge in self-pity, even when he could only watch certain sports, instead o' participatin' in them as he once did. Your mom told me that he packed away all o' his trophies in his room—I guess they were too much a reminder o' earlier days when he excelled in basketball and track."

"Did Roger feel bitter about the war, do you think?"

"I don't think he felt bitter aboot the war. But he dinna understand why people looked doon on him for answerin' the call to serve."

"People weren't rude to him, were they?"

"When Roger first came home he walked with a cane. On one occasion, he was walkin' downtown with his cane and a young man came up to him and asked him if he'd lost his leg in the war. And when he replied he had, the man said, 'Got what ye deserved.'"

"Poor Roger. That kind of treatment must have been hard to take."

"The man who went to war liked to laugh. The man who returned rarely did. Your sister could get him to laugh a wee bit."

"What did my brother look like? Do I look much like him?"

"Ye don't favor your brother . . . very much." Mac looked closely at Richard and then squinted into space, as if he were forming an image of Roger from memory. "While you're tall and slender, Roger was stocky and muscular in build. His hair was dark broon like yours, and his eyes were blue like your father's, while yours are hazel like my dear Kathleen's and your mither Mary's. His face was rounder than yours. Ye both were born with the Hawkins' chin—square jaw with a cleft. He dinna have a mustache as ye do; he had a beard for a while after he returned from Vietnam. And one more thing, like ye, he had a slow smile; as if he had to think aboot it first.

At this point, Mac sat back in his chair, lethargically stirring the half-filled cup of tea in front of him. His mind was on the events that led up to the accident that had taken away some of the dearest people in his life.

"Well, I guess I might as well clear the table," Richard said. He saw that his words interrupted his uncle's thoughts about the past.

"What? Oh, the dishes. Aye. Ye don't have to do that. I believe it's my turn."

Richard got up and picked up his plate. "You made dinner; why don't you let *me* take care of the dishes tonight. Then you can watch one of your favorite TV shows—the *Boston Pops* is on."

"Well, okay if ye're sure." Mac went into the living room, and settled himself before the TV.

3

A Pleasant Interruption

RINSING DISHES IN TIME with a Viennese waltz, Richard was about finished when the phone rang.

"I'll get it!" yelled Mac.

Richard heard his uncle say, "He canna come to the phone right now. Can I take a message?"

"Uncle Mac, I can take it!" Richard yelled.

"It's a lassie on the line. A bonny lass I bet."

"Hello. This is Richard Hawkins."

"Richard, this is Melissa Ingram. You rescued me from those men in the van today. The policewoman gave me your name and phone number. I'm not calling at a bad time, am I?"

"No, not at all, Melissa. How are you? I hope you had no bad effects from your experience."

"Yes, one bad effect."

"Oh . . . may I ask what?"

"*Embarrassment.* I'm embarrassed, because I never thanked you for coming to my rescue. Those men . . . were . . . I don't know who they were. But it's clear they wanted to hurt me. Who knows what they would have done? But for you, they would . . ."

Richard could hear Melissa's voice choke up. Soon he could hear her crying.

"I'm sorry, Richard . . . just . . . give me a minute. I'm sorry . . . to lose . . . control this way."

"That's okay, Melissa. Take your time. I can wait."

Soon the sobbing at the other end of the line lessened. Richard heard Melissa ask someone for a handkerchief.

"I'm all right now. I told myself that I wouldn't lose control. But, here I go, crying in your ear."

"You have every right to feel upset in thinking about those two men."

"But, they're not the reason I was crying. I was crying because . . . of *you*."

"Crying because of *me*?" Richard had often wished that he had a mother and sister to teach him about women. Though his occasional confusion didn't diminish his interest.

"Every time I think about what you did for me . . . the gratitude I feel overwhelms me. I owe you so much."

Now it was Richard's turn to be embarrassed. He had always found it difficult to take praise. He never knew what to say. "I'm glad the Lord put me there to help." As Richard said that, he wondered if Melissa would understand what he meant. The words came out before he realized Melissa might not be a fellow believer.

"I'm glad He did, too." She continued, "My parents would like to meet you, Richard. I believe they want to thank you for saving their only child. I promise they won't get emotional—and I promise not to also—but it would mean a lot to them if you would let them invite you over for dinner. Of course, I'd be there, too."

"Well, sure, that would be nice." Melissa's last words prompted a quick response of agreement from Richard. Seeing the attractive runner again in better circumstances was a pleasant prospect.

Richard and Melissa agreed on a date and time, and said their good-byes.

During the phone conversation, Mac had gone to the kitchen to finish cleaning up. When he walked back to the living room, he found Richard smiling to himself and humming a little tune.

"A bonny lass?" asked Mac.

"A bonny lass, Uncle. My damsel in distress."

The Scot patted his nephew on the shoulder.

"Well, I'm off to my bed, Richard. I'm feelin' a bit tired."

As Mac headed for his room, Richard heard him quoting lines from Robert Burns. His uncle often found occasion to share lines from his favorite poet.

"Ay waukin, O,/Waukin still and weary:/Sleep Ah can get nane,/Fur thinkin' o' my Dearie."

4

Dividing of Time

"OUCH!" RICHARD BELLOWED AS he danced around on one foot. Clad only in a sock, his other foot had come down hard on a nailhead protruding from one of the old porch floorboards.

"I guess city boys are supposed to wear shoes," he muttered to himself.

As the pain subsided, Richard eased himself into the Adirondack chair that stood guard, and planted his feet on the railing, and sipped the coffee from the mug he'd placed on the chair arm. He watched a gray squirrel dig at the base of the 40-foot slippery elm that dominated the front yard. The early-morning sunshine—making amends for yesterday's rain—promised a beautiful day.

"It's gude to see ye relaxin' and takin' time to appreciate God's creatures, laddie," said Mac, making an appearance on the porch.

Richard glanced up, smiling, "Uncle, do you have squirrels in Scotland?"

Richard didn't see the mischievous smile flicker across his uncle's face. "No, no squirrels in Scotland are awaitin' my return. But the countryside has plenty o' them."

Richard, used to Mac's teasing, chuckled at the thought of his uncle keeping squirrels in Scotland. "I thought the Scots raised squirrels to save money on food." In spite of Mac's innate generosity, Richard liked to kid his uncle about Scots being thrifty.

"What a scunner!" snorted Mac in a tone of pretended disgust. "I'll have ye know that Scots make better use o' squirrels than that. We train them to go up in trees and gather nuts by the bushel. It's an amazin' sight to watch these creatures puttin' choice nuts into a sack tied to their necks. And when they get too old to climb, the Scots teach them to sweep porches and walkways with their tails."

Richard laughed and shook his head in acknowledgement of Mac's superior "gift o' the gab." When Mac failed to embroider his story, as he customarily did, Richard turned in his chair to look at him. He saw that his uncle was staring at the neighbor's yard across the street.

"Those poor roses over there," said Mac sadly. "Mr. Galiger simply doesn't know the first thing aboot roses. He prunes them as if he's prunin' a mulberry bush."

"How should he prune them, Uncle?"

"With roses, ye must prune from the inside out, so that the plant grows up and out." Mac extended his arms outward above his head to describe this desirable growth. "He prunes from the outside in, and cuts branches too far above the joint; he leaves stumps where disease and bugs can attack the plant."

"Why don't you tell Mr. Galiger how to prune? He can see how good *your* roses look."

"Di' ye think my head buttons up at the back, laddie?" Mac patted the back of his head. "I canna think o' a better way o' upsettin' a neighbor than to tell him how to grow his roses. No. I must be patient and wait 'til he asks my help, which I would gladly give."

"When do you think Mr. Galiger will come to you for help?" Richard couldn't picture their neighbor, who was always in a hurry, taking time to learn how to tend his roses.

"Well, my boy, when the time is right. Remember, 'To everythin' there is a season, and a time to every purpose under heaven,' includin', 'a time to keep silent and a time to speak.' It's natural when ye're young, laddie, to want to hurry time; waitin' becomes painful. And when ye're older, ye want to slow time doon, and waitin' then has a meanin' o' its own."

"Well, yes, it's true, Uncle. I hate waiting to do something. I mean if it's something that needs doing, I want to do it *now*. Speaking about time reminds me, I need to start looking for a summer job. After all, I'm not independently wealthy."

"Ye may not be 'independently wealthy,' but your folks' estate has enough left to pay your way through graduate school. In the meantime, ye don't have to worry aboot expenses. I've enough money for both o' us. Say, why don't ye do somethin' for fun today and maybe later we can watch a video or play some draughts."

"Draughts? Oh, you mean checkers. Sure. Maybe if we played more often I'd remember. Why don't Scottish people just say checkers?"

"I can tell ye, the Scots wonder why Americans don't just say draughts."

"Touché! My old professor Hans Leitner would call my comment ethnocentric. But he doesn't need to learn to say *draughts*."

Further inactivity encouraged by his uncle, Richard followed the Scot back into the house, careful to avoid the offending nail. Going to his room, Richard selected a book from the well-filled bookcase. He'd purchased *The Eternal Path* a month ago for a time of leisure like the present. The book gave a fictional account of the fight to return prayer to public schools. On the way back to the porch, he grabbed a sofa pillow to make the wooden patio chair more comfortable.

Later, Mac insisted that Richard continue reading while he prepared lunch—coffee and sandwiches, with ice cream for dessert—which they ate together on the porch.

"Thanks for the lunch, Uncle. You can't beat cheese on rye. Say, you know Brent, my friend from the university? He lent me a movie weeks ago. I really should watch it and return it. Would you like to see it? It's called *The Time Machine*—a science fiction film, made in 1960, the box says."

"Let me tidy up the kitchen a wee bit and we'll see what Hollywood did with H.G. Wells' story."

"Oh, have you read the book?"

"Yes, laddie. It was Wells' first novel, and it brought him instant success. Published in 1895, I think. Wells was wise to make one o' his characters, David Philbey, a Scotsman. This character personifies one o' the traits o' true friendship, *loyalty*. After *The Time Machine*, he wrote more books, at least 100. But the more interestin' ones predicted future scientific inventions that seemed to materialize."

"What did Wells ever predict that came true, Uncle?"

"Ye can decide that for yourself. Read his book *The War o' the Worlds*, which he wrote in 1898 and see if he correctly envisioned modern warfare."

"How do you know so much about H. G. Wells?"

"Ye forget, I spent a gude part o' my life in libraries, as a librarian and as a lover o' books."

While Mac put things away in the kitchen, Richard found the video and waited for his uncle. When Mac finally appeared, he was carrying a big bowl of fresh popcorn.

"Show time!" announced Richard, as he inserted a cassette into the VCR. Then he sat on the floor, close to the popcorn.

The film began silently, showing dark, eerie images of various time-pieces. A sundial appeared out of the darkness. Then small clocks came into view, followed by larger clocks. Finally, came the largest clock of them all, Big Ben. The chimes of the great London clock coincided with the onset of thunder and lightning, which seemed to carry an ominous warning. Then orchestral theme music filled the room, as credits flashed across the screen.

Richard and Mac both became engrossed in the movie; it combined romance and adventure in the typical Wells' fashion. The main character, George, time-traveled into the remote future and returned to tell his housekeeper and four friends what he'd discovered. Centuries into the future, he found a very different Earth from the one he left behind. Decades of war had devastated the planet. Two races of human beings emerged, one living above ground and the other below ground. George described the above-ground beings, the Eloi, as handsome, docile, and ignorant, and the below-ground beings, the Morlocks, as monstrous, aggressive, and ignorant. The Morlocks controlled and preyed on the Eloi. George told his friends how he had taught the Eloi to defend themselves against the Morlocks. At the close of the film, George indicated his intention to return to the future to help the Eloi to rediscover the noble ideas and truths of the past that had made humanity humane.

Richard wondered. If H. G. Wells could view our present world, would he see the beginnings of the fictional world of the future he'd imagined? The last scene of the film left him pondering the possibility of time travel. Yesterday's science fiction often becomes tomorrow's scientific truth. But *time* travel? Not even Einstein's space-time continuum made that sound possible.

"Uncle Mac, do you think we will ever be able to travel in time?

"My boy, we can travel in time *now*. Our memory can take us into the past and we can see how it affects the present. And we can ride our imagination into the future, and see what consequences might follow our actions. But it takes more courage for that kind o' time travel than the kind H. G. Wells had in mind. For it isn't the Morlocks we must face, it's ourselves."

Mac's unexpected response drew Richard into a thoughtful silence.

"I enjoyed *The Time Machine*! It was a braw film, so it was. I thank ye for showin' it to me."

"I'm glad you liked it. Do you think the film did justice to the book?"

The Scot cocked his head in silence and stared thoughtfully into space in a familiar look of contemplation.

"I must say this was one film that tried to bring the book to life. Indeed, it did do justice to Wells' story!"

"Uncle, since we'll soon begin a new millennium, do you think God will do something amazing to show His power?"

Mac's eyes twinkled. "We mortals seem to think that God has adopted our calendar and marks off the centuries as we do. Wait a minute, my boy."

Mac left the room, returning in a couple of minutes with a book.

"Here, let me read somethin' to ye in Thomas Mann's *The Magic Mountain*." Mac paged through the book quickly, searching. "I have it now. Listen: 'Time has no divisions to mark its passage; there is never a thunderstorm or blare o' trumpets to announce the beginning o' a new month or year. Even when a new century begins it is only we mortals who ring bells and fire off pistols.'"

"That's an interesting quote. It makes me think."

"What does it make ye think?"

"That we humans suppose we can slow time by dividing it. I don't know. Maybe I'll read that book."

"Ye might enjoy it. But, back to your question. Ye can be sure that the new millennium is part o' God's plan, and He has miracles in store, as He does today. Ye must remember, too, a thousand years is but a wink o' the eye to God. Now, I'm goin' to take a wee kip before supper."

"Oh sure, Uncle. Have a nice nap. I'll go back to my book, and keep things quiet."

A week later, Richard announced, "I have an e-mail for you, Uncle, from someone by the name of MacPherson, James MacPherson. That's certainly a Scottish name."

"Ye have that right, laddie. He lives in Dumbarton, Scotland, on the banks of the River Clyde. I've known Jamey since he was a wee bairn. He's a pure soul, he is. I saw him a few years ago durin' my last visit to Scotland. But he likes to take the mickey."

"You mean he drinks a lot?"

"No!" Mac chuckled at how his nephew had misinterpreted the Glasgow expression. "I mean he likes to tease and make fun o' his friends to make them laugh."

"Sounds like someone I know. Here, I printed his message.." Richard handed the page to his uncle.

Mac quickly read. "Soonds like Jamey awright. He asks, since I've stopped policin' book-borrowers, what have I been doin' with my life? He suggests that I should come to Dumbarton to help him with his shippin' business. He operates out o' the Port o' Glasgow. He says he has plenty o' men with strong backs and strong minds, but he needs a man with a strong conscience to be sure that profits don't exceed ethics. They're shippin' Scottish gudes all over the world in days, when it used to take weeks."

Richard smiled and shook his head. "Goods, people and information are moving faster and faster, but never fast enough to satisfy us. We expect to travel hundreds of miles in minutes."

"Aye. We want everythin', includin' ourselves, to arrive yesterday. We've lost the ability to appreciate the wait between wantin' somethin' and gettin' it. Why, when Thomas Jefferson became president in 1801, Americans couldn't move gudes and information much faster than the ancient Romans. And probably most people expected it to remain that way. In Jefferson's day, it took aboot six weeks for information to go from the Mississippi River to Washington, D.C. When Abraham Lincoln took office aboot sixty years later, a telegraph could convey information nearly instantaneously. Now look, e-mail from Scotland, like *that*!" Mac snapped his fingers. "The more we compress time, the more we shrink space. Whatever happens, happens faster and closer."

"Is that bad, Uncle?"

"Aye, in some ways. It's like a ride in a lift . . . an elevator. Ye go up so fast, ye feel ye've left your stomach behind. We may move so fast that we leave behind somethin' we need and value, and then we won't have much reason to get to where we're goin'."

"Do you think it's inevitable, that we won't be able to help ourselves?"

"No, my boy. Earthly time alone needn't mark the movements in your life. Ye should also give thought to where ye are in God's time. No matter how fast life may seem to move ye along laddie, God remains the same yesterday, today, and tomorrow."

Both men sat silent for a few minutes. Each man used the silence to reflect on those ancient words.

"I guess I don't understand what you mean by 'God's time,' Uncle. In a way I do,   but . . ."

"Richard, I believe the Bible teaches that God expects His children, day by day, to grow in spirit, as they develop physically. But, if Christians focus only on material things—how many pounds, dollars, or honors they've gained or lost—their spirits won't develop, and God's timetable for them will be disrupted. Then, God may put somethin' in their way to slow them doon, so they can see what's important in life."

"Oh yes, I see." Richard nodded to encourage him to continue.

"The Scriptures are plain: 'When I was a child, I used to speak as a child, think as a child, reason as a child; when I became a man, I did away with childish things.' When we're in God's time, laddie, we see and hear what He tells us, and, in *His* time, we come to understand who we are, spiritually, and how we're to use our gifts in His divine plan. 'For now we see in a mirror dimly, but then face to face; now I know in part, but then I shall know fully just as I also have been fully known.' Sometimes, God uses our experience to shine a light in the mirror. Then we see more clearly what He would have us know."

Often in the days to come, Richard would contemplate the verses from I Corinthians that his uncle had quoted.

5

Facing New Challenges

RICHARD WAS NOT A morning person. Except when college classes had required it, he seldom rose before nine. But this morning, crows in the backyard sounded their alarm at the break of day.

Unable to get back to sleep, Richard stared at a brown water stain on the ceiling, picking out the shape of a seagull in flight, as he'd done numerous times since childhood.

Climbing out of bed, he muttered, "Rotten crows!"

He showered, dressed, and went quietly downstairs. Not wishing to wake his uncle, he fixed himself a simple breakfast of coffee, toast, and orange juice.

Guess I'll take a walk. Burn all those calories from that huge breakfast.

Richard slipped on a light jacket against the cool morning air. He closed the front door softly and headed toward town.

Deep in thought, he hadn't realized that he had walked all the way downtown until he suddenly noticed the sidewalks filling with people who, unlike himself, had particular destinations in mind. They rushed to stores just opening or to reach jobsites on time.

"Excuse me!" said a woman after she bumped into Richard in an effort to get around him. The young man's slow pace made him an obstruction.

Since I'm just a block from church, I'll say hello to Cal Jessup and get out of everyone else's way. He picked up his pace.

When Richard appeared at the open door to Cal's office, the youth pastor said. "Do you know I was thinking about you this very minute?"

"Oh? I hope it was something good."

"It was! See!" Cal pointed. "My desk calendar says, '*Call Richard Hawkins*' and here you are!"

"Rich, in all the years I've known you, you've taken every opportunity to serve our church. I wouldn't say this to all our members, but you don't just talk the talk, you walk the walk."

Richard wondered where this was leading.

"I'm leaving for Columbus, Ohio soon. I'll be speaking at a church there. Responsibility for our youth group needs to be entrusted to someone who's reliable. Someone who'll lift up Scriptural truth. But I need a person who can relate to youth! I need someone the kids will look up to."

"Yea, that's the kind of person you need alright. What about Charlie Evans?"

"If I wanted someone who could take the youth group ice skating, Charlie would be fine. But fun isn't my objective."

"I can't think of anybody else right now."

"How about you, Rich? You're the one I had in mind."

"Me? Leading a group isn't my thing. I'd like to help, but . . ."

"I need someone who has a dynamic witness, who regularly spends time in God's Word as I know you do."

"I don't know, Cal. How would I know what to do? I would sure need to pray about this, and talk to my uncle."

"Yes, you *should* pray about it. And speak to your uncle. I've put some notes and other materials in this file folder. Look these over and let me know your decision tomorrow morning. If you decide it's a go, we'll meet for lunch and talk. I'll be leaving for Columbus exactly one week from today. Uh, that would be June 21st. Should give you time to prepare for the group's meeting. You would also have to make yourself available in case any of the kids need to talk with you about a problem. If a problem turns out too heavy," Cal emphasized, noticing Richard's look of concern, "that person could talk to one of the other pastors, or to me when I get back."

"I'll think about it and let you know."

"Hey, my barber told me this joke the other day, but stop me if you've heard it."

"Even if I have, I won't mind hearing it again. A good joke deserves an encore."

"A father drove his six-year-old daughter to school every morning on his way to work. One day he had to be out of town, so her mother took her. When they arrived, the little girl looked puzzled. She said, 'We didn't see any idiots the way we do when daddy takes me to school.'"

Cal laughed. "I hadn't heard that one. I just might be able to use it in a sermon I have to give next week."

"You know, Rich, I've known you for years. This is the first time I've ever heard you tell a joke. Come to think of it, I've not heard you laugh very often."

"No, I guess not."

"In my devotions recently, I read the Scripture: 'Let us be glad and rejoice in every day that God has made.' That isn't the exact quotation, but you get the idea."

"Close enough. Psalm 118:24 has encouraging words for all of us. So, that verse gave you a new outlook."

"Yes, but it was a goal I had. I just didn't know how to get there—not 'til one night when I picked up a book of my father's."

"Oh? What book was that?"

"The title was *Little Rivers*. It's a book of short stories by Henry van Dyke."

"Yes, the nineteenth century religious writer," interjected Cal. "I've read his book *The Story of the Other Wise Man*."

"In one of the stories, a man on a lonely moor finds a twig of white heather growing there. The beauty of the heather encourages him to focus on God, and not on the loneliness of his situation. And then the man feels glad about the day the Lord has made."

"If I follow, you've discovered that you needed to focus more on the white heather and less on the lonely moor."

"Well, I'm trying. I'm the kind of person who's ready to solve the problem, but doesn't know how to enjoy the solution."

"I'd say telling jokes and laughing more is a good beginning."

As he walked back home, Richard thoughtfully considered Cal's request for help. By the time he'd reached his uncle's house, he felt the Lord had led him to a decision. But he wanted his uncle's opinion.

He found Mac in the garden weeding around his roses, sitting on his "weeding stool," a wooden box turned upside down with a cushion on it.

Mac was singing softly to himself: "Oh my luve's like a red, red rose, / That's newly sprung in June; / Oh my luve's like the melodie / That's sweetly played in tune." Richard stood there a few minutes, undetected. He liked listening to his uncle sing.

"It's ye!" exclaimed the Scot, as he turned around on his box and smiled at his nephew. "I felt someone's eyes lookin' doon on my back. Di' ye have a braw walk?"

Richard nodded, then told his uncle about his conversation with Cal and his decision to help. He wondered what his uncle's response would be, since he valued his judgment.

The Scotsman's answer was immediate. "Ye made the right decision, laddie!"

"I'm proud o' ye, so I am. A lot o' young men would have avoided the responsibility, but not ye," he proclaimed as he got up and patted Richard on the back.

Even though his uncle seemed very positive about his decision, Richard himself still felt uneasy. "I wonder, Uncle, if I have time to really prepare."

"Is it more time ye need to prepare? Or, is it more time ye need to get used to doin' the job? People often fear anythin' they canna completely understand, and they want all the answers before they'll take a step o' faith. The great Irish poet, William Butler, once said, 'Life is a mystery to be lived, not a problem to be solved.' Well, I have work to do. And I suppose ye do too."

"Yes, I guess I do." Smiling wryly, Richard looked at the folder in his hands.

6

The Beautiful Runner

A DOG BARKED IN response to the doorbell. Richard waited, but no one came to the door. He pressed the doorbell again and this time he heard voices inside the house. A moment later, Melissa stood in the open doorway. The beautiful runner looked happy to see him.

"Richard, please come in! It's so nice to see you again. My folks are in the backyard, where we'll be eating. Dinner should be ready in about 20 minutes."

"I hope I'm not too early. I made better time getting to your home than I thought I would." Richard spoke these words as he followed Melissa through the living room, into the kitchen, and out the backdoor onto the patio.

Melissa acted as if she found Richard's words complimentary, perhaps because he suggested that he got to her home as fast as he could. She gave him a warm smile.

Richard stood on the patio, feeling a little awkward. He could see Melissa's dad turning steaks on the grill, and her mom placing bowls of salad on a cloth-draped picnic table.

"Attention everyone! This is my rescuer, Richard Hawkins!" Melissa announced. "And Richard, these are my parents, Donald and Helen Ingram."

Helen rushed toward Richard and hugged him. "You dear boy! We can never thank you enough for what you did for our daughter. We're your friends, as long as God gives us life!" Helen took a tissue from her apron pocket and dabbed at her eyes.

"Oh Mom. If anyone should be crying, I should." Melissa went over and hugged her mother.

Suddenly, Richard felt a strong hand grasping his, shaking it vigorously. Donald had followed his wife to the patio to greet Richard.

"The steaks!" exclaimed Melissa, running to the smoking grill.

Still holding Richard's hand, Donald said, "Our home will always be open to you, Richard. I'm thankful that when my daughter called for help, a brave man was there to answer. Thank you, my boy. Now, I hope you brought an appetite. I'm not known as 'the Picasso of the grill' for nothing. It's all in my barbeque sauce. I know you'll love it!"

"My dad believes in helping people make up their minds, so they don't have to bother doing it themselves." Melissa said this as she turned the meat fork over to her father, and patted him affectionately on the cheek.

The meal was nearly ready when Melissa directed Richard to a wooden picnic table with built-in benches, set on freshly mown grass under the shade of a large maple tree.

Richard sat down at one end of a bench while Melissa hurried away to finish preparations.

I hate to look like I'm starving and can't wait to eat, he thought. *But I don't want to be in the way.*

He smoothed a wrinkle out of the white tablecloth, then picked up a spoon placed with other silverware. He tapped it nervously on the table. *I wonder how much of my life has been spent in just waiting. If waiting patiently is a skill, it's one I've yet to learn.*

Richard looked up into the tree, startled by two green eyes in a furry head watching him from out of the foliage.

"I see you up there, Mr. Cat. Don't you know it's bad manners to stare at a guest?"

Bringing a large bowl of mashed potatoes to the table, Melissa shook her head. "I'm afraid Spooker is hopeless when it comes to manners." She pointed at one of the lower limbs of the tree. "Spooker likes to settle down on it and poke at your head if you happen to walk beneath him. You have to watch out for him whenever you're in our backyard," she added with pretended seriousness.

"I'll be on guard." Richard gave Melissa a big smile, happy to hear he was expected to make future visits.

"If you're going to get fed, I'd better help Mom bring the rest of the food."

As Melissa rushed off, Richard pondered, *Does Melissa really hope I'll be here often? Or was she just being polite?*

Donald put the finishing touches on the ribeyes. The women brought the rest of the meal from the kitchen—besides mashed potatoes and two kinds of salad, there was corn on the cob, buttermilk biscuits, and fresh lemonade.

Richard and the Ingrams had finished eating and were chatting when Donald said, "I don't know about all of you, but I'm too full to eat dessert now. What say we have dessert later in the house."

The guest of honor nodded his agreement with a look of relief, having had second and third helpings at Helen's insistence.

"Melissa and I will take care of the dishes and, Don, why don't you show Richard your vegetable garden and workshop."

After the women had cleared the table and gone into the house, the men went over to the barbeque grill.

"I'd better clean up my mess, before I show you the Ingram estate."

"Can I help?"

"Thanks, Richard. This is pretty much a one-man job, but I appreciate having company while I work. You mentioned at dinner that you live with your uncle. I suppose this was a convenient situation for you during your years at college."

"I should have been clearer about my living situation. You see, I've lived with my uncle all my life. My parents, sister, and brother died when I was a baby."

"I'm sorry, Richard. That's rough." Looking uncomfortable for raising such a sad subject, Donald moved the conversation to something more positive.

"What was your major in college?"

"Communication. I minored in political science and I took a lot of electives in music."

"What courses in music did you take? I mean did you study any instruments?"

"I studied piano and guitar. And I found out very soon that piano took a special kind of talent I didn't have. But, I did well in guitar, and got Bs in music theory."

"Melissa has taken piano lessons ever since she was a little girl. At one time, she tried to learn to play the guitar, but she said the strings hurt her fingers. You know, you two should play a number together—you on the guitar and Melissa the piano."

"Sure. I'd be happy to do it."

The two exchanged comments about their churches and what their churches were doing to help people in need. They discovered that each of them had gone to Mexico with groups from their church to build houses for the poor.

"How many houses does your group usually build, Richard? We generally build three."

"I've gone twice and both times we built three houses. They were very basic houses and small, but well built. I do worry, though, that the owners won't have enough money to keep up repairs."

"Yes, I've wondered about that myself. After all, we have people in *our* country who can't afford to pay for needed home repairs. That's why our church has organized a group of men who have the skills to do repairs for folks on fixed incomes."

"Do you have to be a member to join that group?"

"No, you don't, Richard. Think you might want to join us?"

"I'll consider it. I'm a pretty good house painter. Three years I painted houses to help pay tuition in college."

"We always need painters. The group would love to have you. As a matter of fact,   we . . ."

"Dad, there's some coffee made and dessert if you're ready!"

"Okay, Melissa, we're coming!"

In the living room, Donald offered Richard a comfortable recliner. Judging by *Field and Stream* and *Sports Illustrated* magazines on a nearby end table, Richard deduced he was sitting in Mr. Ingram's favorite chair.

Looking at the family seated around the room, Richard felt a kind of peace settle over him. *It must be nice to be part of such a family.* After everyone was served a slice of chocolate layer cake topped with ice cream, Donald said to his wife beside him on the sofa, "Richard told me that his uncle raised him. He was orphaned at an early age."

Both Helen and Melissa looked at Richard sympathetically.

After a brief pause, Helen asked, "Do you have any other relatives who are close to you, Richard?"

"Yes, there's Aunt Jennifer, my father's sister, who lives in Flagstaff. She lives alone. As far as I know, she never married."

"Did you see her very often growing up?"

"I didn't see her at all 'till I was twelve, Melissa. Then one day, she called Uncle Mac and asked if I would like to visit her in Flagstaff for two weeks. Uncle Mac encouraged me to go, so I did."

"Did you ever find out why she didn't contact your uncle sooner? I assume she was told about her brother's death."

"Oh yes, Mrs. Ingram, Uncle Mac got in touch with her right away. He thought Aunt Jenny was afraid that she would be asked to take a baby to raise. For a long time, he was afraid that she would ask for me and he would have to let me go."

"Several years ago," Donald commented, "I went to Flagstaff on a business trip. Nice city. Friendly people. Matter of fact I thought about buying some property there."

"Well, if you had, you might have met Aunt Jenny. She was a realtor and later a real estate developer."

"Did you have a good time when you visited your aunt?" Helen asked.

"Yes, she was very good to me. Though, when I first met her I thought she was kind of unusual. Every morning, after breakfast, she and I would do exercises called T'ai Chi—years later, I learned more about it. At first, I could hardly do it, but after a few days I caught on. When we went to her favorite restaurant, the waitress knew that she was supposed to stand by the table with eyes closed while my aunt prayed."

"What did you do for fun when you were with your aunt?" Melissa asked.

"We went hiking. I had a hard time keeping up with her, even though she was older. We went horseback riding—sometimes we'd race, and the loser had to do the supper dishes. But, what I enjoyed most were our talks about life. She also told me about my dad when he was a boy, and that meant a lot to me. I love my Aunt Jenny—she doesn't allow anyone else to call her Jenny."

"Are you going to visit her this summer?"

"No, Melissa, she's too busy with her campaign. A few years ago, she became interested in politics and ran for a senate seat in the Arizona state legislature, and won. The first time she ran, I helped her with her campaign. I enjoyed it a lot."

"Would you like another piece of cake, Richard?"

"My eyes say yes, but my stomach says no. I couldn't hold another bite. But, thank you, Mrs. Ingram. Your cake is delicious, as was the whole dinner."

"Richard, I wish that you would call Don and me by our first names. All of our dearest friends do."

"Thank you for your kind words, Mrs. Ingram… Helen. Your friendship and Don's and Melissa's mean a great deal. I don't have a lot of friends, so it's nice to make three new ones."

Helen excused herself and left the room with the plates that had held her cake. Minutes later, she returned with another slice of cake and put the plate down near Richard.

"Mother, don't you remember that Richard said he was full."

"Yes, of course, I'm sorry Richard. Just leave it there. Don will eat it later."

"Wait a minute. Finders, keepers. My stomach just got as big as my eyes," Richard said as he reached for the cake.

Melissa flashed Richard a look of gratitude.

The time passed quickly—so quickly that when Richard looked at his watch, he was surprised to see that he'd been there three hours. When the Ingrams refused his offer to help with the dessert dishes, Richard said good night and promised to visit again soon.

Melissa led him to the front door. As she opened the door for him, she took his hand and squeezed it.

Richard smiled his thanks. His cheeks showed rosier than usual in the porch light. "I hope you'll be more careful next time you go running."

"Yes, I *will*! I'm going to run with Otto."

"You are?" Richard's tone conveyed disappointment. "Is Otto your boyfriend?"

"No," Melissa laughed. "Otto is our German shepherd. We had him locked in my room. He has a tendency to jump on our guests."

After another good night, Richard headed for his car. As he walked along, he thought, *Lucky dog.*

7

Meeting About Prayer

MEMORIES OF HIS GOOD time with the Ingrams, one Ingram in particular, monopolized Richard's thoughts for some days. But with effort, he began planning the youth group meeting. Cal gave him some good ideas over lunch one afternoon and Richard completed his preparations in time. He decided the evening's theme would be *prayer*.

"I'd better practice what I'm going to preach," Richard said to himself. He spent an hour praying in his room that the teens who came would hear truth that would strengthen their faith in Christ. Richard claimed God's promise in Isaiah 55:11. He read the verse out loud: "So shall my word be which goes forth from my mouth; It shall not return to me empty, Without accomplishing what I desire, And without succeeding in the matter for which I sent it."

Richard arrived at the church half an hour early to get the meeting room ready. The group, aged 14 to 17, met in Room 21, the Olive Carlyle Room. He glanced over his notes, checking to see if he had marked certain passages of Scripture.

"Hi. Are you the new youth leader?"

This greeting caused Richard to turn from the window, where he had stood while saying a silent prayer. "I'm the youth leader for one night, anyway. I suppose you're a member of the group."

"Yep, for three years. The rest will be along pretty soon. Cal always likes us to be on time."

His prediction proved correct. In a few minutes Richard found himself facing fifteen young people, whose facial expressions showed both curiosity and apprehension.

"It looks like everybody is here," Richard said.

"Except for Jimmy. He ain't all here!" Rewarded by the laughter of the other teens, the jokester added, "And his brain ain't likely to join up with his body for another half hour!"

Richard noticed that the teens directed their laughter toward a boy in the front row, who seemed to take the teasing good-naturedly.

Rising up in his chair, Jimmy glanced toward his tormentor and retorted, "At least, I *have* a brain, Leroy!"

"My name is Lee," muttered Leroy.

Richard waited patiently for this exchange to conclude, then announced, "We're going to sit in a circle. Please move your chairs."

The thundering noise that ensued sounded more like the eight girls and seven boys were remodeling the room instead of simply repositioning chairs.

Moving his chair into the completed circle, he said, "My name is Richard. Tell me *your* names. I know you're Lee, and you're Jimmy." He glanced toward each of the boys who had teased each other minutes before.

After a brief pause, one of the girls said, "My name is Sandra, but I prefer Sandy."

"Okay, Sandy. And the young man on your right? What's *your* name?"

"My name's Chris. Named after Christopher Columbus."

"I'm Jose Ortega. We're really glad that you could take over the group for Cal. He asked us to help all we could."

"That's great, Jose. This is my first time leading this kind of group. So, your help will be appreciated."

Several students then yelled out their names so rapidly, that Richard couldn't catch them all. "Hey not so fast," he pleaded.

"I'm Debbie Martin," one girl said slowly and deliberately, so that Richard would be sure to hear her name correctly.

Soon all the members of the group had contributed names.

"Well, I think I know your names now, but I may have to ask you again. We're here this evening in the name of One whose name 'is above every name,' as we read in Philippians 2:9. Verses 10 and 11 tell us, 'that at the name of Jesus every knee should bow, of those who are in heaven, and on earth, and under the earth, and that every tongue should confess that Jesus Christ is Lord, to the glory of God.' I believe that one of the ways we confess that Jesus is Lord is through prayer. And that is the subject of our lesson this evening. Jose, would you get us started with a prayer?" As Richard made this request, he wished he'd asked Jose earlier if he would mind praying.

Jose offered a simple prayer, asking God to bless their meeting and help Richard.

The circle of teens became very quiet, and a mood of expectancy settled over the group.

"When I was a small boy, my Uncle Mac taught me to pray. You see, my uncle raised me. He told me first to thank God for what He has done for me and for others, including answered prayers; second, to petition God to help me and others, including requests for healing; third, to confess my sins to God—openly and honestly—including the things I've left undone; fourth, to praise God for the wonders of His creation and His salvation through Jesus; and fifth, to listen for God's voice and sense His will, including the whispers of my conscience."

Richard paused for questions, and Lee's hand went up.

"Yes, Lee?"

"What's 'bedtishun'?"

Richard restrained a smile and said, "'Petition' means asking someone who has authority to give you something, usually something that takes a lot of power."

"But like what's prayer, really, Richard? When the minister tells us, 'Let's pray,' I listen to him pray, or anyway, I wait 'til he's finished." Debbie made this comment and paused thoughtfully. Before anyone could say anything, she added, "I just don't have the right words like the minister."

Richard looked around the circle to see all eyes on him, in anticipation of his answer to Debbie's question.

"Prayer is simply talking to God about something important to you . . . in your own words, and in your own way. Clement of Alexandria, a 3rd century Christian writer, said, 'Prayer is conversation with God.' I believe God is more interested in *what* we say, than in *how* we say it."

"I try to understand prayer the way you do Richard," said one of the girls, shaking her head and displaying a sad face, "but I guess I'm not spiritual enough."

"Karen, what is it that you don't 'understand'?" Richard asked.

"I don't know if I can explain it like some of you. I can think it, but I can't put it into words very well."

"We're all learning. That's why we're having this lesson, Karen," encouraged Jose. "So, just say it any way you want to."

"Okay, I'll try. You see, my sister wanted to get a part in this school play, and so did another girl. She wanted the same part. She, the other girl, got it and told my sister it was because she prayed. My sister told me that she forgot to pray, and so that's why she didn't get the part. She thinks now, you know, that God likes the other girl better."

"Well, first of all, prayer isn't a magic formula for getting everything we might want. Some people even pray for parking spaces, expecting God to look out for their convenience. The other girl may have gotten the part because she worked hard to get it, or the person making the decision liked her acting. God gets blamed for answering prayers that He didn't, as well as for not answering prayers that He did."

At this point, Sandy raised her hand. "My stepfather says that faith in God doesn't do any harm, but it doesn't do any good, either. He says all the time, 'If you want something to happen, you've got to make it happen . . . yourself.' And he's very successful, but," Sandy said quietly to herself, "he's not very happy about it."

"I'm sorry that your stepfather feels that way about prayer. Perhaps, in time, you could influence him to give faith in God a chance."

Speaking slowly, as if thinking hard about Richard's words, Sandy responded, "My stepfather does ask me what I'm learning in school and what I'm hearing in church. I always tell him, 'Just the usual stuff.' But next time he asks about church, I'll try to give him the things we've learned about prayer."

"Good for you, Sandy. If you haven't already, you could also invite your stepfather to church." Richard's suggestion brought approving looks from the group.

"Richard," asked Jan, "do you think that prayer really makes a difference when you're sick? Grandmother Bessie prays for everyone in the family everyday. I know she does because once when she was visiting I heard her in her room praying. And, whenever anyone in the family is sick my mother calls grandmother so she can pray for their healing."

"Jan, I believe, first, that God hears every prayer, and second, that He answers every believer's prayer, including those that ask for His healing touch. As much as others might love us, He loves us better. Studies show that prayer makes a big difference in people's healing. Prayer enables people to recover more rapidly from surgery, and to suffer less pain and disability. Prayer is powerful! Pray for each other. Pray for God's blessings in the name of our Savior, the Lord Jesus Christ. Pray . . ."

Thinking that Richard had completed his thought, Kimberly interrupted, saying, "But what if you don't know what to pray for when someone's sick. I mean what if someone wants to die because he has a lot of pain, like my Uncle Gilbert?"

"I wish you'd save questions like that for Cal," pleaded Richard. "I'm not a minister. I'm just a believer with a little more experience than you have."

"That's okay," encouraged Jose. "We'll ask Cal, too, but we want to know what you think. Right?"

Richard smiled in resignation to a chorus of "Right!" from the group. "Kimberly, I believe when we're praying for someone who's ill or, let's say, in trouble, and we're not sure what to pray for, then it's best to simply put that person in God's hands and trust Him to do what's best, rather than to tell God what we want Him to do."

"Yes, but how do you know what God did in answering your prayer?"

"You're Ken, aren't you?" asked Richard.

"Yes."

"Well Ken, that's where faith comes in." Richard thought for a moment and added, "We can believe that whatever is the outcome of our prayer, it's always going to be in the direction of what's best for the person we prayed for. However, we may not recognize the answer to our prayer, because the result is not what we expected. The result may seem negative in physical terms, but in spiritual terms it may be positive. Someone I know had to lose everything—his wife, his material possessions, even his sight—before he could see his need of Christ in his life. After he accepted Christ, his wife eventually returned and found him a changed man. She helped him adjust to his loss of sight. Through it all, his mother and his friends never stopped praying for him."

Brett, who had been silent to this point, suddenly blurted out, "I know it says somewhere in Matthew that we should pray for our enemies. But I don't get it. Like why should I pray for a guy who wants to give me trouble? Seems to me it's a waste of a good prayer."

Brett's question elicited several "yeahs" and nods of agreement from members of the group, as they waited for Richard's reply.

Richard opened his Bible and turned to Matthew 5:44 and read: "'But I say to you, love your enemies, and pray for those who persecute you.' Here Jesus tells us not only to pray for our enemies, but to *love* them."

"Brett's question is a good one. I think the group should answer it, and I believe there are several possible answers. So," encouraged Richard, "would someone like to begin?"

Following a brief pause, Jose said, "We should love our enemies and pray for them because Jesus told us to. After all, He was able to forgive and pray for the soldiers that crucified Him."

Karen raised her hand. "Well, you know, as Christians we should be different than the world that says hate your enemies. We've seen what happens with that in the schools where kids are killing other kids."

"That's a good point, Karen!" offered Lee. "We can win people to Christ by turning the other cheek and caring more about their souls than their insults to us. And that's where prayer comes in."

"If we don't pray for people because we're angry at them for what they've done against us, then that anger hurts us, and we become like them. So, we let them hurt us twice."

"You're absolutely right, Rachael," responded Richard. "I remember something that Norman Cousins wrote in one of his books. He said that negative feelings take up a lot of space in the human mind; they influence our perceptions, our prospects in life, and our pleasures. He also said that the lack of forgiveness can cause physical problems and diseases."

"Maybe by loving our enemies and remembering them in prayer we can help bring them closer to God. Don't you think?" asked Sara.

Richard agreed and waited for someone else to speak.

"It seems to me," commented Jimmy, "that praying for someone who doesn't like you is pretty practical. It's like making up your mind to find something good about the person and not give up on him and decide he's an enemy. As my dad says, 'You don't need another enemy, but you do need another friend.' He used to tell me that when I would get into fights in grade school."

"Yeah," said Lee mischievously, "your dad got tired of seeing you get beat up all the time."

Before Jimmy could give a rejoinder to Lee's remark, Richard said, "Jimmy, I like what your dad says. One of my Uncle Mac's favorite authors is Ralph Waldo Emerson. One quote from Emerson goes like this: 'He who has a thousand friends / has not a friend / to spare, and he who has one enemy / will meet him everywhere.'"

"I like that quote," said Debbie. "Would you repeat it so I can write it down?"

Richard repeated it while several teens in the group copied Emerson's words.

During the remainder of the meeting, the group focused its discussion on the need for discipline in developing a prayer life. As Jose noted, "It's kind of difficult to get prayer from church to home."

In closing the meeting, Richard asked each of the youth to give a one-sentence prayer. One girl gave thanks to God for sending Richard to them to talk about prayer.

After the meeting, Richard received many positive comments from the group and promised that he would stand in for Cal again if he were asked to do so.

As Richard drove home from the meeting, he was praising God and thanking Him for His help. He thought as he came to the familiar driveway, "Lord? Do you want me to be a youth minister?" But his heart gave no answer.

"How'd it go this evenin'?" asked Mac, smiling. "Di' ye keep the lads and lassies' attention?"

"I believe *so*," Richard said confidently.

"Ye seem happy, Richard, what happened?"

"Everything went real well."

"That's gude to hear, but could ye be a wee bit more specific, laddie?"

"Well, before we got started, I was pretty nervous. But after we got into it, it just seemed to come together."

"Like it says in the Gude Book, 'In God all things hold together.'"

"They sure did! There was an amazing thing that happened in particular. After the meeting one of the girls came up to me and said that for the first time she believed that God heard her when she prayed. And a lot of the others told me that I did a good job and they would like me to come back."

Mac nodded and gave Richard a knowing look. "I knew ye'd do just fine. I said a prayer for ye when I heard ye leave the hoose this evenin'. Ye look a wee bit tired."

"I am feeling a little sleepy; I didn't sleep very well last night. So, I'll say good night, Uncle. But I'll be up with the birds."

"Gude night my boy."

8

Working the Graveyard

THE NEXT MORNING, RICHARD sat with his uncle after breakfast to talk about his experience with the kids.

"Di' ye think ministerin' to youth is somethin' ye might want to do with your life?"

"Right after the meeting, I was thinking along that line. But later—this morning actually—I realized I wasn't cut out for it. I don't see it as God's purpose."

"Why di' ye say that, laddie?"

"A youth pastor has to accept how one minute young people act like little children and the next like mature adults. You can't become impatient or frustrated as I did, although I tried hard not to show it."

"I hope ye'll keep an open mind. Remember, in any kind o' work, ye have to develop appropriate attitudes and skills."

"Sure, Uncle Mac. And I'd be happy to substitute for Cal again sometime."

Nodding his approval, Mac suddenly changed the topic of conversation.

"Ye know, Richard I've been ponderin' somethin'. I remember how ye said recently that ye wished ye had more money saved in the bank."

Richard nodded. "Uh-huh."

"I was just talkin' to a friend o' mine whose son works at a vegetable cannery. Well, he says they need more help on two o' their shifts. What di' ye think?"

Richard wasn't sure about working at a cannery; he tried to imagine the kind of people he'd have to work with. He knew that some of them would be pretty rough types.

"I guess I could check on it."

"That's the spirit! Look into it, and if ye found ye dinna like it or they dinna need ye, nothin' is lost. And, it just might turn out to be somethin' gude."

Richard knew full well that his uncle understood his hesitation, that he felt such a job was beneath him. For the past two years, he had worked in the university library in a white collar job that his uncle had helped him get. But this summer the library didn't need him.

"I'll go apply tomorrow."

Dressed neatly and armed with his resume, Richard ate a quick breakfast, and started for the cannery. Twenty minutes later, he spotted the cannery's sign and pulled into the company parking lot, nearly hitting a heavily-loaded truck that was pulling out. The driver of the truck yelled something at him that Richard wouldn't repeat in polite society. *I'd better concentrate on my driving or I won't need a job.*

He parked and got out of the car in time to meet one of the employees who was hurrying toward an old pickup truck. He stopped the man and asked, "Could you tell me where I might find the general manager?"

"You go through that door over there," the man pointed, "and then you turn to the right and Jangle's office is third—no fourth—door down. His name is on the door. You can't miss it."

"Thank you," said Richard, encouraged by the man's courteous manner.

Richard quickly found Mr. Jangle's office door and knocked.

"Yes? Come in!" called a loud, high-pitched voice.

The short, middle-aged man with a round, red face and a fringe of red hair around a shiny pate was seated at a battered wooden desk, covered with papers and stained coffee cups.

"Yes, come in! Take a seat. I've been expecting you."

Richard found this remark strange, since he hadn't made an appointment. "You've been expecting me?"

"Yes, of course. You want a job don't you? And, if I'm not mistaken, and I rarely am, you're holding your work record. Let me have it, and then we'll talk turkey . . . or rather vegetables."

"Well, I *am* looking for a job."

"Good!" said Mr. Jangle, slapping the papers on his desk, and taking the resume from Richard's out-stretched hand. "I like a man who's decisive."

"Hmmm, says you've got computer skills. That could be handy. I see you sold home-canned peas and carrots at the County Fairground. Don't see any reason for folks to can their own vegetables in this day and age. Do you?"

"Well I don't . . ." began Richard.

"Glad you agree, my boy! You got to be loyal to our business. Besides, the average homeowner gets the temperature too high or too low." Mr. Jangle spoke these words as fact.

"I suppose that's possible," said Richard in an agreeable tone.

"More than possible. More than possible," answered Mr. Jangle. "Nothing worse than overcooked vegetables! Wouldn't you agree?"

"Oh yes!" Richard hated mushy vegetables.

Visibly pleased that he had elicited such a positive response from the young applicant, Mr. Jangle waved Richard's resume and said, "I can see by this that you're neat, orderly, careful about detail. I believe we can use you. Yes, you're hired! See J. S. Packer just down the hall. I'll give Packer a call before you get there."

"Thank you, Mr. Jangle. I'll do my best."

Mr. Jangle, already on the phone, smiled and waved Richard out of the office.

"Hmmm, 'Packer.' Good name for someone working in a cannery," Richard mused as he stopped at the door that held the nameplate: *J. S. Packer, Foreman.* He knocked on the door.

"Come in, Mr. Hawkins!"

Richard obeyed, surprised to be called by name. The surprise apparently registered on his face.

"You probably didn't expect the foreman to be a woman. That right? Please sit down," J. S. Packer requested in a soft voice.

"Oh well," replied Richard, sitting down across from the foreman seated at a table with a stack of time cards in front of her. "I . . . uh was surprised that you knew my name."

"Mr. Jangle just called and gave me your name. He said you would be here in a couple of minutes. Actually, he put it more colorfully: He said you would be here in 'two shakes of a lamb's tail.'"

Feeling a little dumb, Richard asked, "When do you want me to start?"

"I would *like* you to start tonight. However, when *can* you start? I have an opening on the graveyard shift."

"Excuse me, but what's the 'graveyard shift'?" Richard's tone betrayed some uneasiness at hearing the word 'graveyard'.

"That's the shift that begins at midnight and goes to 8:00 AM. You'll have a half hour to eat and, of course, the usual breaks."

"Okay," said Richard. He provided social security information and signed three papers, including one that listed rules. "I'll be here tomorrow night at midnight."

"Good. Let me give you a note to give to our shift leader, Ben."

While Packer wrote the note, Richard leaned back and looked at her more closely. She had short, dark hair, big brown eyes, a nice complexion, and gold-rimmed glasses on a slender nose. When she stood up to give him the note, Richard could see that she was tall, slim and somewhere in her 30s.

Richard stood up and took the note. "Thank you, Ms. Packer. I'll give this to Ben tomorrow night."

"Good luck, Richard." With these words J. S. Packer shook his hand.

She has a strong grip, he thought as he left the office and headed for the parking lot.

When Richard got home, he left the car in the driveway and slumped down on the steps of the porch, wondering if his decision to work at the cannery was the right one. Soon the front door opened and Mac came out.

"Well laddie, what do ye have to report? Di' ye get the job?"

"Yes I did, Uncle Mac. I hope I made the right decision. I'm supposed to go to work tomorrow at midnight, on the graveyard shift."

"Then ye get off at 8:00 AM. I'll have some breakfast ready for ye when ye get home, and see that the hoose is quiet so ye can sleep."

"Thanks, Uncle. Since this is my last night of freedom, let's see a movie after supper. What do you say?"

"I think that's a gude idea, Richard. Whatever ye choose it will be fine with me."

"There's a John Wayne move on TV tonight that I don't believe you've seen, or at least, not in a long time. *The Alamo.*"

"I do hope John Wayne stuck to the facts in tellin' how the brave men at the Alamo fought and died. The truth o' their heroic defense doesn't need any Hollywood embroidery to be interesting."

"They held out for weeks against thousands of Mexican soldiers, didn't they?"

"Not weeks, Richard. Aboot 180 men held back General Santa Anna's well-equipped army for 11 days. Now aboot supper this evenin'. Aroond 5:00 o'clock I'll call and have pizza delivered."

"Sounds good. Right now I'd better go downtown and buy some cannery clothes and sturdy work shoes. I'll be home before supper."

After shopping and a short walk, Richard took a quick shower and sat down with Mac for pizza. Then they relaxed in the living room, Mac reading Robert Burns and Richard reading a biography of Abraham Lincoln while waiting for the movie to start.

About an hour into the film, Mac said, "Uh-huh, it does look like the Alamo. They've built a very gude replica for their movie set."

"Have you been to the Alamo, Uncle Mac?"

"Aye, I visited the Alamo a number o' years ago durin' a conference o' librarians in San Antonio."

At the end of the film, Mac sat in silence, shaking his head.

"What did you think of the movie, Uncle Mac?"

"It was a gude film, but it left out an important fact. There were four Scots among the defenders, and one o' them, I believe, was an ancestor o' ours, John MacGregor. He played the bagpipe while the men were fightin'. Davy Crocket was quoted as sayin' that his playin' inspired the men and lifted their spirits."

"I bet if John Wayne had known about John MacGregor, he would have put him in the movie. Having one of the defenders playing the bagpipe would have given the movie . . . a human touch."

"As far as puttin' a Scottish bagpiper into the script, Bob's your Uncle," responded Mac.

"I agree that it could be quite easily done," said Richard, interpreting his uncle's Scottish expression. I remember you used to tell me about John MacGregor, but I guess it didn't register that he played the bagpipe at the Alamo. Imagine having a combat piper in the family."

"There was also Bruce MacGregor who served in World War I; he was a soldier in the Royal Scots Fusiliers. When his regiment charged the enemy in France, he was in the front line playin' his bagpipe. The

Germans, seein' the pipers in their kilts, called them the 'ladies from Hell', because the fierce Scots would use the soond o' their bagpipes to signal an attack."

"Did Bruce MacGregor live through the war, Uncle?"

"No, I'm afraid not. He was shot doon in 1918. He was one o' 1,000 pipers who died durin' that great war."

On the day he was scheduled to report for work at the cannery, Richard tried to take a nap to prepare for his all-night shift, but sleep could not loosen the tense muscles of his body. *I might as well give up and get up. I just can't stop thinking about tonight. I hope I can stay awake on the job.*

He proceeded to busy himself with a series of chores around the house—he washed the Chevy hatchback he shared with his uncle, did a load of laundry, and made dinner for his uncle and himself. Three hours before midnight, at his uncle's suggestion, he sat down in the living room to relax a while.

"Wake up, Richard! It's time to go."

Richard sat up abruptly. "What time is it?"

"It's 11:15. I have a lunch packed for ye."

Twenty minutes later, Richard was in the car, heading for the cannery. On his arrival, he parked, and walked swiftly toward the main building. Inside he encountered several people talking together.

"Excuse me, I'm looking for Ben, the shift leader," Richard said, interrupting the conversation of four men and a woman.

The woman smiled at Richard and pointed toward a middle-aged man in bib overalls standing nearby.

"Ms. Packer told me to give you this."

"Oh she did, huh. Well, let's see what the foreman has to say."

Ben stared at the note so long that Richard began to wonder if he knew how to read.

Nodding his head in satisfaction, Ben pocketed the note and gave Richard a welcoming smile. "Well, we can sure use another man on the shift, Richard. With you on the job, I can have an eye on our operation, without having to pitch in myself. Let me show you around the plant and have you meet some of our people."

Ben gave Richard a quick tour of that part of the plant where he would work, including the location of the lunch room, restroom, and first-aid kit. Occasionally, he would stop to introduce Richard to someone. Then he led

Richard to a woman seated on some sealed cases of vegetables. A small paperback held her attention so well she didn't notice their approach until Ben spoke.

"Connie, this here is Richard Hawkins. Keep an eye on him so he don't get hurt, will ya?"

Richard accepted this introduction with a look of gratitude.

"I'd be glad to."

"Thank you, Connie, that makes me feel better. I'd be happy if you would give me any pointers about the job. I've never worked in a cannery before." In making the last comment, Richard knew he was probably stating the obvious.

"I'm sure you'll do just fine. Did you think to bring any ear plugs?" Connie asked.

"Well no. Do I need them?"

"You'll want to protect your hearing, Richard. Here," Connie said, digging into a pocket of her sweatshirt, "take these ear plugs. They're new. I'll wear my old ones."

At Connie's insistence, Richard took the ear plugs, a decision he was glad of when the machines started up and the graveyard shift went to work. The din was deafening, as Connie had warned him.

"Come with me, Richard," Ben yelled above the noise. "I'll show you your station for the time being. Do you have gloves?"

Richard nodded and pointed at his pocket.

"Here's a hat. You wear it," Ben yelled close to Richard's left ear, "to protect the product and keep it sanitary!" Ben handed Richard a round, white paper hat.

Ben next grabbed Richard's left arm and towed him toward a machine where a man pushed silver cans of peas without lids onto a large revolving circular plate from metal trays that contained a dozen cans.

"Jack, Richard will take over. You go back to your usual station."

"Glad to!" Jack gave Richard a look of pity and sauntered away.

"Now Richard, keep feeding the cans in these trays onto the turntable," Ben said loudly. "Make sure they move smoothly onto the conveyor. When the stack of trays gets low, someone will bring more. And make sure every can is full."

"What do I do if the can *isn't* full?" yelled Richard at the retreating shift leader. But Ben continued to walk, apparently not hearing Richard's question.

9

Friendship With Tony

W**HEN LUNCH BREAK CAME** Richard was surprised that time had passed so quickly. *Maybe that's one advantage of having a repetitive job, you lose track of the time.* He got his sack lunch from the car and slumped down wearily on a bench at an unoccupied table. He was surveying the contents of his sack when he suddenly became aware of someone standing behind him.

"Alright if I join you?" a voice asked.

Richard turned to see a man who had the appearance of an old hippie. He sported a short, scraggly beard and a long pony tail of gray hair; he wore a white, tie-dyed dress shirt tucked into faded jeans, held up by a wide belt with a large oval buckle bearing the peace symbol in brass.

"Sure! Glad to have the company."

"Food goes best with conversation," responded the stranger, as he seated himself across the table from Richard. "Don't you think that's so?"

"Yes, I . . ."

"I'm glad you agree, friend." The stranger nodded his approval. "We human beings were designed to herd together and help each other. But we're more and more separate. Say, my friends call me Tony. What's your handle?"

"Oh, my name? Richard."

Tony pulled an apple out of his sack and took a bite. "You know, Bob Dylan was right on. His songs warned us where this society was goin'. And it's finally got there!"

"Where's that?"

"Where? Right under the thumb of the establishment, that's where, man! See that camera up there on the wall? That's 'Big Brother" with his eye on you."

"You mentioned Bob Dylan. I especially like his song *Tambourine Man*. I sometimes play it on my guitar."

"Right on! You dig Dylan, heh?"

"I taped some of his songs from the radio several years ago for my collection of 60s songs. I think he represents that era better than any other singer of that time."

"Yeah, that's it, man! I heard him sing in concert a couple of times. He and Joan Baez caught the soul of our movement in their songs."

"What was the 'movement' as you saw it? I mean what was your goal?"

"In one word, *love*," said Tony, as he stared into space as if seeing something long past. "Me and my friends would get together on warm summer evenings, and talk about love. We'd sit in the shadows of the Douglas firs. And we'd talk about the beauty of love; how we could keep it alive."

"Alive?" Richard chewed a bite of sandwich thoughtfully. "I don't understand."

"You see, Richard, we knew it was dyin'. Lookin' back, we didn't know how right we were." Tony dropped his head sadly and munched on a piece of celery.

After drinking juice from his small thermos, Richard asked, "When did you and your friends start seeing that love was dying?"

"At Berkeley. There was this huge rally on the campus against the Vietnam War. That was 1966. We could see that the killin' in Nam was just a symptom of the problem. We could see that the establishment was to blame."

"The 'establishment'? When I came across that term in my reading, I could never really figure out what you people meant."

Tony smiled indulgently. "You know, that artificial machine we call society—that's the establishment. It tries to stamp everybody with the same face and outlook. Every soul is expected to spend 24 hours a day on a capitalistic hunt for the almighty dollar. Our movement centered on love, not bank accounts and *prized* possessions."

"I don't see how you separated yourself from society since, as you say, it had stamped its patterns on you. Didn't the establishment create the love you saw dying, in the first place?"

"Oh man. You're too young to know what I'm sayin'. You see Richard, nowadays, we hear about crime, greed, pollution . . . *and* we don't think anything about it, 'cause we're desensitized."

"In other words, we've come to see it as normal."

"Yeah, we see what's goin' on as 'normal'. Funny thing about the word *normal*. *Norm* gives a group a standard how to act. Whatever the group accepts as normal is normal, or whatever it sees as true is true. It doesn't matter how bad it really is, either. So, we can't assume that most people, even the majority, know what's true. If we can't have the truth from our society, we have to go out and *find* it for ourselves."

"Well how do we do that?"

"I'm glad you asked me that," smiled Tony. "You find truth in the natural, and in the spontaneous."

"I think I know what you're getting at."

"That's just it," said the other. "You don't have to '*think*' about it. Just *feel* it."

"Feel *what*?"

"Richard, don't you get it? You don't analyze a thing like *love*. You let it come to you. You're tryin' to grasp what I'm sayin', but you're tryin' too hard. And that's the influence of the establishment. It creates a regulated, controlled environment that dictates how to act and what to think. It forces you to conform. 'One size fits all' reads the label."

"Well there are certainly a lot of people who let others think for them," said Richard, still not sure if this was what Tony was getting at. Suddenly glancing at his watch, Richard let Tony know that the lunch period was nearly over.

"See what I mean? The clock says jump and everyone goes to their pigeonhole." Tony spoke with the tone of one whose point had been proven.

As the two men parted company to head for their respective stations, they both expressed interest in talking further about the social revolution of the 1960s and '70s. Tony saw the revolution as a continuing objective in society, one not fully realized; whereas Richard saw it as a dissipating influence in society, losing ground to traditional forces. In college he had written research papers on it, which he believed, made him something of an authority.

The days seemed to pass faster and faster with little change in routine for Richard. What did change was his growing respect for his fellow workers. The men and women who worked the graveyard shift, he came to realize, were industrious, good humored, and helpful to one another. They showed knowledge and skill in their jobs that came not from books but from experience.

Richard especially looked forward to lunch periods when he could converse with Tony, whose first-hand recollections of the "hippie era," as Tony called it, transported Richard back in time. During one of their conversations in the lunch room, Richard decided to satisfy his curiosity about Tony's attire.

"Say Tony, would you tell me why you always wear tie-dyed white dress shirts?"

"Ah, you noticed."

Richard thought that the brightly-colored dress shirt could hardly escape notice, but said, "I've never seen anything like it."

"I wear these to protest white-collar greed, which consumes the days and nights of the people in this country."

"Yes, but if it weren't for the profit motive, we wouldn't have a . . ."

"By the way, do you know what day this is?" interrupted Tony.

"No, I can't say that I do. Is it your birthday?"

"It's kind of a birthday, but not mine. It was 30 years ago today, on August 15, 1969, that we met near Woodstock, New York—three hundred thousand of us!"

"So you were at the Woodstock Music Festival! I've read about that." Richard was obviously impressed to know someone who was part of such an historic event. "You say, three hundred thousand hippies!"

"Well, no. We weren't all hippies. There were students, too, and those who opposed the war in Vietnam among us. But, it was like one big love-in, man. Woodstock was a gathering of many types of people who put out good vibrations, 'cause they had it together, unlike the older generations."

"Had what 'together'?"

"Man, I've got to go through all this with you sometime—so you know where I'm comin' from. For now, just follow along as best you can, Richard." Tony closed his eyes. "I can still see the huge field, all of us standin' as far as the eye can see, mostly people your age, packed tight before a long platform. I was, I don't know, 'bout a hundred feet from the front of the platform. We were crowded together with so much love—I mean nobody shoved you. People you didn't know put their arms around you. Sometimes the crowd would surge forward in anticipation of the next band, like when the Grateful Dead came on. But the crowd's movement really worried the cops," said Tony, a sneer in his voice.

"Cops?" queried Richard.

"Oh yeah, well, there was a bunch of cops all around, 'cause the people in the towns close by thought we were goin' to riot or somethin' and so they sent all these cops to watch us. They didn't trust us 'cause of the establishment's propaganda. They should've believed how the event was advertised: 'Three Days of Peace, Love, and Music'—I still have one of the original posters. But they figured they had somethin' to fear. And they did, but not what they thought."

"What *did* they have to fear?"

"That we had the power to turn the world around—through the power of love," said Tony with a look of mixed confidence and sadness. "You know, Richard, all those people comin' together didn't make any trouble, even when it started to rain and the food and water ran out. I can still remember the smell of wet grass and flowers in my girlfriend's hair."

"How come the food and water ran out? Didn't the promoters prepare well?"

"I suppose they didn't expect so many of us to show up. I have to tell you, the music was outta sight! It stirred the soul, man! Folk. Rock. I was one lucky cat to experience Woodstock. For years afterward, we called ourselves 'Woodstock Nation.'"

"It sure must have been an interesting time to be alive. I wish I could go back in time and see it for myself," Richard remarked, more to himself than to Tony.

"I wish you could, man. I wish we *both* could. It was groovy. We celebrated life." As Tony said these words, he slapped Richard gently on the shoulder. "In those days, we wanted to be self-sufficient, independent of the establishment—findin' identity and direction within ourselves, and not from the discordant voices of authority."

As Richard drove home at the end of the shift, he pondered the conversation with Tony and asked himself if anyone can ever be completely independent of social institutions. He wondered if Tony had been one of the thousands of hippies who'd relied on government food stamps to eat.

10

Prelude to Crisis

THE BRIGHT, WARM DAYS of summer were fading into fall with cooler nights and the smell of wood smoke in the air. The cannery responded to signs of the new season with slower production and reduced hours for workers such as Richard. The resulting freedom meant that Richard could once again plan weekend activities with Mac and others, including his new friend Tony. Richard found Tony's descriptions of the hippie era fascinating. Although it became increasingly apparent to Richard that Tony, to a great extent, lived in the past. Once when Richard hinted at this in a conversation, Tony replied, "Well, everything groovy happened twenty-five years ago." When Tony spoke of the protest marches, university sit-ins, draft-card burnings, speeches against the Vietnam War, and the music of the period, he conjured up vivid images that made those times live again for Richard. As their work at the cannery came to an end, both men expressed their desire to maintain their friendship.

The third-night after his cannery job ended, Richard thought, "I feel like I should be getting ready for work." Weeks of that routine had been ingrained into his system. Though it hadn't taken long to adjust to the graveyard shift, he wondered how long it would take his circadian rhythms to re-adjust.

Alone in the living room, he relaxed in a comfortable, old rocking chair. From a nearby table, he took a novel he had started and soon became engrossed. He had just reached a point where the hero confronted his nemesis when he felt a hand on his shoulder.

"*What!* Oh, Uncle Mac! I didn't hear you come up behind me."

"I'm sorry laddie, I dinna mean to startle ye. But I wanted to let ye know. I have your family's photo album I'd been searchin' for. It has pictures o' your mither and father and your brother and sister. I thought ye might have time now to look at it."

"Sure."

The two men sat down on the sofa, and Mac put the album on Richard's lap. As Richard turned the pages, Mac commented, sometimes saying where and when a photograph was taken.

"I certainly had a nice looking family," said Richard sadly. Pointing at one photo, he declared, "I like this shot of the whole family. It looks like I'm included too, because my mother is expecting. Wait a minute though—that couldn't be, my brother and sister are too young." Richard looked at his uncle for an explanation.

"You're right, o' course, laddie. At the time this photo was taken, your mom was carryin' her third child. In this photo, I think . . . she's aboot seven months along. If it turned out to be a boy, she planned to name him Douglas. I canna tell ye what went wrong, but your brother was stillborn. I'm sorry to have to tell ye, but ye should know. We should always remember Douglas."

"You know, Douglas and I have something in common—we both never knew our parents or brother and sister."

"I was thinkin' aboot him just last night. Ye see, my boy, if Douglas had lived, tomorrow would be his birthday; he'd be 39 years old."

Richard and his uncle looked at, and talked about, family members in the album until past midnight. Richard concentrated hard on the faces of his relatives, imprinting them in his mind in an effort to see them as a family that would have loved him, rather than as strangers who didn't know him. He wondered how they would view God's purpose for his life.

"Over the years, I've seen how the things you do, Uncle Mac, always come back to the purpose God has given you for your life. I wish I knew God's purpose for my life. The only purpose in *my* life has been my physical survival, and that of the people I love."

"Stay close to the Lord, laddie, and He will show ye, in His gude time, how your life can have a larger purpose than just survival, as vital as that is."

"By 'larger', Uncle, do you mean something important?"

"Not necessarily; 'larger' in the sense that it will give priority to the spiritual over the material. It will enable ye to please God and serve others ahead o' your own comfort."

"If my family had lived, maybe they would have taught me to be less self-centered, so that I could see now what He'd have me do with my life."

"Aye. Your dear family would have been a benefit to ye. But, son, remember what the Word tells us, 'And we know that in all things God works for the gude o' those who love Him, who have been called according to His purpose.'"

"I want to find God's purpose for my life—I realize I'll never be truly happy until I do."

"We may find God's purpose, or it may find us, as it found Paul on the road to Damascus—like a light from Heaven."

Mac suddenly looked at his watch "It's been a bonny chin wag, but it's time I called it a day, laddie. I'll see ye at breakfast."

"Okay. Thank you for showing me the album," said Richard, starting to hand the album back to his uncle.

"No Richard, the album is yours now. I saved it for ye." As Mac said this, he patted his nephew's hand, smiled, and turned to head up the stairs.

Richard was up early the next morning; Tony was coming to pick him up for a drive to the site of a hippie commune where Tony had lived in the 70s. After dressing and spending time in devotions, he headed downstairs to discover that Mac had already eaten breakfast and was outdoors working in his garden. Richard ate a cold breakfast that sacrificed nutrition for speed, then went out and sat on the porch step to wait for the old Volkswagen van to appear. "Tony's van will give the neighbors something to talk about," chuckled Richard to himself.

At that moment a red Volkswagen van pulled up in front of Mac's house. On the side of the van, facing Richard, Tony had painted a large yellow peace symbol. It seemed to Richard that the peace symbol looked like an upside down rake. He wondered what hippies wanted raked up. Underneath the peace symbol was the picture of a salmon jumping out of a stream. Printed under this scene were the words: "SAVE OUR ENVIRONMENT."

Cranking down the van window, Tony yelled, "Hi, Richard! Your limo is here!"

Richard stood up and waved. Walking briskly toward the van, he paused at the sidewalk and turned to try to catch a glimpse of his uncle. Unsuccessful, he hurried around the van and climbed into it on the passenger side, as Tony held open the door.

"Use this rope, Rich, to tie the door shut. This here is a customized van," laughed Tony.

As the van swiftly left the curb, Tony's loud greeting to Richard brought Mac hurrying from the backyard, hoping to catch Richard to say goodbye before he left. He reached the front of the house only to see the van drive off down the street. Standing motionless, a sudden premonition seized Mac. It was the same feeling he'd had when Richard's family had left on the fateful evening of their fatal accident. Entrusting his words to the wind, he called, "Be careful, Richard!"

"Hey, man! You're lookin' good! Enjoyin' your freedom since leavin' the cannery, are you, Rich?"

Before Richard could reply, Tony continued talking.

"Freedom, Man. That's where it's at! Rich, if it weren't for havin' to buy food and gas, I'd never restrict my life with a forty hour week, I can tell you that."

"What would you do if you could?" asked Richard, somewhat amused at Tony's view of work.

"I'll tell you, I'd be back makin' leather belts, wallets, and wristbands. Man, that was cool, 'cause it was on my terms. If I wanted to do it, fine; if I didn't, fine."

"Why did you give up leather craft then?" Richard queried.

"Couldn't compete with the big stores with their cheap, machine-made junk! Why, each belt, wristband, or wallet I made was a hand-crafted original. See this belt I'm wearin'—I designed and made it."

Richard looked admiringly at the belt. When he saw that Tony was looking at it too, instead of the road, hoping to sharpen Tony's focus on the highway, he observed, "That's an interesting brick building up ahead on the right."

Tony looked up, but still seemed to be in his own world.

"Freedom is what all humans are searchin' for and most of 'em think they'll find it by workin' hard, savin' money, and collectin' a lot of material stuff, but it's all an illusion, 'cause the more they collect, the more tied down they are and the less freedom they have. See, Rich?"

"I guess you're right. I once heard a professor say that he didn't have time for his family, because he had to write articles to get promoted."

"Right on, Rich! I knew a few like that, too."

After driving for over two hours, the men devoted more attention to the countryside than to each other. Richard broke the silence that enveloped them.

"Say Tony, I need to get back to town early this afternoon. I found out last night that my mother had a stillborn baby many years ago, and today would be his birthday. I thought maybe Uncle Mac and I could do something in remembrance of Douglas."

"Heavy, man. I'll get you back on time, never fear." With that declaration, Tony increased speed. "By the way," he asked, "how old are you, if you don't mind me askin'?"

"No, I don't mind. I'm 24—born in 1975."

"Well, Rich, you look younger and act older than your age. Hmm, the hippie era started to end when the war in Nam ended in '75." Tony fell into a brief silence, as a mourner might at the death of a friend. Then looking up, he yelled, "Hey Rich! There's a sight you don't see with your head down, countin' your money. See him up there? A goshawk. He's as free as any creature can be, floatin' on the air currents."

When Tony and Richard looked up, they were approaching a sharp curve at a high rate of speed. Becoming aware of this, Tony applied the brakes and, as the van began to skid, he struggled to keep from going off the highway. For some seconds, driving with two wheels on the level shoulder seemed to work. But when the shoulder inclined, the van, as if by an irresistible force, careened toward the telephone pole looming in its path.

Tony screamed, "Oh no! We're goin' to . . ."

A man driving a parcel delivery truck saw the red van strike the pole. He watched, horrified, as the driver was thrown from the vehicle, unrestrained by a seat belt. He heard the sounds of metal against splintering wood and shattering glass. There was nowhere he could safely park to try to help, but he called the state police immediately to request an ambulance.

Sitting on his weeding stool, working in his garden, Mac muttered to himself, "I know that Albert Schweitzer, in keepin' with his reverence for life, wouldn't allow flowers to be cut at his mission hospital in Africa, but I hope he would have allowed pesky weeds to be pulled." Quickly he straightened from his crouching position. *That's the phone ringin'. Maybe it's Richard.* He hurried into the house.

Mac rushed to the telephone in the living room, picked up the receiver, and anxiously said, "Hello . . . No, I'm sorry ye have the wrong number." As he sat down by the telephone, he tried to shake off the uneasiness he'd felt, when Richard drove off with Tony. The front doorbell's sudden ring upset his thoughts. On the porch stood a police officer.

"Good afternoon, sir. I'm Kenneth Morgan of the state police. I would like to speak with the spouse or close relative of a Richard Hawkins."

"I'm his uncle, Stuart MacGregor. Richard isn't married. Is Richard . . . hurt?"

Speaking sympathetically, the officer responded, "The information I have sir, is that he was in a car accident on Highway 99 and taken by ambulance to Mountain View Hospital. I'm sorry, I don't know the extent of his injuries."

"Thank ye, Officer Morgan. Di' ye know aboot when the accident happened?"

"Well . . . as I understand it, state police arrived on the scene . . . maybe, an hour ago.

"Thank ye, Officer. I'm goin' now to see my Richard."

11

Despair and Prayer

O N HIS WAY TO the hospital, Mac prayed hard and drove fast. He shaved 20 minutes off the usual trip to Riverfield; the ambulance took Richard to Riverfield Hospital, due to its proximity to the accident.

When he arrived, Mac parked the car and rushed toward the building's entrance. Standing aside only to let two women holding bouquets exit the front doors, Mac hurried to the information desk. He started to speak to the woman behind the desk, but instead turned to see who had touched his shoulder.

"Are you Mr. MacGregor?"

"Aye, I'm Stuart MacGregor, Richard Hawkins' uncle."

"Yes, a policeman called and said you were on your way, Mr. MacGregor. I'm Dr. Schiller. Your nephew is unconscious. We've X-rayed his jaw and neck and didn't see any sign of fracture. I have called in a neurologist, and will need permission to continue treatment."

"Ye have it, Doctor. Please do whatever is necessary to help my Richard. Di' ye think I might see him for just a minute?"

"Yes, of course. Come this way." The doctor led Mac to the Emergency Room, to a position just inside the door.

Mac fought back tears as he gazed at Richard lying on a wheeled cot, with a doctor and two nurses working over him. His shirt was off, revealing a large bandage over his ribs. His pants had been removed leaving him lying in his shorts. The petite, dark-haired doctor had treated cuts and abrasions on both legs and applied a cast to his ankle. While Mac watched, she examined Richard's head. Mac heard her tell a nurse to bandage a wound that was above Richard's right temple. He was receiving IV fluid, through a tube, attached to his arm.

The doctor examining Richard's head glanced up, saw Mac and Dr. Schiller and came over to them.

Dr. Schiller turned to Mac, "Mr. MacGregor, this is Dr. Karen Olson. Dr. Olson is the neurologist I called. I'll leave you with her. When you're finished, please see someone in Patient Receiving. You'll need to fill out some forms."

Mac nodded his response and turned to Dr. Olson. "Is Richard badly injured?"

"It's too soon to say. But I need to ask you several questions now. Does Richard use any medication, I.V. or recreational drugs, or alcohol?"

"No," answered the Scot emphatically.

"Does Richard have a history of chronic liver, kidney, lung, heart, or other medical disease?"

"No, he's always been very healthy."

"That's good. Now why don't you go to the waiting room and try to relax. I'll get back to you as soon as I review some tests. I've ordered a CAT scan and an MRI."

Mac gave Patient Receiving the required information and found a seat in the waiting room. Paging aimlessly through a magazine, he tried to follow Dr. Olson's advice and relax. Finally, he picked up a Gideon Bible and turned to Romans 8:28. He read the words several times: "And we know that in all things God works for the good of those who love him, who have been called according to his purpose."

Then a voice beside him asked, "How are you getting along, Mr. MacGregor?"

Mac turned to see a nurse standing near him. "I'm awright. Thank ye for askin'."

"Dr. Olson asked me to look in on you and see if you would like a cup of coffee or tea."

"Aye nurse, a cup o' tea would be nice. And could ye find out somethin' aboot my nephew Richard and his friend Tony—I was so worried aboot Richard I neglected to ask after Tony."

"I'm sorry, Mr. MacGregor. I thought you had been told. The man in the car with your nephew, identified as Anthony Kline, was dead on arrival. He died of internal injuries. His family has been informed. Was he a friend of yours?"

"No, not o' mine. He was a gude friend o' Richard's."

"I'll get you that cup of tea," said the nurse softly as she left Mac.

A little later, Dr. Olson appeared carrying Mac's tea and placed it on a coffee table near him. "Nurse Ella sent this to you. I wanted to tell you what I know at this point about Richard's condition."

"Aye, whatever ye can tell me, Dr. Olson."

"Richard remains comatose, Mr. MacGregor. This means he is in a state of extreme unresponsiveness; he shows no voluntary movement or behavior. He's been unconscious now about four and a half hours, which is not unusual after severe head trauma. The assessment we've made is a concussion."

"And the concussion," Mac said thoughtfully, "causes the coma."

"Well, yes. When a severe blunt force is applied to the skull," replied Dr. Olson, touching the top of her head, "as in a car accident, communication pathways between parts of the brain are disrupted, resulting in loss of consciousness. The concussion causes bleeding and tissue damage, which, in Richard's case, has produced a diffuse injury to the cerebral cortex."

"A 'diffuse injury,' ye say, Dr. Olson."

Noticing the confused look on Mac's face, Dr. Olson explained, "This means that the injury was spread out rather than concentrated in one spot. Based on tests, structural damage appears limited. We've assessed basic reflexes, including his eye responses to light, eye movements, gag reflex, and his breathing drive. What we learned did not suggest primary or secondary brainstem damage, since there seemed to be control of those involuntary functions."

"So, you're sayin', Richard's condition could be much worse."

"Yes, his injuries could be considerably more serious. But his head injury *is* serious. It's true people who suffer head injuries generally do better than those who become comatose from other causes. However, Mr. MacGregor, only about 15 percent of patients who remain comatose for, say, 12 hours recover all of their physical and intellectual functions. And adults, whose coma lasts more than four weeks have little chance of coming out of it with their former abilities intact." Wanting to sound more optimistic, she added, "On the other hand, I've had cases of children and young adults who've beaten the odds and have regained good functioning even after eight weeks in a coma."

"When di' ye think I might see my Richard again, Dr. Olson?"

"I've had Richard moved to the Intensive Care Unit. Nurse Ella is with him. I'm going there now. When I'm ready, I'll have someone notify you that you can come up. He's in room 507. Will you be here?"

"Aye, I won't be movin' from this spot."

An hour later when he received word that he could see Richard, Mac found his way to the Intensive Care Unit. Opening the door of room 507 slowly and quietly, Mac peered in. He could see Richard in bed, lying motionless, Dr. Olson bending over him. On receiving her signal to enter, he moved close to the bed and watched her put a cotton wisp under Richard's nostrils. Speaking to Richard as if he were awake, Dr. Olson said, "Richard I'm going to tickle your nose to see how you will respond, so that I'll know more how to treat your problem."

"Oh, he's movin' his head to get away from the tickle," observed Mac.

"Would you step out into the hall with me a minute?" prompted Dr. Olson.

Mac followed her out of the room and stood by her, next to the closed door. "Is anythin' wrong, Doctor?"

"No. I just wanted to explain, out of your nephew's presence, why I spoke to him as if he weren't comatose. You see, we can't be sure of how much Richard is aware, so everyone giving care to him will tell him what is being done and why. We also do this because he deserves the same respect as a fully awake patient."

"Aye, that's gude. But Dr. Olson, would ye try that tickle test again on my Richard? He's always been a wee bit stubborn."

"Well, you understand, it's not a matter of stubbornness," replied Dr. Olson with a smile. "But I'll try again and see how he responds."

With Mac looking on, she performed the test again and, this time, he moved his hand to his nose and shifted his shoulders.

"Aha, as your uncle thought, Richard, you needed a little coaxing. Now, I'm taking your right hand in mine and I'm going to press hard on your knuckles for just a moment. I want you to respond to the pain." Saying this, she pressed down on his knuckles, which elicited from Richard some unintelligible sounds. Pressing his knuckles a second time, she exerted more pressure. Richard responded with a few disconnected words. "That's just fine," she said, patting his arm.

"Excuse me a minute, Mr. MacGregor." Dr. Olson said this, as she walked across the room and spoke quietly to Nurse Ella, who was observing machines monitoring Richard's vital signs.

While Dr. Olson talked with the nurse, Mac leaned over to Richard, placed his hand gently on his forehead and quietly prayed, "Dear God, please heal my boy's body. Protect his brain from any permanent damage, so that he might serve ye all o' the days o' his life. Guide the doctors here, as they help Richard get well again. Thank ye Lord; I know ye have heard my prayer. In the name o' your Son, Jesus. Amen."

Returning to Richard's bedside, Dr. Olson didn't speak until she saw that Mac had finished praying. "Mr. MacGregor, I've got to be away from the hospital for a couple of hours, and when I return, I plan to discuss Richard's case with Dr. Schiller and Dr. Johnson, a brain specialist. The three of us will examine test results. As soon as I have news, I'll have you paged. I suppose you'll be in the waiting room."

"Aye, I'll be there."

"Why don't you get out of the hospital for an hour or two and get a bite to eat—that's *my* prescription. You have to keep your strength up, you know." Dr. Olson's tone showed sympathy and concern for her patient's uncle.

"Thank ye, Doctor, I think I'll take your advice." Mac suddenly felt tired. He realized that, for the last three hours, he had been getting by on adrenaline.

A simple meal at a nearby restaurant boosted his energy, and Mac returned to the hospital. He was directed to a private telephone and called Richard's Aunt Jennifer. He assured her that all she could do now is pray. He promised to keep her informed. He then called a number of Christian friends, telling them about Richard's accident and requesting their prayers. He called the senior pastor of their church, who promised to organize a 24-hour prayer chain, including members of the youth group. Mac also called Melissa's home and spoke to Helen Ingram. She assured Mac that she, her husband Donald, and their daughter would be in prayer for Richard. Helen's voice revealed that Mac's bad news had upset her. "I know that this will hit Melissa very hard," she said, "she thinks a lot of Richard—we all do. Please let us know when we can visit Richard at the hospital."

"Aye, I will Mrs. Ingram, and I thank ye for your prayers and friendship."

After placing a few more calls to former colleagues to ask for their prayers, Mac returned to the waiting room. When two more hours passed without any word from Dr. Olson, he became worried and began slowly pacing the length of the spacious room. He had walked from one end of the room to the other several times, when a young man sitting in a secluded corner spoke to him.

"It's the waiting that's so hard, isn't it?"

Mac stopped pacing and looked in the man's direction. "Di' ye say somethin' to me, sir?"

"Oh," said the man, "I just said that it's the waiting that's hard."

"Aye, I'm no gude at waitin', though I've had a gude deal o' practice in my life. I suppose you're waitin' to hear aboot a patient yourself?"

"I am, yes. A few hours ago, my father went in for bypass surgery. I'm waiting for him to come out of the operation. The surgeon said Dad was a good candidate for the operation. But, he's not as young as he used to be."

"I would like to pray for your father. What's his name?"

"That would be very nice; thank you. My father's name is Bruce Grant. I'm John Grant."

"'Grant' is a braw name for a man to have, so it is. The clan o' Grant has a great history in Scotland. The Grants and the MacGregors—I'm a MacGregor—come from the same stock. Where was your father born?"

"Dad was born in Los Angeles. But his parents were born in Inverness, which, I believe, is in Scotland."

"Aye, Inverness is in the highlands. Ye can take a ruler and draw a straight line doon a map o' Scotland and intersect Glasgow, where I was born. I can tell ye, any Scot in Scotland knows the Grants are tough fighters, and that weighs in your father's favor, as he fights to live."

"You're right about Dad, he's tough. Thanks for reminding me, Mr. MacGregor. I feel a lot better."

Mac was about to respond, when he heard Dr. Olson paging him. As he hurried toward the elevators, he called, "I'll remember to pray for your father."

As directed, Mac went to Dr. Schiller's office where he saw Dr. Olson. He entered and, at her invitation, took a chair near hers.

"Dr. Schiller was supposed to be here, but he received an emergency call and had to leave. And Dr. Johnson was due in surgery. I did talk with both of them before they left."

"I see, Dr. Olson. I appreciate everythin' that ye and the ither doctors are doin' for my nephew."

"Frankly, Mr. MacGregor, we all expected to see signs that Richard was coming out of the coma. He's been comatose nearly ten hours." Seeing the discouraging effect of her words on Mac, Dr. Olson added, "We do expect him to wake up. It's just that the longer Richard is comatose, the greater the impairment is likely to be. Dr. Johnson used a pinprick on the bottom of Richard's foot, and got him to open his eyes for a moment. Speaking loudly to him, however, did not get Richard to open his eyes—that would have been a better response."

"Ye will keep tryin', won't ye, Dr. Olson?"

"Yes, we will. Results from these tests may vary from minute to minute. Richard is under 24-hour observation, with all of his responses recorded. We're monitoring his fluids, and his body functions. The nurse is keeping Richard's eyes moist to protect them. We'll also make sure he stays nourished."

"My poor Richard. He always enjoys his food, and he's a gude cook."

"Well, Mr. MacGregor, he'll enjoy his food again. As I said, we all feel he'll wake up, especially since he had a score of eight on the Glasgow Coma Scale."

"Ye say 'Glasgow Coma Scale'? I know Glasgow has some gude hospitals."

"Yes it does. Researchers there developed a scale that helps us assess patients like Richard. We total up a number of points for our test results: opening the eyes, speaking, and moving a part of the body."

"Aye, I see. So if Richard had opened his eyes when Dr. Johnson spoke to him, he'd have gotten more points."

"We would have given him one more point," replied Dr. Olson in a tone that suggested the importance of the additional point.

"Di' ye think he'll be gettin' more points soon?"

"We *hope* so. We'll let you know about any change, Mr. MacGregor. Can we reach you at home?"

"No, I'll be in town, stayin' at a motel. I'll leave my phone number at the information desk. Di' ye think I might peek at Richard before I leave?"

"Yes, of course, Mr. MacGregor. You know his room number."

Leaving Dr. Olson, Mac went directly to Richard's room and quietly looked in. Standing at the foot of Richard's bed, Nurse Ella was obviously praying silently for his nephew. He carefully closed the door with a look of gratitude on his face. *Well, Lord, you're hearin' from a lot o' people aboot Richard.*

12

A Different Reality

TONY SCREAMED, "OH NO! We're goin' to . . ."
Richard's warning cry was lost in the din of the crash. He felt
a moment of pain before losing consciousness and suddenly felt he was
afloat in a quiet sea—dark and warm. Abruptly his body was subjected
to light, sound, and cold. These sensations signaled the beginning of a
different reality.

The doctor held the wet newborn up by his ankles. He gave him a
little slap on his bottom to start respiration, but the baby remained silent. "Come on. Come on," urged the doctor. The doctor once again gave
the baby a gentle slap that once more proved unsuccessful. Obviously
worried, the doctor tried a third time and this time a loud cry filled the
room. "We can be grateful it's not a stillborn," mumbled the doctor to
himself. "Mrs. Hawkins," the doctor announced, "you've given birth to a
fine baby boy. What's the little fellow's name?"

"Richard John."

"Well, now, it sounds like you took the first names of the two candidates for president—Richard Nixon and John Kennedy."

"No. I never thought of that. May I see my boy, Dr. Ferguson?"

"Of course, Mrs. Hawkins. After you have a look at him the nurse
will take him and clean him up."

Victor Hawkins waited in the lounge area reserved for expectant
fathers. Speaking to an acquaintance sitting next to him, he said, "This
is the third time I've waited for Mary to have a baby and each time I'm
more nervous than the last. I wish I could relax like these other chaps.
Some of them look young enough to be waiting for their first."

A nurse suddenly appeared at the lounge entrance, and gave each man a searching glance. Her eyes finally rested on Victor.

"Mr. Hawkins," the nurse softly called, "you can see your wife now."

Victor followed the nurse to a room in the maternity ward, which Mary shared with one other woman.

"Don't stay too long, Mr. Hawkins. The doctor gave your wife something to help her rest."

Mr. Hawkins assured the departing nurse he would only stay a couple of minutes.

"Hello, love," said Mary as Victor crouched by her bed.

"Hello, Mary. How's my girl feeling? A little sleepy, maybe?"

"You have a son, Victor. Did they tell you?"

Victor grew silent and showed Mary a concerned expression.

"Is there something wrong? Aren't you happy we had a boy?"

"Oh yes! A boy *or* girl would make me happy. I was just thinking that there must be *something* I could do for you."

"There is *one* thing you might do," replied Mary with a smile.

"What's that?"

"The staff is very kind and efficient here, but they aren't paid to be affectionate toward their patients. And well, I thought . . ."

"Oh, of course, how stupid of me!" And Victor bent over the bed and gently gave Mary a hug and a kiss.

Two days later, Victor took Mary and baby Richard home. The baby received a happy reception from his big brother and sister, who enjoyed helping their mother take care of him.

Surrounded by a loving family, Richard seemed to develop at a faster rate than most young children. Watching him play one day when he was three years old, Mary said to her daughter, Cathy, "He learns so fast. His vocabulary is four times what yours was at the same age."

"Well," chuckled Cathy, "I remember doing a lot of dumb things, like the time I borrowed Uncle Mac's antique Indian peacepipe to blow bubbles with. Boy, was he *mad*!"

"Only at first, Cathy. I didn't help matters when I said that the pipe needed a good cleaning anyway," recalled Mary with a smile and a shake of her head. "But you didn't do 'a lot of dumb things.' You were just being a little girl. Look there, Cathy. He's holding a ball in each hand as if he were weighing them. You know, the other day, I showed him how to spell his name—his whole name—with his letter blocks, thinking that he wouldn't understand what I was doing. And do you know, the next day he spelled his name out with his blocks for your father."

"Maybe, he's a genius, Mom."

The days, months, and years seemed to compress for the Hawkins family. Watching Richard grow and develop appeared to mark the passage of time for them. He did above-average work in school and had good health. Then one afternoon, shortly after his eighth birthday, Richard complained to his mother.

"I feel funny, Mom," said Richard slowly, as if the words were painful to utter. "I'm hot. Can I have a glass of water?"

"Come here, Son. Let me feel your head." Mary touched her hand to Richard's forehead. My goodness! You're *very* warm. Let's get you to bed, and I'll call Dr. Barker."

Mary helped Richard climb the stairs to his room. The doctor told her to give Richard liquids and keep him cool. When she returned, she had a glass of water and a thermometer. "Here Honey, put this in your mouth, under your tongue," Mary directed.

"For how long?"

"Not long." Mary patted his small hand that clutched the arm of his teddy bear. "I'll be back in a minute. Now, you keep that in your mouth."

Mary returned, holding a cold compress, which she applied to Richard's forehead. Then she removed and read the thermometer. "Hmm," Mary said to herself.

"What does it say, Mom?"

"103°," Mary told Richard in a tone of concern. "Here," she urged, "take a drink of water." She lifted the glass to Richard's lips and he drank deeply. "That's a good boy," Mary said, trying not to sound worried. "Do you think you could sleep for a little while?"

"I am a little tired." Richard put his teddy bear beside him and closed his eyes.

Mary left Richard's bedside.

When she checked on him a half hour later, she saw that he was awake.

"Mom, I'm . . . real . . . hot," Richard said, so softly he could hardly be heard.

Mary offered him a drink of ice water, then took his temperature again.

"Oh my goodness!" she cried. "Your temperature is up to 105°. Let's get this blanket and sheet off you."

Mary then grabbed the sheet, ran out of the room and returned in a few minutes with it, still damp from being rung out in cold water.

"This will cool you down, Honey," Mary assured her son, praying that she spoke the truth. After spreading the wet sheet over him, she hurried away again and came back with a pan of ice water and a wash cloth. Sitting beside his bed, Mary applied the cloth, dipping the cloth in ice water every few minutes for a fresh application.

"Where's my bear?"

"Why, he's right beside you, darling. Are you feeling a little cooler?" Mary asked with a hopeful tone.

"Better . . . put . . . cold wa . . . ter . . . on my . . . bear . . . We're both . . . hot."

Anxiously, Mary took Richard's temperature again. "Oh dear Lord, help me to know what to do," prayed Mary. The thermometer read 107°. She knew that a temperature above 108° could cause irreversible harm to the brain. "I wish Victor wasn't out of town," she said to herself.

"Mom, I wish . . . I wish . . . I . . . could jump . . . into the . . . at . . . beach."

"What darling?"

"Cold waves," said Richard, smiling as if he could visualize himself in the cold ocean water.

Suddenly, Mary scooped Richard out of his bed and carried him to the bathroom where she placed him in the tub and turned on the cold-water faucet. Holding his head up, she ran in enough water to cover him. Every now and then she would gently squeeze water from a sponge over his head. Ten minutes into this treatment, Mary fished for the thermometer in her apron pocket and took Richard's temperature. She sighed with relief. 104°. "Thank you, Lord," she silently prayed. Ten minutes later, his temperature had dropped to 101°. At this point, Mary lifted Richard out of the tub and dried him and the teddy bear that he had kept hold of, and carried them both to Roger's room, where she could put them into a freshly made-up bed. As Mary looked down at Richard whose temperature now showed normal, she said out loud, "I wonder if it got above 108°."

"What, Mom?" asked Richard sleepily.

"Nothing, Dear. Now try to get some rest."

Richard awoke to see his mother standing by his bed. "Hi, Mom. Do you want something?"

"I just wanted to see how you were feeling. I want to take your temperature one more time to be sure the fever has broken. But, you look fine."

"I feel fine, Mom." Richard opened his mouth for the thermometer.

Mary put her hand on Richard's forehead. "You feel nice and cool. But I want you to stay in bed for a while. I'll bring your supper."

Richard shook his head to show his objection.

"Yes, you will, young man. You were a pretty sick boy for a while. I'll be right back. I want to get something for you."

Mary left the room, and a few minutes later, came back carrying a large glass of what appeared to be juice. She put it down on the night stand and took the thermometer out of Richard's mouth. "Good. Your temperature is 98°. Still normal."

"Can I get up, now I'm normal?" Richard asked hopefully.

"No, Richard, not yet. You see, the high fever you had removed nutrients your body needs. So we have to put them back in. I brought you a glass of apple juice that has a tablespoon of blackstrap molasses in it. It should taste pretty good, but, even if it doesn't, drink it anyway."

"Mom, feel Teddy's head to see what he needs."

Mary felt the teddy bear's head. "Yes, well, I think what Teddy needs is to sit in front of the heater and dry out."

Richard relinquished his bear, and took a drink of juice. "So, this will put magnesium and potassium back in my body. Right, Mom?"

"Where did you learn about those?"

"I don't know. In school, I guess," replied Richard matter-of-factly.

Mary shook her head. "I didn't know that they taught things like that in the third grade. I'd better get supper started. Now, be sure to drink all of your juice. Oh, and I'll bring you in a pitcher of ice water and a glass, so you can take a sip now and then." As Mary was leaving, she said over her shoulder, "The doctor told me you were to drink plenty of fluids."

"See how Teddy feels, Mom!" yelled Richard.

"I'll check on him," Mary called back somewhat impatiently.

Days later, Mary entered the living room and stood behind her husband.

"Vic, would you turn down the TV for a few minutes? I want to talk to you about something. I'll let you get back to *Get Smart* after the commercial," Mary said with a smile.

"Oh, sure, Honey. Is something wrong?"

"Not exactly, Dear. It's just nice to see Richard over there, playing with his fire truck, like a normal child. Ever since his fever, he's been . . . well, different. Sometimes talking to him is like talking to another adult."

"Well, now, he certainly is precocious. But he's normal enough. The other day, he was asking me about baseball—he wants to learn to play," Victor offered with a tone of approval.

"Do you know the other day I found him in your study reading one of Shakespeare's plays?" Mary countered.

"I doubt he was *reading* much of it. He wouldn't have understood the Elizabethan English."

"Oh? Well, I asked him what 'periwig-pated' meant in . . . I think it was *Hamlet*, and he *told* me. I know he was correct, I looked it up."

"He likely knows the word 'wig', so he guessed. Still, I'm surprised he knew the word 'pate'. One of these days I'll test him on *Hamlet* to see how much he understands." With a tone of confidence Victor added, "It won't be much, I'll wager."

Mary was about to respond, but she saw Richard get up and walk towards them. Not wanting her son to hear them talking about him, she said, "We'll talk later."

Turning the TV back up, Victor said, "I'm sure it's nothing to worry about."

Richard carried his fire truck to his mother. "Mom, could I get a more modern fire truck? Then my friend Billy could use this antique one, and I could use the new one."

"Richard," Victor said, "that's an exact copy of the *latest* fire trucks in this city. You can see one just like it at the fire station over on 10th Street!"

Shaking his head, as he walked back to where his toys were on the floor, Richard muttered, "Then the city needs a new truck."

Mary gave her husband a knowing look. "See what I mean, Vic?"

"Does your head hurt, Honey?" Mary asked, when she saw Richard shaking his head and rubbing it.

"No, Mom, not really. I just keep hearing a sound in my head; kind of a beeping sound."

"How long have you heard this, 'beeping' in your head?"

"Well, I guess, it started the day after I had my fever," Richard said thoughtfully.

"You mean it's bothered you for two weeks and you didn't tell me?"

"Well, you see, it seemed to go away, but it came back. At least, it got so low, I didn't notice it anymore."

"Is the beeping very loud?" Mary asked, obviously worried.

"No. Most of the time, I don't notice it. I just tell myself, it's my motor going," said Richard with a wry smile.

"Tell me, if it continues, and I'll take you in to see Dr. Barker," Mary said. Then, more to herself than to Richard, "I think I'll call now and ask him about it."

13

An Explosive Episode

T WO DAYS AFTER RICHARD mentioned the beeping sound, Mary
asked him, "How are you feeling? Does that beeping sound you
mentioned still bother you?" Her tone suggested that she expected a
negative response, since he hadn't complained again.

"No, it doesn't bother me." But, Richard didn't mean that he didn't
hear it anymore.

"I'm glad it went away. Be sure to tell me if it bothers you again.
Honey, will you get your father and tell him supper's nearly on?" Mary
returned to setting the table.

Richard knocked on the door of his father's study and heard a
friendly, "Come in."

As he entered, Richard saw his father pacing up and down, obviously agitated.

"I don't know what this society of ours is coming to. I'm afraid,
son, you're going to inherit a mixed up world from my generation," said
Victor, shaking his head.

"What's the matter, Dad? Did something bad happen?"

"Richy, I see how this day of peace in the country is being misused
to further the agendas of certain groups."

"You mean the Moratorium on Vietnam?"

"Yes. In spite of observances of the Moratorium on campus, classes
were supposed to meet. But then I hear that some departments cancelled
classes, so their students could march to City Hall to hear speeches
against the war and President Lyndon Johnson. And, as you'd expect,
the SDS urged students to boycott classes. SDS stands for . . ."

"Yea, I know, Dad—Students for a Democratic Society. Roger told me that the marchers were chanting about the President."

"Oh, he did. What was it? I suppose something pretty uncomplimentary."

"You can say that again! 'Hey! Hey! Hey! LBJ! How many kids have ya killed today?' They just kept saying that over and over."

"One other thing. Roger told me it was the SDS that marched to ROTC headquarters at James Monroe U. Roger thought you must have seen them, since their hangout is near your office."

"No, I *didn't* see them . . . or *hear* them. Did Roger say they were peaceful?" Victor looked worried. "Depends on what you call 'peaceful'. About a hundred entered ROTC's building. I guess they were singing and chanting; they also shouted some pretty bad anti-ROTC slogans. I know one of 'em, but I don't think you'd want me to say it. I bet they were disappointed that the ROTC guys didn't try to beat 'em up!"

"Yes. Never mind their slogans. I've heard them, too. Did you want to talk to me about something, son?"

"Oh, yes. Mom says supper's nearly on."

"Well, in that case, we'd better get washed up." Victor put his arm around Richard's shoulders and steered him out the study door.

A short time later, Victor and Richard sat down to supper in the small dining room of the Hawkins home.

"Where are Cathy and Roger?" asked Victor.

"Don't you remember, Dear?" responded Mary. "Cathy is eating at Darcy's house tonight, and Roger has a date."

"Ah, yes. I remember. Then, let us pray. Silently." When Victor was sure Mary and Richard had finished, he said, "Amen."

Richard gave more attention to his father than to the food. It was the first time that he had ever seen his father say grace silently. "He probably wanted to pray about the trouble at the University," thought Richard. Richard marveled at his father's erect posture when sitting—it made him appear taller than his 5' 10" height. The eight year old looked closely to see if his father still appeared worried. Victor's brow was worry wrinkled above his horn rimmed glasses, and he periodically ran his hand through his dark brown, wavy hair—sure signs something was bothering him.

Smiling to himself, Richard thought, "Dad's the only prof in the Communications Department who wears his hair short and doesn't have a beard. No wonder his students ask him if he's joined the *establish-ment*." Richard knew his father's standard reply: "Establishment has two meanings: One is a permanent settled position, and the other is an act of bringing into existence. The first is static, inflexible; and the second is dynamic, ever-changing, which describes a normal society and a healthy life. I prefer the second meaning. How about you?"

Richard broke the silence, "Say, Dad, did you go today to hear that prof from California speak? The one with his picture in the student paper."

"As a matter of fact, I did, Richy. The speaker seemed determined to create controversy rather than offer constructive ideas about improving education. He suggested that children are taught a lot of myths about important figures in American history, such as George Washington, Thomas Jefferson, and Abraham Lincoln. He also said new technologies have made social studies and humanities unnecessary to teach in public education. I disagree, Richy. I believe that new technologies make social studies and humanities all the more necessary."

"Why?" Richard asked with an interest beyond his years.

"Take new technologies in medical science, for example. Philosophy can help us deal with ethical issues new medical advances raise."

"You know, Dad, I bet you one of these days, the schools won't even teach about Washington, Jefferson, and Lincoln."

"Well, Richy, I don't think things will ever get *that* bad; at least, I hope not," said Victor, slightly amused at such a thought.

"I don't know about that," Mary interjected. "After all, our youth to-day will be tomorrow's teachers. Look what they're learning from people like Spock."

"Mr. Spock from *Star Trek*?" asked Richard.

"No, Richy. Dr. Benjamin Spock is an elderly baby doctor, who wrote a famous book on caring for babies."

"What did he do, Mom?"

"I heard on the news that he's under a federal indictment—he's been charged with conspiring to counsel and help our young men to avoid the draft. Do you know what *conspire* means?"

"Sure, Mom, it means you meet secretly with others to plan a crime. Did Mr. Spock tell 'em to burn their draft cards?"

"I don't know, Richy, And he's *Dr.* Spock. I do know, he told them to break the law and not support their country or the troops. As famous as he is, the American Civil Liberties Union decided not to defend him. Now, let's have a moratorium on these serious topics, and talk about more positive things, while we enjoy our supper."

"I second the motion," said Victor good-humoredly, as he helped himself to more mashed potatoes.

Richard smiled and nodded, and also attacked the mashed potatoes, as Mary looked on with approval.

After supper, Richard helped his mother clear the table and clean up the kitchen, while Victor headed for the study. He liked being near his mother or simply watching her work.

"Richy, scoot out of here, and find something fun to do. Thank you for your help. You're always a good helper."

"I'm glad you think so, Mom," said Richard, as he left the kitchen, munching on a leftover biscuit.

Richard settled in a chair in the living room, and picked up *Time* from a nearby table. He was there when Roger came home.

"Hi, Squirt!" greeted Roger, in an affectionate tone.

"Hi, yourself. I thought you were on a date or something."

"I did have a date for dinner. But, I took Nancy home early. I have to work tonight at the University. Say, did you want to come along and help? I have to do my custodian job tonight, cleaning classrooms in the sociology building."

"Sure, Roger! What do you want me to do?"

"Well, you could empty wastepaper baskets, for starters. How's that sound?"

"Sure, I can do that," Richard said enthusiastically.

"Then listen, tell the folks that you'll be with me, so they won't wonder where you are. Okay?"

"Okay. I'll go tell Mom, and be right back. Don't leave without me."

"What? And lose my assistant custodian? I wouldn't think of it!"

Richard hurried off to ask Mary if he could go, and returned in a few minutes with word that he couldn't be out late.

"No. We won't be gone very long."

Roger parked the car near an old gnarled oak tree, which, in the shadows, seemed to reach toward Richard with leafy arms. The area was dark and secluded, its only light coming from a distant street lamp.

As they got out of the car, Roger warned, "Watch your step, Richy. This part of the campus is kind of dark. There's the sociology building over there." Roger pointed at a large red brick structure with white painted trim a short distance away.

"Style, looks Georgian," said Richard.

"Oh, is it? You might be right, little buddy," replied Roger, putting his arm around his brother's shoulders.

Roger led Richard up some steep concrete steps. "The building should be unlocked. That's funny—entrance lights are off. Hold the door open, Richy, and I'll see if I can find the switch." A couple of minutes later, Roger called, "I found it!"

Richard was relieved to see the entrance lights come on. He hurriedly joined Roger inside. "This is a spooky building. You say there's nobody here? Then, how come I hear creaking sounds?"

"Don't you know, Richy, *all* old buildings creak. You get used to it. Nothing to be worried about, except maybe the ghost of an old professor, looking for his glasses."

"You're just kidding about the ghost, aren't you?" asked Richard nervously.

"I *hope* so." Roger headed up the stairs in semi-darkness; Richard stayed very close behind.

"Do we have to go upstairs, Roger?"

"Yep. That's where the classrooms are that we have to clean. The light switch is just at the top of these stairs."

Reaching the second floor, Roger soon located the switch, producing a dim light down the lengthy hallway. This light did little to increase Richard's feeling of security, since it left the large classrooms dark behind their doorways.

Richard stood outside the first classroom, sure that he'd heard a strange noise emanating from its black recesses.

"Roger, I think I heard something in this room."

"What? Oh, don't worry. It's nothing. The sound is probably coming through an open window. I know where the lights are." Roger stepped into the room and it became brightly lit.

"Say, little buddy, check to see if all the windows are closed. I'll put the trash cart in the hall. It'll contain two big cans; dump the wastepaper in them. I'll push the cart along."

"Okay, Roger."

Roger assigned one side of the hall to Richard and took the other side himself. Armed with cleaning materials and a push broom, he entered the first classroom and began cleaning the chalkboard.

An hour and a half later, Richard had finished his job, and Roger had a good start on his.

"On your side, Roger, I'm going to start at this end!" yelled Richard from down the hall.

"Okay! That's groovy!" yelled back Roger. "I'll be working toward you! You're makin' good . . ."

A man's voice, yelling loudly, was suddenly heard, coming from the first floor. "Get out of the building! A bomb's going off in *five minutes!*" Roger and Richard were startled to near disbelief.

"Richard, did you hear *that*? We've gotta get outta here. Come on! *Run!*"

Richard started to run down the long hallway, when the lights went out. This left the two brothers in total darkness.

"I'll keep talking! Just follow my voice, little buddy! Slide your hand along the wall as fast as you can!"

"Yes . . . I'll try!" called Richard. "Ahh!"

"What's the matter, Richard?! Are you alright?!"

"I'm alright, I think," said Richard. "I ran into the open door of the broom closet!"

"Okay. Keep coming. Fast as you can. We maybe got only three minutes!"

Finally Roger could hear Richard's steps getting closer. He could also hear his brother breathing loudly.

"I'm here, *here*, Rich. Take my hand!" A small hand obeyed, and Roger grabbed it.

"Let's move as fast as we can toward the steps. I'll lead. You stay behind me, and don't let go of my hand," cautioned Roger.

The brothers reached the steps and were taking them two or three at a time, without the aid of the entrance light.

At the bottom of the stairs, Roger quickly felt for the double doors. "We made it!" he exclaimed. He began to push open one of the doors when, with a sound like thunder, an explosion made the building shake as if struck by a tornado. The bomb had been placed on an upper story. A shock wave from the blast roared down the stairwell toward them, carrying a dense cloud of dust and debris with it.

Roger got to his knees, and picked Richard up, trying to shield him from falling pieces of plaster. Roger butted his head against the door to keep it open while stumbling out with Richard in his arms. Light from the distant lamppost, revealed blood oozing from above Richard's right temple.

As sirens filled the night air, Roger realized that Richard was unconscious.

14

Back in Time

T HE ATTRACTIVE YOUNG WOMAN with the blonde ponytail observed a middle-aged gentleman, as he sat in the waiting room, head bowed in prayer. She waited at some distance. When he raised his head, she walked toward him. She recognized him from the picture Richard had shown her.

"Mr. MacGregor, I'm Richard's friend, Melissa Ingram. I thought I might be able to visit him."

"Aye, Melissa, thank ye for comin'. I know Richard would appreciate it. Visiting hours start in a few minutes."

"May I sit here and wait with you?"

"Aye, I'd be pleased if ye would. It gets a little lonely waiting' by myself."

Turning to Melissa, Mac asked, "Did ye come by yourself?"

"Yes. My parents are planning to come this evening, but I didn't want to wait for them. I wanted to come sooner, but didn't want to share my cold."

"Richard has told me a lot aboot ye. He thinks ye are very nice. He likes your parents, too."

"You say that Richard thinks I'm 'very nice,' Mr. MacGregor?"

"Aye, that he does." Mac nodded and smiled knowingly.

"I think Richard is, too. I hope he's well soon."

"Aye, we all want our Richard to come back to us."

"We should be able to visit him now," Mac declared, looking at his watch. "He's in room 507."

The two left the waiting room with Mac leading the way to the elevators.

Mac and Melissa exited the elevator at the fifth floor, and as they headed toward Richard's room, Dr. Olson suddenly appeared, walking rapidly toward them.

"I'm glad you're here, Mr. MacGregor. I was going to call you." Dr. Olson spoke these words as they met in the hallway.

"Is somethin' wrong with my Richard, Doctor?" Mac asked worriedly.

"Could I speak to you briefly in private?"

"I'll wait for you by Richard's door," Melissa said and walked down the hall toward room 507.

"Richard is stable now. But a short time ago, his temperature went very high—although it didn't remain at a high level very long. At this time, we don't know why he had this rise in temperature."

"How high did it go?" asked Mac, expecting to hear the worst.

Dr. Olson remained silent for a moment. A worried frown showed on her face. "Richard's temperature reached 107°."

"That's serious, isn't it, Doctor," responded Mac softly. His tone betrayed the depth of his fear.

"Yes, it's serious. A temperature that high could injure the brain," said Dr. Olson, putting her hand on Mac's arm. "We won't know more until Richard wakes up. Right now, I must visit another patient, then I'll stop in and see Richard. I think it would be better if you and the young lady visited tomorrow."

"Just as ye say, Doctor."

Mac found Melissa waiting for him at the door of Richard's room. "I'm sorry, Melissa, but Dr. Olson thinks we should wait until tomorrow to visit Richard. He had a high fever until a short time ago."

"Is Richard going to be alright? Has the fever hurt his condition?"

"Dr. Olson dinna say that." Mac sounded more optimistic than he felt.

The next morning, Mac quietly opened the door of 507, and peeked into the room to see a nurse he hadn't seen before washing Richard's face. She looked up as Mac entered.

"I hope I'm not disturbin' ye, Nurse. I saw Dr. Olson downstairs and she said I could come up to see Richard. Is there any change?"

"No, you're not disturbing me at all. You must be Richard's Uncle Mac. Dr. Olson said you would be visiting your nephew. We are expecting to see some positive change any time. I'm sure that Richard will let us know soon, how he is feeling. Right, Richard?" With her last comment, the nurse patted Richard's hand.

"Aye, laddie, all your friends are prayin' for ye."

"Richard," said the nurse, "I'm going to wash your ears now. And I promise not to hurt you. I still remember, how my mother used to wash my ears when I was a little girl. She used a *thick* washcloth, which didn't feel very good. And, I didn't like the water running down my cheek into the collar of my dress."

After she had gently washed Richard's ears, the nurse, gesturing to Mac to come closer, said, "Mr. MacGregor, would you like to comb Richard's hair? I'm sure he would rather have you do it, since you know how he likes it."

"Aye, I used to comb his hair when he was a wee lad, and he still combs it the same way." Just as Mac took a comb from the nurse's outstretched hand, the night sky brightened for a moment outside the hospital room's windows, warning of a more impressive event—in another moment a loud thunder clap filled the room.

"That sounded like an explosion! But I guess it was just thunder." The nurse spoke these words with some nervousness. "Last year at this time, we had a lightning strike that started a nearby fire."

"When the thunder sounded, my Richard moved his head and said somethin'," reported Mac.

The nurse went quickly to the monitors, but saw no change in the readings.

As Mac listened to their steady beeping, they seemed to chant, *not yet, not yet.*

"What did Richard say, Mr. MacGregor?"

"It sounded like he said, 'It was loud.'"

"I'll make a note of that on his chart for the Doctor," commented the nurse.

"I wonder if Richard heard the thunder, or was it somethin' else?" Mac said more to himself than to the nurse.

Roger carried his brother a safe distance from the building—smoke and fire billowing from its roof. He tenderly laid him on a patch of grass near a lamppost. In the lamplight he could see Richard's eyes open and his head move.

"Take it easy. Don't try to get up yet. Something fell on you I think, and knocked you out."

"What . . . happened? All I remember is running down the stairs and stuff falling on me," said Richard, dropping his head and shoulders back down on the grass.

"Don't you remember the explosion?" asked Roger in a worried tone.

"Uh . . . yeah. The explosion. It was loud."

"Let me look at your head, little buddy. Hmm, there's a cut, just above your right temple. It's bleeding a little. Here, Richard, here's a clean handkerchief. Keep it folded against your head . . . right there," and Roger gently touched a spot close to the cut.

"Ow," responded Richard.

"Sorry, Richy. Now, I'm going to carry you to the car, and take you to emergency at the hospital."

"Hey, I can walk, Roger. Just give me a minute to rest—I feel a *little* dizzy."

"Oh, sure, I know you can walk. But, I would like it better if I carried you. You know Mom and Dad would want me to."

"Yea, I guess you're right. Well, if it would make you feel better," replied Richard, secretly relieved.

Roger picked him up and started toward the car. He reached it in time to see fire trucks and police cars entering the campus. After laying Richard in the back seat, Roger got behind the wheel and drove to the hospital.

At the hospital, the physician in Emergency, bandaged Richard's cut and quickly examined him for other injuries.

"Mr. Hawkins, your brother appears to be alright, except for the cut on his head," the examining physician reported. "He should take it easy for a couple of days to be on the safe side. If there's any change, have your family physician look at him. But, he looks fine."

"I'm glad to hear that," replied Roger. "Thank you for helping my brother, Doctor."

"You're quite welcome. Now, excuse me, Mr. Hawkins. It looks like I have another customer." The doctor said this as he glanced through a window at an ambulance just pulling up, its lights still flashing.

As the doctor walked away, Roger put his hand on his brother's shoulder. "How you doin', Richy?"

"I'm feeling okay, Roger. Can we go home now?"

"Yea, little buddy. Can you walk to the car if I steady you a little?"

"Sure. I can walk. Maybe hang on to your arm."

As the two brothers walked slowly toward the car, Roger was quietly rehearsing how he would explain Richard's injury to his parents.

Inside the car, Richard lay down again in the back seat. "I'm just going to rest a little on the way home."

"Yea, good idea. I'll have us home in a flash!"

Roger kept his word by driving faster than the speed allowed. "Here we are, Richy. Can you walk or do you want me to help you?"

"I can manage on my own, Roger," replied a tired-sounding voice.

"Okay, but let me explain what happened. I don't wanna upset Mom and Dad."

"Alright," said Richard, as he slowly got out of the car.

As the two boys walked through the front door, they heard their father on the telephone in his study—he was talking to someone about the explosion on campus. They heard him mention their names.

The sound of the front door closing brought Mary into the room. The brothers stood waiting to report their adventures to their parents.

"Oh *there* you are! We were beginning to *worry* about you! We heard the explosion, and then your father turned on the radio and got the news. He's on the phone talking to a colleague about it. He told me a few minutes ago that a building close to where you were working got bombed."

Richard had been standing with his hand over his bandage. "Oh, no Mom, the building where we were working *was the one* that got bombed!"

"Richy," spoke up Roger, in a tone of irritation, "I'll explain all of it to Mom when Dad is off the phone. Richy's right, Mom. It was *our* building."

"What's that?" inquired Victor, as he came out of the study. "Let's sit down in the living room and get the story."

Roger eased his brother onto the couch to rest.

Putting his arm around Roger and giving his shoulder a squeeze, the father said, "I'm mighty glad to see you two." Victor then walked over to Richard, and patted his arm. Noticing his younger son looked a little pale, he asked, "Are you alright?"

"I'm *fine*, Dad," said Richard with a brave smile.

Mary suddenly noticed Richard's bandage.

"Richard!" Mary exclaimed, as she quickly got up from her chair and hurried over to him, "Did you get hurt in the explosion? Is it painful? How do you feel?" She bent down to look more closely at the bandage.

Richard looked at Roger with an expression that invited him to answer his mother's questions.

"Richy's alright, Mom. I took him to the hospital, so a doctor could look him over, and he said Richy was okay, that he should take it easy for a couple of days and call our doctor if you noticed any change. But, he's fine."

"Richy, you'd better go right to bed," Mary said, in response to this disclosure. "I'll help you get ready."

"When you get back, Love," Victor interjected, "Roger can tell us all about their experience."

"Be sure to tell them how the explosion knocked me down," Richard called over his shoulder.

Nodding his head, Roger replied, "Sure, I'll tell 'em."

"You both certainly had a close call. The Lord was with you and kept you safe. And your parents are grateful," Victor said. "Before Richard goes to bed, Mary, let's spend a few minutes giving thanks to God for their deliverance."

On the Saturday morning after the bombing at the University, Victor came home with good news. Standing in the living room, he shouted, "Where is everybody?"

Mary, hurrying from the kitchen, asked worriedly, "What's the matter?"

"Nothing's the matter," answered Victor with a chuckle. "Where are the children? I have some good news to share with the family."

Mary rounded up Richard, Roger, and Cathy.

With the family assembled, Victor announced, "We're moving into our own house, no more renting. The sale's gone through, and the house is ours! Richard will go to a new school, I think a better one, and we'll be close to the campus. And by the way, we'll also be closer to Mac."

While Richard and Cathy expressed their pleasure at the news, Roger remained strangely silent.

"That's wonderful, Vic," Mary responded. Then speaking more seriously, she added, "But, Roger has something to tell us too."

"What's that?" questioned Victor, sensing a change in mood.

"Well, Dad, I've been drafted into the Army. I have to report very soon." Roger spoke these words with forced cheerfulness.

"Here it is 1968, and the war in Vietnam is still going on," Victor said, shaking his head sadly. "I never thought it would last this long. How long do you have before you have to go?"

"About two weeks."

"Wow! They don't give you much time, do they?"

"No, little buddy, not too much. But, we'll still do some of those things we talked about."

Impulsively, Richard ran over to Roger and hugged him around the waist, tears starting down his cheeks.

"Hey now, I'll be okay." Roger gave Richard a gentle pat on the head. "I'll be in the states three months for training before I'm sent overseas. And by that time, who knows, the war may be over. Say! How about that movie you wanna see."

"You mean *2001: A Space Odyssey*?" prompted Richard.

"Yeah, that's the one. Tell you what, get cleaned up, and we'll go see the movie and afterward we'll get a hamburger for lunch. Whatta you say?"

"Neato!" The prospect of spending time with Roger temporarily cheered him.

Mary smiled her approval at Roger. Then turning to Cathy, she said, "You'll be home for lunch, won't you?"

"No, I won't be, Mom. I have to eat at Darcy's so I can help her with a writing project for school. It's due tomorrow. But I should be home soon enough to help with supper."

"Don't you worry about supper. I'll ask your father to help me," replied Mary with a twinkle in her eye.

"I'm your man! But I *must* be fed," Victor said with mock seriousness.

"I think we can manage that for someone who has gotten us a new home." Mary complemented these words with a kiss on Victor's cheek.

"Uncle Mac's going to be pleased about having us closer," Victor noted. "He's been pretty lonely since cancer took Kathleen."

"Well, Mom, I guess Richy and I will take off—we should make it to the matinee."

"Just as soon as Richard combs his hair and changes his shirt."

"Oh, Mom! Do I *have* to? It's just a movie," Richard whined.

"That's no excuse not to look neat, young man," declared Mary in a tone of finality.

Understanding argument was fruitless, Richard hastily left his family and hurried to his room where he altered his appearance according to his mother's wishes. Then he called his goodbyes, and ran out to the car. Roger was waiting with the motor running.

"Pass inspection, little buddy?"

"I guess I would have if Mom had seen me. I don't see why I have to look neat in a dark theater though," puzzled Richard.

"What Mom always told *me* when I would answer that way, was that even if nobody else saw me, *I* would see me. She'd say somethin' like that." As Roger provided this explanation, he backed the Nash Rambler out of the driveway and headed down the street.

"Did you like the movie? Was it as good as you thought it'd be, Richy?" asked Roger, as they walked out of the theater.

"Sure did!" Richard shaded his eyes against the bright sunlight that greeted them.

"Wait a minute, Richy, I wanna give my eyes a chance to adjust to the light."

"To adapt our vision to the dark theater, our photoreceptors increase our sensitivity to light ten thousand-fold."

"Where in the world did you learn that, anyway?" asked Roger, impressed.

"I don't know. Maybe I read it in one of Dad's magazines. Are your eyes adjusted yet," asked Richard, anxious to have the promised hamburger.

"Yea, I'm fine—my photoreceptors are getting back in shape. Let's go eat! Is A&W okay with you?"

"Sure, Roger. I love their root beer."

As the two brothers left the theater, Roger turned to the right. "I think we parked down the block *this* way."

"No, Roger, it was the *other* way."

Richard's confident tone convinced Roger to turn around. "I never did have a good sense of direction," he said, shaking his head with a smile.

"Roger, I'm afraid that you might get lost if you went to Vietnam," said Richard, looking and sounding worried.

"Tell you what, I'll stick close to the other guys I'm with, so I don't head in the wrong direction." Roger said these words with pretended seriousness. He rubbed his brother's head. "Hey, I'm gettin' hungry. Let's walk a little faster."

"There's the car just down the block. Let's race," challenged Richard, starting to run.

Roger trotted along, being careful to stay behind Richard. When he saw that his brother had nearly reached the car, he speeded up. "Phew! I must be gettin' old. You beat me fair n' square."

"Oh no, Roger. You're not getting old. It's just that I started ahead of you. You know, after running, I'm even *hungrier* now."

"Me too!"

15

Between Two Worlds

THE TWO BROTHERS SAT in the front seat eating hamburgers. Attached to the open window on each side of the car was a tray holding a frosty mug with what was left of their A&W root beer.

"Say, little buddy, do you want a piece of pie to go with the rest of your root beer?"

"No, I'm full, Roger. But thanks. That was a super lunch."

"Well, okay. Let's drink up, and I'll honk for the carhop."

"Roger, why do they call the waitresses at the drive-in restaurants carhops? They don't *hop* or anything."

"Don't know, unless it's because they have to hop to it to wait on customers. You could ask her when she comes for the trays," Roger suggested with a mischievous grin.

"No, I wouldn't do that. I just wondered," replied Richard, embarrassed at the thought.

A few minutes later, Roger honked and the carhop appeared quickly.

"See, she *hopped* to it," Roger observed with a mock seriousness.

"Shall we head for home?" asked Roger, as they drove away minutes later.

"I guess . . . so," hesitated Richard. "On the way to the restaurant, I saw a couple of garage sales. Could we stop at one of them?"

"Tell you what. We'll pick up Cathy at her friend's place then find a sale."

Roger drove to Darcy's house. Cathy was apparently watching for them, since she immediately came out of the house and hurried to the car.

Richard climbed into the back seat, so Cathy could sit in front. Roger began the search for a garage sale.

"Did you help Darcy with her writing project, Cathy?"

"Yes, I hope so, Richy. All she has to do now is make a few corrections and type it up."

"Did you show Darcy about APA footnoting and quoting?"

"Where in the world did you learn about APA? Sometimes, Richy, you *amaze* me." Cathy looked over her shoulder at Richard as she made this response, smiling and shaking her head.

"I don't know, I guess . . . Stop Roger! There's one of the sales! See on the right, the *red* house there?"

Roger pulled up in front. They all got out of the car to have a look at the wide assortment of objects displayed on tables in the driveway.

Richard and Roger headed for a table full of hardcover and paperback books.

"Look here!" said Roger. "A leather-bound edition of Shakespeare, and it's in great condition. I bet Dad would like it. I'm gonna get it for him."

Next to the books was a table of hand-crafted jewelry—the kind that hippies made. A silver chain and pendant caught Richard's eye. On closer examination, he could see that the pendant looked like a cross and a star at the same time. "I've never seen a cross like *this* before," said Richard to himself. "I wish I had enough money to buy it for Mom."

As Roger passed the jewelry table to buy the book for his father, Richard grabbed his arm.

"Roger, would you lend me enough money to buy this necklace for Mom?"

"Sure, pretty soon I'm not gonna be able to spend much of my *own* money, anyway. Uncle Sam will pay me all I need." Looking at the necklace in Richard's hand, Roger nodded approvingly, "A real eye-catcher! You know what it is, Richy?"

"No, I guess it's some kind of cross."

"It's a Maltese cross. It was the emblem that the knights of Malta had on their shields a thousand years ago."

"Do you think Mom will like it, Roger?"

"Sure she will. I bet she'll wear it to church. Here, let me have it, and I'll pay for *it* and Dad's book at the same time."

Glancing down at the jewelry table, Richard spotted a hand-made belt that was modestly priced because it was made for a child. Impulsively, Richard picked it up and hurried after his brother, who had walked away to find the person in charge of the sale.

Catching up with him, Richard said, "Roger, . . . would you please buy this belt too? I'll pay you back."

"Okay. But you don't have to pay me back. We'll call it a little gift from your big brother." Roger patted Richard on the shoulder.

"Thank you, Roger. It's just like a belt a friend of mine made."

When the brothers returned to the car after making their purchases, they found Cathy in the car waiting for them.

"I guess you couldn't find anything, huh, Sis?" asked Roger.

"Yes, I did," answered Cathy in a tone of satisfaction. "I found something really nice, and at a good price, too. It's in the trunk."

A week after the garage sale, Richard approached Roger, who was dozing in a chair in the living room.

"Are you asleep?" asked Richard softly.

"If I was, I'm not now," replied Roger with a chuckle. "What's up, little buddy?"

"Oh, I just wanted you to see my new belt. What do you think of it?" asked Richard, directing Roger's attention to the belt he was wearing.

"Real hip. It's definitely you."

"Thank you for buying it for me."

Roger observed Richard start to hug him—and then stop himself. "That's okay, you can hug me if you want. I won't think you're less of a man if you do."

But Richard stood embarrassed in silence.

Changing the subject, Roger said, "I'm glad you like the belt. Say, you said that the belt was like one that a friend made. Who was that? I might like to have him make *me* a belt some time."

"His name, his name is . . . That's funny, I just can't think of his name."

"Well, that's okay. It doesn't matter. When you think of it, let me know."

"As Mom says, it's on the tip of my tongue. He was my good friend. I don't know why I can't think of his name. I can't think how he looks, either." As Richard spoke, he put his right hand on his temple. The room started to spin. "Roger," he said in a small voice, "I feel like . . ." The floor suddenly moved toward him.

Dr. Olson stood at the foot of Richard's bed, staring intently at her patient. "Richard," she called softly, "can you hear me?" But, she received no answering response. She then looked at his chart, shaking her head with concern. But suddenly, out of the corner of her eye, she saw a movement under the blanket. "Yes," she thought, "there it is again." Seconds later, Richard brought his right hand up to his temple. He held his hand to his head for a moment and then dropped it forward onto the blanket, as if the effort fatigued him. "That's good, Richard. I'll just record that on your chart."

Dr. Olson didn't see Mac slip into the room.

"I know it's not visitin' hours, Dr. Olson. But I thought I could peek in to see my Richard."

"Yes, of course, Mr. MacGregor. Please come in and tell Richard hello. A minute ago, he put his hand up to his head. *Didn't* you, Richard?"

"Aye, that's gude, isn't it, Doctor? I've been a wee bit worried. This is the fourth day and . . ."

Dr. Olson interrupted Mac. "We can talk about that later. Richard, here is your Uncle Mac to visit you."

"Look there! Richard turned his head to look at me. How are ye doin', laddie? The church has organized a 24-hour prayer chain for ye. And ye have a braw and beautiful doctor to help ye get well."

"Will the young woman be back today to read some more to Richard?" asked Dr. Olson. "I'm sure he appreciates that. Don't you, Richard?"

"Aye, that would be Melissa. She plans to come often as she can to read to him."

As Mac replied, he walked across the room to get a chair. Glancing in Richard's direction, he saw that his nephew followed him with his eyes.

"Dr. Olson," whispered Mac, "Richard kept his eyes on me as I moved. He seems to know me."

"Yes, he started tracking our movements with his eyes yesterday. At this point though, we can't say that he knows you. After you talk to Richard, perhaps we could talk out of his hearing."

"Aye. I'd like that."

As Dr. Olson left the room, Mac pulled a chair close to Richard's bed, and said, "Laddie, Melissa will be comin' by to read to ye. She's a bonny lass, as ye very well know. She thinks a lot o' ye, so she does."

"I told ye aboot Mr. Grant, Bruce Grant, who is in this same hospital for bypass surgery. I've been prayin' for him, as I promised his son I'd do. Well, he came through the surgery fine. I visited him yesterday, and he said he would come and see ye, maybe tomorrow. I brought with me my book of Robert Burn's poetry, so I could read ye some o' the poems ye like."

Mac read several poems and had just finished reading Burns' "My Heart's in the Highlands" when he noticed Dr. Olson waiting for him. Mac leaned over and gently patted Richard's arm. "I've got to go now, but I'll be back later."

Out in the hall, Dr. Olson suggested that they go to the hospital cafeteria for their talk.

As they stepped into the elevator, she said, "You read Burns' poetry beautifully. I wish you would read for some of our other patients."

"Well, I thank ye for the nice compliment. Are ye a fan o' the Bard o' Scotland?"

"Yes, I am—ever since my college days. After a long, hard day at the hospital, I enjoy relaxing with a cup of tea and my friend, Robert Burns."

Leaving the elevator at the second floor, they walked a short distance to the cafeteria. There, they each ordered a cup of tea and sat down at a nearby table.

"I wanted you to know that Richard's increased responsiveness has encouraged both Dr. Schiller and me. We think—I repeat *think*—that he shows signs of coming out of the coma. Now, I don't want to raise your hopes too much, but we do see cause to be hopeful."

"Dr. Olson, ye told me that when people wake up after 12 hours in a coma, most o' them recover fully. But, my Richard has been in a coma almost eight times longer. When he comes out o' it, will he be very . . . affected?"

"Mr. MacGregor, my father, who is also a physician, was told by his doctor that, on average, the people who have his condition live about a year—that was 11 years ago. Statistics help those of us in the medical profession make educated guesses about what we're up against and how to recommend treatment. But, you don't practice medicine very long before you learn that some people beat the odds, especially when it comes to the human brain."

"So, Richard could come out o' the coma normal, even after that long. Is that what ye're sayin', Doctor?"

"He might have some deficiency after he wakes up, but often therapy can enable the patient to overcome the deficiency, if it isn't too acute. I've studied the human brain, the *living* human brain, for 20 years, Dr. Schiller has for 30 years. We have met with the best physicians in our field all over the world, and we all agree that there is more we *don't* know than we *do* know about the human brain. Remember, someone as brilliant as Aristotle believed that a person's center of thought was in the heart and that the brain simply functioned to cool the body. Many experts agreed with Aristotle for centuries. It's fair to say that we've probably learned more in the past 25 years than in all of medical history. In the final analysis, the Great Physician determines the prognosis."

Getting up, Dr. Olson said, "I should be getting back to my rounds. Stay and finish your tea. If there's any change in Richard's condition, I'll let you know. Try not to worry." She lightly touched Mac's shoulder, and received a pat on the hand back.

Mac followed her departure with his eyes. *Juvenal was right: Beauty and modesty is a rare combination.*

16

A Loving Family

RICHARD SLOWLY OPENED HIS eyes and looked searchingly around the room.

"How did I get here? Why am I on my bed?"

Richard put these questions to his brother, who was sitting on the bed, peering down at him anxiously.

"How are you feeling, little buddy? You fainted on me, so I carried you in here. And you're getting to be a heavy guy. Are you feeling better, now?"

"How long was I out, anyway?" asked Richard, sounding embarrassed.

"Oh, just a few minutes. I think your blood sugar might be a little low." Roger tried to think of a logical reason for his brother's fainting spell.

"Say, does Mom know I fainted?"

"No, not yet. She's still packing stuff out of the kitchen cabinets for the move to the new house. Matter of fact, Richy, I promised to carry out some boxes for her. So, I better shake a leg, that is, if you're okay."

"Yea, sure, Roger. But do me a favor, don't tell Mom I fainted—I don't want her to worry."

"Okay, I guess I don't have to tell her. If you don't want me to, I won't. It's no big deal to faint. I did it once, myself."

"You did, Roger?"

"Yep. I sprained my ankle really bad, playing basketball. The day after it happened, early in the morning, I headed for the kitchen and tripped over my crutches. I came down hard on my swollen ankle, and, boy, the pain was so bad I fainted. I was in the living room, close to the piano. So when I fell, my fingers dragged over the piano keys and woke up the whole house. It was my first and last concert!"

"It must have been painful, to make a big guy like you faint," said Richard, feeling better.

"Yeah! It sure was! Tell you what, when you feel up to it, come out and help me with the boxes. I could use an extra pair of hands."

"I'll be *glad* to help, Roger."

Roger left while Richard got off the bed, and put on his shoes.

After spending a few days packing and moving, the Hawkins family was finally settled in their new home. They discussed the event in their living room.

"It would have taken us a lot longer to move," Victor told Mary and the three children, "without Mac's pickup. And we saved a bit of money by not hiring professional movers."

Mary shook her head. "I didn't know we had so many things, until we had to pack them all. I discovered that many of the things we brought over we don't use anymore—in fact, I had forgotten we even had them."

"Well Mom, one thing I sure found a *lot* of, and that's *books*!" Roger said, rubbing his back. "I think I carried fifty boxes to the pickup."

"I'm probably responsible for ninety percent of them, son. It may have seemed like fifty, but we loaded fourteen. But they're the tools of my trade. And I certainly appreciated your help. Though I'm sorry you had to work so hard when you're leaving for the Army soon."

"That's okay, Dad. It was a good workout for me. I needed an excuse to get a workout before reporting, anyway."

"You and Richard were a lot of help with the books and other things, and . . ."

"Hey, what about me, Dad!" interrupted Cathy. "I dusted a lot of your books when you were gone, and I packed a few of them, too."

"Yes, I know, Cathy, your mother told me. And so I was about to say 'and so was Cathy.' I wouldn't forget my girl," said Victor, with a loving look. "I know you're always ready to help your family," he said, as he noticed the appreciative look on his daughter's face. "I'm a fortunate man to have such a great family." He gave each family member a grateful smile. "And I say that in my prayers every day. A week from today is a big day for Roger and Richard—Roger heads for Fort Lewis, and Richard heads to a new school."

Mary added, "And since Richard's birthday is really two weeks from now, he and I thought we would celebrate it early so that Roger can be with us. I'm planning to serve one of Roger's favorite meals this evening—spaghetti and meatballs. For dessert, we'll have cake and ice cream. I called Mac this morning and while he can't come to dinner, he says he will be happy to join us for the party."

"Neato!" responded Richard to the news. 'Maybe he'll tell us more stories about his days in Scotland."

"I'm sure he will, Richard," said Mary. "Your Uncle Mac never needs much coaxing to talk about his beloved Scotland. Now, everyone stay close by, because we'll have an early dinner. And Cathy, if you'll help me decorate the cake I can work on dinner, so we can eat around 4:30."

As the women left the room, Victor got up from his chair. "I guess I should get busy too, fellows. I have to give a test tomorrow, so I'd better put something together. I'll see you at dinner." With these words, he headed for his study.

When he was sure that his father wouldn't hear him, Roger commented, shaking his head and smiling, "Dad never needs much of a reminder to go to work. I bet he's spent half his life in his study. I'll tell you, Richy, teaching in a university isn't my bag. Not that I'm smart enough, anyway."

"Do you think Dad enjoys teaching, when he has to work so hard?" asked Richard.

"Oh yeah! He *loves* it. The only thing he doesn't like about it, that I've heard him say, is the grading. It's tedious work—and he doesn't like to give low grades. He tries to help the weaker students. But you know how life is," said Roger shrugging his shoulders, "he can't get good work outta *everybody*."

Richard suddenly felt sad, as he thought that soon Roger would be too busy to give him much attention; he would have to get ready to leave for the Army. "When you leave for the Army, Roger, what time of day do you have to go?"

"Very early, little buddy; before you're up. I have to catch a bus to Portland, to the induction center, and then all the guys will be on a chartered bus to Fort Lewis. There we'll do our basic training."

"Where exactly is Fort Lewis?"

"It's outside Tacoma. You know where Tacoma is."

"Oh, sure, it's in Washington. That's not far away. Maybe we could come and visit you," said Richard in a hopeful tone.

"I should get some leave after I finish basic, and then I'll tell you all about it. And we can write each other letters! You can keep me posted on how things are with the family. You can tell me how you like your new school."

"Well, I guess so. But, I'd rather come and see you."

Noticing that his words hadn't cheered Richard up, as he'd hoped, Roger offered a sudden suggestion. "Hey! How 'bout a game of checkers? You've won the last two times we've played, but I'm feeling lucky."

"That's a good idea. Maybe this time you can beat me." Although he always played to win, Richard suspected that Roger sometimes let him. He wanted to concentrate on the game, and try to forget that his brother would be gone for a long time.

The brothers were on their third game when Mary called them to dinner.

"And get your father!" yelled Mary. "He's probably lost track of the time."

When everyone finally got to the table, Victor said grace and included a prayer for Roger and Richard. His prayer reminded the family that Roger was leaving, which caused the conversation to sound forced, until they were able to put it out of their minds.

Cathy helped when she commented, "Mr. Kettle in our social studies class was telling us about ideas of Arnold Lazlow and Colin Borgers; you know, how to find yourself and relate to people. Pretty interesting."

Roger looked at his father's face and saw the dawning of an opinion. "What do you think about that, Dad?"

Victor, gesturing with his fork, took the bait. "Well, we hear a lot of talk these days about freedom and openness, but we see the same people practice license and behave disorderly. Many of our young people today are looking for simple formulas to explain complex issues. But, after all, gurus, such as Colin Borgers and Arnold Lazlow, said that they could create their own reality, and they have. Now, as a result, we have a society full of . . . self-centered *lifestyles*, to use Borgers' favorite term."

Richard spoke up when his father paused: "But, didn't Arnold Lazlone say something smart about self-esteem?"

Victor gave his son a surprised look. "His name is pronounced Laz*low*. But yes, he did. We have to give him his due, son. How did you know about his work on self-esteem?"

"Oh, I don't know. I guess I read it, maybe."

Cathy, who looked as if she were thinking hard about her father's comment, said, "Mr. Kettle didn't say anything about 'reality,' when he spoke of Lazlow and Borgers."

"Next time he talks about them, you might ask him about that," suggested Victor.

Observing the conversation was getting rather heavy, Mary interjected a practical concern. "We forgot to dig up my tulip bulbs before we left the house. I told myself to do it, but I forgot. I suppose it's too late now."

"Yes, my dear, unless we went over to the old house at night with a flashlight." Perceiving that his flippant remark was not well received he quickly added, "You can buy some new bulbs, and I'll help you plant them. How's that, Honey?"

"That would be nice," responded Mary, sounding happier.

"Yes, and think how surprised and pleased the people in the old house will be when your tulips come up and they see the beautiful blossoms." Victor said this, thinking to encourage Mary. But her facial expression made it obvious that she was sad again. "Well, one thing we're going to have to do is build a fence around the backyard."

"When I'm home on leave, I can help," offered Roger. "Say, when do we celebrate Richy's big birthday?"

"Right after dinner. Your father and I will clear things off," responded Mary. "Then we'll bring out the cake and we'll sing happy birthday to our boy. I think we can find a few presents for this young gentleman, too."

With that incentive, the family ate more and talked less. When Mary was satisfied that everyone had eaten seconds, she and Victor cleared the table, and Cathy brought out the cake that she had decorated with red roses and the words: "Happy Birthday Richy From Your Loving Fam." The candles burned in a circle around the edge of the cake. Cathy explained to Richard that she did not have enough space to complete the last word.

"Cathy, that's the *fanciest* cake I ever saw," said Richard admiringly. "I bet it tastes as good as it looks."

"Well," chuckled Cathy, "I can't take credit for how it tastes, since Mom made it, but I tried to give it the tasty look it deserves."

"It looks groovy," interjected Roger. "Very sliceable!"

The family started to sing happy birthday to Richard when the doorbell rang.

"That must be your Uncle Mac, Richard. Let him in. He might just have a present for you," said Mary with a knowing smile.

Richard hurried to the door, pleased that his uncle had made it to his birthday party. "Come in, Uncle Mac, it's time to sing happy birthday to me!" Richard said as he opened the door.

Richard soon returned to the table, holding his Uncle Mac's hand.

Noticing a small, white package sticking out of Mac's jacket pocket, Roger asked, "Well, little buddy, did you return with a present?"

"No, but Uncle Mac is a good enough present for me."

"Thank ye, laddie, but I don't rate myself so highly, that I could get by on my gude looks," responded Mac with a twinkle in his eye. "So, I brought ye a wee present." With that, he placed the small, white package on the table, next to another small package from Victor and Mary.

"Now that we have added a strong tenor to our group, we are ready to sing a happy birthday," Victor announced.

They all gave him a hug, and he blew out the candles so he could make a wish.

Mary took charge of slicing the cake, giving the first piece to Richard, with two scoops of ice cream.

The cake and the ice cream disappeared quickly amid the sound of family chatter and laughter. Soon it was time for Richard to open his presents.

Carefully and slowly opening Uncle Mac's gift first, he discovered a watch case in which nestled a Mickey Mouse watch. "Oh, neato!" Richard exclaimed. "Now I can tell when it's close to recess." He next picked up the gift from his parents. "It's sure heavy—and something in it rattles." Richard's curiosity aroused, he opened this gift faster to find a chain and padlock.

"That's to keep you chained to your desk at school, little buddy," Roger joked.

"Wait a minute, I know what *this* is!" Confident in his theory, he ran to the front door, opened it and gave the porch a close look; then undaunted, he ran back, went through the kitchen and out the backdoor. A loud yell of joy showed his discovery of a shiny bicycle in the backyard.

When Richard came back, the table held a small guitar case with a green bow. As he walked up to the table, Cathy pushed the case toward him. "Happy birthday, Richy."

Richard's eyes grew large and a slow smile appeared. His hands touched the case lovingly. He unfastened the case, opened the lid, and exclaimed, "It's a guitar!" He gently removed the small guitar from its case and examined it. Though a little scratched, it appeared to be a fine instrument. Still looking at it, he ran his fingers over the strings. It produced a nice sound.

"That day, you know, that we went to the garage sale, well that's what I bought and put in the trunk of the car," said Cathy proudly. "I had it restrung for you," she added.

"Thank you, Cathy. I've been wishing I could play an instrument. And this is just what I need."

"I'm glad you like it, Richy," said Cathy cheerfully.

Looking at his family, Richard's face showed his gratitude. When he thought about all the gifts, especially the guitar, it was hard to keep from crying. "Thank you for all these neat presents. They're just what I wanted. I need them all, including the new belt you gave me, Roger. See? I'm wearing it now!" He stood looking happily at his family, when suddenly they seemed unreal, as if posed in a family portrait. He shook his head. The beeping sound seemed to get louder. For a moment, a mist appeared to engulf them and obscure them from sight. But then the beeping sound subsided, and the mist lifted and he was once again with a family that loved him.

17

Making Music Together

O N HIS FIRST DAY at Applegate Elementary, Richard got acquainted with Sarah and Jeff, who had also transferred from another school. The teacher, Miss Kindskill, writing their names on the chalkboard, welcomed the three pupils to the class and encouraged the other children to do the same. At recess, they found out they had something else in common.

"Sarah, Richard, Jeff, if you'll come with me, I'll show you the cafeteria where we eat lunch. Then we'll go to the playground for recess."

The three children followed their new teacher , who acquainted them with the building.

"Do you have any questions before I leave you?" Miss Kindskill asked.

Richard replied, "I was wondering if I could practice my guitar sometimes during recess."

"Me, too," chimed in Sarah.

"You also play the guitar, Sarah?"

"No, I play the autoharp. But some days my music teacher doesn't *think* I do."

"I understand it's a difficult instrument," Miss Kindskill said. "I'm sure you do very well." Then turning to Jeff, she said, "I don't suppose you play an instrument too."

"Well, no I play three."

"Three!" exclaimed Richard. "What are they?"

"Drums, guitar, and piano."

"It sounds like some talented children have come into my class," Miss Kindskill said with a warm smile for each child. "Perhaps you could practice together and prepare something to play for the class. Would you like to do that?"

After receiving nods from Sarah and Richard, Jeff responded, "Sure. But you might change your mind when you hear us play."

"I'm willing to take that chance. I'll see you in class in a little while." She spoke over her shoulder as she walked away.

At the end of the day, as the children filed out of the classroom, Richard grabbed Sarah and Jeff. "Could we get together tomorrow during recess somewhere?"

"I *think* so," said Sarah with a little smile.

"I don't know." Jeff showed less interest in the idea.

Richard got the impression that meeting new people in a new place made it too soon to ask Jeff about this. But Richard was determined. He asked, "Could you at least come and watch?"

"Well, alright," said Jeff hesitantly.

"Good," said Richard, encouraged, "then we'll meet tomorrow during recess. I'll ask Miss Kindskill if we can use the music room."

"Are you sure this school *has* a music room?" asked Sarah teasingly.

"I'm sure it does. And I'll ask the teacher where it is." Richard saw that he was more enthusiastic about making music together than the other two. But when Richard set his mind on a goal, he was slow to give it up.

The next day, Richard went to school, looking forward to practicing music with his new friends. He learned that the music room wasn't far from their classroom.

"The room is kept locked," Miss Kindskill told Richard. "But I'll see that it's unlocked during recess for you."

For a boy of his age, Richard showed unusual determination to see the music group formed. It was almost as if he knew they would be successful. He fully expected Sarah and Jeff to share his confidence and interest, and was unprepared for any lack of enthusiasm on their part. This attitude was consistent in all of his activities.

When recess came, Richard went looking for Sarah on the playground and found her on one of the swings.

"Hi!" said Sarah cheerfully.

"Hi. Do you remember what we planned for today?"

Thinking a moment, she said, "Oh *that* old thing! Yeah, I'm ready."

"Are you sure?" he asked in a tone of authority.

"Yes. But, I'm playing on the swing right now."

"For how long?" asked Richard, tapping his music case with irritation.

Sighing, she said, "Alright. I'll come."

The playground was down a slope from the school building. While the two went up the cement steps of the slope, Richard remarked, "You probably didn't even remember to bring your autoharp."

"I did too!" snapped Sarah.

Following her to an entrance, he asked, "Well, where is it?"

"It's on the shelf thing where we hang our coats. I'll *show* you!" she insisted, grabbing his arm.

They went into their classroom to the place where all of the students put their coats, hats, and lunch boxes. It was at the back of the room and the teacher referred to it as "the cloak room."

She reached above the coats and hangers, and pulled down a large black case with a handle. The shelf was high and the case was heavy.

After she took it down, Richard remarked, "You should have let *me* do that."

"Then why didn't you?" asked Sarah with a little smile.

Richard headed for the doorway, allowing her to pass in front of him.

"Is Jeff going to join us?"

"I don't know. I asked him to come and watch us play. I figured he'd listen to us and decide he'd want to play, too."

Richard led the way. Halfway down the hall on the right was a doorway, which led into an open room with a high ceiling. Hanging from the ceiling were small, old-fashioned chandeliers. Gazing up at their stained glass covers, Richard said, "I bet this was a dining room at one time."

"It's a *music* room now!" yelled someone.

Startled, he turned to see Jeff, sitting some distance away behind a set of drums. "Hey there! I heard you two coming, and I stayed quiet to *surprise* you!"

"I thought you weren't that interested in playing with us!" said Sarah curiously.

"I wasn't. But I changed my mind."

After reading a basic book on guitar playing Cathy had purchased for him, Richard found he could pick out melodies instinctively, like someone who had once played the guitar well and given it up for a period.

They first experimented with harmonizing various chords together. Richard had prepared to sing *Michael Row Your Boat Ashore*, so the three worked on it. After a few times through, Jeff said, 'I think we're getting the right sound!"

"I think so too!" said Richard. Their session went better than he'd expected. He sang while the other two just played their instruments. When they stopped, he asked Sarah, "Can you sing as well as play?"

"Sure. I sing at home all the time."

Just then, Richard happened to look at a clock on the wall. "Hey, we'd better get back to class!"

The recess period was thirty minutes. This particular clock said they had five minutes until class. Richard and Sarah hurriedly put their instruments into their cases. Jeff moved his drums to an out-of-the-way corner. Then they ran to their classroom, getting to their chairs just as the teacher walked in.

The three practiced folk songs during recess every Monday and Wednesday. After rehearsing for five weeks, they felt ready to perform for their class. On the fifth Monday, after school, they talked about what songs they might present. At one point, when the conversation went silent, Sarah thoughtfully observed, "We need a name like all the groups have."

Richard agreed. Trying to show leadership, he immediately said, "I have *just* the name for us!"

"What's that, Richy?" asked Jeff.

"How 'bout 'Birds of Play'?"

Sarah shook her head. "I don't know. It's *pretty good*, but if you say it fast, it sounds like 'Birds of Prey.' And, we don't want to *scare* people."

"I kind of like it, but Sarah's right. We need a friendly name," observed Jeff.

"I suppose so," responded Richard disappointed.

Then Sarah got an idea. "How about *The Love Bugs* for our name?"

"Sure!" expressed Jeff. "Look at *The Beatles*! I'll tell you what. I'll paint *The Love Bugs* on my bass drum."

"Well, if you two are sure. But maybe there's a *better* name," said Sarah.

"No," said Richard thinking about it, "*The Love Bugs* is right on. If you want me to, I'll tell Miss Kindskill we're ready to play for the class."

Two weeks later, Miss Kindskill announced to the class that in place of their math lesson, a new musical group called *The Love Bugs* would perform. The teacher encouraged the class to welcome the new group with applause. The children responded enthusiastically to replacing math with music.

Before Miss Kindskill could introduce the three musicians, Sarah got up from her desk in the front row and said softly, "Miss Kindskill, we have to go out for a couple of minutes to change."

Receiving a smile and a nod of permission from their teacher, Sarah, Jeff, and Richard made a quick exit. They carried small duffel bags that contained new outfits each child's parents had provided.

The three children soon returned, outfitted in costumes of dazzling green and gold. Their appearance at the classroom door brought yells of excitement and anticipation from the children. Yells of "Neato!" "Oh boy!" "Wow!" filled the room. Sarah walked in first wearing green bell-bottom pants, and a gold blouse with flared sleeves. Both Richard and Jeff wore green bell-bottom pants, and a gold turtleneck shirt; Jeff also wore a brown leather vest. The enthusiastic reception bolstered their confidence.

"We're privileged today to hear the first performance of *The Love Bugs*," announced Miss Kindskill.

Following the children's applause, Richard said, "Our first number will be *Michael Row Your Boat Ashore*, with Sarah doing the vocal. Then we'll do *This Land Is Your Land*, and Jeff and I will join Sarah singing."

After they had performed the two numbers, they had to repeat the performance to please the children, who called out, "Sing it again!" "One more time!"

Before they sang *This Land Is Your Land* again, Richard told the children, "We'll sing it once ourselves and then we'll sing it a second time and you join in, and Miss Kindskill, too."

When everyone had sung, Miss Kindskill thanked *The Love Bugs*. "You sounded very professional. Now, we had better let you change clothes and get back to work."

As the three performers left the classroom to change, Jeff spoke up, "You know, we sounded pretty good!"

"Yes, I think we did," replied Richard. "And a little more practice will make us sound even better."

"My mom thinks we ought to play for some folks at a nursing home, where she volunteers," observed Sarah. "She says we're so loud, the old folks won't have any trouble hearing us."

"I think I'll take that as a compliment," Jeff said laughing.

Two weeks after *The Love Bug's* presentation in class, Miss Kindskill told Richard, "Before you leave school today, will you drop by the principal's office—Mr. Hillstern wants to talk to you, Richard."

"I'm sorry, Miss Kindskill that I was late getting in my last two assignments. Our group had two gigs on the weekend at nursing homes. And, we had to learn three more numbers for our repertoire, and . . ."

"No, Richard, that's not what Mr. Hillstern wants to talk to you about. He just wants to ask if *The Love Bugs* would give a presentation to the whole school."

"Oh, sure," replied Richard, sounding relieved. "I'll talk to Sarah and Jeff about it. I'm sure they will be glad to do it."

Richard walked away from this conversation with a light step and a whistle; he gave his guitar case a loving pat where he had pasted a hand-made ad. It carried the message THE LOVE BUGS, and a telephone number. Coming to some stairs, he descended two steps at a time, hurrying toward the principal's office.

"Uh!" Richard exclaimed, as he stumbled on the last step and fell forward on his guitar case. He lay there at the bottom of the stairs a minute, then started to get up when he felt a piercing pain in his ribs and a moment later his ankle.

"Oh, man, I think I . . .," he groaned, as a swimming dizziness overtook him and a loud beeping sound welcomed him into the darkness.

The nurse in Room 507 had just finished washing Richard Hawkins' face when she heard her patient say, "Oh, man, I think, I . . ."

Recognizing the sound of someone in pain, she asked, "Richard, does something hurt? Are you in pain?"

Although there was no response to the nurse's question, Richard spoke: "Beeping never . . . stops." He opened his eyes and stared at the ceiling.

The nurse thought she made out the words "chest," "hurt," and "can't move." She knew Richard was experiencing pain, because his words were mixed with groans. She gave his hand a reassuring pat and he closed his eyes.

Nurse Ella placed a chair beside Richard's bed and took his hand in hers. "Aren't you going to thank me for washing your face, Richard?" She paused, and continued, "I want you to look your best when your Uncle Mac and Dr. Olson come to see you, which should be any minute." Again, she paused before adding, "I can see that you are due for another shave. Since I haven't cut you yet, maybe you'll trust me to give you another shave this evening."

Richard suddenly groaned and said, "Ouch!"

"Now, you can do better than that, Richard," the nurse said, smiling and patting his hand again. Then she rose up and leaned over to whisper in Richard's ear, "That pretty young lady, Melissa, is coming to visit you later today. Won't that be nice? She's going to read some more to you and play a tape of your guitar music that you made for your uncle."

At that moment, Dr. Olson and Mac entered. "Here's your uncle now, Richard," Ella said.

Mac carried a chair near the bed. Sitting down, he pulled a small book out of his coat pocket. "I hope ye had a gude night, my boy. I brought poetry to read to ye. If ye suppose it's by Robert Burns, you'd be only half right. It's by Robert Frost."

The doctor read the chart at the foot of Richard's bed. Next, she took his pulse and placed a stethoscope over his heart. "Any change, Ella?" she asked.

"Just before you came, he said a few words and groaned and opened his eyes. He said 'Ouch,' but I don't think he was responding to anything I said or did."

"Ella, take Richard's pulse in about an hour. A couple of minutes ago, it was abnormally fast."

"Yes, Doctor."

18

Professor Barnhart's Class

"WELL, RICHY, YOU'RE NEXT," Dan said, after driving Sarah and Jeff to their homes.

"We're really lucky, Dan, to have a good driver like you take us places."

"Thanks. I enjoy doing it. Besides your dad pays me well."

"You're his teaching assistant this year, aren't you?"

"Yep. I see you rubbing your head. Are you feeling okay?"

"I have another headache," confided Richard. "Lately, when I get one of these things, I close my eyes and I see a bright light and shadowy images, kind of like photo negatives."

"Sounds to me like a migraine," observed Dan sympathetically, as he navigated through five o'clock traffic. "Maybe your mom should take you to see a doctor. Of course, it might be just a reaction to the bright lights at the TV studio. By the way, the program you and your friends gave at the studio was far out! Even the camera guys applauded."

"I'm glad you liked our music. Too bad it's just a local TV channel."

"Yea, but a lot of people watch it to see community stuff. And, remember, I put up flyers around town a couple of days ago—to let 'em know about your TV appearance."

"That's right, you did. I'd forgotten."

As they drove up in front of Richard's house, Dan asked, "How's your headache?"

"Better. A lot better. Thanks for asking. Dad told me you're taking a psychology class now. Would it be okay if I went to class with you sometime? I think I'd like to study psychology when I've grown up."

"Be glad to have you along. You might find it entertaining at that. We can always count on Dr. Phillip Barnhart to say something farout. Would you like to go tomorrow? It's a late afternoon class, so it won't interfere with school."

"Sure! But would it be okay with the professor?"

"Yea, Barnacle likes to have visitors. He finds it flattering. He'd especially like to have a colleague's kid attend his class."

"Why do you call him 'Barnacle'? Don't you like him?"

"All the guys call him that. I don't know, maybe because he *grows* on you. He's alright, I guess. You can tell me what you think of him tomorrow."

Richard nodded, as he got out of the van. "Thanks for the ride, Dan."

"You're welcome. Now, I'll pick you up tomorrow at about three o'clock at your classroom."

"Okay, I'll be waiting!" yelled Richard, as he walked quickly to the front door of his home, guitar case in hand.

He stood a moment on the porch, waving good-bye to Dan. Then he turned to see his mother standing in the open doorway.

"You're a little late, Richy. Did everything go alright?" Mary asked, while allowing her son to pass.

"Oh sure, Mom."

Closing the door behind Richard and putting her arm around him, Mary said, "I bet you're hungry, love. Why don't you wash up and I'll give you a glass of milk and some cookies I just took out of the oven. They're your favorite kind—chocolate chip."

"Thank you, Mom. That would be great. You're a wonderful mother. I hope I never lose you. Sometimes I worry that some morning, I'll open my eyes and find that my family has disappeared."

"Don't you be silly, Richy," Mary said, patting both of his cheeks with her hands. "Now, wash up, so you can eat the cookies while they're still warm."

Dan appeared promptly at the appointed time. He motioned to Richard and the two hurried out of the room.

Richard practically had to run to keep up with Dan, who moved quickly down stairs, through hallways and out to a parking lot, where he'd parked his Volkswagen bug. Getting into the car, Richard, breathing hard, asked "Are we late?"

"No, we're fine. I'm just being careful not to *be* late. Barnacle thinks it's a personal offense, if you're late, so, I *never* am," Dan added, as he drove onto the street.

Minutes later, looking at the speedometer, Richard asked innocently, "Should we be going this fast?"

"Huh? No, I suppose not," replied Dan slowing down. "I guess I didn't realize I was speeding. Richy, I should warn you, Barnhart has some pretty extreme ideas, so don't let it bother you."

"Like what? What kind of ideas?"

Dan thought for a moment. "Well, he feels he must enlighten as many people as possible, about the terrible effects of traditional beliefs, or, as he puts it, 'outdated voices,' in American society. Barnacle says that one way traditional beliefs are harmful, is that they contribute to mental illness. He thinks they force people to conform to standards they can't possibly meet, because they go against human nature. They also contribute, he says, to racial prejudice, gender inequality, material greed, rejection of the poor, and, *especially*, war."

"What do his students have to say about his ideas when they discuss them in his class?"

"Well, students have learned that Barnacle doesn't like to hear disagreement. He believes that anyone who disagrees with him on the solutions to man's problems, contributes to the problems themselves. I disagreed with him in a paper I wrote for him one time, and I got a 'D' for my trouble."

"You think he graded you down, because you disagreed with him?" asked Richard, shocked.

"Think? I know. He *told* me so!" Then shaking off feelings of anger, he said suddenly, "Here we are." Dan made this announcement as he turned into one of the University's parking lots, guiding the car near one of the older buildings on the campus. "Usually, I can find a parking space close to the entrance at this hour. Yep, here's one." Dan parked and rushed Richard out of the car. "We have ten minutes. If we move along, we can just make it."

The man and the boy entered the building and immediately confronted a large bulletin board containing a multitude of posters and flyers. One large poster in the center of the board declared: "**PROTEST MARCH AGAINST WAR! MARCH ENDS AT COURT HOUSE! THIS FRIDAY! BRING A SIGN!**"

"Come on, Richard. We've got two flights of stairs."

They reached the classroom minutes before Professor Barnhart's arrival, and took seats in the back of the room.

When the professor entered, Richard blurted out, "He looks like Gregory Peck, the actor!"

Looking around to make sure no one overheard Richard in the loud din of talking, Dan whispered, "Keep your voice down. You gotta be careful what you say."

Richard nodded and closely observed the students sitting around them. The young man in front of him wore a black leather jacket, his ponytail partially obscuring the peace sign painted neatly in white. Most of the men had long hair, and sported long sideburns and beards. A number of the women had long, straight hair, with head bands and wooden love beads. Richard turned his attention to the professor, who was writing a reading assignment on the blackboard. His graying hair was full, messy, but not long; he had close-cropped sideburns. He wore a green turtleneck sweater and a brown corduroy jacket over dark brown slacks.

Looking up from his notes that he had arranged on the lectern, Professor Barnhart said loudly, "I want to remind everyone that class is dismissed this Friday, so you can participate in the protest march! I'll be in the march myself and expect to see many of you there too."

"Sounds like an order," Richard whispered.

Dan nodded with a slight smirk.

"Also," continued Barnhart, gesturing with his horn rimmed glasses, "give particular care in reading chapter five," and he pointed toward the reading assignment on the board. "And I say that, not because Woofington quotes one of my articles in the chapter," he added with a knowing chuckle.

Picking up the cue, several students in the first two rows laughed. One of those laughing, who seemed to have some rapport with the professor, said, "Dr. Barnhart, I've been wondering about something."

"Oh? What's that, Steve?" Barnhart asked good naturedly.

"Well, I've been wondering why you have so many coffee mugs," Steve replied with a pretended puzzlement. "You seem to have a different one every class period."

Professor Barnhart held up the mug he had brought this day, so that all could see it. "The handle of the cup is shaped like 'P' for 'professor," he said. He took a sip of coffee out of it. "You see, Steve, these cups are my bribes. Whenever a student feels too stupid to get a good grade the normal way, he offers me a coffee mug. And, if it isn't one I have, I raise his grade." Smiling impishly, Barnhart added, "Now, you believe that, don't you?"

The class rewarded Professor Barnhart with a ripple of laughter at Steve's expense.

Steve, looking embarrassed, responded, "I guess that was a dumb question."

"Well, I had a little fun with your question. But when it comes to our work in this class, there are no 'dumb questions.' Every question is a cry for knowledge. Speaking of work, in our last session, we touched on the subject of *transactional analysis*. We discussed this concept in three parts. And the three parts make up the *ego*. Now, who can tell me what those three parts are?"

After a brief silence, Richard started to raise his hand. But Dan noticed the movement out of the corner of his eye, and grabbed his hand, shaking his head disapprovingly.

A woman sitting in the front row raised her hand. Her dark brown hair was arranged in a tight cone on the top of her head and red plastic discs—the size of half dollars—dangled from her ears. In a confident tone, she said, "The three parts are *child*, *adult*, and *parent*, Dr. Barnhart."

"Excellent!" judged the professor. "It's students like Deborah that prevent me from changing my profession." With this, he drew a diagram on the blackboard, representing the concept with three overlapping circles, in a column. Each he labeled with the three terms Deborah had given. Then, tapping with a piece of chalk the top circle labeled *Parent*, he stated, "The *Parent* category refers to the kind of relationship that the grown-up has, or had, with the parents."

Before Dan could stop him, Richard had his hand up.

Catching sight of the small raised-hand, Barnhart called, "Yes, young man—there in the back row."

"What if the child had only one parent?"

"Ah yes, a very good question. In that case, the one parent's influence would be doubly great, since there would be no other corrective influence. You might want to remember my answer for the next exam."

Dan sighed with relief and wrote something on his notebook, which he showed Richard. It said: "No more questions!"

"Now, the *Adult* category," continued Barnhart, "refers to all the things that are present in a human being that comprise what he is as a grown-up—for instance, your experience in this very room."

Richard took Barnhart's words as an invitation to make a visual examination of the room. Cracks showed in places on the faded plaster walls. Three large double-hung windows provided a view of a row of tall spruce trees. Glancing up, Richard saw water-stained tiles and dusty fluorescent lights. One brown water stain caught his attention. It looked like a seagull in flight. *I've seen that bird-shaped stain before*, he thought. *But how could I? I don't remember being in this room before . . .*

Suddenly, Richard realized he had tuned Barnhart out. But his attention picked up again when he heard the word "*you*."

"Let me repeat, the adult circle is in the middle of the diagram, because it is *you*," Barnhart stressed. "It represents the bridge between yourself as a child, and the person or people who raised you. Make no mistake. *Everything* you are is the result of environmental influences. If you forget everything else in this class, remember *environment* shapes behavior, and thus is the basis of mental health."

A hand shot up. A man who appeared to be in his late 20s, looking out of place in a white shirt and tie, had a question. Encouraged to ask, he said, "You're not saying that people become criminals, because they've been environmentally shaped that way, are you?"

"Mr. Peterson, never mind what I'm '*not* saying,' pay attention to what I *am* saying. And what I am saying is that any behavior, including deviant behavior, is predictive by environmental influence."

"Yes, but what about inherited characteristics, Dr. Barnhart?" Mr. Peterson queried. "Doesn't inheritance have a role?"

"You inherit certain physical characteristics that become subject to the forces within your peculiar environment. Let us say, Mr. Peterson," Barnhart said smugly, "that you were born with a nicely-formed nose and that you were raised in a rough part of town where you frequently got into fist fights, which left you with a broken nose and affected your speech. As a result, the way you look and sound may aversely affect your self-image and your opportunities for success. Do you see? You may even feel forced by circumstances to enter a life of crime."

"But, Professor Barnhart, what about personality characteristics? Surely, a person inherits some of those from his parents," Mr. Peterson insisted. "Or, what about a person's conscience?"

Using a tone that one might use in speaking to a child, Barnhart replied, "What we call 'personality' is simply a learned pattern of behavior, and 'conscience,' is merely a collection of rules conditioned into us from childhood. Be careful, class, about developing a theory around the notion of conscience. Because, I can tell you, it's often an excuse for *dogmatism*, especially when combined with religion. The dogmatic person is often the product of old-fashioned parents, who believes in narrow-minded absolutes."

Dan was doodling in the middle of his notes and failed to see Richard raise his hand. Suddenly he heard the professor call on the young visitor.

"Professor Barnhart, don't you have absolutes in your syllabus that students have to obey to pass?" Richard asked politely.

The professor paused, that question coming from a child apparently taking him aback. "Yes, you could say that," he answered slowly. "But, they are expressed in time-tested statements, agreed on by the academic community."

The leather-jacket clad man sitting in front of Richard, not bothering to raise his hand, spoke up, "I think the kid is right on. Your absolutes *might* be just as narrow-minded as any we get from the establishment for this war. The class should have the right to question requirements in the syllabus, so we can agree on what's fair."

Before Barnhart could respond, Mr. Peterson commented, "The absolutes my parents taught me came out of the Ten Commandments, and they're time-tested over thousands of years."

"Remember to raise your hand if you want to participate," scolded Barnhart, looking at Mr. Peterson. "I believe Duke raises an interesting issue. The educational experience should be a shared experience. Next Monday, we will discuss the requirements and come to a mutual agreement. Now, let's consider the third part—the *child*. The child we were, remains in all of us. The adult acts in ways that reveal what the child learned years before from the parent. Mr. Peterson, it's interesting that you spoke of what your parents taught you as a child. This is the child in you speaking, as the child speaks in all of us."

Steve raised his hand, with a smile on his face.

"Yes, Steve?"

"Yes, I was wondering if we ever hear the child speaking in you."

"Well, doubtless you do. I suppose . . . well, in fact I know, that my formative years find expression, at times, in my teaching." Adjusting his glasses, he continued, "When you hear my views about the military, you hear what I learned from my father who was a captain in the Marine Corps. Sadly, the Corps was more important than his own family. I saw what hyperpatriotism did to him. I learned from him the danger of loving your country more than humanity."

"Were you ever in the Marines yourself?" blurted out Duke.

Barnhart was quiet so long that Richard was beginning to think he hadn't heard Duke.

"No. My father wanted me to join someday. He was very disappointed when I said I didn't want to. He used to give me sermons on why the country needed men like him to fight its battles." Barnhart's tone taking on a bitter edge, he added, "He was killed in the Korean Conflict. But, I'm not sorry I told him that I didn't want to be a Marine."

At that point, a young woman with long hair, wearing a miniskirt stood up and said, "I'd just like to stand up n' say how much your words speak to my heart. And what you've said proves that, love means never having to say you're sorry."

Professor Barnhart displayed a look of humility and said, "Uh, *thank* you, Karen." Then speaking more forcefully, he asserted, "You've no doubt heard those of the traditional establishment say that the ideologies of the past are noble. Well, don't allow yourselves to be brainwashed! Our so-called founding fathers built this country on a foundation of two things—religious *prejudice* and capitalistic *greed*. What we need is a philosophy of one world that has Indians, Whites, Asians, and Blacks *coming together!*"

"Ah-huh!" yelled a man in the back of the room. "Speak the *word,* man!"

"Instead of honoring the United States of America," Barnhart ranted, "we need to honor the United States of the World." Receiving sounds of agreement, he continued his rant, "And, if you want to find a place for a religious experience, I strongly recommend you go on a pilgrimage to the United Nations building. You'll probably learn more about world peace there—than anywhere else."

Richard listened to Barnhart in shocked silence. He knew that his father would disagree with practically everything he'd said.

Noticing that Richard was shaking his head in disbelief, Dan whispered, "I warned you."

The positive responses of students put a look of satisfaction on Barnhart's face. He looked at his watch and though several minutes in the session remained, he announced, "It's time to go our separate ways. But I hope we get back together at the protest march. And remember, as I've said before, the personal is political—it's okay to shout what we think of leaders in our government. If we hate war, it follows we hate those who take us into war."

As students began to file out of the room, Dan looked for a chance to leave undetected with Richard. They had nearly reached the doorway when they heard Barnhart call Dan's name. Turning back, Dan replied, "Yes, Dr. Barnhart?"

Approaching the two, Barnhart reached out his hand and placed it on Richard's shoulder. "So, how did our little visitor like my lecture?"

Richard thought for a moment. "I think it was very *revealing*."

"Well, I'm glad you liked it," Barnhart said, a pleased expression on his face. "Your questions, my boy, were as good as any adult's. I've been concerned about the difficulty of my assignments—we don't want any of the men flunking and losing their draft deferment, do we!"

"I asked Dan if I could visit your class. I hope it was okay."

"Yes, of course. Feel free to visit anytime . . . uh?"

"Richard, sir. Richard Hawkins."

"Richard is Dr. Hawkins' son," noted Dan.

"Ah, that explains your excellent questions. I admire your father, even if we don't always agree in faculty meetings," Barnhart was about to say more, but a student interrupted with a question.

"Come on, Richard, we'd better be going," urged Dan, as he gently pushed Richard ahead of him out of the room.

When the two had reached the entrance of the building, Dan asked, "What did you think about my psychology teacher?"

Richard frowned thoughtfully. "I think he needs his own therapy."

"Right on! Richard," Dan responded, laughing.

Soon they were both laughing, as they walked toward the parked car. Professor Barnhart would have been surprised to see the effect of his lecture.

19

Inward Journey's End

SITTING IN THE LIVING room with his sister, Richard asked, "Cathy, do you ever feel like life speeds up the older you get? Like watching yourself on a merry-go-round that goes faster and faster 'til all you see is a blur of color and shapeless forms."

"Well, no I never felt . . ."

"Today is my 15th birthday," interrupted Richard, "and it seems that the last five or six years have compressed into a few snapshots and random memories."

"I suppose a lot of people feel that way from time to time, only they express it differently," responded Cathy, uncertain as to Richard's meaning.

"Yeah. I suppose you're right. I *am* looking forward to my birthday party. But, I worry that Mom is working too hard—she's so close to having the baby. I noticed when she was mixing up my cake this morning that she looked tired."

"Well, she might be a little tired. But, keep in mind that Mom has had practice being pregnant and knows how to pace herself. Besides, you know how Mom is—she likes to be busy. If she weren't working on your birthday party, she'd be working on something else. In fact, I heard her singing to herself in the kitchen a little while ago. And, I'll tell you what, I'll take pictures of your birthday party—I'll make a record of it, so you can relive all of it when you look at them."

"That would be very nice. I guess I never told you, but I love you very much."

"Thank you, Richy. Now, I must get busy and wrap your gift, 'cause if you don't get it tonight, you just might think I don't love you too."

"Oh no, I would never think that," objected Richard, taking her words seriously.

"I know you wouldn't," Cathy winked and said, as she got up from her chair. "Now, you forget all those years that went by so fast and concentrate on today, on your birthday," she advised, as she left the room.

"Right on!" Richard said out loud to himself, and he leaned back in his chair. He thought about his family—he thought about his brother coming back from Vietnam with one leg, and how Roger had learned to walk with his artificial leg without a limp. He thought about his father and mother and how they worried about him and expressed their love in many ways. He thought about his sister, who encouraged him when he felt down. He thought about the success of *The Love Bugs* and the enjoyment that the group had brought to many people over the years. He closed his eyes and, on the verge of sleep, became more conscious of the beeping sound, which seemed to grow louder and fill his mind with strange images of figures in white, moving around him, peering at him. He strained to hear what they were saying, but they spoke too softly. Suddenly, one figure came closer and spoke his name.

"Richy! Can ye hear me? It's your Uncle Mac."

"Yes, Uncle Mac. I can . . . see you . . . but you're fading. Why are you . . .?"

"Nurse! Di' ye hear *that*? Di' ye hear my Richard *speak*? He *knew* me. He must be comin' out o' the coma. Where is Dr. Olson? Could she come and examine Richard?"

"Yes, Mr. MacGregor, she will want to know immediately about Richard's response. I know she's in the hospital. I'll have her paged."

"Thank ye, Nurse Ella. I believe the Lord is aboot to answer our prayers," said Mac, nodding his head and smiling.

Mac pulled a chair close to his nephew's bed and took hold of his hand. "Can ye hear me, laddie. It's your old Uncle Mac," he said softly, close to Richard's ear. "We've all been so worried aboot ye. Melissa came to visit ye this mornin' and read from the Gospel of John."

Richard suddenly squeezed his uncle's hand, as if in reply.

"That's it, Richard. I'm *sure* ye heard me. Dr. Olson will be here soon to check on ye, my boy."

"Uncle Mac. I must have drifted off," said Richard, shaking his uncle's proffered hand.

"I canna let ye sleep on your birthday. There's a time for sleepin' and a time for celebratin' and this is a time for celebratin."

"You're right! I guess I got so comfortable in this big chair, I went to sleep. You know, I had a funny dream, and you were in it."

"I hope I kept my dignity in your dream, laddie," chuckled Mac.

"Oh, yes. You were trying to help me do something, but I can't remember what. And thanks for coming to my party. It wouldn't seem like a birthday party if you didn't come."

"I'd have to be dead to miss it. Your birth is a celebration o' the comin' o' a soul from Heaven. A wee bit o' poetry comes to mind:
'Our birth is but a sleep and a forgettin':
The Soul that rises with us, our life's Star,
Hath had elsewhere its settin',
And cometh from afar;
Not in entire forgetfulness,
And not in utter nakedness,
But trailin' clouds o' glory do we come
From God, who is our home.'
Can ye tell me the poet's name who gave us those gude lines?"

"Robert Burns?"

"No, my boy, but the Bard himself is a gude guess."

"Wait a minute, now I remember—it was William Wordsworth, and the poem is . . . 'Intimations of Immortality.' Right, Uncle Mac?"

"Ye called it right, laddie."

"Yes, I remember that you read that poem to me once—I think more than once. But I don't remember when. I always remembered that one line: 'Our birth is but a sleep and a forgetting.' It used to make me wonder what we forget. Sometimes the dreams we have in sleep, seem more real than our lives when we're awake."

"Aye, laddie, 'There are more things in heaven and earth, Horatio, than are dreamt o' in your philosophy,' Shakespeare reminds us in . . ."

The appearance of an excited Victor prevented Mac from completing his thought. "Excuse me, Mac, but Mary has to go immediately to the hospital. We think the baby's on the way." Victor spoke hurriedly, as he left the living room. "We'll have to postpone your birthday party for a while, Richard. I'll call when we get to the hospital. Roger and Cathy are going with us."

"Don't ye be hurryin' faster than ye *need* to Victor!" Mac called, looking worried.

"I want to go too, Uncle Mac," Richard said, getting out of his chair. "Do you think I can?"

"Aye, ye should go. Ye can squeeze into the back seat with Cathy and Roger. Tell your mither I said Victor should drive carefully."

"I will, Uncle Mac," responded Richard as he rushed after his father.

Richard caught up with his father and made known his desire to come along. But, his father didn't answer, which, to Richard meant that he had no objection. The family quickly headed for their car, parked in front of the house. Richard followed Cathy and Roger into the back seat.

"I hope I'm not crowding you too much," Richard said quietly to his brother and sister. But neither of them answered. This left Richard to wonder if they would have preferred that he stay home. He sat anxiously with his silent siblings in the evening glow of the outdoor lamplight, as the father maneuvered the car into the street.

"Will it take us long to get to the hospital?" Richard asked, to anyone who might care to answer. Strangely, nobody did.

A sudden feeling of loneliness gripping him, Richard stared out the window and tried to give shape to the dark forms of people and things that the car sped past. As he stared into the night, the beeping sound began to grow louder in his head and seemed to blend with the racing engine of the car. His loneliness gave way to inexplicable anxiety as the speeding car devoured distance.

Turning to look at his sister and brother, Richard asked softly, "Should we be going this fast?" But once more, his words brought only silence. He strained to see the faces of his family, but the darkness of the car's interior made them indistinct.

"What are those two bright lights ahead of us?" Richard heard his mother ask.

Then a moment later, the headlights of an oncoming truck filled the car with a brightness that obscured Richard's family from sight. The car swerved in a hopeless attempt to avoid the inevitable.

"We're going to crash!" Richard cried.

"Di' ye hear that, Cal? It sounded like Richard was relivin' the accident that killed his friend Tony."

Cal, who had been at the foot of the bed in a posture of prayer, replied, "Yes, I saw his hand come up in front of his face, as if to protect himself."

"We must tell the nurse what we heard when she gets back," Mac said, more to himself than to Cal. "I believe our prayers are bein' answered. I see more and more signs o' Richard comin' out o' the coma. The little kirk that I attended in Glasgow as a wee bairn has been prayin' for our laddie, since I told them aboot his accident."

"And, not only has our church been in prayer for Richy, but two other churches in the city have also devoted time to pray for him. You may not have heard," Cal added, "but the youth group has had a 24-hour prayer chain for the past three days. They remember and appreciate the time he spent with them, when I had to be away. I'll be leaving you now. I have some calling to do, but I'll be back tomorrow."

"Thank ye, Cal, for your support and prayers. And thank the members o' the church for me. I know Richard would be grateful for your prayers. He knew . . . knows the power o' prayer."

Cal showed Mac an encouraging smile. Then, looking at his watch, hurriedly left the room.

Minutes later, an orderly poked his head into the room and held the door open. A man in a wheelchair entered.

Mac got up and walked over to the visitor and greeted him with a handshake. "It was gude o' ye to come again to visit Richard."

"Well Mr. MacGregor, I would be ungrateful in the extreme if I returned your kindness with disregard for someone dear to you," Mr. Grant replied solemnly. "I will never forget how you prayed for me during my heart operation. And later, when I was hit with an infection, you continued to pray and encourage my son. What do you say we get on a first name basis? My friends call me 'Bruce,' and I would like to think of you and your nephew as my friends."

"I know Richard would be pleased to have ye as a friend, Mr. Grant . . . Bruce. Ever since he was a wee bairn, he's reached out to ithers to help and encourage. Ye see, Bruce, I've taken care o' Richard since he was a *baby*—he lost his whole family in a car accident. He's like my own son."

"When he comes out of the coma, he's going to need a lot of help and encouragement from his friends. And, if you will permit me, I would like to take care of Richard's hospital bills and assist him when he wakes up to make a good recovery. Money's something I have plenty of and I can't think of a better way to spend it."

Mac's gentle eyes moistened with tears. "Thank ye, Bruce, I have been worryin' some aboot the bills. The insurance only covers part o' the cost. God bless ye. You're as generous as the Grants in Scotland."

"We Scots have to stick together. Well, Mac, I'd better be getting back to my room. I promised my nurse I wouldn't be gone long. I'm still a little unsteady. But, I expect to be able to check out of here tomorrow— I'll take care of Richard's bill when I do. Here's my card. Please call me when Richard wakes up."

After Bruce Grant left the room, Mac sat down again beside Richard's bed. He stared at his nephew's face, hoping to see some subtle movement signaling that he was about to awaken. He reached out and patted Richard's hand, and watched in vain for a reaction.

"It's your old Uncle sittin' here beside ye, laddie," said Mac, hoping to hear a response. "I had a nice chin wag with Mr. Grant, I mean, Bruce. He wants to help ye with the hospital bills. When I spoke to him before, he said he would give ye a job in one o' his companies—if ye wanted one. O' course, he meant after ye regain your strength. Oh, and Richard, I brought some more tapes o' some o' your favorite songs to play for ye."

Mac was suddenly aware of someone else's presence in the room. Turning, he saw Dr. Olson, who had entered quietly moments before. She smiled and nodded at Mac and examined Richard's medical chart.

"I see our patient is showing signs of waking up. *Aren't* you Richard," she said encouragingly. She leaned over him and put a second pillow under his head.

As Dr. Olson started to rise up to answer Mac, the stethoscope hanging around her neck brushed against Richard's arm, which brought an immediate reaction. He opened his previously closed eyes, turned his head to look up at Dr. Olson, and moved his lips without producing a sound.

"That's it, Richard," said Dr. Olson softly. "How are you feeling?"

Richard nodded his head slowly, and moved his head to glance around the room. The frown on his face was replaced with a smile when he saw his Uncle Mac.

"I'm right here, laddie. You're goin' to be alright."

Richard widened his smile; then wearied by his efforts, closed his eyes in sleep.

Dr. Olson motioned for Mac to follow her out of the room. When the door was closed behind them, she said, "I believe our wait is over. I believe that Richard is coming out of the coma—perhaps within a few hours. Remember, when he wakes up, he'll be confused and disoriented. Let him adjust to his new circumstances at his own pace."

"Di' ye think Richard will have serious effects due to the length o' the coma, Doctor?"

"I really don't know. My experience with similar cases would suggest that we can expect some light to serious effects from his injury. I want to go now and speak with Dr. Schiller and Dr. Johnson, and inform them of Richard's progress. After I've consulted with them, could you come to my office? I want to talk about Richard's condition and what we can do to help him in his recovery. Could I see you, say, in about an hour?"

Mac nodded.

As she hurried toward the elevator, Dr. Olson passed Melissa Ingram. "Mr. MacGregor has some interesting news about Richard."

Reading the doctor's tone as positive, Melissa picked up her pace to catch up with Mac, who was headed toward a small waiting room at the end of the hallway.

As soon as Mac took a seat, Melissa joined him.

Melissa, sounding anxious, asked, "Is Richard going to wake up? Has he shown signs of waking up? I've been so *worried* about him!"

"Aye, Melissa. Dr. Olson thinks he may wake up in a matter o' hours. Ye could go in to his room and sit with him and if he opens his eyes, talk to him. Maybe he will speak to ye."

Encouraged by Mac's words, Melissa quickly rose to her feet. "I'll go right in, Mr. MacGregor. I brought a book to read to him."

Left alone, Mac bowed his head and began to pray. When he had finished, he looked at his watch and was surprised that nearly an hour had elapsed.

"It's time for me to see Dr. Olson aboot Richard—so it is," Mac said out loud.

He hurried to the doctor's office and knocked.

"Come in, Mr. MacGregor!"

Entering, Mac asked, "How di' ye know it was I at your door, Doctor?"

"You knocked like a Scotsman," Dr. Olson replied, smiling. "And besides, I knew you would be prompt for our visit to talk about Richard. Please take the easy chair. That's where I sit when I want to relax."

Mac sat, and waited for Dr. Olson to speak.

"I was able to consult with both Dr. Schiller and Dr. Johnson."

"How long di' ye think it will be before Richard wakes up?"

"We don't think long. I'll administer a simple test to see if I can get Richard to respond."

"Could I be there when ye test Richard, Doctor?"

"Yes, I think that would be okay. But, you need to remember that your nephew has had a serious brain injury that may cause some degree of impairment in his usual cognitive communication."

"What exactly di' ye mean?"

"I mean, a patient who has suffered brain trauma may experience impairment in one or more abilities, associated with cognitive communication. Sometimes brain trauma affects perception, memory, thought organization, problem solving, reasoning, or self-awareness. When Richard communicates, he may have trouble in one or more of these abilities."

With a worried expression in his eyes, Mac asked, "How will we know if Richard's communication is impaired? I mean, what will be a sign o' impairment? And, isn't it possible that he will be completely normal?"

Dr. Olson paused, choosing her words carefully. "After weeks in a coma, there's a high probability of temporary incapacity," she said. "For instance, his speech might be slow and difficult to understand for a few months. And later, after he has his speech facility back, he may have trouble expressing himself when he's under stress."

"That would bother my Richard. He's very particular aboot the way he expresses himself," observed the Scot, shaking his head.

"There are early warning signs that would indicate that Richard needs special help from a speech and language therapist."

"What are they, Dr. Olson?"

"I can tell you, but you have to be careful that you don't imagine you see them, because you *expect* to."

"One warning sign is trouble concentrating, when he usually concentrates well."

"Aye, my laddie has gude concentration."

"Another warning sign is that he may find it difficult to process new information or retain new facts. He may become confused in dealing with an unexpected situation. Disorganized speech or writing is the most common sign. I've seen that one many times in patients, who had been comatose for several days. I wanted you to know the difficulties Richard faces. He probably will have some disability that, with professional help, can be made less severe. It may take him a while to adjust to the limitations involved."

"My Richard is a fighter, Dr. Olson."

"I'm sure he is. Let's go see if we can help him start fighting."

20

Awake to Life

"RICHY. I'M GOING TO start reading in Chapter Three. You should recognize the story. It's one of your books—your Uncle Mac gave it to me to read to you."

Melissa moved her chair closer to the bed and began. She'd read only a couple of pages when she saw him suddenly reach out as if trying to touch something.

"Do you remember reading this book, Richy? You told your uncle you liked it." Melissa gently took his hand as she spoke.

Richard responded with some unintelligible sounds and then turned his head toward Melissa. He opened his eyes, and uttered the words: "Mom . . . where?" Then with sadness in his voice, "Gone . . ."

Melissa waited for Richard to say more, but several minutes of silence elapsed while he looked at her, without moving.

Melissa started to read again, but stopped when Richy shook his head. The book slipped to the floor when Richard squeezed her hand and spoke.

"My . . . head . . . it has . . . hurt . . . I feel . . . I feel . . . weak. Melissa?"

"Yes, Richy. I'm here."

Nurse Ella had entered the room while Melissa was talking. "Did I hear Richard speak?" she asked excitedly.

"Yes! And he *knew* me! He's coming out of the coma! I'm sure he's coming out of it. Aren't you, Richard?"

At that moment, Richard looked around the room and said, "What . . . place? Beeping . . . always heard . . . What . . . makes . . . it?" Richard asked, speaking slowly.

"The 'beeping,'" Nurse Ella replied, "comes from monitors that check your pulse and other vital signs, Richard. They've been guarding your health."

Richard nodded and smiled. "My mouth . . . feels . . . thirsty."

Ella gave Richard a sip of water. "You have been sick for a while," she said, "but you're better now. You're in a hospital room. Dr. Olson and your Uncle Mac will be in to see you soon. Before they arrive, would you like us to help spruce you up?"

Richard nodded his consent. "How . . . long . . . time?" he asked.

"You want to know how long you've been ill?" Ella asked.

"Yes . . . how long?" Richard appeared to speak with much effort.

"Dr. Olson will tell you all about that when she comes. Let's see if we can help you feel better. Melissa will wash your face and comb your good-looking hair."

Pleased that her compliment had elicited a smile, Ella left the room to notify Dr. Olson of her patient's remarkable improvement.

"If Richard wakes with impaired speech, select a therapist to help him who has worked with brain injured patients in his age group... " Dr. Olson's phone rang.

"Excuse me."

A minute later, she gave Mac a big smile. "It's Ella. Richard is *awake* and talking a little."

"Canna we see my laddie now?"

"Yes, just as soon as I inform Dr. Schiller and Dr. Johnson about Richard, so that they can examine him as soon as they're available." The doctor left messages, then said, "Let's go see how your nephew is doing."

"Aye! I want to welcome him back to life."

During the elevator ride down, the two people stood in silence—but, Mac was not silent toward God. When the elevator stopped, and they walked in the direction of Room 507, he said, "I hope and pray, Richard's brain injury didn't affect him seriously."

Dr. Olson returned a hopeful glance, and walked ahead of him to the door of Richard's room. She opened it and waited for the Scot to enter first, so that he could have first sight of the young patient awake.

Mac quickly made eye contact with his nephew. Richard was propped up in bed; face washed and hair combed. Tubes providing nutrition and hydration had been removed.

Smiling, Richard raised his hand to greet his uncle. "It's good . . . uh . . . for me to . . . see you, Uncle Ma-c."

Mac stood silently a moment, nodding his head and smiling. He pulled out his handkerchief and wiped his eyes. "It's gude for me to see ye too, Richard. The dear Lord be praised for bringin' ye home to us all."

"Yes . . . back . . . here . . . but I, but I . . . got . . . with . . . my mo-ther, fa-ther . . . sister, bro-ther . . . You . . . also . . . You looking . . . young, more young."

"I see, laddie. Ye were dreamin' o' your family."

"No . . . wasn't . . . dreaming . . . Real! . . . God gave me . . . a chance . . . grow with . . . all . . . my family. They taught . . . me." Richard put his hand over his heart. "I really . . . there . . . gone now . . . Happened . . . Melissa . . . Believe me, you do?"

"Yes, Richy, I believe you. We all believe you. All things are possible with God," Melissa answered, while holding his hand.

"I feel . . . different. I can't say it . . . what I think . . . to make it right." Fear replaced an expression of frustration on Richard's face. "What's . . . happening . . . with me? I can't . . . sound like . . . like . . . me."

"Richard, I'm Dr. Olson. You've been under my care, since the accident. What you're experiencing in expressing yourself is temporary. Do you remember the accident?"

"Accident? Accident? No . . . remember . . . no . . . head hurting . . . chest feels, feels . . . funny."

"You were in a car accident, Richard. And, you received a head injury that put you in a coma for several weeks. You also sustained a fractured left ankle and a cracked rib." Then, looking at the nurse, Dr. Olson added, "We'll give you something to relieve the pain."

"Am I . . . hearing? . . . Several weeks? . . . No waking . . . all the time . . . These things . . . I remembered . . . happening . . . happening to me . . . weeks, only weeks . . . Don't I understand . . . And . . . I can't think . . . to say it."

"Try not to worry, Richard, about your speech," Dr. Olson said encouragingly. "Give yourself time to do some relearning. You can regain your previous fluency with some professional help. I'm sure you can make a good recovery. A lot of people will help you, and I'm one of them," she said with a warm smile.

"Thank you," replied Richard, flashing a look of gratitude. "I know I'm with . . . others, who are . . . friends for me."

"Aye, laddie, we're all here to help ye."

Dr. Olson, wanting to examine Richard, announced, "I think the best way I can help now, is to give you a little check-up. Mr. MacGregor and Miss Ingram, I have to ask you to leave for a while."

The doctor took Richard's pulse and listened to his heartbeat.

"Raise your right arm and take hold of my hand," Dr. Olson instructed. "Now, squeeze my hand." Seemingly satisfied, she asked her patient to repeat the exercise with his left arm. "Next, Richard," she said, "I want you to raise your right leg a few inches." After Richard complied, she asked him to raise his left leg, but try as he might, he could not manage it.

"Why does my leg . . . move . . . not? . . . What . . . matter is it?" Richard sounded worried. He tried again to move his leg, but once more his leg disobeyed his will. "What is it . . . meaning? Will I be . . . uh . . . you know . . . moving my leg?"

"Richard, your head injury may have caused some motor dysfunction on your left side," Dr. Olson said, avoiding the word paralysis. "You showed difficulty moving your left arm. But, you're young and strong, so you should, with time in therapy, be able to teach those muscles to move when you want them to."

"Ella, would you please uncover Richard's feet? I want to check his reflexes."

Ella pulled the covers loose and folded them back.

Using the pointed end of a pencil, Dr. Olson touched the bottom of each foot, drawing a line from the heel to the toes. This action brought appropriate responses from Richard.

"That's very good, Richard. Now, move the toes of your left foot."

Richard easily twitched the toes of his right foot, but seemed unable to do the same on his left foot.

"Try again, Richard. Think hard about moving your toes."

Nodding to show his willingness to try, Richard clenched his teeth and strained every muscle. "Come do it, . . . *move* toes!" he said. When he was about to give up, suddenly some slight movement was evident.

Smiling at this simple achievement, Richard said, "Never, I thought . . . I would . . . feel . . . proud by . . . move my toe."

Nurse Ella then patted the obedient toes as she recovered Richard's feet.

Three weeks after his awakening, Richard, with Mac's and Melissa's constant encouragement, had progressed in mobility from a wheelchair to a walker. Back on solid food, he was regaining his lost weight and increasing in energy needed to move his left leg as he walked.

One day, laboriously moving through a hospital hall, he saw Dr. Olson walking toward him. He stopped to wait for her.

Dr. Olson smiled, nodded and said, "You're walking very nicely, Richard. I don't think I've ever had a patient improve so fast."

"Well, that's glad . . . to hear. I think, . . . I guess the credit is . . . for my . . . physical therapy. He, uh . . . Ken Ki-yo-shi. I came just from a . . . workout with Ken's help."

"Yes, Mr. Kiyoshi is a very good therapist. But, he has a very cooperative patient. He tells me that you spend a lot of time working out with weights, and now you're swimming in the pool."

"Yes, I enjoy . . . the water. But, I do more . . . splash than I swim," Richard laughed. "But I never was much . . . to swim, . . . a good swimmer, you know."

"I can see, you're getting some good movement with your left side, as you walk."

"I was thinking it . . . and Ken said it too, but I am . . . glad to hear it . . . the same, from you."

"Oh, a few minutes ago, I saw Mr. Grant downstairs in the waiting room talking with your uncle. I believe he plans to visit you soon. I told them you would be in your room."

"Well, I'm heading . . . there *now*, . . . so I'll be there . . . when he gets there, too . . . I guess I'd better get . . . on going . . . Good-bye, Dr. Olson."

Richard started to walk and then stopped to say something before taking his leave. "Thank you, Doctor, for . . . all the encouraging of words

. . . to what I'm doing." Then shaking his head with frustration, he complained, "I'm trouble talking today, . . . but you know what I said."

"Yes, of course, you're expressing yourself very well. I'm sure, as you continue to work with your speech and language therapist, you will soon be as articulate as you were before the accident. I'll stop by to see you this evening," Dr. Olson said, as she parted from Richard.

Richard nodded with an expression of confidence and determination. He tried even harder to move his left leg as he walked.

Not allowing himself to stop and rest, he reached his room before Mr. Grant arrived. He dropped with relief into a chair near the window. His new room was located in the rehabilitation wing of the hospital, which looked out over a rose garden.

The mild pain in his legs—a good sign he realized—disappeared by the time he heard a knock at his door.

"Come in!" he called.

The door opened and Bruce Grant entered, fully recovered from his heart operation. He stood a moment without speaking, a big smile on his face. Nodding in agreement with his thoughts, he said, "You're looking *great*, Richard! You're a whole lot better than you were a few days after you came out of the coma."

"I'm feeling better, a lot. Uh, my strength, . . . I'm getting back—more, every day, a little."

"Are they taking good care of you, my boy? You let me know if there's something you need that you don't have."

"Mr. Grant," Richard began, picking his words carefully, "I want to thank you . . . for everything you've done to me, . . . paying all my expenses . . . I just don't know, the way I could pay you back."

"Well, it so happens, Richard, I *do*."

"You do?"

"Yes. I want you to come to work for me, in one of my companies. Richard, I see you as someone who will make a fine leader in our corporate office—you're a fighter, who sets his mind on a task and gives it his all to achieve it—the way you've done in coming back from your injury."

"Well, Mr. Grant, I would love . . . to have a job for you . . . I sure would work the *best*, uh, I could do," Richard said enthusiastically.

"It's a deal, then. That reminds me. I brought you a little present that I thought you might find useful. Give you something new to think about."

With that introduction, Richard watched Mr. Grant take a laptop computer out of a carrying case he had been holding.

"Here, my boy," Mr. Grant said, putting the computer and case on a table. "This belonged to Mrs. Haverstock, my private secretary. It's only two years old, I believe. I bought her a new one. Oh, and here's my card with our corporate web site. When you're out of the hospital, you can use it to see if one of our operations appeals to you. For now, you can bring up the file 'Grant Corporation' to see our U.S. companies, as well as job descriptions in management. I've written my home number on the card in case you want to call me."

"Thank you, Mr. Grant. I don't know how to say my appreciation . . . It's sure a beauty," observed Richard, opening the lid of the laptop. Touching the keys, he repeated, "It's sure a beauty."

"I'm glad you like it. Keep me posted on your progress. Oh, and Mac told me to tell you that he'll be paying you a visit later today. Well, good-bye, my boy." Bruce Grant shook Richard's hand, and left him examining the laptop with great interest.

21

The Mind's Eye

Mac knocked softly at the door of Richard's hospital room. When he received no answer, he quietly opened the door a few inches and peeked in. Richard was asleep in his chair. Trying to close the door quietly, Mac accidentally rattled the doorknob.

"Uncle Mac, is that you?"

"Aye, it is your clumsy Uncle Mac. I'm sorry my boy I woke ye. I was goin' to leave, but . . ."

"Oh, come in, Uncle."

Mac entered and said, "It's gude to see ye lookin' more yourself, laddie."

"Sit down, Uncle, and tell me what . . . news. How's Melissa? How's the church . . . going?"

"Everyone's fine," said Mac, pulling a chair closer to his nephew. "Melissa, that bonny lass, is bakin' cookies to bring tomorrow. The church has hired another pastor to serve the seniors. His name is Lynch, Michael Lynch."

"Pastor Lynch should get . . . contact with Melissa's dad. His church makes seniors . . . repair their homes, or uh makes repairs on seniors' homes . . . they own. I hope, Uncle, you've thanked the people in the church for their . . . praying for me."

"Aye, that I have. Richard, there's somethin' I've been wantin' to ask ye aboot, when ye felt up to it."

"Sure, Uncle, it's okay. Ask me."

"When ye came out o' the coma, ye told us ye saw your family. What di' ye mean ye saw your mither and father?"

"Well, Uncle, I don't know how I can explain, . . . but can try. It was like I started over in another life, . . . growing up again, but . . . with my father and mother and . . . Kathy and Roger were there too. In this other life, I was a baby, and then a small boy, and . . . I think, a teenager. I played guitar . . . in a little band, with two friends . . . at the school. And you were there, Uncle . . . I was in the car when the accident killed them, killed my family and I couldn't do anything . . . to make it stop. Now I know, my family loving me—how they would take care of me, as someone in the family. It's made me feel different about me. No longer feeling unhappy, as I guess I was, down deep in me, because, my family was taken away . . . but, I've thanked God lots of times I had you though; you've been my family."

"Durin' your weeks in the coma, laddie, di' ye feel any pain or discomfort from your injuries?"

"No, I don't think so . . . I... a sound, a beeping in my head kept bothering. Nobody could help about it. When I woke up, . . . I found the beeping in the room, in a machine . . . that uh, monitored . . . me. But, I never knew . . . in the coma where it comes from," Richard said, smiling and shaking his head.

"It sounds like ye had somethin' amazin' happen to ye, Richard. Maybe somethin' ithers in a coma never experience."

"I feel older, somehow. It's like, I've lived longer than my own age. I can understand better, I think, how the 60s and 70s influence our life, the culture . . . and other cultures."

"Aye, the 60s and 70s influenced the whole world. And not for the better, I'm thinkin'." Mac glanced out the window, as if to see evidence of his words.

Changing the subject, Richard asked, "Did you know about Mr. Grant . . . offering a job to me?"

"Aye, I knew he was goin' to ask ye."

"Well, I said yes. And, Mr. Grant gave me a laptop computer. This is it," Richard lifted the case from the floor. Looking at it, he said, "I can use it for... to look for a job in his corporation."

"I'm sure it's a braw computer, but I canna tell 'til I see it."

Richard quickly pulled the laptop from its case and held it for his uncle to see. "I haven't plugged it in yet."

"Di' ye want me to plug it in for ye, laddie?"

"Yes, please do it and we'll see . . . what it does. I'm going to have to learn about it."

"There now. Ye can see what Mr. Grant's corporation has for ye."

Richard, smiling with anticipation, turned it on. He intended to bring up the file on the corporation's U.S. companies, but suddenly a look of pain contorted his face and a groan escaped his clenched teeth. He pressed his hand against his chest momentarily, and then dropped it on the computer's keyboard. His head back, he gazed intently at the ceiling. It was as if he saw something above him.

"What is it, Richard?!" cried Mac, rushing to his nephew. The uncle peered down at his face. "Shall I call the doctor for ye?"

Richard shook his head. He then waved his hand to signal his uncle to wait.

Mac stood beside Richard, ready to call for medical assistance at a moment's notice.

Richard no longer seemed to be in pain. But he continued to gaze at the ceiling. His hand rubbed across the keys of the laptop. Then he said, "I'm alright, but Mr. Grant's secretary—she isn't. I think she's . . . had a heart attack. She's on a floor, but not dead. She . . . needs help. Now. When I touched her computer, I saw it. It looks like bedroom, . . . not an office. Here. Mr. Grant's card . . . with private number. Call right away! Tell him . . . send doctor. . . ambulance!"

Without asking Richard how he knew such a thing, Mac grabbed the phone and reached Bruce immediately. Putting down the receiver, Mac announced, "He said he would have an ambulance sent to his secretary's home right away."

That evening, after his uncle had gone, Richard reflected on one of the most extraordinary occurrences in his life. Somehow, his mind made physical contact with someone in a life-threatening situation. In his vision, he saw the room and the person in it clearly. The experience raised questions that nothing in his background prepared him to answer. While the unexpected experience confused and unsettled him, the call from Mr. Grant that his secretary was out of danger, made him happy. His vision helped the woman live. *Is this psychic ability part of God's purpose for my life?*

Becoming weary from pondering implications of his vision, Richard put his mind on something he considered more relaxing. He sat down at a small table, where there were writing materials that his uncle had provided for his correspondence.

"I guess I'll see to writing a letter of . . . con-dolence for parents of Tony. Uncle Mac got . . . hospital for their address." Soon, crumpled stationery littered the floor around his chair. He couldn't write a letter that he thought sounded right.

"It's one thing, write for friends, another thing, write for strangers . . . not knowing injury of mine." Shaking his head, he dislodged tears of frustration. "I can't just fit thinking with, with words. I try it, and try. I can't . . . do it . . . right! Why God, did this let happen to me? *Why*? What purpose is this? Just trouble is making . . . for everyone."

Getting up to pick up the wadded paper on the floor, Richard moved too fast and fell on his back. He hammered the floor with his fist. Tears of anguish welled up.

It suddenly occurred to him how ridiculous he must look. Often, when his uncle heard him sounding sorry for himself, he would say, "Laddie, your spirits sound heavy. Ye need to lighten up the burden ye're carryin.'" Sometimes then he would quote G. K. Chesterton: "Angels can fly because they take themselves lightly."

Holding on to his cane, Richard stood up and sat down at the table. "I have to . . . lighten up. Start again . . . fresh." This time, he began the letter with a statement about his inability to write well, due to the accident that took Tony's life.

On the third attempt, Richard was satisfied. In five pages, he talked about their friendship, the good qualities Tony had, and his future plans. Richard told them how happy and carefree their son was just before the accident. He looked at the sealed envelope, propped against the lamp with a sense of accomplishment. "I did it!" he said.

Richard rewarded himself with a stroll to the cafeteria for a cup of coffee. After he returned, he was thinking about writing a letter to Cal, when he heard a knock at the door. Smoothing his hair and shirt collar, he called, "Come in!"

"Hi, Richard! May I come in? The nurse said I had only fifteen minutes before the end of visiting hours."

"Sure. Come in, Mr. Grant."

Waiting for Richard to return to his chair, Bruce Grant sat down and gave the young man a long searching look before he spoke.

"You were right about the heart attack, Richard. The paramedics reached her just in time to save her life." Mr. Grant's face showed his gratitude. "Your Uncle Mac said you had a vision. Do you mean you saw an image of her having a heart attack?"

"Yes, just an instant could I see her. I knew . . . a bad . . . heart attack happened . . . to her, because I felt strong pains in my chest . . . and hard . . . to have breath."

"Do you often have these visions, Richard?"

"No, that was the only time. I've never been intu, uh . . . had intuition very good," smiled Richard.

"How did you know that the woman in your vision was my secretary?" asked Mr. Grant.

"I don't know," Richard said, shaking his head. "But I right away knew . . . I think, because I touched the laptop . . . belonging to her . . . and it gave me a contact somehow . . . I don't know."

"Richard, before I leave, would you do me a favor? Would you look at a photograph and point out Mrs. Haverstock for me? It's a photo of some employees at a company picnic. There are eleven women pictured."

"Sure. I'll see if I can see her," replied Richard, reaching for the tendered photograph.

"Take your time," encouraged Mr. Grant. "She might look different to you, since this was taken more than ten years ago."

A quick glance at the photo, and Richard observed, "Her hair is longer and darker, and she's thinner back then, . . . but I see which one she is. She stands in the back row, and she is the third person, . . . I mean the third woman, looking from the left."

"So, you're saying Mrs. Haverstock is standing in the back row, the third woman from the left side of the photo." Mr. Grant's tone conveyed his amazement.

"Yes. She's the one—I saw her in my vision."

"Well Richard, I want you to know how thankful I am. You saved a good friend and a trusted employee of the firm—I can't imagine trying to replace her."

"I'm glad I could help, Mr. Grant. I'm sure the Lord . . . gave me the vision."

"I'd better be going now, before the nurse gets after me. Oh, and if you get any more visions," said Mr. Grant standing in the open doorway, "I'm ready to listen. As of this morning you're on the payroll of the firm as a consultant—no consultant has ever advised me as importantly. Have a good night's sleep."

"Thank you, Mr. Grant. It's good . . . to have a job," said Richard with a big smile.

22

Man of Mystery

Two weeks after the vision that saved Mrs. Haverstock's life, Richard sat in a wheelchair in the court yard behind the hospital, reading a Christian novel Melissa had brought him. While enjoying the sunny day, he smelled the fragrance of the nearby rose bushes.

"I think I'd better give this leg a little exercise," he muttered to himself. He took hold of a cane that hung on the back of the chair, and used it to steady himself.

"You're sure doing well in your recovery, Mr. Hawkins!" an orderly called from inside the building as he walked past.

"Thanks Jim," answered Richard as he took several steps with confidence. Though leaning heavily on his cane, he knew he was making progress.

Richard stayed on the path that wound through the rose garden. He occasionally stopped and smelled a blossom. *Someone in my condition has to stop and smell the roses.*

"You like roses don't you!" proclaimed a voice behind him. He turned to see Mr. Grant standing there.

"Yeah I do!" said Richard enthusiastically. "My Uncle Mac has a rose garden at home . . . Oh. I've been wondering. How is Mrs. Haverstock doing?"

"Well, Richard, I'll let her speak for herself. She knew I was coming to see you, so she sent you this note." Mr. Grant handed Richard a small envelope.

Putting the envelope carefully into his pocket, Richard said, "I'll read it later in my room . . . I'd better head back to my wheelchair now."

Richard turned to retrace his steps and, as he did so, nearly fell.

"Can I help you, Richard?"

"No thank you, Mr. Grant. It's tempting, but I'd better do it on my own."

Back at his wheelchair, Richard permitted Mr. Grant to help him sit back down.

Reaching into his jacket pocket, Bruce Grant drew out several brochures and gave them to Richard. "These brochures," he said, "describe a few of our companies that I thought you might find especially interesting." He then took a seat on a nearby bench, so he could answer any questions the brochures might raise.

Looking at one colorful brochure, Richard commented, "The picture of your headquarters is sure . . . impressive. I wouldn't think you would use, or need seven stories."

"Yes, the building's design is 'impressive'. We find it functional as well as attractive. It was built for us just this last year. And, Richard, we need every square foot of space in the six stories above the shops on the first floor. The Grant Corporation is highly diversified—companies range from oil to cosmetics. We have companies in nine states, mostly in the West and South. Our international holdings provide jobs for thousands of people in six countries. We're planning now to make large investments in Eastern Europe."

"I guess I didn't realize how big your corporation was, Mr. Grant."

"Yes, it's big and getting bigger. That's why I'm continually on the lookout for men and women who would make good managers. We're looking for someone to manage those first floor shops I mentioned. If you're interested in applying for the job, let me know, and I'll see that you're accepted into our management training program."

Richard smiled and nodded. "Okay," he said, "I'll let you know, Mr. Grant. Thank you for thinking of me." Then, he looked at another one of the brochures and shook his head as if perplexed. Pointing at a man pictured in the brochure, he asked, "Who's this guy with the beard?"

"Let me see." Mr. Grant got up and came close enough to see which brochure Richard was looking at. "Yes, he's employed at our small electronics company in Dallas. We bought it four years ago. It's doing okay, but it hasn't proven to be as profitable as expected. We've had a good offer for it. We'll probably sell if I can get assurances that nobody will lose his job as a result. But, why do you ask about this man? Does he look familiar?"

"No, but when I touched his picture, I felt a powerful, I don't know, *mental* energy, radiating from it. For an instant, I could see an image of him in what looked like the future. He was receiving an important honor, I think in science. You shouldn't sell that company and lose *him*, Mr. Grant. Now, that man is going to invent something big! Something *real* big! I think . . . something that could affect our national security. I can't see what it is, though."

"But, I haven't had any report from the company about anything he's working on that's important. As a matter of fact," Bruce emphasized, "their R and D department hasn't produced anything useful."

"What's 'R and D'?"

"Research and development."

"I don't know why you haven't gotten a report. If I could meet him, I believe I could tell you more."

"I'll arrange that immediately," Mr. Grant promised. "I'll have him flown here, so that you can talk to him. Then you can let me know what you find out about the work he's doing."

"Okay, but I think you'll have to be careful not to worry him. I sense that he's nervous—easily frightened."

"I'll ask his manager to have him come here to tell you about the company, so you have an opportunity to consider a job there. I'll take your advice and hold on to the company. Well, I'd better be going. It's been a very interesting visit. Take care of yourself, Richard."

Richard watched Mr. Grant walk out of the garden. Left alone with his thoughts, he wondered, *What's happening to me? What did the coma do to me? I see things in my mind that haven't happened yet. Has God given me this ability? And if He has, for what purpose?* Back in his room, Richard watched TV for a while and then went to his physical therapy session.

At the end of the session, Ken said, "You're doing well, Richard! Making good progress!"

"When do you think I can drive a car?"

"When you develop more strength and mobility on your left side."

"And, pretty soon I should be able to walk without a cane, don't you think?"

"That depends. Every case is different. You may find that for some months, or even years, walking any great distance will require the use of a cane. But, you should, in time, be able to walk faster and with greater ease. You should also one day be able to raise your left arm higher."

"Well, I'm grateful I can walk at all. But, my goal is to hang my cane up some day."

"Okay, but you know, the cane makes you look interesting. Gives you a distinctive look."

"I never thought of that," replied Richard, prepared to accept a new perspective.

"Why, there was a time in our history when every gentleman of high standing carried a walking stick."

"Sure. I've seen that in old movies that were set at the turn of the century."

When Richard left Ken with a parting word of thanks he felt better about using a cane. Then he thought about what it would look like in his favorite color. "I wonder if I could get one in blue. One with a more comfortable handle." On the way to his room, he tried to limp less every time someone passed him in the hallway.

As a nurse passed, she said, "I noticed a note taped on your door."

"Thank you, Ella. I'm sure it's a message from my uncle."

Richard picked up his pace. He had the habit of timing himself in walking from therapy to his room. At the door to his room, he looked at his watch. *Two minutes off my record.*

The note, as he expected, told him that his uncle would stop by in the morning. It suddenly reminded him of the note from Mrs. Haverstock. Inside his room, he took the envelope from his pocket.

> Dear Richard,
>
> Mr. Grant told me about your vision where you saw my heart attack and immediately contacted him. I am grateful that I survived and that you were obedient to the will of God. I am a widow with a nine-year-old son, who suffers from diabetes. There is no family member who could care for him, if something happened to me. So I also thank you on his behalf.
>
> I was glad to hear from Mr. Grant that you accepted a job with our company. Please consider me your friend. And if I can ever be of help to you, please let me know, for I will always be in your debt.
>
> Sincerely,
> Judith Haverstock

Richard smiled at the thought that his vision proved helpful to a small boy who needed his mother's care to survive a serious disease. *It must be that a personal object, or a person's picture transmits an image to my mind, when there are intense feelings about something. Maybe it's especially strong when more than one person is involved. I wonder if this ability is permanent . . . or just temporary.*

The telephone interrupted his thoughts. He moved as quickly as he could to answer it, and heard Mr. Grant's voice.

"The man in the picture is Karl Lester. He will be at the hospital to see you tomorrow evening."

"I've just had a thought. I believe it would be helpful if I could see pictures of his office and where he does his research."

"Alright. I'll see that you get those photos as soon as possible. If I can arrange it, I'll have Lester bring the photos with him in a sealed envelope. He won't know what's inside it."

"I may be putting someone for trouble . . . for nothing . . . But, I'm feeling the photos, and Mr. Lester himself, will… reveal . . . important work he's doing."

Still not saying things quite right. But it's getting better.

Late next evening, coming into the hospital from a stroll in the rose garden, Richard headed for an elevator. When the door slid open, he heard a man call, "Hold it! I need to go up."

A bearded, chubby, middle-aged man stepped into the elevator just before the doors closed. He started to press the button for the third floor, but saw that the other occupant had pressed it ahead of him.

Richard observed the stranger standing beside him and recognized Karl Lester. Again, he felt the same mental energy emanating from him that he had felt when he touched his picture. He started to speak, but decided against it. Instead, when the elevator stopped at the third floor, he stepped out and headed for his room. He left Lester standing in front of the elevator, wondering which direction to go.

Richard had time to get to his room, wash his face and comb his hair before he heard a knock at his door.

He smiled to himself. He didn't need any psychic ability to know who was knocking.

Opening the door, he saw the bearded man standing awkwardly in the doorway. Richard asked, "Yes? Are you looking for someone?"

"Yes, I'm looking for Mr. Hawkins," the man replied, in a tone suggesting he had doubts he'd come to the right room.

"I'm Richard Hawkins. Come in. You must be Karl Lester."

"Well, yes I am," Mr. Lester said, entering the room and sitting down at Richard's invitation. "I was beginning to think I had the wrong room," Mr. Lester said, with a sheepish smile. "My boss, that's G. H. Grifith, said something that made me think you were older," Mr. Lester hastened to say. "But our company could use young men like yourself with fresh ideas and youthful energy."

"Well, thanks for your vote of confidence. I *am* looking forward to working for Mr. Grant in one of his companies."

Mr. Lester stared hard at Richard a moment. "Haven't I seen you somewhere else?"

"You saw me in the elevator. We rode up together a little while ago."

"Of course! I'm afraid I'm not very observant today," Lester said, looking embarrassed. "I was deep in thought."

"Oh, that's alright. I suppose you were thinking about your work. If you don't mind my asking, what's your current project?"

"You see, Mr. Hawkins, I'm not supposed to talk about my work. Not even with my mother."

"Sure. I understand," said Richard encouragingly. "I probably wouldn't have the scientific knowledge to appreciate it anyway."

"Well, uh, no. You'd just find it boring."

Richard noticed Mr. Lester taking a bandaged hand out of his pocket. "Did you hurt your hand while doing your work?"

The other man replied, "Yes I uh, *did* hurt my hand. It's nothing serious though. Just a burn."

"The doctor gave me some pills for the pain. It's not too bad. But, never mind me. I understand Mr. Grant wanted me to tell you about our electronics company. This year, we should make a nice profit—the last few years I guess we've broken even. I brought along three job descriptions that Mr. Grifith thought might interest you. I also picked up some brochures from the Dallas Chamber of Commerce. I believe, Mr. Hawkins, you would like Dallas. I've lived there only a short while myself. But, I like it. I like everything, but the humidity. You see, I came from Alaska, and I'm not used to it."

"I should think not," commented Richard. He did not say anything, but he continued to wonder what caused the injury to his hand.

"Here is an envelope that Mr. Grifith asked me to give you." Lester carefully took a sealed envelope out of his inside jacket pocket and handed it to Richard. "I believe it contains information about our product line."

After asking several questions about the company, Richard asked, "When are you returning to Dallas?"

"Tomorrow morning. Can I give you any more information, Mr. Hawkins, before I leave?"

"No, you've been very helpful. Thank Mr. Grifith for me."

"Yes I will. It's been nice talking with you, Mr. Hawkins. I hope you will decide to apply at our company. We have some nice people."

Following his guest's departure, Richard closed the door, and immediately began thinking about what kind of work he did. Richard quickly opened the envelope. He examined the photographs of the lab where Lester worked. In his mind, Richard suddenly saw a series of images: Lester in a laboratory with an intense light. Lester accidentally burning himself. A moment later, he saw an image of Lester reading a notebook. In the notebook he saw the words: "a beam of concentrated photon particles generated by electricity rather than chemicals." *So that's it! He's working to develop an electric laser!*

Richard didn't know much about lasers. He did know that an electrically-generated laser would be an important scientific breakthrough. He picked up the phone, called Mr. Grant's private number, and left a message on his voice mail. He described what he believed was the nature of Lester's work. He also offered advice.

"I don't think you should . . . uh confront Lester with what I've . . . told you. I would say, give him help . . . or resources he needs, and . . . special security to guard him and his project." *After all, it's advice he's paying me for, at least, at the moment.*

23

Pastor Burton's Message

RICHARD, THROUGH CONCENTRATED EFFORT, improved his verbal skills to a level of pre-accident effectiveness. Regular physical therapy increased strength and movement in his left side. Occasional panic attacks, a side effect from his coma, were gradually overcome, as he learned to feel calm and secure going outside the hospital for short walks or to shop at nearby stores. A few sessions with a psychologist proved helpful. Observing his progress, his Uncle Mac had returned to Verity.

After a while, he could ride the bus without worrying he would lose his balance getting on and off. Today, he took the bus to one of Riverfield's local restaurants.

"I'm sorry I'm late, Richard," Melissa said, as she approached his table in the restaurant. "I had trouble finding a parking place. Saturday traffic seemed heavier than usual."

Richard rose quickly to greet Melissa with a hug. Stepping away from the table, he responded, "You're not late. I'm glad . . ." His words were cut off, as he lost his balance and fell.

"Are you *hurt*, Richard?" Melissa asked as she hurried to where he lay. "Let me help you," she said, offering her hand to him.

His first impulse was to refuse her hand and ask for his cane. But resisting his feelings of pride, he told her, "Let me get on my knees."

By holding on to the table and Melissa's hand, Richard got to his feet and gave Melissa a big hug.

When they were seated, Richard said drily, "Guess I forgot my disability."

"Oh, Richard, you're not disabled. You just need time to regain your strength on your left side. And you're making great progress."

"I appreciate your encouraging words, Melissa. But for now, and probably for a long time to come, I *am* disabled—but I can manage. I've come to terms with it, now I have to learn to live with it. Did my uncle tell you I'm moving?"

"As a matter of fact, he did. I know he wanted to find you a comfortable place close to the hospital, so you could continue your therapy with Ken Kiyoshi."

"He sure picked out a nice apartment. At first, I thought it was too expensive, but that was before I got my first paycheck from Mr. Grant. I was surprised to get so big a salary. I wonder what my five months in the hospital cost Mr. Grant? I imagine plenty."

Melissa reached across the table and took hold of Richard's hand. "I think Mr. Grant is a wise judge of character. He knows you're a good investment. Besides that, he *likes* you." Softening her voice, she added, "And he's not the only one." A squeeze of his hand emphasized her words.

Richard gave Melissa a warm smile and squeezed back. "You know," he said, "we'd better order lunch. In about two hours, I've got to meet with Mr. Grant's son, John. He's going to help me move stuff from the hospital to my apartment, then we're going to hear Pastor Jacob Burton preach at a local church. How about joining us?"

"I'd like to, but I've got to get back, so I can prepare for a history exam."

"He's an evangelist. Our youth pastor, Cal Jessup, encouraged me to hear him preach to the young people in the church. Cal will be on hand to introduce him."

Lunch gave each the opportunity of enjoying the other's company.

Getting into a red sports car near his apartment, Richard asked, "John, are you sure you don't mind going to church with me?"

"No, not at all, Rich. It'll do me good. I haven't been to church, since my mother died."

"When was that?"

"Well," John began sadly, "I guess it was almost eleven years ago. It doesn't seem that long." John paused for a moment—as memories filled his mind. Changing the subject, he asked, "Are you looking forward to hearing this preacher guy?"

"Yes, I am," Richard answered enthusiastically. "My friend Cal told me I'd like his style of preaching."

Looking concerned, John said, "I'm sure he's alright and all that, but if you don't mind, could we sit in the back?"

"Oh, sure."

Starting the car, John boomed, "Okay, here we go. Let's burn rubber."

He revved the engine, and took off fast.

Richard thought he'd better say something. "You don't need to drive fast. We don't have to be early."

"You're not concerned about my driving are you? You're as safe with me, as you would be with your Uncle Mac. Besides," chuckled John, "this car has a lot of horses under the hood—and they like to run!"

Thinking of a tactful way of putting it, Richard remarked, "I used to like fast cars too . . . until my accident."

After the two rode together at a more sedate pace, John asked, "What led up to the accident? I mean if you don't mind my asking. Was another car involved?"

"No. My friend, Tony, lost control. We were driving along and talking, and the next thing—he was dead and I was in a coma." Looking at John, he added, "Recently, I realized I've taken the gift of life for granted. I don't want to ever again."

"I've done the same thing, now that I think of it. You know, you have a habit of making me think more deeply than I'm used to doing. In fact, sometimes I feel like I'm talking to an older brother. And it's amazing, since you're so much younger than I."

Cal Jessup was about to introduce Pastor Burton, when Richard and John found seats in the back row of the church's fellowship hall. The two men listened to Pastor Jessup's introduction: "Pastor Jacob Burton spent ten years as an Air Force chaplain, and in that time saw many people brought to the Lord. Most recently, he worked with youth in Los Angeles, who were involved in the city's gangs. On one occasion, when preaching on a street corner, a gang leader knifed him in the side—he was angry at Jacob for helping members of his gang find a new leader in Jesus. Jacob led that gang leader to Christ. It's a great pleasure to have my friend, Pastor Burton, speak to us today."

A man in his early 50s of below average height and solid build, with dark hair, wearing a neat gray suit, stepped up to the pulpit. "Thank you, Cal, for that kind introduction. You mentioned my knife wound. I'll resist the temptation of showing you my scar."

The audience laughed.

"I know what he means," John whispered to Richard. "Dad takes great delight in showing friends his scar from his heart operation."

"It's a little warm up here on the platform," Pastor Burton announced. "So, I'd like to take my coat off." Removing his coat revealed a very striking vest.

"With that vest on," John whispered, "he'd never be lost in a crowd."

"That's for sure. With that vest, he could *attract* a crowd."

Pastor Burton looked down at his vest, which presented a red-and-black checkered pattern. "I see by your expressions that my vest has aroused some interest. Well, my vest tells a story. It probably reminds you of a checkerboard. And in many ways, life is like a game of checkers. But it's a game between you and yourself! Between sinful desire on the one side, and moral purpose on the other side. The moves you make show which side is winning in your life. I'm here to tell you that Jesus can help you start a new game!"

Richard looked at Pastor Burton's vest with new respect.

"One good thing about my vest is, it stays in your memory. I realize my vest is more memorable than my face. So, if, someday, you don't remember me, you may remember my vest and what it represents. It's vital that you do."

The speaker's words and his visual aid produced laughter and applause.

"It's great to be here. Thanks for your warm welcome. I especially like applause at the beginning—it's a vote of confidence. At the end, it could be a sign of relief." Again the pastor was rewarded with laughter.

"Not many people know it, but I grew up in this town. When I was a kid, Verity was a place where not much happened. Seeing the town makes me feel like a kid again, although I'm not allowed to act like one."

The young people laughed.

His voice and demeanor becoming more serious, Pastor Burton declared, "I'm a man with a sense of calling. I listen when my wife calls me to supper, and I listen when God calls me to share the good news of salvation in Jesus Christ. You might think of me as a reporter with a headline that's always current—*Jesus Saves!* Times have changed since I was young, but human nature hasn't. Young people like yourselves, and adults too, have always looked for something solid to build their lives on."

At that point, Richard glanced at John, who was leaning forward, nodding his head.

"A lotta people in my generation were out trying to save the world. We didn't know that God, through His Son, had already taken care of that. Friends, if you want to find something in this world to believe in, you need to look to Someone who is higher than yourself. Because the cruelty of this world," he said sadly, "is far stronger than you are. Let's hear Jesus' words in John 16:33. 'These things I have spoken to you, that in Me you may have peace. In this world you will have tribulation, but take courage; I have overcome the world.' We don't have to face life's problems alone, if we have Jesus to walk beside us."

John turned in Richard's direction and said softly, "I see that kind of faith in you, Rich."

Pastor Burton stated, "A lotta people look for their security in stuff. They spend their lives collecting stuff. They get all they can, can all they get, and then keep the can. And like the pharaohs of ancient Egypt, they think they can take it with them when they die." Looking closely at the faces in the audience, he added, "I've never seen a hearse pulling a u-haul."

John, speaking with his head down, so that it was hard for Richard to hear him, said something like, "He looked right at *me* when he said that."

"The Bible says, we're all sinners. But we don't have to read the Bible to *know* that! We can look around us and see for ourselves. Just turn on your TV," Pastor Burton suggested, "and you'll hear of murder, rape, theft, lies, perversion, corruption, drug abuse. Our churches are constantly looking for new members, but our prisons are filled to over-flowing capacity."

Richard looked around the room, trying to see what effect the pastor's message was having on the two hundred or so youth and adults in the room. What he saw convinced him that the pastor's message was getting through.

Pastor Burton went on to explain the plan of salvation in Christ, clearly and compellingly. He concluded his message saying, "It is the desire in most people's hearts, to find a purpose in life. And those who seek Jesus in their hearts will find a new life of purpose. Won't you this day, this hour make the most important move in your life? As the pianist plays *Just as I am*, stand up for Jesus, as He stood up for you, and come forward to accept the risen Christ. Don't bet your soul on an uncertain tomorrow by waiting for another opportunity that may not happen; come today to receive God's gift of salvation, to become a new person in Christ."

Two young teenagers made their way to the aisle and went forward, and three more young persons followed—in a few minutes, many youth and some adults stood before Pastor Burton.

Richard, who was praying that more hearts would be touched, suddenly felt John's hand on his shoulder.

"I'm going forward, Rich."

"I'll walk with you."

When the audience had finished singing *Just as I am*, Pastor Burton said, "I want to pray for you and then I want to give each of you a *New Testament*, a devotional guide, and a booklet that will help you to grow in Christ.

After Pastor Burton prayed, Cal distributed the literature. Cal told the group, "Be sure to attend church regularly and get involved. You don't have to attend this church, but, I'm sure, the folks here would love to have you do so. But find a church that preaches the Gospel of Christ."

As Richard and John left the church minutes later, John said, "I'd like to attend church with you, if you wouldn't mind."

"Of course. I'd like to have you go to church with me. I go to the early service, so that I can attend Sunday School."

"Well, I can see I'm going to have to get accustomed to rising early Sunday morning. But, that's okay. I need to reexamine my use of time. I'd like to be your transportation."

"Sure. Thank you, John."

24

Muggers Carry Guns

AFTERNOON RAIN CLOUDS THREATENED Richard with a soaking as he got off the city bus and started to walk the half block to his apartment.

What I used to call walking briskly, I now call running.

Richard had spent an hour with Ken, his physical therapist, exercising to strengthen his left arm and leg. Ken had him sit and hold the tip of his cane with his left hand, and with his right on the handle, push his left hand above his head, forcing muscles in his arm to function. He had him stand and raise a three-pound weight with his left arm from his side to a position straight out in front of him. As instructed, he did similar exercises at home. He was determined to do his part to improve mobility.

He reached his apartment just ahead of the rain. But a short time later, he was reminded of the fickle nature of Oregon weather—bright streams of sunlight poured through his windows and lit the room.

Standing at the picture window in the living room, Richard watched joggers on the sidewalk, the sun's appearance luring them outdoors.

Good thing the rain held off. Being from Arizona, Aunt Jenny isn't used to it.

She had called yesterday to say she would like to visit him today if he were free. He was always free for Aunt Jenny.

Richard looked at his watch. *She should be arriving in two hours by taxi, unless the plane's late. For Aunt Jenny, punctuality is a religious commitment.*

He read for awhile, then got up and traded his jeans and t-shirt for slacks and a dress shirt. *Should I wear a tie? Yes, I'd better. Aunt Jenny will likely wear one of her fashionable suits, looking as if she'd just delivered a speech in the state legislature.*

Aunt Jenny arrived at about the time she was expected. She stood a moment in the living room, smiling at Richard. She took his hand and patted it. "You look fine, Richard, handsome as ever. I see you still have your mustache. It suits you."

The two sat in the living room, chatting about Jenny's political activities and Richard's Grant Corporation employment.

"In a few weeks, I'll be heading to San Diego to get training, so I can apply for a management position in one of the Grant companies."

"That should be a good opportunity for you . . . You know, Richard, I'm sorry I didn't see you last month. I wanted to be with you and Mac at Christmas. I had a cold I couldn't shake, even using my grandmother's cold remedy."

"What's that?"

"Hot sarsaparilla tea with lemon and brown sugar four times a day."

"Sounds better than some remedies I've heard of."

"I thought we might go to McGrath's Fish House for dinner. How does that sound, Richard?"

"Sounds like fish and chips!"

"We probably should go outside and wait for the taxi I ordered, in case he's early."

Richard helped his aunt put on her jacket, and got one for himself.

As they left Richard's apartment, it was getting dark—rain clouds obscured the moon.

"If the taxi driver's on time," Jenny said, looking in both directions, "he'll pick us up in a few minutes."

They stood waiting with their backs to a closed Starbucks. Suddenly, a man, who had slipped behind Richard, growled, "*Don't* turn around! What ya feel against your spine, fella, ain't no candy cane. Get your wallet and hold it behind ya."

"Do what I tell ya, if ya want to keep living, lady. Slide your purse to me under your left arm."

Richard changed his position slightly to take the weight off his left leg.

"I said, *don't* move. Move again, and ya'll need *two* canes."

"I was just . . ."

"Shut up! You got anymore cash on ya?"

"No. You have it all," Richard said.

"I'm gonna take only the cash. You can keep the credit cards." Chuckling evilly, he added, "Don't bother to thank me. Stay where you are *five* minutes. Get curious and turn around, I'll kill ya!"

He dropped the wallet and purse behind his victims and left so quietly neither Richard nor his aunt heard him go.

"I guess that's about five minutes." Richard, shaking a little, turned to pick up his wallet and Aunt Jenny's purse.

"Thank goodness, all he took was cash; he didn't take our ID and credit cards," Aunt Jenny said, as she checked the contents of her purse. "How much did he take from you, Richard?"

"I think about sixty-five dollars. Did he get much from you?"

"Your aunt is one hundred and seventy-five dollars poorer."

"I'm sorry, Aunt Jenny."

"I still have money for a taxi," she said, opening her jacket and unpinning a fifty dollar bill from the lining.

"Good for you, Aunty!"

"Your old aunt hasn't lived all these years without learning a few tricks."

"There's our taxi!" Richard waved at the driver.

Looking at her watch, Jenny responded, "Yes, and his promptness has earned him a tip. How do we report we've been mugged?"

"I'll ask the driver to notify the police. Too bad we can't describe the mugger."

"That's why we're still alive," Jenny replied, getting into the backseat of the cab.

Later, at the restaurant, good food and pleasant conversation gradually eased their nerves.

Accepting a warm-up on his coffee, Richard shook his head sadly. "I'm sorry, Aunt Jenny. You had a bad welcome to Riverfield. I wonder if that mugger really had a gun."

"Muggers carry guns. They need that kind of fire power to intimidate or hurt an uncooperative victim. I know. This was the second time I've been mugged."

"It was? What was the first time?"

"A few years ago, I came out of my office in Flagstaff late at night. My car was in a well-lit parking lot, so I wasn't worried. I was about to get into my car, when a voice behind me said, 'Hold it.' I turned around and a man with a gun shined a flashlight in my face. He told me, 'Do as I say and you won't get hurt.' My purse was in my briefcase, so he took both. It contained important papers, more important than the money."

"That's a shame. Did you have copies of the papers?"

"No. But as it turned out, I didn't need them. Couple of days later, a package appeared at my office door, containing my briefcase, papers, and purse . . . and a note from the mugger."

"The mugger wrote you a *note*?"

"Yes. He wrote he'd used my visa card to '*borrow*' a hundred dollars, besides taking a hundred and fifty from my purse. Get this. He said he read the papers in the briefcase and was so impressed, he planned to vote for me in the November elections. Needless to say, I didn't advertise his endorsement."

Richard chuckled. "It wouldn't sound good on the 6:00 o'clock news."

"Were you scared, Richard, when the mugger stuck a gun in your back? You didn't act scared."

"I started to feel scared, but then I felt a strong reassurance that we wouldn't be hurt. It was as if God were saying, 'Don't worry, I have plans for you. You survived the car accident for a purpose.'"

After saying goodbye to his aunt that evening and returning to his apartment, Richard thought about the mugging. He suddenly felt a sense of helplessness. *Even if I'd been in top physical condition*, he told himself, *I couldn't have done anything. The man had a gun in my back.* But, the feeling persisted. He realized he made a vulnerable target for any bad guy who might want to rob or harm him. Moreover, he couldn't effectively defend anyone with him—Melissa, Uncle Mac, Aunt Jenny.

Feeling tired, he turned in early, but couldn't get to sleep until past 2:00 AM. His anxieties about his inability to defend himself and others filled his mind with busy thoughts.

The phone woke him the next morning. Aunt Jenny called to say goodbye. She'd be driving to Verity to visit Mac a couple of days before heading back. He told her he would stop at the police department to give information about the robbery on his way to the hospital.

In his PT session with Ken, he did the exercises with less enthusiasm. *More strength and mobility on my left side won't make that much difference*, he reasoned. *I'm still going to be crippled.*

"Are you feeling okay, Richard? Let me know if I'm pushing you too hard."

"I'm okay, Ken. I'll try to get with it. I guess I've been worrying about something . . . Last night, my aunt and I were mugged."

"Did he get much from you?"

"It's not the money. It made me realize for the first time, my disability makes me *vulnerable*."

"I see . . . Did you know I operated a martial arts school?"

"No, I didn't know that."

"On weekends, when I'm not at the hospital, I teach tae kwon do—that's a Korean style of karate. Right now, you couldn't do the kicks and jumps, but I could teach you how to turn your hands into weapons of defense."

"As you know, I'll be leaving in three weeks for management training."

"That would give us three weekends—enough to get you started. After you finish your management training, you could continue tae kwon do with a good instructor I know in Verity. Think about it."

"I thought about it. I'd like to get started."

"Sometime, you might want to look up a guy who teaches 'cane-fu' self-defense to people who use canes."

"I'll keep it in mind."

25

Deciding on Dallas

Three months after his visit with Aunt Jenny, Richard looked around his bedroom in Verity at objects that held many happy memories. He had arrived the day before at his uncle's house, unannounced, a surprise.

Smiling, he thought of the response he'd received when his uncle opened the door. Mac's hug had nearly knocked Richard over. "Ye're lookin' like your old self," he'd said.

He absent-mindedly rearranged objects on his desk, and grimaced at the sight of unanswered letters, sitting beneath a prized piece of obsidian he'd found near Bend, Oregon when he was ten.

After he'd talked about the obsidian to his fourth grade class, his teacher, Mr. Jackson, complimented him: "You made a piece of black rock more interesting than recess." His success, he knew, was due to his uncle's advice, "Keep your attention on your listeners, not on yourself." He'd followed that advice all through his communication major in college.

Turning to his mirror he saw a man leaning on a cane, who looked older, but who would never again look like his "old self."

"Well, at least I look more mature."

"How aboot havin' some breakfast, Richard! I've made your favorite breakfast!" Mac called.

"Coming!"

Richard descended the stairs, chuckling to himself. *I hope that's the stairs creaking and not me.*

Mac stood at the foot of the stairs, waiting to greet his nephew. "Di' ye sleep well last night, laddie?" he asked, as Richard joined him on the first floor.

"Sure did. It was nice to be back in my old room. I noticed you hadn't changed anything."

"Nooo. It's just the way ye left it. It will always be your room, my boy, and some day this house will be yours, too."

The two men went into the kitchen and sat at the little formica dinette set.

"Looks delicious!" Richard said, eyeing the French toast and bacon.

After Mac said grace, he got up from the table to pour coffee for each of them. "I have a pitcher o' fresh-squeezed orange juice for ye in the fridge, Richard," Mac announced proudly.

"Oh, you shouldn't have gone to so much trouble for me, Uncle. But, I'm glad to have it. You heated the maple syrup!"

Between savored mouthfuls, Richard shared the story of John Grant's conversion.

"Ye did a gude work by taking John to church, Richard."

"Actually he took me, since he drove. And, he found the Lord through Pastor Jacob Burton's preaching. I was just there."

"Aye, but ye witnessed by your life what it means to be a Christian."

"Speaking of Mr. Grant, Uncle, I wanted to let you know about a decision I've made, a decision about a job offered to me." Richard paused, wondering how his uncle would take his news. "I've decided to take a job in Dallas, at a small electronics firm Mr. Grant owns. The job is human resource manager. I called him a couple of days ago. He seemed very pleased about it. But, I'm going to miss you and Melissa and my home, Uncle Mac."

"I'm goin' to miss ye too, my boy. But I'm sure Bruce can use ye in Dallas; it will be a gude opportunity for ye." Mac swallowed hard, trying to keep his voice from betraying his sadness at the thought of Richard moving so far away.

"I don't kid myself that HR management is God's ultimate purpose for my life, but, I'm hopeful it may lead to something that is. For now, it's a good job, which I need. Last week, I read in Isaiah: 'I have good plans for you, not plans to hurt you. I will give you hope and a good future.' I claimed that promise in going to Dallas."

"I believe ye mean Jeremiah, not Isaiah."

"Yes, Jeremiah, Jeremiah 29:11. I have to say, I've been wondering, more truthfully, worrying, if I can hack it as a manager, when I don't have any management experience."

"Remember, son, ye have the greatest human resource to draw wisdom from—the *Bible*."

"Yes, that's true, Uncle Mac."

"But, laddie, your college classes, and all those recent weeks o' trainin' surely gave ye some gude preparation."

"Yes, I think I have a good basic understanding of management responsibilities. And, as I wrote you in my letters, the people at the Grant company there in San Diego were very helpful. The one thing that all six of us in the training program heard from everyone though was, 'We can teach you the theory, but it has to be adapted to every situation.' And, that's where experience comes in, I imagine."

"I suppose in your trainin' they gave ye books to read. A gude book sometimes is better than experience."

"We were given a lot of material to read. That's for sure. I think I read more than the other trainees, from what they told me. But then, they had more experience than I."

"What did Bruce say to ye when he offered ye the job?"

"Well, he said half of human resource management is communication and, since that's what I studied in college, he was sure I'd do well."

"Bruce is a good judge o' character and talent. If he weren't, he wouldn't be so successful."

"I just wish I were as confident about me, as he is. But, you're right, Uncle Mac, Mr. Grant knows the kind of men and women he needs in management. I'll trust his judgment and stand by my decision. He spoke to the trainees in our last training session. He told us, 'If you don't make mistakes, it'll mean you're not trying anything new.' I think it's more likely I'll make mistakes trying something old."

"When will ye leave for Dallas?"

"This coming weekend." Richard saw again the sadness in his uncle's eyes.

"That means then, we have five days, countin' today to enjoy ourselves and arrange for your trip. Ye're goin' to need to buy some clothes, laddie, so ye'll look presentable in your new job. Have ye told Melissa aboot your decision?"

"No, I haven't come right out and told her, Uncle; I only talked about the possibility."

"Why don't ye invite her over tonight? I'll plan a nice dessert, and then ye can tell her, and see what she says aboot it."

"Good idea. Thank you, Uncle. I'll call her as soon as I've eaten and helped with the dishes."

Mac glanced at Richard's cane. "No, I can manage by myself, laddie."

Richard, who had seen his look, insisted.

"Aye, my boy, just like old times. I'll wash and ye dry."

As his uncle put away the clean dishes, Richard phoned Melissa.

"Hello?"

"You're the prettiest girl I've ever met, in or out of a coma."

"Thank you, Richard, that's very nice. Let me get Melissa for you," Helen Ingram said with a giggle.

In a moment, Melissa was on the line. "I've been expecting you to call," she told him. "How are you feeling? Have you recovered from training?"

"I'm fine. I just haven't recovered from my embarrassment. Your mother and you sure sound a lot alike on the phone. I never know which one of you I'm talking to."

"Mom told me what you said and we both thought your compliment was sweet. Could you come over for dinner tonight, Richard?"

"Well, actually, Melissa, Uncle Mac and I wanted to invite you to the house for dessert. I want to talk to you about something."

"You're alright, aren't you?"

"Oh sure, I'm okay. It's nothing about my health."

"Okay, I'll be there at 7:00. I should warn you though, my hair has looked better. When you see me, you may want to take back your compliment."

"I promise I won't. See you at 7:00."

As he hung up the phone, Mac came into the room. "A bonny lass, Melissa is," he said, smiling broadly.

"How'd you know it was Melissa?"

"I could tell by the look on your face."

Thinking about Mac's remark, he stated, "She *is* a bonny lass. I'm going to miss her a lot when I'm in Dallas. I'll miss you both."

When Melissa arrived that evening, the first words out of her mouth were: "What is it, Richy? It sounded serious."

"Let's sit in the living room; my uncle's in the kitchen fixing dessert."

Richard, taking Melissa's hand, told her about his decision. "The company is Advanced Development Electronics."

Melissa looked sad for a moment and then her face brightened. "I have a good friend in Dallas. Amy Kellog has often invited me to visit her. I think that this would be a good time for me to say, yes. I'll talk to my boss at the book store about vacation days I've got coming. Then I'll call her. And, I'll tell her about you, too, so she knows I have an ulterior motive for accepting her invitation. She'll want to meet you. She's quite a character."

"Dallas is looking better already. I think your hair looks beautiful."

"Well . . . I did work on it a little . . ."

Richard leaned over and gave her a kiss, just as Mac started to enter the room. The Scot quickly retreated and called from the kitchen: "Your dessert is ready, if ye'd like apple pie and ice cream!"

After the three had enjoyed Mac's dessert, they listened to him talk about his visits to Dallas.

"Were the people in Dallas friendly?"

Mac chuckled. "Aye, Melissa. In my experience they were. When Richard was a wee lad, I presented a paper at the Jonsson Central Library in downtown Dallas—I spoke on the importance o' letters and journals in research. Afterward, I visited the Dallas Museum of Art. While admiring the work o' an impressionist painter, an attractive woman rushed over to me and gave me a big kiss."

"What did you do then?"

"Bein' a gentleman, Richard, I kissed her back."

"I was tryin' to remember who she was when she called me Henry. Not wantin' to embarrass her, I was Henry for aboot an hour. I shared my limited knowledge o' art with her, as we strolled around the museum. When she had to leave, she said it was wonderful to see me after so many years."

"Uncle Mac, didn't she notice your Scottish accent?"

"Aye, Richard. I told her I'd lived many years in Scotland." The recollection made him smile. "I never had such a pleasant welcome in Edinburgh as I did in Dallas."

"I hope Richy's welcome to Dallas isn't that friendly," Melissa said teasingly. "I suppose I should be going. I have to be up early in the morning for class before my job at the book store. Thank you, Mr. MacGregor, for the delicious apple pie and ice cream."

"Ye're very welcome. Your presence made dessert more flavorful. As the Bard says, 'Theres nought but care on every hand, /In every hour that passes, O: /What signifies the life o' man, /And twere not for the lasses, O.'"

"Robert Burns had that right, Uncle Mac. I'll walk you to the car, Melissa."

Standing by her car, Melissa asked, "What poem was Mac quoting from?"

"One of his favorites: 'Green Grow the Rashes.' I used to know all six verses myself."

"What are 'rashes'? Is that a Scottish word?"

"'Rashes' just means 'rushes'. Those plants that grow near water." With that explanation, Richard took her face in his hands and gently kissed her forehead.

"You understand, Melissa, I'll be spending most of my time this week with Uncle Mac. I'm so glad I'll see you in Dallas. As soon as I have an address there, I'll call you, so we can write."

"Of course. You should spend time with your uncle."

During the next few days, Richard and Mac spent some happy times together. They watched movies, shopped, prepared meals together, visited Cal Jessup and his wife, Karen, so Richard could say good-bye to them. They worked in the garden, and gave special attention to Mac's roses.

The evening before Richard was to leave, Mac asked about his nephew's coma.

"Does it still seem that your life started over with your mither and father, and your sister and brother?"

"Yes," said Richard, rethinking what happened to him. "It was as if I took the place of Mother's stillborn baby, Douglas, and grew up in the family back in the 60s and 70s. Everything seemed as real as it does talking to you now. I can't explain it, but in my mind I feel I knew them, and even saw them die."

"Your mither and father looked like their pictures in the album? Is that right?"

"Yeah! I even saw them age."

The two men sat in silence a few minutes, each alone with his thoughts and memories.

"Richard, have ye had any more visions o' the kind that saved Judith Haverstock's life, and revealed Karl Lester's project?"

"No, Uncle, I haven't. Actually I've been wanting to talk with you about these . . . visions, as you call them. I've been concerned about having this ability."

"What aboot it, Richard?"

"Well, can I be sure that it comes from God?"

"I can understand your concern. But, remember laddie, every gift that God has bestowed on man, has been used for good or evil purposes. Every person chooses. Ye have used this gift o' yours for good purposes. In the case o' Mrs. Haverstock, it was to save her life. And it so happened to protect her son too. In the case o' Mr. Lester, it was to make sure he got resources and security to aid him in his work."

"Uncle Mac, you know the Bible better than I do. What does it say about the ability to see visions?"

"Di' ye have your Bible handy, Richard?"

"Yes, it's over there on the table. I'll get it."

"Read Acts, Chapter 2, verse 17—and see what God says."

Richard read: "God says, 'That I will pour forth of My Spirit upon all mankind; And your sons and your daughters shall prophesy, And your young men shall see visions, And your old men shall dream dreams.'"

"You're saying this verse applies to me and the visions I've had?"

"Aye, laddie."

The day of Richard's departure for Dallas came all too soon for Mac. They left the house early for the airport, so Richard would have plenty of time to check on his flight and get help with his baggage.

Mac made good time getting to the airport, stopping the car near the terminal entrance to save Richard some steps. He removed two heavy suitcases from the trunk and got someone to carry them for Richard.

"I'll not go in with ye. Take care o' yourself. If ye should need anythin', let your old uncle know."

"I will, Uncle Mac. I'll call you soon after I arrive. Good-bye. Oh, and tell Cal Jessup I'll be calling him, too."

"Aye. Ye have a lot o' friends who will want to know how ye're gettin' along. One friend *especially*."

"Yes, I know," responded Richard with a smile. "I'll be calling Melissa, too. Her folks plan to invite you over for dinner some evening soon."

"That's nice to hear. I'll look forward to it. T'will be lonesome without ye."

"Well, good-bye, Uncle. Take care of yourself, and don't worry. I'll be fine." With these words, Richard took a light suitcase from the backseat of the car. Holding it in one hand, and his cane in the other, he turned and headed for the terminal doors, wondering what life would be like for him in Dallas.

26

Conflict at ADE

IN DALLAS, RICHARD CLAIMED his luggage. He had to wait only five minutes before he saw Karl Lester heading in his direction.

Karl, with a big smile on his face, greeted him like an old friend. "It's good to see you again, Richard!" he exclaimed. "I was happy to hear from Mr. Grifith that you had decided to take a job at ADE." As if to emphasize his words, Lester grabbed Richard's left hand and shook it gently—Richard's right hand held his cane.

"I appreciate your willingness to pick me up, Karl. I hope it didn't cause you too much inconvenience."

"Not at all, Richard, not at all. Actually, I offered to get you. I was looking forward to seeing you again, after our nice chat in the hospital. The company needs younger employees like you. You and I will be the youngest employees at ADE. Most have been there since it started nearly two decades ago. Say, I bet you'd like to get going." Picking up Richard's three suitcases, he said, "Shall we head for the car?"

"Yes, that sounds good."

Walking slowly so Richard could keep up with him, Lester explained, "The company has reserved a suite for you in one of Dallas' nicest hotels. I took the liberty of looking for an apartment for you, but didn't have very good luck. I'll keep looking."

As Karl slid behind the wheel, he noticed Richard rubbing his leg and asked, "Are you feeling okay?"

"Huh? Oh, sure. Just a little stiff from the flight. Say, thanks for carrying my luggage. I'm sorry you had to get stuck with it."

"I'm glad to help. Well, let's head for the hotel, so you can get a look at your temporary home. There's a fine restaurant in the hotel."

"I see your hand has healed."

"Yes. I'll try to be more careful in the future. It's not only the pain I want to avoid, it's the inconvenience to my work."

"How's your work progressing?"

"It's going well. Thanks for asking. Main reason is because of my new lab. What a surprise that was! Without any overture on my part, the Grant Corporation informed me I needed better lab equipment and a well-equipped lab at home to be more productive. So they took the makeshift equipment in my home basement and turned it into a state of the art lab, after my specifications. Unlike my lab at work, it's specialized for my particular research."

"When did you get your new home lab, Karl?"

"When I got back from seeing you in Oregon, I was told Bruce Grant, himself, authorized the new lab for immediate attention—oh, and also installation of a security system."

"Any explanation for giving you the lab?"

"No, not really. Just something about the Corporation's new policy of more emphasis on R and D. Funny thing. I heard that G.H. wasn't consulted before the decision was made."

Ten minutes after this exchange, Karl pulled up in front of the Clareton Inn. He got out of the car and carried Richard's luggage into the lobby.

"If I didn't have to get back to the office, Richard, I'd take you out to lunch," Karl noted apologetically.

"You've done enough for me. It's I who should take you out to lunch, and I will, once I get a routine going."

Karl smiled and nodded and left Richard standing in the lobby.

Richard glanced around, suddenly feeling alone in a new world of strangers. *As soon as I get to my room, I must call Uncle Mac.*

After a brief telephone conversation with his uncle, followed by a short nap, Richard ordered coffee and a sandwich in the hotel restaurant. He enjoyed the sandwich, but he would have enjoyed it more in the company of a friend. *Had Melissa been sitting with me, my sandwich would have tasted like a banquet. At least I can talk to her on the phone this evening. I'd better be careful what I say, until I'm sure I'm not talking to her mother.*

The next morning, Richard took a taxi to ADE and arrived at 8:00 a.m. He learned from G.H. Grifith's secretary that her boss would be out of town for two weeks.

"Mr. Grifith instructed me to show you your office and to tell you that you should feel free to order any new furniture or equipment that would make you more comfortable."

"That's very thoughtful of him."

"All you have to do is tell me what you would like and I'll see that you get it."

"I'll remember that. Thank you."

"Oh, Mr. Hawkins, my name is Kelly, Kelly Worley. I'll be your secretary until you hire your own. If you'll follow me to the elevator, I'll take you to your office."

The two stepped into the elevator, along with a young man in a security guard's uniform. He nodded at Kelly and gave Richard a curious glance.

Kelly and Richard left the elevator at the fourth floor and walked down a hallway a short distance, while the guard entered a door marked SECURITY.

"I'm sorry this hallway is so dark," Kelly said. "It's slated to have new light fixtures and a paint job. The first two floors have just been done, so it won't be long before this floor will be brighter. Here, this is your office." She handed him a key. "I'd better be getting back downstairs— I'm expecting a call from Mr. Grifith. I'll let him know you've arrived. Oh," she added, as she turned to leave, "this used to be Mr. Comstock's office, the founder of our company. He liked being able to look out the windows at the city of Dallas."

Richard found, to his surprise, that the door to his office was unlocked. Entering, he saw a huge desk of polished walnut, ornately designed in 19th century style. A comfortable-looking leather chair stood at attention behind it. A large, round conference table, surrounded by eight leather-padded chairs, complemented the desk in style and finish.

I imagine some pretty important meetings took place in this office.

Walking across the dark green carpet to windows flanked by green and gold print drapes, he looked out at a panoramic view of gleaming buildings, sidewalks full of hurrying people, and busy streets of fast-moving traffic.

"Wow! What a view. I can see why Comstock liked this office," Richard said out loud.

"Yes," said a voice behind him, "great view."

Turning quickly around, Richard saw a smiling Karl Lester, standing in the doorway.

"I thought I'd better answer, so nobody walking by would think you were talking to yourself," Karl said with a chuckle.

Matching Karl's spirit of fun, Richard responded, "I talk to myself when I'm looking for someone to agree with me. Say, what are you doing up here on the fourth floor?"

"Looking for you. I'm kind of surprised that Grifith put you up here. I figured he'd park you in the administrative wing on the first floor. In fact, there's an empty office near his that's just been remodeled."

"I don't mind being up here, Karl. I think I'm going to be very happy in this office."

"Well, it is a pleasant office—a little old fashioned, but spacious."

"And, on this floor, I have security guards just down the hall to protect me," Richard remarked jokingly.

"You know, the owner's son, John Grant, came in here several weeks ago, looked around and said we needed to beef up security. The security office you see down the hall is the result."

Recalling the advice about security he'd given Mr. Grant, Richard asked, "Do you know what prompted John Grant to worry about security?"

"I don't know, except I had just developed new software that predicts what company B will do when company A introduces a new product on the market. Right now it's a secret project until all the bugs are worked out."

"I didn't think software was your field," Richard replied with surprise.

"You're right, it isn't. I hit on the idea for the program purely by accident. I'm a chess champion, or, at least, I used to be, and one night I was working on a new strategy for a chess game when this idea came to me. Now I hear the company expects to make a lot of money on the software."

"Has the company shown its appreciation in a tangible way?"

"You mean in addition to my new lab? Yes, surprisingly so. Grifith told me John Grant said I could work on any project I chose to and I could have all the resources I needed for my research."

"That's great. I'm happy for you."

"G.H. was pleased, too, that the cost of my research would not be deducted from ADE's budget."

"Obviously, Mr. Grant knows you're a good investment." Richard spoke these words with sincere conviction, born of his vision of Karl's future success.

"It's nice of you to say so. Between you and me, I am working on something that could prove very important. And what do you think? John Grant personally checked my home security system his father authorized. He said we have to be careful about industrial espionage."

"Good for John. You don't want someone stealing a discovery you've worked hard to make."

"I must admit, Richard, I have been worried."

"Well, now you don't have to be. You can put that energy into your work." With this response, Richard moved toward the conference table. "I think I'll try one of these chairs," he said. "Do you have time to sit down with me a few minutes? I want to ask you something."

"Sure, I'm busy here welcoming a new employee." That said, Karl dropped into a nearby chair. "Ask away."

"I'm worried that personnel won't accept a young, inexperienced manager like myself. What's your opinion?"

"If it says MANAGER on your door, employees will accept you, and, as you treat them fairly, they'll *like* you. Don't advertise lack of experience—they won't know unless you tell them. Do you have glasses?"

"Yes, I often wear them when I read."

"Start wearing them all the time. They'll give you a more serious, wise appearance, which people connect with age. If you didn't have a moustache, I'd say grow one."

"I don't mind wearing my glasses, but you think they'll make me look older?"

"Yes, I know from experience. When I taught science at a community college in Anchorage, I wore glasses. In those days, I looked younger than I was. Now that I'm older, I'd like to look younger," Karl mused.

"Did you grow a beard to look older?"

"I grew a beard because every scientist I ever met had one."

The next day, Richard asked Kelly to help him arrange an area in his office where he could make and serve coffee to visitors.

Richard added books, plants, and pictures to give his office a personal touch. His obsidian paperweight flanked a picture of Melissa, displayed on one side of the big, green desk blotter.

At the end of his first week at ADE, Richard, standing in the doorway of his office, smiled and nodded his approval after a visual sweep of the interior. "I'm ready for guests," he thought. "I'll invite a couple of supervisors in to talk about the company and have a cup of coffee."

The following week, Richard met with most of ADE's supervisors and a few lower-level employees. He sought their opinion on having more personnel involved in hiring. He wanted to know, too, what they thought of testing applicants on communication and problem-solving skills.

When Grifith had been back a couple of days following a two-week absence, his secretary told Richard Mr. Grifith wanted to see him.

He probably wants to welcome me aboard. Leaving his office, he stopped at the elevator and used his cane to push the "down" button.

Mr. Grifith met him at the door of his office. "Come in, Mr. Hawkins. I hope staff have taken care of you while I've been gone. I'm sorry I wasn't here to greet you when you arrived."

Shaking Mr. Grifith's outstretched hand, Richard replied, "Everyone has been kind and helpful, especially Miss Worley. Thank you."

"I need to bring something to your attention, so you'll get started on the right foot." Suddenly glancing at Richard's cane, he said, "I don't want you to make any trouble for yourself."

"I'd appreciate any advice you have to give me."

"What I have to say is stronger than 'advice,' Mr. Hawkins. Let me be frank. You're new here and inexperienced, which is not all bad, since you don't have a lot of wrong notions to unlearn. That means you're here to learn, not take over what you don't, as yet, understand. Talking to our employees about our hiring process, before you even know what it is isn't what you should be doing. Do I make myself clear?"

"Yes, Mr. Grifith, you do. I'm sorry I didn't consult you first. I meant only to get feedback from coworkers who could tell me if a new process was a good idea, one worth talking with you about."

"I see. Well, I can tell you we *don't* need a new hiring process at ADE. The one we have works fine. What we *do* need is someone to describe job openings, collect resumes, interview applicants, screen out unqualified people, and refer the best two or three to me for final selection. Think you can handle all that?"

"Yes, I'm sure I can."

"Good. I appreciate your desire and drive to be helpful. But, take time to get acquainted and become familiar with our operation, before you try to change it. Miss Worley will give you books on the two electronic components we manufacture. Study the books. But don't take them home—the components are classified by the military."

"Is this a private wake or can anyone with a mournful expression attend?"

"Come in, Karl! Glad to have your company. Guess I was feeling down a little. But, I've reason to feel good about the furnished apartment you found for me. Rent's reasonable and it's conveniently located. Thanks for your persistence in looking."

"You're welcome. One of our employees put me on to it. What's up?"

"Guess I was feeling sorry for myself. Got an e-mail today from Mr. Grifith—Karl, please close the door . . . it looks like I've ticked him off again. It's a sure sign when he calls me 'Mr. Hawkins' instead of 'Richard.' He wants to see me this afternoon."

"You haven't told him how to do his job, have you? I've learned there are several ways you can do that, without intending to."

"I don't know. Maybe I have unintentionally. He doesn't like me to show initiative by making a suggestion. And, the couple of times I've brought to his attention a personnel problem, he's gotten put out with me and reminded me of my inexperience. I get the impression he wants to handle HR himself. I believe he doesn't trust my judgment, and hasn't since the time, months ago, when I mistakenly talked to employees about the hiring process."

"Well, have you told him about a personnel problem?"

"Yes, yesterday I sent him an e-mail regarding one of our supervisors. Two men in his team came to see me and they said they spoke for the whole team. They said the supervisor—I'll call Bill—treated them 'like dirt.' Their words. One of the men said, working under Bill made him 'feel like a third-class passenger on the Titanic.'"

Karl whistled. "Strong language. To do your job, you *had* to report it to G.H."

"Yes, I thought he would want to talk to Bill and get training for him."

"I think I know who Bill is. G.H. hired him against the previous HR manager's advice. Bill is also the top bowler on the company bowling team, of which G.H. is captain. Might be a connection."

"Well, I'll find out something this afternoon. I have a 3:00 o'clock appointment."

When Richard arrived for his appointment, Miss Worley asked him to wait in the outer office. "Mr. Grifith will be with you in a few minutes," she said. A half hour later, he was still waiting.

Reminds me of the time I had to go to the principal's office for talking back to my 2nd grade teacher. I won't let a long wait make me nervous the way it did then.

"You may go in now. I'm sorry you had to wait so long."

"That's okay."

"Come in and take a seat. Mr. Hawkins, I'll come right to the point. You seem determined to find fault with ADE's personnel. A couple of weeks ago, you were complaining about a little good-natured shoving. If our employees knew you were reporting on them, they wouldn't appreciate it."

"When I told you about the shoving, Mr. Grifith, I didn't intend to complain. It may have been good natured, but one person lost his balance and fell. I simply wanted to bring it to your attention, as I thought I was supposed to do."

"Then there's this e-mail about one of our best supervisors. There are 26 men and women in his team and you heard from two, who don't like him or don't like to take orders. I can tell you that he has a high performance evaluation."

"He *does*?"

"Yes. Now, I want you to be less critical. I want you to focus on filling the lab supervisory position. That's what should occupy your time."

"We're close to filling that position. I'll get the names of the top three applicants and their files to your desk later this afternoon. I want to add some comments before I send them."

"That's what I like to hear, Richard! Never mind the comments, you've done your work. I'll have Miss Worley come to your office and pick up the files."

"I'll get them ready."

A rueful smile flashed over Richard's face as he left Grifith's office. *At least the conversation ended on a positive note.*

27

Hiring Mr. Murkey

IN HIS KITCHEN, RICHARD sat on a stool at the sink, washing dishes. *If Uncle Mac could see this stack, he'd say, "Did you sprain your arm, Richard?" I think I know now why bachelors let dirty dishes pile up. It's no fun washing dishes alone.*

Finished in the kitchen, Richard gave the living room a critical glance and saw jackets on chair backs, an empty potato chip bowl, a pop can on the coffee table, and peanut shells on the carpet beside the recliner. "I wonder how much of this I can blame on my disability," he said, chuckling.

He cleaned the room. When he sat down in the recliner to rest, he smiled. A line from a woman's comedy routine came to mind: *Bachelors are bears with furniture.* He adjusted the recliner. "This bear," he muttered, "just cleaned his den."

Sinking back into the comfort, he closed his eyes. *I'm just going to rest my eyes. I don't want to fall asleep.* But intention soon gave way to siesta.

"What?" Richard sat up—waking to a loud knock at the door and someone yelling.

"There's the knock again," he said. Though farther away, this time he made out the words: "Fire in the building! Use the stairs!"

He grabbed his cane and, in the bedroom, put on his coat and stuffed a small photo album and his wallet into the pockets.

He hurriedly went out into the hall. Sniffing the air, he exclaimed, "I can smell smoke." He could hear the faint sound of a smoke detector coming from above.

As he headed for the stairs, several people ran past him. To them, he yelled," How many stories up is the fire?!"

A woman in the group slowed her pace, and yelled back, "I don't know! Close enough to see smoke!"

When he reached the stairwell, the people had already disappeared. He shook his head, a worried frown on his face as he thought about the five flights of stairs that separated him from safety.

Moving as fast has his disability permitted, Richard reached the fifth floor. When halfway down to the next level, he heard heavy foot steps running up the stairs toward him—two firefighters laden with equipment rushed past him.

Minutes later, three more firefighters appeared. As they passed, Richard called, "Where's the fire located?"

"Eighth floor!" one of the men yelled.

Richard received this information with relief. He sat down on a step, steadying himself with his cane. After a brief rest, he got up and continued his descent—this time going more slowly and keeping close to one side to avoid a collision with firefighters coming up or tenants going down.

He reached the first floor with a sense of accomplishment. Two flights back, he had turned down a firefighter's offer to call for assistance. He believed he could make it on his own, without creating a distraction for the brave men and women working to save the building.

Making his way around firefighters and their equipment toward the open door, Richard stood on the sidewalk with other tenants, who, by their remarks, expected to be allowed to return to lower level apartments relatively soon.

Spotting an elderly man with whom he'd had a brief conversation in past days, Richard asked, "Do you know if everyone got out safely?"

"Yes, I heard nobody got hurt. They contained the fire pretty fast. But all the folks who live in apartments on the top three floors aren't supposed to return, until they do some checking and get rid of the effects of the smoke."

"Guess that makes me a man without an apartment," Richard said, smiling ruefully. "I'm on the sixth floor."

"Say, I can offer you a shakedown on my sofa. I have extra blankets and even pajamas I keep handy for when my son visits."

"That's very kind of you. But I think I'll head for a hotel. My leg puts me to extra trouble."

"Oh yes, of course. Here's my card. Call me and I'll keep you posted on the apartment cleanup, Mr . . .. ?"

"Hawkins, Richard Hawkins." Then seeing a cab at the curb, Richard signaled his need for transportation. Glancing at the name on the card given him, he said, "Thanks again, Mr. Hanson, for your offer."

"I'm Jerry to my neighbors."

"Good night, Jerry," Richard responded, before walking to the cab that would take him to his temporary home.

Richard left the hotel early the next morning and walked to a nearby men's clothing store. A short time later, he left the store, outfitted in new clothes. "I needed new slacks and shirts, anyway," he noted, as he waved down a cab.

At ADE, he stood impatiently at the elevator, hoping to get up to his office without being seen. He was an hour late for work.

"Good morning, Mr. Hawkins."

"Good morning, Kelly."

At that moment the elevator opened. *There must be a law that the less you want to see anyone, the more likely it is that someone will turn up*, Richard thought, as he stepped into the elevator. He looked at his watch. *I have an hour before my first interview of the day.*

In his office, Richard made coffee and put a leftover bear claw on a paper plate. *I don't think Uncle Mac would approve of my breakfast.*

He had just finished going through the interviewee's file, when Karl called, having heard about the fire on the radio. "Tell you all about it later, Karl. I have an interview I have to get ready for." Richard hung up with a smile. "At least 'a fire' is a good conversation starter."

After preparing for the interview, Richard looked at the clock on his desk and thought it would be a good time to call his uncle. After several rings, his uncle answered.

"Hello, Uncle Mac. I'm glad I caught you at home."

"I was on the porch about to close the door when I heard the phone ring. I said to myself, I better answer it in case it's my laddie callin' me."

"Uncle Mac, I have big news that will make your day."

"Aye?"

"I'm going to ask Melissa to marry me."

"That's wonderful news. Di' ye plan to ask her father for permission? It's still a good custom."

"Yes, I do. Do you think it would be okay if I asked for his permission on the phone?"

"Aye. Donald will be happy to get your call."

"I knew you'd be pleased, Uncle. I had to leave my apartment for a few days. I'll call you soon and tell you about it."

He next called Donald Ingram's real estate office and received a positive response from his future father-in-law.

"Helen and I were hoping your affection for our daughter would, one day, culminate in a proposal."

"Donald, don't tell Melissa about my call. I'm planning a surprise."

The two men said their goodbyes and Richard put the phone down in time to hear a knock at the door.

"Come in," Richard invited.

A tall, slender man who appeared to be in his middle 30s entered. "I'm George Murkey," he said, removing his cap. "I heard you on the phone, so I didn't knock."

"That was thoughtful of you. Please sit down, Mr. Murkey. Can I make you a cup of coffee or tea?"

"No thanks. Don't care for tea. Coffee gives me a headache."

"Then you must certainly avoid it. I read your application and resume and noticed that you worked as a deputy sheriff in Atlanta. But you stayed with it for only 16 months. Could you tell me why you left that position?"

"Yeah. It was a good job. I liked the guys I worked with. But I got tired of going on calls to break up domestic arguments. Besides, my aunt and uncle were planning to go to Europe and invited me along. And since they were pretty elderly, I thought I should go and keep an eye on them."

"Did you enjoy your time in Europe?"

"Oh yeah! It was a blast! My uncle and aunt did the usual sightseeing tours, which left me to operate on my own. One of these days, I'd like to get back to Paris. And I will. As soon as I get enough money."

"You stated in your letter of interest, Mr. Murkey, that you're not concerned about money, that you just want a job. Does that mean that you'd take a job anywhere?"

"Yeah, that's right, Mr. Hawkins."

"How do you feel about working at night, which you likely will be required to do?"

"I don't mind the night shift. Everything's quiet—I can catch up on my reading."

"Do you know anything about our firm? What products we produce?"

"Not much. Just that you produce electronic stuff—valuable things that need to be guarded."

"Yes, that's true, Mr. Murkey. There are overseas competitors that would like to get their hands on some of our innovative developments."

"I bet. They'd pay plenty to get a hold of them."

"Yes. Well, Mr. Murkey, you've answered all my questions. I've arranged for you to speak to Sam Dill, our Superintendent of Security. He will see you right away. His office is just down the hall on the right."

Standing up with the aid of his cane, he shook Mr. Murkey's hand.

"Thank you for your time, Mr. Hawkins. If you have any more questions, let me know."

After George Murkey left the office, Richard phoned Sam Dill and let him know Murkey was on his way. "When you've completed your interview, give me a call and let me know what you think. I want to give Mr. Grifith our recommendations before he interviews Murkey tomorrow."

Following his call to Sam, Richard got up and walked to a window and gazed down at the sight of Dallas commerce. He thought about his meeting with George Murkey. He didn't like the man's answers to certain questions. But more than that, there was something about Murkey that disturbed him. *I don't think I'm prejudiced against him, because he misspelled a few words on his application. No, it's something about the man himself. I'll see what Sam says about . . .*

A young woman's voice suddenly interrupted Richard's thoughts. Turning from the window, Richard responded, "Please come in. You're one of our lab technicians, Carol . . ."

"Atkins. I'm sorry to disturb you, but I was wondering if I could speak with you a minute."

"Certainly. Won't you sit down?" Richard pointed to a chair near his desk.

She described a conflict that had arisen between herself and another employee who was once a good friend.

Drawing on conflict management theory and common sense, Richard suggested ways to resolve the conflict between the two women. Choosing his words carefully, he said, "Remember that she may feel as troubled about the end of your friendship as you do. Let me know how it goes. If things don't improve, I'll talk to her also. I'm also prepared to discuss this with both of you together, if need be. Anyway, I'm sure we can resolve the disagreement."

After she thanked him and left his office, Richard thought, *If Miss Atkins could forgive her coworker, it would be a good first step in saving the friendship. The closer the relationship, the more painful it is to hold a grudge.*

Richard was making notes on his meeting with Miss Atkins when his phone rang. It was Sam Dill reporting on his interview with George Murkey. Sam said, "After meeting with Mr. Murkey, I would not recommend him for the job. I spoke to the sheriff of the county where he was deputy, and listening between the lines, I got the impression they were glad to see him go."

"Did the sheriff comment on Murkey's performance?"

"No, but as you know, sometimes it's what someone doesn't say, that's important."

"True. I have to say that I came to the same conclusion. I don't think Mr. Murkey is right for the job. Tomorrow, I'll give you the names of two other applicants," said Richard, as he hung up the phone.

Richard left a message with Grifith's secretary that Sam and he did not approve of Murkey's qualifications for security guard—they would interview other applicants.

Having taken care of the Murkey interview, Richard made one more call to Verity. Directory assistance gave him the number of a bakery, famous for its chocolate cake. He spoke to a clerk and ordered a cake, decorated with red roses and, in white frosting the words: "MELISSA, WILL YOU MARRY ME? RICHY."

The next day, Richard, returning from lunch, stopped at his mailbox and picked up a memo from Grifith.

Surprised and perplexed, Richard read:

Mr. Hawkins:

While I value your input and that of Mr. Dill, I have learned over many years of experience to trust my judgment of character and competence in hiring personnel. Therefore, on this occasion, I must overrule your recommendation and hire Mr. Murkey. I believe he will prove to be an excellent security guard, given his experience as a deputy sheriff. I know I can count on you to show him the ropes and help him to succeed.

   G. H. Grifith

He went to Sam's office to give him the news.

Sitting down at Sam's invitation, Richard announced, "Mr. Grifith has rejected our recommendations and hired George Murkey. He wants us to help him do a good job."

"Oh he does. Mr. Hawkins, would you please close the door?" Sam was obviously annoyed. Looking down at his desk momentarily, he said, "Did he give you any reason for his decree?"

"Well, the only thing Mr. Grifith mentioned was that he liked the man's experience as deputy sheriff."

Sam shook his head, but didn't say a word.

Seeing the intense look in Sam's face, he asked, "Are you angry about Murkey being hired?"

"A little, but more *concerned* than anything. I think Mr. Grifith will live to regret his decision," Sam said, shaking his head.

"Mr. Hawkins, I'll keep a close watch 'til we know this man better."

"I know you'll help him all you can, Sam. But I think you're right to give him close supervision, at least for his first few months. He starts Monday of next week."

Back at his office, Richard checked his e-mail and found Melissa's response: "YES!!!!!!!! MELISSA."

"Now, that's the kind of mail I *like* to get!"

Twelve weeks later, Sam Dill stopped by Richard's office to report on Murkey. "I don't care much for his attitude. It's like he thinks the whole world is a big joke and he's the only one in on it. But, since he chooses to work at night, his attitude isn't all that important. At this point, I don't have any serious complaints about him. I'm beginning to think I was wrong about him."

"I hope we were both wrong, but continue to keep a close watch on him for the present, Sam."

A loud, familiar voice in the hallway interrupted this exchange.

"Excuse me, Sam, but I think a friend of mine is about to pay me a visit."

The office door, standing ajar, suddenly opened wide, framing John Grant, who looked pleased at the obvious surprise his appearance had caused.

"Rich! How's the company man? It's great to see you!" Observing Sam in the room, he added, "I hope I'm not interrupting anything."

"No—not at all!" assured Richard. "Come on in. Sam and I are finished. John, I believe you know Sam Dill."

"I sure do! I had something to do with *hiring* him! How are you, Sam?"

"I'm just fine, Mr. Grant. I'll be running along now, Mr. Hawkins. I'll keep you posted on Murkey."

"Okay, Sam. Talk to you later."

"Take a chair at the conference table, John. I'll join you as soon as I make a note."

A few minutes later, Richard pulled a chair near John's, and shook his hand before sitting down in it.

"You're looking good, John. You've lost some weight, haven't you?"

"Yes, fifteen pounds. Thanks for noticing."

"When did you arrive in Dallas?"

Looking at his watch, John replied, "About two hours ago. I talked with Lester and spent a little time talking to Grifith. He spoke very highly of your work."

"That's good to hear."

"Lester tells me you had a fire that kept you out of your apartment a few days."

"Yes, two floors up. It was good to get back to my apartment, but not to my cooking."

"Grifith plans to offer you an office in the administration wing."

"You didn't say anything I hope," said Richard anxiously.

"Not a word. It was entirely his idea. If I were you, Rich, I'd take his offer. Besides, you should be on the first floor, where you can be more accessible."

Richard looked around him with a satisfied expression. "I think you're right, John. I've liked this office, but one downstairs would be more convenient. And I think I could get to know more of my coworkers better—get closer to the action. Say, how long do you plan to be in Dallas? You don't have to hurry back to Oregon, do you?"

"No, you're likely to see a lot more of me, at least in the foreseeable future. You're looking at the new vice president of Grant Corporation, Southwest. Dad thinks I've demonstrated the ability to handle the job. He told me that since I became a Christian, I've taken hold of responsibilities with a new enthusiasm. I have tried, Rich, to show a Christian witness in my work."

"Congratulation, John! I know you'll do a fine job. The companies in the region will benefit from your leadership. Where will you make your headquarters?"

"Right here in Dallas."

"Does that mean at Advanced Development Electronics?"

"I'm afraid not. Corporate offices for the region are at BG Oil Company. This reminds me—I'd better check in over there. I think they're planning a dinner for me this evening to introduce me to the team. I'll call you in a couple of days, as soon as I'm settled. Then we can see about getting out to lunch."

"Good, John, let's do it."

John paused at the door. "Oh—and when we get together, you can tell me about your church. I plan to attend there and join your Bible study group."

"I'm sure you'll like our church. Our senior pastor is a dynamic preacher of the Gospel."

"I'm sure he is. You wouldn't attend any other kind of church." As he left the office he added, "See you soon."

"Would you let Mr. Hawkins know that Sam Dill would like to see him?" This request was addressed to Richard's newly-hired secretary.

Hearing Sam's voice through the open office door, Richard called, "Cindy, send Sam in."

Cindy kindly pointed toward Richard's doorway.

Sam entered the office and looked approvingly around. "If I may say, Mr. Hawkins, it looks like you've come up in the world by coming down to the first floor! How do you like your new office?"

"I like it a lot!" remarked Richard. "There is one thing I miss though. My old office on the fourth floor had a better view. But here it's more convenient. And having a secretary helps me to use my time better."

"Would you like to sit down?"

"No thanks, Mr. Hawkins. I just wanted to let you know that George Murkey is leaving. He told me that his mother is very sick and that he has to go to Oklahoma immediately."

"Of course, he should go. Does he want us to hold his job until he gets back?"

"He feels he has to quit," said Sam, looking concerned. "He asked me for a letter of reference and I said I would write one for him."

"Looks like I was *wrong* about him, Sam."

Sam leaned forward and, lowering his voice, said, "I don't think you were wrong. I still sense that there's something not right about him. But from what I hear, he did well at his job, so I'll have to give him a good reference letter."

"Sam, it's not like you have to be sorry. If you believe he earned a positive letter, then he should get one."

"I know but, there's just something about the man that doesn't add up."

"I understand that you were concerned, and I was, too. But as you say, his work was okay."

"I guess you're right," said Sam, sounding embarrassed. "I guess I was nervous for nothing. Well anyway, I just wanted to let you know about Murkey." With these words he left.

Minutes later, Cindy passed along a message from John Grant. "He wanted to know if you were free today for lunch."

"Cindy, would you let him know that I can't make it today, but can day after tomorrow. And also, please order a dozen roses and have them delivered to the address on my calendar where my fiancé will be staying. I'm off now to pick her up at the airport. Oh, and call a taxi for me—I'd like to get to the airport early. I should be back by 4:00, but don't tell anybody that, in case I don't make it."

"I understand, Mr. Hawkins," Cindy replied with a smile.

Richard then made a couple of business calls to confirm appointments for the following week. He winked at the picture of Melissa on his desk, and started to walk out of the office.

"Oh, Mr. Hawkins, Mr. Grant called and said that he could make it for lunch day after tomorrow."

"Thanks, Cindy. Please put it on my calendar. I'm off to the airport to meet a pretty lady."

Richard arrived at the airport considerably ahead of Melissa's expected arrival. Taking a seat, he thought, *These benches are designed for maximum discomfort.* He glanced down at the floor and picked up a flyer at his feet. It featured a musical ensemble that comprised one woman and two men, who looked to be about Richard's age. The flyer announced the group's appearance at a local nightspot. He gazed intently at the woman and one of the men. They resembled Sarah and Jeff, his two friends who performed with him in his coma. *As Uncle Mac used to say, "Your imagination is working overtime, Richard." But, I should start playing my guitar again. I might have Uncle Mac send it to me.*

Richard put the flyer on the bench beside him, and took a small New Testament out of his jacket pocket. Several chapters into the Gospel of Luke, he heard Melissa's flight announced and stood up to catch sight of her in the crowd. Moments later, he saw her and waved. Realizing she hadn't seen him, he waved his cane, and this time received an answering wave back. Soon they were hugging each other and heading for a taxi that would take Melissa to her friend's home. Once inside the taxi, they kissed and made plans for the next day.

"Tomorrow, Lovely," Richard said softly, as they neared the friend's house, "we have shopping to do. I picked out a jeweler where we can look at engagement rings and maybe find one you like."

"That's wonderful, Richy. When I get back home, I can show off my ring and prove I have a claim on an eligible bachelor in Dallas."

"The bachelor part is right anyway, but not for long," Richard responded, putting his arm around Melissa's shoulders.

When the taxi pulled up in front of her friend's house, Melissa gave Richard a good-bye kiss, and gave him her friend's phone number.

"I'll call you later this evening."

"I'll be waiting."

28

Investigating a Disappearance

"I'M NOT SURE I should be along when you meet your friend, John, for lunch," Melissa said while driving Richard and herself. "I feel I'm intruding. He doesn't even know I'm coming."

"Now, I know John will be glad to see you. He'll consider your presence a bonus, Sweet Face. It'll give him a chance to talk about some of the funny experiences he's had. He's traveled all around the world for his dad, to places like Bombay and Istanbul. He tells about the time in London when this little dog followed him into a high class hotel. And the clerk refused to believe it wasn't his dog."

"What happened then?" Melissa asked.

"Well, you'll have to ask John," Richard said with an impish grin.

"I guess I'll have to eat lunch with you guys now, if only to hear the punchline."

They arrived at the restaurant ahead of John. On entering, they discovered that he had made a reservation.

"I'm surprised John isn't here. Usually, he's early for an appointment," Richard said as they were seated.

A half hour passed quickly while they chatted over coffee. Richard suddenly looked at his watch and exclaimed, "What could be keeping John? It's not like him to be late. Excuse me," he said to their waiter. "Would you check to see if John Grant called to say he'd be late?"

A few minutes later, the waiter returned with a negative reply.

"I think I'd better give his office a call, Melissa. He probably got held up in a meeting. Go ahead and order for both of us—I'll have the prawns with a baked potato."

Richard left Melissa and located a public telephone. Ten minutes later, he returned with a puzzled expression on his face.

"Is he on his way?"

"I guess so. His secretary said he left there more than an hour ago. She thought he might have stopped off at the hospital. One of the employees at BG Oil had an accident this morning and had to be rushed to Emergency."

"Would he forget to call?"

"I suppose, if he were sufficiently upset about his employee. Yes, he might. Did you order for us?"

"Yes. I said you wanted sour cream on your potato."

"Thanks for remembering, Hon."

When their meals came, Richard said grace and, between bites, encouraged Melissa to update him on city happenings in Verity. Outwardly, he appeared relaxed, but inwardly he harbored uneasiness about John's absence.

After they'd finished eating, they remained in the restaurant another half hour in the hope that John might yet arrive.

"We might as well leave, Melissa. John's not coming. I'm beginning to think something has happened to him. He may have had an accident—he does sometimes drive too fast."

"How can we find out?"

"I think you'd better drop me off at the office. Maybe G. H. has received word. I'll call you as soon as I hear anything."

Melissa let Richard off at ADE's front entrance. He entered the building and encountered Mr. Grifith, wearing a worried expression.

"Richard! Was John Grant with you?"

"No, Mr. Grifith. He was supposed to meet me for lunch, but he never showed up. I thought he might be at the hospital, looking after an injured employee."

"The people at BG Oil contacted the hospital—and he isn't there. They called here and they've called other locations trying to find him, but so far no luck. That's not all. They found his car in BG's parking lot. It was unlocked and his briefcase was on the front seat."

Speaking more to himself than to Grifith, Richard said, "He might have had car trouble, but then he wouldn't have left his briefcase in an unlocked car."

"His secretary said it contained important papers. What do you think it means? I don't know him very well myself. Of course, he's only been out of touch with his office a few hours. What do you think we should do?"

"I can tell you this, Mr. Grifith; it's not like John to take off without telling people where he's going. He's a very considerate person, and he wouldn't worry us by just disappearing. No, something's happened to him."

"Do you think we should call his father?"

"Yes, I do. And I think we should call the police, even though it's too soon for them to classify him as a missing person."

"Richard, I know that you and the Grants are friends. Would you call Bruce Grant and give him the facts we have. And I'll let BG's management know what steps we've taken."

"I'll do it right away. Is it possible that management at BG Oil has already called him?"

"I was told they haven't. When you talk with Mr. Grant, let him know we'll do whatever he advises."

Richard nodded his response, and hurried to his office. Mr. Grant's secretary connected him immediately. Bruce agreed that it wasn't like his son to take off without telling anybody, or to leave important papers unguarded.

"Do you suspect foul play, Richard? Do your psychic senses tell you anything?"

He didn't reply for a moment.

"Are you there, Richard? Did you hear what I asked?"

"Yes, I did, Mr. Grant. I was just asking myself the same questions."

"What do you think has happened to John?"

"I think Mr. Grant . . . he's being held against his will. But, I haven't had any kind of a vision that tells me that. I do feel that he's alive... though I also feel he's in danger."

"Richard, if you haven't heard anything in, say, two hours, call me and I'll catch a plane for Dallas. And, I'll get in touch with some friends of mine on the Dallas police force and ask them to investigate."

Following his conversation with Mr. Grant, Richard contacted Mr. Grifith and told him what his boss had said. Then he sat at his desk and prayed for his friend. He was still praying when he heard a knock at his door.

"Come in!"

Mr. Grifith entered, obviously upset. "I have some bad news. BG's manager, Harley Fuller, just told me that security guards found a kidnap note on the floor of John's car. He's being held for ransom."

"Have they notified the police?"

"No, they haven't. The note said if the police were notified John would die. Harley called Grant and told him what the note said. He'll have to make the decision to bring in the police."

Soon after Mr. Grifith left his office, Richard left also. He walked to the elevator and took it to the fourth floor and let himself into his old office with a key he had retained. Inside, he paced up and down, occasionally stopping to look out a window. With difficulty, he cleared his mind of all concerns in an effort to open his mind to a vision of John's location or an impression of his kidnappers. But after some time had elapsed with no images or thoughts of John's situation, Richard, speaking out loud, said, "I guess I've lost my psychic ability, or maybe I need to handle something that belongs to John. If Mr. Grant would give… me…"

The ringing telephone interrupted Richard's train of thought. Thinking that it likely concerned John, he quickly answered it. It was Kelly, Mr. Grifith's secretary.

"Mr. Hawkins, I'm glad I found you," Kelly said. "Mr. Grifith placed something confidential on your desk that he wants you to see as soon as possible. He said when he returned from BG Oil, he would meet with you."

"Alright. Thank you, Kelly. I'll be right down." As he hung up the telephone, he thought, *What could it be?*

Richard picked up a large Manila envelope from his desk. It bore his name and, in bold print, the word *confidential*. Cutting open the envelope, he pulled out a typed note, encased in transparent plastic. A small post-it note from Grifith was appended. It indicated that the envelope contained the original kidnap note and that Mr. Grant had given orders to show it to Richard and nobody else. Typed all in capital letters, the kidnap note stated that John's family was to pay one hundred thousand dollars for his safe return and that the money was to be in small bills. *I wonder how they will contact Mr. Grant with instructions for delivering the money?* Richard puzzled. The note's last line filled Richard with dread. It read: "IF YOU WANT TO SEE YOUR SON ALIVE AGAIN, DON'T CALL THE POLICE."

Putting the kidnap note back into the envelope, Richard realized he was handling important evidence that eventually would be given to the police. *Mr. Grant probably thought if I handled the kidnap note, I might get a vision that would help us find John. But, I can't seem to get an image. I just feel strongly that John's alive.*

Richard resealed the envelope and sat back in his chair in a prayerful posture in an effort to relax his mind and body. *I won't be able to help John very much if I'm tense and anxious.*

The phone rang the very moment he started to get an idea about the kidnap note. But now it was gone. With some irritation, he picked up the receiver and growled, "Yes!"

"Mr. Hawkins," Cindy reported, "Melissa Ingram is on the phone. She wants to speak with you."

"Oh yes. Sorry, Cindy. Please put her on."

"Richard. Is everything alright? I thought I'd better call when I didn't hear from you."

"We've had some trouble here. I'll be able to tell you more when I can speak with Mr. Grant."

"Is John still missing?"

"Yes, he is."

"I'd better let you go. I've been praying for John."

"That's good. He needs our prayers. Love you. I'll call as soon as I can."

Replacing the receiver, Richard wondered how Mr. Grant would deal with the kidnappers. *I hope he decides to bring in the police.* He knew that kidnappers usually killed their victims.

Walking out of his office, Richard stopped at Cindy's desk and told her that he would be in his old office. "I'm not available to anyone, except Mr. Grant or Mr. Grifith," he added.

29

Threat of Death

Back in his old office, Richard paced across the room, trying to recall his thoughts about the kidnap note when Melissa's call had interrupted. Out loud, he said, "It may have been useful; we always think the idea that gets away from us is our best."

Eventually his bad leg forced him to rest. Realizing early evening hours had darkened the room, he switched on the desk lamp. "Maybe if I went back to my office and I looked at the kidnap note again, I'd remember."

The door opened suddenly. G. H. rushed toward him.

"Richard! I've just talked with Mr. Grant."

"Is Mr. Grant in Dallas?" he asked.

"Yes. His private plane landed minutes ago. He wants the two of us to meet him at the airport."

The two men made good time. Bruce Grant was waiting for them, standing just inside the front entrance of the terminal, talking to a young man whom he seemed to know. Richard and Grifith quickly joined their boss and his friend.

Greeting his employees with a grim smile, Bruce said, "Thank you for coming." He then introduced Ron as his pilot. Turning to Grifith, he said, "G. H., contact Harley Fuller and tell him to have one of our helicopters fueled and ready to fly in an hour. Ron here will pilot it and I'll be aboard with him." Noticing the puzzled looks of his two listeners, Bruce continued, "Soon after we landed, I was paged to take a phone call. I, of course, thought it was one of you two. It was the kidnappers calling to give me instructions about delivering the money."

"They must have had one of their confederates here watching for you," observed Grifith.

"Yes, I suppose so. We're to fly some distance from Dallas, over a wooded area and drop the money in a backpack at a point where we see a light flash three times. Ron has the information on direction and miles."

"Mr. Grant," queried Richard, "have you notified the police?"

Bruce was silent for a moment. "No, Richard, I haven't. The kidnapper told me that if I called the police, they'd kill John, and I believe him. He said they would have no reason to kill John if I paid the money. He told me that when they had the money, I would be contacted at my hotel and given John's location. I told him where I'd be staying."

Dropping his voice, Grifith said, "You must have the money with you."

Nodding, Bruce patted the small suitcase he was carrying. "But, I need to pick up a backpack," he said.

"Well, I had better make the arrangements for the helicopter right away," Grifith said, looking at his watch. "Will you be coming with me, Richard?"

Before Richard could reply, Bruce answered, "No, G. H., Richard won't be. We'll take him with us and see that he gets to his apartment. I've rented a car."

After Grifith left, Richard asked, "Did you want me to go with you in the helicopter after all, Mr. Grant?"

"Just Ron and I are going. I wanted to talk to you a minute, Richard. Ron, would you get the car for us and bring it around to the front?"

"Yes, Mr. Grant. I'll see to it," Ron responded, and hurriedly left.

"I wanted to ask you in private, Richard, if you have had any visions that would tell us anything about John?"

"No, sir. I've tried to keep my mind calm and prayerful, to see if an image or a strong impression would come to me."

"And nothing has?"

"Nothing except . . . I have this feeling, that John is alive and well. Beyond that, I can't get a picture of where he is or anything about his kidnappers."

"Before I left Portland, Richard, I spoke to your Uncle Mac on the phone, and he told me that you need a personal object belonging to the one you're trying to help. So, I brought along this pen. It was a birthday gift to John from his mother. He keeps it on his nightstand by his bed. Here, Richard," Bruce said, placing the pen in Richard's shirt pocket. "Maybe it will help you learn something about John."

"I'll do my best, Mr. Grant."

"I know you will. Ron's probably here with the car. Call my cell phone, if you think of anything."

Back at his apartment, Richard sat quietly in the living room, close to the phone. He took John's pen out of his pocket and held it tightly. He freed his mind of all thoughts in order to coax it to show him John's condition or whereabouts. After waiting a half hour without success, he started to put the pen back into his pocket, when suddenly an image flashed in his mind. It was an image of John bound and gagged.

Have I seen a real vision of my friend's danger? Or, has my fear for John's safety caused me to imagine what I saw?

Richard rose from his chair and, without the aid of his cane, walked carefully to a nearby table. He picked up a notepad and pencil, returned to his chair, and began to write a description of what he'd seen.

He wrote: "John tied to heavy wooden chair. Handcuffs on wrists. Duct tape covered mouth and eyes. Head was down against his chest. Behind him was workbench with wrenches and other tools. In front of him was a mechanics' hoist for working underneath cars. Toward back of room were two stacks of tires."

Reading what he had written, Richard pondered, *I'm sure that it was a real vision. I feel John is in great danger. It looks like he's being held in an auto repair shop, probably in or near the city. But where? I don't know if I should call Mr. Grant or not. It might be more upsetting than helpful. I wish I could tell him where John is.*

Richard got up from his chair and began to pace back and forth, stopping at times to lean on his cane. During one of these stops, he looked at his watch. *By now the kidnappers likely have their money.*

"Their *money*." Something about that word. He recalled that the word bothered him when he read it in the kidnappers' note. *But why? What was I about to think of when Melissa called?*

Then without warning, he lost his balance and fell to the floor. Lying on his back, he reached the cane that had slipped from him. "Now I know how a turtle feels," he muttered.

As he pulled himself up, it suddenly came to him. "Yes, that's it!" he yelled. "In their note, the kidnappers spelled *money*—'MONY,' the same way Murkey spelled the word in his job application. And one of Murkey's references was a man who owned a local garage!"

Richard quickly telephoned the security office at ADE and reached Sam Dill. Finding it hard to control his excitement, he said, "Sam, would you please get George Murkey's application from your files. I need the name and address of a reference of his who operates an automotive repair shop. I'll hold."

Minutes later, Sam had the information for him. "Is Murkey in some kind of trouble?" Sam wanted to know.

"I'll fill you in later, Sam."

He hung up then and called Mr. Grant's cell phone.

"Is that you, Richard?"

"Yes,   sir."
"We just dropped the money. Do you have anything to report?"

"I believe I know one of the kidnappers and where John is. Call the police right away and give them the address I'm going to give you. John is in danger."

Following his brief exchange with Mr. Grant, Richard prayed while he waited to hear some word about John. "I hate to wait," he told the walls in his living room. "I've never been good at it. Some people like suspense; I don't."

It's been an hour and a half. You'd think the police would know something by now. I suppose they would need a warrant to search the garage. Maybe they couldn't get it. Or, maybe my theory was wrong and Murkey isn't involved.

Another hour seemed like three. *I wonder if the police didn't get to John in time, maybe the news is bad. People don't hurry to give bad news.* This thought made him start to pray again.

He was still praying when the telephone rang. He lifted the receiver with trepidation and said weakly, "Hello?"

"Richard, I just heard from the police. They found him just where you said. John is okay—he has a few cuts and bruises where they knocked him around. You were right about his being in danger. The police found a grave dug behind the building. John heard the kidnappers say they planned to kill him after they got the money. I thank God for His gracious help and for yours in saving my son's life." ` `

"Well, I'm glad I could help my friend. God answered the prayers of all of us, including John's."

"Yes. I'll be seeing John soon. When the helicopter lands I'll head for the hospital. I'm sure they'll keep him overnight to check him over. I'll tell him how you helped in his rescue. I know he'll want to talk to you tomorrow."

"Let him know I'll be at ADE."

After Richard said goodnight, he leaned back in his chair. His eyes began to fill with tears at the thought of his friend's rescue. He knew he had come close to losing a brother in Christ, as he had lost his family. His tears, he knew, were not only tears of relief, but were also tears of mourning for the family he saw killed in his coma. Unashamed, he allowed his grief to spill down his face—tears no longer held back by the conviction that strong men don't cry.

30

Diamonds and Roses

THE DAY AFTER HIS rescue, John called Richard to thank him for his help and update him on his condition. "Dad and I thought I'd be out of the hospital tomorrow," John said, "but the docs found two cracked ribs and a broken toe. So, it looks like my coming-out party is postponed."

"How are you feeling, John? I mean how are you doing?"

"Oh, I'm fine. I had the shakes for a while last night in the hospital; more mental than physical, I think. But, I'm fine now. For a while there, it looked like I wouldn't need my pension. I was glad I'm a Christian. I knew where I'd be in the next life if I didn't make it in this one."

"Yes, I'm thankful that we're still in the same world."

"Me, too. When I'm able to navigate with crutches, I want to take you and Melissa to dinner. Dad told me she was in town.

"I can tell you, Melissa will be happy to have a personal invitation. Oh, and when we go to dinner, you'll have to tell her about the dog that followed you into the London hotel."

"You know, John, Melissa and I will be married after she finishes college—unless she changes her mind."

"She'd better not. On my recent trip to Berlin, I bought you two an expensive wedding gift."

"That's very nice. I wanted to ask if you'd be my best man?"

"I would be honored to stand beside you in your wedding. I count you and Melissa among my dearest friends. You know, I'm well trained; I've been a best man three times. You know the old saying, 'Always a best man, never a groom.' Of course, I realize it's my own fault."

"John, I believe the 'old saying' you're referring to is: 'Always a bridesmaid, never a bride,'" said Richard, laughing.

"Well, I must admit your version sounds more familiar. Dad's always hinting he'd like to become a grandfather."

"By the way, Cal called last night to see how I was doing. He told me there's some trouble at the church."

"Next time Uncle Mac and I talk, he'll probably tell me about it. I'll see you soon. Take care of yourself. I'm heading out for coffee with the boss."

"Okay. Give my regards to G.H. Tell him, I appreciate his role in my rescue."

"Yes, I will."

John should thank G.H. himself. But he'll have to wait awhile before he can do it personally.

"Cindy," Richard said as he left his office, "I'm out to coffee with Mr. Grifith. I'll be back for my 10:30 appointment with Karl."

Walking to a nearby cafe, Richard entered and spotted Grifith in a booth. "I see you beat me, Mr. Grifith," he said, sitting down.

."By an hour. I wanted to get here early and work on a letter to Mr. Grant. I'm taking responsibility for hiring Murkey and telling him I did so over your objections and Sam Dill's. I can only say, I sincerely thought I was doing the right thing."

"Could I make a suggestion?"

"Yes, of course."

"I know you want to be open and candid with Mr. Grant, but why not wait until he asks you about Murkey? In other words, give him time to put things into perspective. Besides, it isn't likely Murkey took a job at ADE with the idea of kidnapping John."

"I suppose you're right. But I just want to keep the record straight."

"Well, as far as the record goes, neither Sam nor I gave you any solid reason why you shouldn't hire Murkey. All we had against him were our hunches."

"Maybe so, but your hunches about the guy were better than mine. Okay, I'll take your advice and scrap the letter."

The two men next turned their attention to job announcements to replace three employees soon to retire. They agreed that the positions required people with more technical knowledge than the employees had who now filled the positions.

"I believe we should open applications to disabled people. The research I've done proves they are excellent workers. They're punctual, industrious, loyal and, as a group, they have less absenteeism than the non-disabled. And, I'd like to encourage disabled veterans to apply."

"I'd be in favor of that, generally," replied Grifith, though his tone wasn't convincing.

In Richard's meeting with Karl, his friend disclosed the progress he had made in his laser experiments. Pleased that Karl had shared the nature of his research with Mr. Grant, Richard congratulated him on the breakthrough that his experiments promised. He assured Karl that he would keep his research a secret.

After Karl left his office, he started to make a brief record of their meeting, but changed his mind. *I'd better not make notes on our conversation*, he thought, *in case they fall into the wrong hands.*

Getting up from his desk, he rubbed his bad leg and did some stretching exercises. Then, glancing at Melissa's picture on his desk, he opened his door and said, "Cindy, please get me a cab."

Several minutes later, Cindy reported that his cab had arrived. "Will you be gone for the day, Mr. Hawkins?" she asked.

"Yes, I will. I believe I've done enough today to get off two hours early."

Richard didn't hear Cindy say softly in a knowing tone: "From what I've heard, you've done plenty for this company."

Getting into the cab, he instructed the driver to head for the nearest florist and then to stop at the jewelers so he could pick up Melissa's newly sized engagement ring.

Arriving at Melissa's friend's home, Richard, holding a bouquet of red roses with his left hand, used his cane to knock on the door.

"Whatever you're selling, Mister, I'll buy it," Melissa said teasingly.

"No charge to pretty women."

"Flattery will get you everywhere. Richy, would you grab the mail?"

"Okay. The letter on top is for you."

"Let me see," she said, as she escorted Richard into the living room.

"That's funny. Nobody knows I'm here except my folks—it couldn't be from mom, since she never types. I bet she gave my address to the

Indian charity I contribute to when they phoned for a donation. I'll read it later."

While Richard stood in the middle of the room, Melissa kissed him and said, "There. With your hands full, you can't defend yourself," and she laughed affectionately.

"I guess you're right. If you want to kiss me again, there isn't anything I can do about it. If you reach into my jacket pocket, the right side, you'll find a little box containing something. It's beautiful, bright, and . . . expensive."

"Oh, you're sweet. You picked up my ring!" Melissa exclaimed, as she pulled the box out of his pocket. "Now, let me take these flowers. I'll put them in a vase and be right back, so you can put the ring on my finger."

When she put the bouquet on the dining room table, she said to Richard, "They're lovely! And I'm sure my friend Amy will enjoy them, too."

When Richard put the diamond on her finger, he observed softly, "Your pretty hand does a lot for the ring." The look in his eyes spoke volumes of his love.

She returned his gaze and replied, "Thank you, Richy. I hate to leave you, but I must show Amy my ring. There are coffee and fresh-baked cookies in the kitchen. Chocolate chip—especially for you."

"Awesome! My favorite cookies. Say, did you tell your parents we wanted to wait to get married so you could finish getting your interior design degree?"

"Yes, they know. They think that's wise. I'll be right back."

In Melissa's absence, Richard looked around the living room and adjoining dining room, and noticed two oil paintings of extraordinary power and beauty. He was standing in front of one of them when Melissa returned.

Turning around, Richard asked, "Melissa, do you know who painted these beautiful oils? I know enough about art to know real artistic ability when I see it. I wonder if the artist would sell me one?"

"I know her pretty well. And I don't think she'd *sell* you one. Although, she did sell the two you like to Amy's parents—who are now in Europe."

"Why wouldn't she sell *me* a painting?"

"Have you looked at the signature in the lower right corner?"

Richard walked closer to the painting and peered at the signature. He read: "*M. Ingram.*"

"*You* painted these pictures?!" Richard exclaimed. "When did you learn to paint like this? I'm *really* impressed."

"I'm so glad you like my paintings, Richy," Melissa said, taking hold of his hand. "I've studied painting since I was a child. When I was sixteen, I spent a summer in Italy, studying under a fine painter who helped me develop my style."

"Boy, you're sure modest. If I could paint the way you do, I'd conduct tours of my work. How come I didn't know you could paint until now?"

"There're a lot of things you don't know about me. When we're married, you'll have fun finding them out."

31

Demolishing an Apartment

O N THE WAY UP to his apartment, Richard found a telegram. It read:

> City plans to demolish Garden View Apartments to widen av-
> enue, build bus stop. 18 seniors and disabled living there can't
> afford higher rent elsewhere. Many attend our church. Started
> Save-Garden-View Fund. Sure you would want to contribute.
> Have ideas how to fight this? Mac

Richard dropped the telegram as he unlocked his door. Picking it up, he thought, *As Uncle Mac would say about somebody else, 'He may have taken on more than he can bite, chew, and swallow.' I'd better see if he needs a hand.*

Seated in his recliner, Richard phoned Cal and, in a brief conversa-tion, learned his uncle had assumed the major responsibility of raising needed funds. Uncle Mac had attracted generous people to help him in his fight with the city. Richard told Cal he would visit Verity soon and help if he could.

Funny thing, the only view Garden View gives its tenants is that of a parking lot.

Talking to himself, Richard said, "I'd better call Melissa and let her know I might be heading home in a few days."

Amy answered the phone. "It's Richard. Could I speak to Melissa?"

"I'm glad you called, Richard. She's upset because of a letter that came a few days ago. She's trying to convince herself not to take it seri-ously. She can take your call upstairs. Hold on a minute."

"Melissa. What's this about a letter?"

"Richy, that letter for me you found in the box?"

"Yes."

"It said something awful! It said: 'If you don't break your engagement, you'll be sorry, I promise you. I warned you.' It was postmarked 'Dallas'. Do you think we should contact the police?"

"Yes, I do. It might be a hoax, but it doesn't sound like something a friend would send as a joke. You said yesterday only your parents knew Amy's address?"

"Yes."

"I'll pick up the letter in the morning and take it to the Dallas Police Department."

"Okay, if you think that's what we should do."

"Wait a minute—come to think of it, there are people at ADE who know you're here and might know your address—I've had your name and Amy's address on my desk. Not knowing my way around Dallas, I asked one employee where your friend's address was."

"What would be their motive?"

"G.H. told me, we have employees who don't like my management style—I'm too critical, they say. I suppose one of them might write a threatening letter to you to get back at me. I would hate to think that's the case. It's such a mean, cowardly thing to do. Well, soon you'll be heading back home, and that should be the end of it."

"I'm sure you're right. Amy was more concerned about it than I was. Did you have some reason for calling?"

"Oh, yes. Uncle Mac is working on a community problem. I think I can get off a few days to get home and give him a hand. Why don't we go back together?"

"I'd like that, Richy. You're not concerned about my safety, are you? You know, because of the letter?"

"No, I'm just making sure a beautiful woman is sitting beside me on the plane. I'll call after I talk to G.H."

As Richard expected, G.H. allowed him to take a few days off. He had only to reschedule some appointments and arrange travel to Verity.

At Verity's airport, Melissa's mother picked her up to shop for a birthday present and Mac met Richard at the baggage claim carousel.

"Ye're as welcome as the roses in spring, laddie," Mac said, giving his nephew a hug. "I was hopin' ye could come home. Folks in the church and community are in a dither aboot gude people losing their home."

"Is there reason to believe that the city will actually widen the avenue and demolish the apartment building?"

"I'm afraid there is, laddie. I'll tell ye aboot it as we walk to the car."

"Is there another route that can be used, which would bypass the apartment?"

"No. And even if they took out the bus stop, which they won't do, Garden View would still have to go. On either side of Garden View for blocks are houses. The residents don't want the avenue widened, because it will increase traffic."

"I suppose they feel more traffic will endanger children and pets."

"Aye. Ye may remember there's a school nearby."

"Yes, I remember driving through the neighborhood and seeing lots of bicycles after school let out."

As they climbed into the car, Mac asserted, "One man has been the main force behind widening streets and changing two-way streets into one-way."

"Who's that, Uncle Mac?"

"His name is Billy Bulwer. He also happens to be runnin' for mayor."

"What do you know about Mr. Bulwer?"

"I know he's a wealthy businessman in his early 50s. I know he's a former hippie, who protested against the Vietnam war, and he's retained a lot o' his hippie ways, such as wearin' his gray hair in a ponytail and advocatin' the legal use o' marijuana."

When they pulled into the driveway of Mac's home, Richard asked, "Is there a more traditional candidate running against him?"

"I canna say for sure. There's been talk o' a retired attorney runnin' against him, who's a Christian, but she likely won't, because she canna match his campaign funds. And there's one thing more. Bulwer has a reputation in business o' fightin' dirty. They say he turns data into dirt and then spreads it, disguised as truth. His tactics have driven a couple o' competitors out o' business."

"Well, if the man has such a bad reputation, how is it he can run for major?"

"He's clever. He gives money to charity and sponsors community projects. When he does it, he makes sure he gets lots o' publicity."

The two men got out of the car and entered the house.

Looking around, Richard observed with satisfaction, "Everything looks just the same. It's nice to be home, Uncle Mac."

"Aye, laddie, our home looks the same with ye in it a standin' there, so it does. Now, why don't ye sit doon, and I'll fix ye a wee snack. Ye must be hungry."

Before Richard could object to his uncle going to extra trouble, Mac left for the kitchen. So, following his uncle's wishes, he sat down in the living room. Then he thought about Billy Bulwer and the people in Garden View Apartments.

Soon Mac returned with a plate of sandwiches and a pot of tea. "I have ice cream if ye care for dessert, my boy."

After munching on a cheese sandwich, Richard asked, "Uncle, do you know anything about Billy Bulwer's beliefs? Does he believe in God?"

"A week ago, I couldn't have answered your question, Richard. But today, I can."

"Why's that, Uncle?"

"Because three nights ago, I saw Bulwer interviewed on television. The interviewer asked him, 'Have you given any thought to the possibility God will be angry with you for wanting to tear down an apartment filled with the elderly?' He laughed and said, 'I don't believe in God, Santa Claus, guardian angels, or the tooth fairy.' So he wasn't shy aboot tellin' the world he was an atheist. He did say he was sorry progress required the destruction of the apartments."

"I would think, though, that Bulwer has some kind of a belief system. My hippie friend, Tony, had a belief system that he lived by. He based all his values on his view of love—which, I guess you'd say was attachment without commitment."

"I learned somethin' aboot Bulwer's belief system when the interviewer asked him who had influenced his philosophy o' life. And he said Plato."

"Plato?"

"Aye, Plato. He said Plato taught him that a good cause has harmony o' the human soul with universal ideas that have proved useful to people, such as a majority vote that puts a candidate in office."

"Sounds like Plato, alright. I suppose when he speaks of harmony, he means on his terms."

"Aye. He said, according to Plato, 'only the philosopher-leader who understands what is good and noble, is capable o' leadin' a city.' And that's why he said he was runnin' for mayor."

"So, while you and I follow the teachings of Jesus, Billy Bulwer follows the teachings of Plato."

"Well, laddie," Mac responded with a rueful smile, "I think Plato's friend, Socrates, would have harsh words to say aboot Mr. Bulwer's business practices."

Soon after this conversation, Richard complained of a headache and his uncle suggested he go up to his bedroom and rest a while. He lay down on his bed and fell asleep, only to be awakened some time later when his uncle called his name.

"Richard! A friend o' yours has come to pay ye a visit!"

Coming downstairs, Richard found Cal Jessup sitting in the living room. Shaking his hand, he said, "Great to see you, Cal."

"Excuse me, Cal," Mac said. "I'll leave ye and Richard to talk. I've got some work to do."

As his uncle left the room, Richard sat down in a chair near Cal's and took stock of his serious manner.

"I'm sorry to barge in on your visit with Mac. I'll just take a few minutes."

"That's okay. Take as much time as you need. I suppose you want to talk about Garden View."

"Yes. Many of us in the church and community don't believe the avenue needs widening, or the neighborhood needs another bus stop. What's needed is for 18 people to retain their homes in Garden View. They live on small, fixed incomes, mainly their social security. Living somewhere else, they'd pay much higher rent."

"What about the owners?"

"A local company manages it for the owner in California. The company told me the owner won't allow it to raise the rent and is quick to provide funds for repairs on the building."

"How does the owner feel about his property being destroyed?"

"Very much against it, and plans to send a substantial contribution to the Save-Garden-View Fund, according to the folks who manage the property."

"I'm only here for a few days, Cal, but whatever I can do to help during my stay, I'll be glad to do. Since Uncle Mac told me about the situation, I've been thinking what might be the best approach, in case anyone wanted my input."

Giving Richard an encouraging nod, Cal asked, "And what did you conclude?"

"You need public opinion on your side. Encourage citizens to contact city officials."

"Right. How do we get the word out?"

"Use contributions coming in to buy an effective TV ad—effective, because it gets attention—professionals know how to do it."

"Yes, that should arouse public opinion."

"Also, get some of your supporters to give an interview to the local newspaper. The reporter should talk with several tenants about the hardship a forced move would impose on them. Then do the same with a TV reporter and get the story on the evening news. The story line could be: Widening the avenue means narrowing the lives of 18 elderly persons."

"Thanks, Richy, I knew you would have useful ideas. I'll pass them to Mac's group."

The next day, a middle-aged, African-American woman in Mac's group came to see Richard. Mac introduced her as Mrs. Mildred Hopkins.

Getting up from an easy chair in the living room, Richard shook her hand, saying, "Please sit down, Mrs. Hopkins. Is there anything I can do for you?"

"Yes, Mr. Hawkins, there is something."

"Oh, the contribution I promised! If you'll give me a few minutes, I'll go up and get my checkbook."

"I don't believe Mrs. Hopkins is wantin' a check, laddie."

"Mr. Hawkins, our group liked your ideas to get public attention on our cause to save Garden View."

"I'm glad you found them helpful."

"We want you to represent us to the press—do the interviews with reporters and prepare tenants to speak for themselves."

Seeing Richard give his uncle a rueful smile, Mrs. Hopkins said, "Mr. MacGregor excused himself when our group started to talk about the notes with your ideas. He wasn't present when we decided to ask you to represent our cause."

"Mrs. Hopkins, I'm sure if you look, you'll find someone more qualified than I and," Richard said, tapping his left leg with his cane, "better able to get around."

"Won't you at least think about it?"

Giving her an indulgent smile, Richard replied, "Okay, I'll think about it. But, you really need to look for somebody else. I'm heading back to Dallas in a few days. I'd be happy to help with money, ideas about strategy, and lining up support. And please tell the folks in your group who wanted me to be their representative, I'm pleased they thought of me in that way."

"When you think about it, Mr. Hawkins, I'm sure you'll see you're the right man for the job. Good bye and thank you for your help."

"Good bye, Mrs. Hopkins."

32

Meeting the Press

"Uncle Mac, has Mildred Hopkins lined up someone to talk to reporters about Garden View?"

"No. The people she asked said they were too busy."

"Well, you can tell Mrs. Hopkins I'll do it. I came home to help and if that's the kind you need, okay. I want the names of four or five Garden View tenants . . . today. I've got to get started. As you know, I'm expected back at ADE in three days."

"I can give you two names right now, laddie. Both are members of our church."

"June Higgins is an elderly widow who has only social security to live on. Then there's Abe Cohen, a veteran whose wounds in the Korean Conflict have left him disabled. His wife is in a nursing home."

"Do you think they would be willing to help us?"

"I'm sure they would. They would know others who would help, too. I'll give them a call now."

The next day at Garden View, Richard and Abe and tenants Bill and Cornelia met in June's apartment. Richard asked each to express why moving would be a hardship. He made notes about remarks that seemed especially compelling. Then he gave each person his or her lines to go over before the next day, when he hoped to have reporters on the scene.

"Time yourselves to stay within a minute or two," he told them.

"I don't see why we need to say our piece in two minutes," Abe complained.

"Two reasons: First, news has to compete for space in the papers or on TV. Second, reporters need to hear only what will promote our cause—anything extra is just noise."

"I'll ask *Verity Banner News* and local TV channels to send reporters tomorrow to hear your side of the story. As soon as I have a news conference scheduled, I'll give June a call and she can pass the word. At the conference, after I introduce you, I'll ask for contributions to our fund and encourage Garden View neighbors to tell city officials where they stand on this issue."

"I hope I can say what you want me to, Mr. Hawkins, and not break down and cry."

"You'll be fine, Cornelia," Richard responded, thinking, *I wouldn't blame Cornelia for crying; she's lived here 16 years.*

After the morning news conference at Garden View, Richard stopped off at the book store where Melissa was working.

"How'd it go, Richy?" a voice behind him asked.

Turning around, he smiled and replied, "It went well, Melissa. Much better than I expected, considering how little time we had to prepare. The tenants spoke with emotion, but didn't sound bitter or angry. I think most people could identify with what they said."

"Did the reporters ask questions?"

"Oh, yes, quite a few. They even had questions for me."

"Why would they be asking *you* questions, Richy?"

"One reporter wanted to know if I were a 'paid consultant'; another wanted to know if I had any connection with the property. Questions like that. Watch the news tonight and read the morning *Banner*—tell me how *you* think it went. I'd better let you get back to work. I'll call you this evening."

Richard first thought he'd take a taxi home then decided to ride the bus.

He boarded the bus, rather pleased with himself. *Good to prove to myself getting on a bus doesn't make me anxious, as it used to, because of my disability.*

He reached home in time for lunch—the aroma of Uncle Mac's creamy mushroom soup verifying that fact.

"I was thinkin' I'd have to eat this delicious lunch by myself."

"Uncle Mac, your company and your homemade soup are two things I'm always happy to come home to."

"That's nice to hear, laddie, but before ye eat, ye'd better call the man at the TV station. I put the message by the phone."

"I wonder what that's about?" Richard said in a tone of mixed puzzlement and irritation. "Well, I suppose I should call and find out. Excuse me, Uncle. It should just take a couple of minutes."

"That was interesting," Richard said, locating Mac in the kitchen. "Matt Crouch invited me to appear on *City Talk* tomorrow."

"I presume it has something to do with Garden View."

"Yeah. Apparently, a reporter at the news conference told Crouch I would be an entertaining guest, that I have a sense of humor."

"What did ye say that made people laugh?"

"Nothing much. A reporter asked me did I 'really need a cane?' I said, 'Only when I walk.' Everybody laughed."

Mac grinned.

"What time do ye have to be at the TV station?"

"Not my favorite time of the day—6:30 A.M. The show begins at 7:00. I hope my circadian rhythms allow me to function that early."

"I've never seen *City Talk* myself, but I've heard it's very popular. Ye can tell the audience Garden View tenants will become displaced persons if their apartment is demolished."

"I'll do my best, Uncle Mac."

"Right now, my boy, let's see what ye can do with a bowl of soup."

Dressed in pajamas and slippers, Mac hurried down the stairs and turned on the TV. He'd overslept and missed the first half of Matt Crouch's show.

A quick channel search showed Richard, sitting beside Crouch, laughing at something the show's host had said. Mac realized Crouch had featured Richard in the early part of the program.

"I hope you'll plan to come back, Richard, and update us on what's happening to the folks at Garden View," Crouch was saying. "You've helped us to better understand the plight of a group of citizens in our city and the efforts of another group to help them. It's an issue that's become all too common—cars vs care."

The studio audience applauded loudly as Richard walked off camera.

Showered and dressed, Mac started to fix himself breakfast when a series of calls kept him busy writing phone messages complimenting Richard's appearance on *City Talk*.

Finally, a lull in the calls allowed Mac to eat his now cold eggs and limp toast.

Some callers he knew, others he didn't. He asked one of the latter how she'd found Richard's number and she replied Richard had mentioned his uncle's name. Most of the calls stressed two things: Richard seemed genuine and he made good sense.

Mac was talking to a caller when he heard Richard come in the front door. "Here's my nephew now, Mr. Chavez; I'll let him know ye want to speak to him—it'll just be a minute."

"Richard! Ye have a phone call. A Mr. Chavez wants to speak with ye aboot your appearance on *City Talk*."

Mac, sitting nearby, heard Richard thank the caller for his kind words and hang up.

"Carlos and Marie Chavez have volunteered to help support the Garden View tenants. I told them that your group would contact them."

"Aye, we need all the help we can get. One of the callers this morning was Donald Ingram. He said Melissa, Helen, and he saw ye on the news last night and they thought ye did a gude job. He was surprised when I mentioned your appearance on *City Talk*. Ye should have told the Ingrams, laddie, especially Melissa."

"At 7:00 A.M., Donald and Melissa are getting ready for work and Helen is getting ready for her volunteer job at the Red Cross. I decided not to bother them about it."

"It's up to ye, Richard, but I think ye should have told them."

"I could probably get a video tape of the program if they want me to."

"I'm sure they'd appreciate . . ."

The ringing phone interrupted Mac.

Richard picked up the receiver and braced himself for compliments that generally left him feeling uncomfortable.

Listening to his nephew, Mac heard words and vocal tone that didn't mesh with compliments. He heard: "He did?" "Doesn't make sense." "Yes, sure." "I believe I can." "I'll leave tomorrow."

"That was John Grant. I have to get back to Dallas. John said Grifith fired an employee of ADE, Sam Dill, for insubordination. It doesn't sound like anything Sam would be guilty of. John let me know Sam was defending me."

"Before ye leave for Dallas, let me know what ye think we should do next to save Garden View."

"Four things, Uncle Mac. I've drafted a flyer you can print and distribute to Garden View's neighbors. Ask church members and others to write letters to the *Banner*'s editor. Produce a short, simple TV ad to get the word out to more people—that's Matt Crouch's suggestion. And someone needs to write a thank-you note to June, Abe, Cornelia, and Bill—they did a great job."

33

Victim of Stalking

A LONE IN THE HOUSE on her day off, Melissa peered out a front window at the street. Seeing no cars parked nearby, she breathed a sigh of relief, sat down on the bed and tried to relax. Still dressed in her nightgown, she leaned back and shook her head.

I shouldn't bother Uncle Mac with my troubles. But, I don't know anyone else I can turn to, except Dad and Mom, and I don't want to upset them when it may not be necessary.

Melissa looked at the phone, undecided. Then she picked up the receiver and called Uncle Mac. She learned that the group working to save Garden View was at his house, but would soon be leaving. "Come over when ye can," he told her.

Mac ushered Melissa in, obviously pleased to see her.

"Ye're always welcome my dear. Is there somethin' ye wanted to talk to me aboot?" he asked, as they sat down in the living room.

"Uncle Mac, I wanted a chance to talk with you about Richard."

"Has my laddie done somethin' ye find disturbin'?"

"No, nothing like that. I'm looking for some inside knowledge about my future husband. He doesn't say much about his childhood, except how much he owes you for taking care of him. What was Richy like growing up?"

"Ye've come to the right person, my dear. Since he was a wee bairn, Richard's been quick to defend the weak. When he was eleven, a boy his age bullied a smaller boy in the neighborhood. Richard told the bully to stop it and got a punch for an answer. I didn't hear aboot his fight with the bully, until I asked him aboot a bloody handkerchief in the laundry. I asked him if he'd turned the ither cheek? He said, 'I was too busy defendin' myself.' The bully must have hit your nose to make it bleed, I said. Richard replied, 'No, I hit *his* nose. When it started to bleed, I lent him my handkerchief. I figured ye'd take it better aboot the blood on my gude handkerchief if it was the ither kid's blood.'" Mac shook his head, smiling at the memory.

"That's a cute story, Uncle Mac. The other night when we went out to dinner, Richy found a ladybug on our table. He coaxed it on to a napkin and put it on a plant. I told him it was a nice thing to do, and he said, 'We don't want ladybug soup.' I knew he did it because he has a kind heart."

"Aye, that he does."

"I've never seen Richy angry. Does he ever lose his temper? I do sometimes."

"Richard generally is gude natured. But he *can* lose his temper if he believes he or someone he knows is treated unfairly. In high school, Richard hung around with Mike, who had asthma. Mike came late to P.E. class three times, and the teacher punished him with 10 laps around the gym. After seven, Richard thought Mike looked like he was havin' trouble breathin'. So Richard asked the teacher to let him rest and he refused. Richard lost his temper and called the teacher 'pigheaded.'"

"What happened after that?"

"The principal sent him home after tellin' him to apologize to the teacher, who accepted his apology. He was put on three weeks' probation, which kept him off the soccer team for two games. After his probation, he apologized again to the teacher o' his own free will. He knew he was wrong to resort to name callin'."

"Do you think Richy would mind our talking about him this way?"

"No. Richard said I should share things aboot him or the family with ye. He said I remember better what he did as a kid than he does—probably, because he dinna have a mither to tell him."

Looking closely at Melissa, Mac asked, "Di' ye want to talk to me aboot anythin' else? On the phone, ye sounded . . . anxious."

"There is something, Uncle Mac. I need your advice. I think I'm being stalked."

"Ye say, ye '*think*' someone is stalking ye?"

"I *know* someone is. I wasn't sure at first. But I am now."

"Di' ye know who it is?"

"Yes, I met him about one year ago. His name is Parker Carrington, Jr. He helped me with an assignment in my first interior design class. He seemed nice; I dated him twice. On the first date, we went to a movie and he said I was wearing the wrong kind of shoes for my feet. On the second date, we went to an expensive restaurant for dinner and he insisted on ordering for me. He was very attentive, but, at the same time, controlling. After the two dates, I always had a reason why I couldn't go when he asked me out. I figured he'd catch on I wasn't interested and he seemed to—he stopped calling."

"Later, though, ye would have *accidental* meetings. Right?"

"Yes, I thought they were 'accidental' at first. One time on campus, my car had a flat tire. Parker came along in a few minutes and saw my problem. He put the spare tire on for me, and offered to have the flat tire fixed. I thanked him and said I would take care of it myself. The guy at the service station inflated it and it stayed inflated."

"Carrington must have let the air oot o' your tire, so he could show up and play the role o' a helpful friend."

"Yes, that's what I believe. Since then, I've seen him in his car, parked close to my home."

"Were there any ither accidental meetings?"

"Yes. Last week, I was alone in an elevator on the fifth floor and when it stopped on the fourth, Parker entered. He said, 'Nice to see you, Melissa. It's a small world.' Then he started reading a newspaper. We both got out in the lobby and went in different directions."

"The wife o' a friend o' mine was stalked. Sometimes the stalker wanted her to see him; ither times he didn't."

"Parker's stalking angered me, but didn't frighten me. I figured it would stop after Richard and I were married. But, yesterday I got a letter that frightened me, and, I think, Parker sent it. It said, if I married Richard, he'd soon be a widower. It also said, 'The world is small, you can't hide from me.' That sounded to me like Parker's 'small world' remark."

"Aye, Melissa. He gave ye a clue to his identity. Maybe he meant to."

"The letter looks very similar to a letter I received in Dallas—the typing and paper look the same. It sounds crazy, but I believe Parker followed me to Dallas."

"Could he leave his job and fly to Dallas?"

"He doesn't have a job. He just takes classes. His parents are wealthy. They give him whatever he wants."

"And right now, ye're what he wants. I take it Richard doesn't know aboot Parker."

"I almost told him before he went back to Dallas. Then I worried that he might confront Parker himself rather than let the police do it. Parker told me he has a license to carry a gun, because sometimes he carries valuable bonds to his father's clients in places like Miami Beach and Cape Cod."

"Tell ye what. Write Richard an e-mail and tell him Annie Anderson, who has the popular radio talk show, wants to interview him aboot Garden View."

"When did that happen?"

"I heard aboot it today from a member o' our Save Garden View group. Ask Richard to try to come home this weekend. When he does, ye and your parents and Richard and I can meet to discuss how to handle this stalker."

34

Unraveling a Betrayal

John Grant had a car waiting for Richard when his plane landed at the Dallas airport.

The driver waited until Richard got into the car, to say, "Mr. Grant doesn't want you to contact people at ADE or let them know you're in town. I'm supposed to take you directly to Mr. Grant's office at BG Oil, if that's okay with you."

"Certainly. Thanks for picking me up and taking care of my luggage."

"Glad to help."

On the freeway, the driver exceeded the speed limit.

Is someone chasing us? Richard mused. *I bet this driver could qualify for a NASCAR Winston Cup race.*

After Richard arrived at BG Oil, his driver said, "Sorry I couldn't make better time, Mr. Hawkins. The traffic was heavier than usual."

"You made *very* good time."

"Thanks. When you're ready to leave, I'll be available to take you to your apartment."

Wondering if he wanted to risk another ride like that, Richard entered the administrative offices building, and took the elevator to the third floor where John's office was located. John was on the phone but waved him in.

"Be with you in a minute, Rich."

Hanging up, John said, "Have you ever noticed that to reassure some people you have to say the same thing three times?"

"No, but now that you mention it. . ."

"Let's go next door to the conference room; we shouldn't be disturbed there. Sorry I had to interrupt your time with Mac and Melissa to bring you back early, but I thought I'd better have your help in clearing this business up."

Once they were seated, Richard asked, "What's this about Sam Dill being fired for insubordination? There are a few employees at ADE whose temper might cause problems, but Sam isn't one of them."

"I'd better start from the beginning. Dad called G.H. and asked him about the process used in hiring Murkey. G.H. said you hired him against his advice, and Sam Dill agreed with you. G.H. told Dad he had misgivings, but nothing he could put his finger on. You look like you want to say something, Rich."

"I want to *say* something, alright! But you go ahead and finish. I want to know how Sam ended up fired."

"G.H. also mentioned that you felt bad about hiring Murkey. Dad replied that Murkey's work record showed no criminal tendencies and that he had complete confidence in your judgment, as do I."

"By any chance, did G.H. tell your father he encouraged me not to feel bad?"

"I believe he did."

"Uncle Mac had me look up the definition of 'rascally,' because I had used it wrong. I know what it means now."

"Sometime after talking to Dad, G.H. told an ADE employee what he'd told Dad. And it eventually got to Sam Dill. He went to G.H. and accused him of lying to Dad about who hired Murkey. That's when G.H. fired him for insubordination."

Richard sat listening, his facial expression showing shock, hurt, and anger.

"How did you find out what Sam said to Grifith?"

"Sam wrote me a letter. In it, he stated you and he recommended *not* hiring Murkey. G.H. overruled you and hired him."

"Sam told you the truth."

"I thought as much. Anyway, can we *prove* it?"

"Never would have believed Grifith would have pulled such a *dirty* trick. I was pretty sure he didn't like me. But, why lie about me to your father? Mr. Grant wouldn't have blamed him if he'd taken responsibility for hiring Murkey."

Did Grifith really intend to write a letter to Bruce Grant telling him he'd hired Murkey? Did he tell me about it, so I would talk him out of it?

"I know Grifith was up for promotion. He may have thought putting the decision on you helped his chances. Did you make notes on how you felt about Murkey? Or do you have e-mails from Grifith that would prove he did the hiring?"

"I made notes on all my interviews and meetings. They would include Grifith's decision to hire Murkey. No e-mails though."

"I'll send the chap who drove you here, my driver, Joe, to pick up the file. Write a note to your secretary to let him take the file. How's it labeled?"

"SECURITY GUARD HIRING."

When the note was written, John left the conference room and returned five minutes later.

"That was fast."

"Joe stays close by. He's my bodyguard as well as my driver. My father hired him after the kidnapping."

"While we're waiting, tell me how the church is coping with its problem and what you're doing to help."

"John, it's a problem for several members in the church, rather than for the church itself. The city plans to demolish apartments where the members live, so it can widen the avenue and build a bus stop. I've been talking to the media in behalf of the tenants to enlist public support in opposition."

Small talk consumed an hour and a half between the two men before Joe returned with the file.

"Have any trouble?" Richard asked.

"No. Your secretary wasn't around, so I walked into your office and helped myself to the file."

Richard took the file and examined its contents.

"Joe's not the first person to take the file—the notes are gone."

"Are you sure?"

"I'm sure, John. Somebody has removed them and I think I know who."

"Griffith."

"Yes."

"Well, I don't need any proof. Your word is good enough for me and will be for Dad. I'll make sure Sam has a good job here. And I'll work on a transfer for Grifith."

"Wait a minute! There's a slim chance. John, Joe needs to go back to ADE."

"Okay. You don't mind, do you, Joe?"

"No sir."

"Joe, go to the fourth floor. Turn right out of the elevator. Enter the last office on the right side. Look for an envelope with my name on it in the top desk drawer. Just maybe it's still there. It's a memo from Grifith I forgot to put in the file."

Richard fished in his pocket for his keys—he removed one from the ring and gave it to Joe.

"Here's the key to the office—it's vacant. If a security guard asks what you're doing, show him the key and tell him I asked you to pick up something. If he needs confirmation, he can call me here."

This time while Joe was away, Richard and John had coffee and a cinnamon roll at the BG cafeteria.

"If I indulged myself like this every day, I'd be overweight again."

"Next time we have coffee, I'll try to be a better influence."

When they got back to the conference room, Joe was waiting for them.

"What luck?" John asked.

"All good! Didn't see a security guard, and the envelope was where Mr. H. said it was."

John took the envelope from Joe.

"Looks like Grifith's handwriting." Taking the memo out of the envelope, John read from it with a triumphant smile. "Listen to this: 'Therefore, on this occasion, I must overrule your recommendation and hire Mr. Murkey. I believe he will prove to be an excellent security guard, given his experience as a deputy sheriff.' Grifith's initials are here. This proves his deception."

"What will you do with the memo, John?"

"If you'll let me borrow it, Rich, I'll fax it to Dad. He needs to know Grifith lied to him about you and fired an employee for telling the truth."

"It's yours. What action do you think your dad will take?"

"I can tell you this: He doesn't like liars, especially in positions of leadership. He'll likely transfer Grifith to another company—to a lesser position of authority, and put him on probation."

"Looks like you have the situation figured out. Okay if Joe takes me to my apartment?"

"Sure thing. Joe, take Mr. Hawkins home and when you get back I'll be ready to head for home, too. Rich, I'll call you this evening, after I talk to Dad about Grifith."

"Yes, I'd appreciate that, John."

Richard was in the middle of his devotions when the phone rang. As he expected, John was on the line.

"Did your father get your fax?"

"Yes, he called me a short time ago."

"How'd he take it?"

"He was disgusted and very disappointed in Grifith. He's asked him to fly to Portland tomorrow. When Dad has to talk with an employee about integrity, he prefers to do it face-to-face. He already has someone in mind to take Grifith's place."

"John, I received an e-mail from Melissa. She says I'm needed back home this weekend. Okay if I take a couple of days after that? I'd be back in my office Wednesday."

"Sure. I'll keep an eye on your department while you're gone. You'll see Sam Dill on the job when you return, that is, if he wants his job back."

"Well, I'm glad to hear that. Sam's a good man. And thanks, John, for the extra days off. Before I leave, I'll make sure there are no loose ends. This Thursday, I'm doing another Information Session at Southern Methodist University—I think it's a great way to interest seniors in a career in the Grant Corporation."

35

To Catch a Stalker

SATURDAY AFTERNOON IN VERITY found Richard home alone. Uncle Mac had a meeting to attend and Melissa had a college assignment to complete. Feeling a need to rest after his flight from Dallas, Richard stretched out on the sofa.

He stared with disinterest at the fast-changing images on the TV.

Suddenly a face on the screen caught his attention—his. He saw and heard enough to realize the ad's producers had culled his remarks from the 6:00 news and *City Talk* to create an effective plea in behalf of the Garden View tenants.

Uncle Mac and his group took Matt Crouch's advice and produced a TV ad. Good for them! It has emotional appeal, but not at the expense of facts. After I just relax a bit I'll call Annie Anderson about the interview on her show.

Richard felt a gentle shake of his shoulder. He opened his eyes to see Uncle Mac bending over him.

"I'm glad ye got in a nap. I'm sorry I wasn't here to greet ye, but ye got my note, laddie."

"Yes, I did. How'd your meeting go?"

"It was a gude meeting overall. We would have finished sooner, except for one member o' our group who's a pettifogger."

"A what?"

"Pettifogger. He quibbled about small details and missed the key points, which got our discussion off track. Bless his heart, he thinks he's bein' helpful."

"We have a pettifogger or two at ADE."

"I didn't mention it in my note, but the Ingrams invited us to dinner tonight. We have to be there in two hours."

"Boy, I'd better move," Richard said, scrambling off the sofa and heading upstairs. "I have to shower and I'd better shave again."

"Helen, that was delicious," Richard said. "I think that's the first time I've eaten chicken and dumplings."

"I never became a gude enough cook to fix ye chicken and dumplings. I mostly had to rely on modern culinary technology, known as canned goods."

Although good food and pleasant conversation made the dinner enjoyable, Richard could tell something wasn't quite right.

When they'd all finished their meal, Donald said, "Melissa has a problem that she's shared with Helen, Mac, and me. We were waiting for you to come home before discussing what we should do. Let's go where we'll be more comfortable."

Richard took Melissa's hand and gave her a reassuring smile. He knew the problem must be serious, because no effort was made to clear the table.

Once they were seated in the living room, Donald said, "The problem is, Melissa recently realized a man who was in one of her classes is stalking her. For the past several weeks he's followed her at times and, we believe, written her two threatening letters."

"Is one of them the letter you received in Dallas?" Richard asked.

"I feel sure he sent it and followed me to Dallas."

"I'll tell you what we know, but it's not a lot. His name is Parker Carrington, Jr. He's a young man, about your age. Melissa says he occasionally takes a class at the university. He has a license to carry a gun; when he travels for his wealthy father, he often carries valuable items. That seems to be his only work."

"He's from New York City, where his father's business is," added Melissa.

"What brought him to our town?"

"Presumably, he had friends at the university."

"I spoke to our attorney today and his sources told him Carrington doesn't have a criminal record. He's had numerous citations for traffic violations—recently, he was belligerent with a police officer, who cited him for speeding. Carrington's silver Mercedes is well known by police on traffic duty."

"Could we get a restraining order against this . . . creep?" Richard asked.

"What we have now is suspicions, Richard, but not evidence convincing to the authorities. Occasionally parking on our street; sharing an elevator with Melissa; putting a spare tire on her car; or, going into a restaurant where Melissa is eating with her girlfriend likely wouldn't be seen as stalking. In a town the size of Verity, it's possible to run into someone you know."

"It would be different if we could tie him to those threatening letters."

"Yes, Mom. I *know* he wrote them. I think he wants me to know he did it, but not be able to prove it."

Clenching his fist, Richard said vehemently, "I'd like to punch his lights out!"

"Now, Richard," cautioned Mac, "ye must not have any contact with the rogue. I think I know how ye feel, laddie, but he might shoot ye and claim ye threatened him with your cane."

"Mac's right, Richard. We need to let the law handle it. At the same time, you and Melissa need to stay on your guard. He may or may not be making empty threats."

"Don, didn't you say you planned to hire a private investigator to keep tabs on Carrington?"

"Yes, my dear. I have an appointment to meet with a P.I. tomorrow; somebody our attorney recommended."

"I know the Lord will take care o' ye, Melissa. But, I believe He expects us to do our part. Ye need to go aboot your business and not live in fear. I think, though, ye should not go out without one o' us with ye, at least for the time bein'."

"That's sound advice," Donald said, in quick agreement.

Helen said, "We've talked about Melissa quitting her job at the book store, so she and I would have more time to prepare for the wedding."

Melissa nodded her assent. "Makes my decision even easier. I'll do as you all say."

"I'm glad to hear that. And if one of us could take you to your classes and bring you home . . ."

"Oh, *Dad*," Melissa said, her tone registering her objection. She looked at Richard for support, but he was nodding his agreement.

"I got to thinkin' last night after we left the Ingrams. It might be a gude idea to head back to Dallas a couple o' days sooner. Ye don't want to jeopardize your job when ye're goin' to be a married man."

Richard gave his uncle an affectionate smile. "You're not worried about me, are you? Could it be you're thinking I might go after this creep alone and end up shot? Well, you don't have to worry, Uncle Mac. Last night I thought about doing it, even made plans. But today, I realized I'd be taking things out of God's hands and playing right into this Carrington's. We can't let him manipulate us."

"Gude. I won't worry then—at least, not too much." "You'll be happy to know I contacted Annie Anderson about Garden View. She'll interview me at the studio."

"Our friends at Garden View will appreciate it, laddie. I'll make sure to get the word oot that ye'll be on the radio tomorrow"

"Don't expect me home for lunch. Melissa will be picking me up in a half hour."

"Well, my boy, if ye're not goin' to be home for lunch, I'm thinkin' I'll go oot for a wee bite myself."

"Good idea. There's a new place . . . There's Melissa," Richard said abruptly. "She's a little early."

Saying a quick goodbye, Richard took his cane from the umbrella stand and headed out the door toward the waiting car.

As they drove off, Richard gave Melissa a searching look. "How are you feeling today?" he asked.

"I keep looking in the rearview mirror," she said and laughed nervously. "If I see the same car behind me for several blocks, I imagine I'm being followed. Driving over, I became worried when the car behind me turned twice when I did. Then it occurred to me: Parker wouldn't be caught dead in such an old car."

Richard gave Melissa's knee a reassuring pat. "I'll keep a lookout for Carrington, Sweet Face."

By the time they reached the restaurant's parking lot, Richard and Melissa had ceased to think about the stalker and focused on Annie Anderson's radio talk show.

"Would you mind if I came with you to the studio?"

"Nope. Not in the least. Your presence would inspire my best efforts—which may not be saying much."

"Thanks to your 'best efforts' people in the community have been contacting city officials and asking them to save Garden View."

"Really? How do you know?"

"I heard it on the radio and read it in the *Banner*."

"That's nice to hear," Richard said, as they entered the restaurant.

Melissa asked the hostess for a corner booth.

"These days, I like to sit with my back to the wall, so nobody can come up behind me."

"I understand," Richard said, giving her shoulder a pat.

Melissa ordered a cheeseburger, fries, and a Coke. And Richard ordered a bowl of potato-ham soup, salad, and coffee. Eating and talking consumed almost two hours.

"I should warn you, Richy. If I go to a restaurant feeling nervous, I order comfort food."

"I'll try to keep that in mind. I would say though, your figure tells me you're not often nervous."

"I'm glad you like what you see. Running every other day has taken care of unhealthy meals. Or at least . . . used to."

"You'll run again. This stalking problem will pass like a bad dream. In time, you'll forget."

"Yes, 'forget,' after I learn from it."

"What do you expect to learn?"

"To trust my instincts and be more observant of a person's values, or lack of."

"Got room for a piece of pie?"

"No, just room for my last French fry."

"Refill on your Coke?"

"No, I'd better not."

"In that case, I guess it's time to leave. I probably should get home and prepare for my radio interview."

"How can you prepare for something like that?"

"I'll try to anticipate Annie's questions and make notes on how I might answer them."

Richard paid the server for their meals and Melissa took care of the tip.

As they started to walk out, an incoming customer, a well-dressed young man, held the door for them.

Richard was about to thank him, when Melissa gasped, "Parker!"

"Hello, Melissa. Fancy meeting you here. Is it very crowded? Doesn't matter; I have a reservation. See you around. Oh, and good luck with your karate, Richard."

Deep in thought, Richard and Melissa walked slowly to the car. Neither one said anything until they'd left the parking lot and were heading for Mac's house.

"How did that creature know we were there?" Melissa asked. "Nobody followed us, as far as we could tell."

"Maybe he has help. He could pay someone to keep an eye on us and report to him."

"I suppose so. But why go to that much trouble?"

"It gives him a sense of power—a high—Melissa. He's playing a game of control. He knows now we're talking about him. I plan to give Cal a call this evening. I want to know what he thinks about this stalker. He's a wise man."

"Do you think Cal might have any advice? We could sure use his prayers. And what did Carrington mean about 'your karate,' Richy?"

"I've taken a few lessons. That's all." While Richard tried to make light of Carrington's comment for Melissa's sake, he couldn't ignore the knot in his stomach that had nothing to do with indigestion. *I understand his interest in Melissa, but how and why does this criminal know about the karate?*

Later at home, Richard made notes on the answers to questions similar to those he'd heard Annie Anderson ask interviewees. Mac hadn't returned; for company, he put on the TV and saw the Garden View ad again.

One thing for sure, my gestures certainly show up with that cane in my hand. Wonder if it makes me look too aggressive?

Richard started to turn the set off when a rerun of *I Love Lucy* came on. He sat back and enjoyed the classic comedy series. It was followed by *Get Smart*, which had him laughing aloud. In this episode, Agents 86 and 99 track enemy spies to a toy store, where talking dolls smuggle out top secrets. He recalled this episode from his coma.

I must be getting old. I'm beginning to like the old comedy shows better than the new ones. The old shows are still funny, decades later.

A call from Helen Ingram interrupted his thoughts.

"Richard, I'm sorry to bother you with my troubles, but I had to talk with someone right away. Don's not here . . . he took Melissa to her late class."

"What is it, Helen?"

"A little while ago, a dozen roses were delivered. At first I thought they were from you. Then I noticed the card."

"Yes?"

"Richard, the card said: 'Thought you should enjoy these flowers before you're gone.' And there was no name."

"We don't need a name. We know who sent them," Richard said, an angry edge to his voice.

"Do you think I should tell Melissa about the flowers? She was upset after seeing Carrington at the restaurant."

"How was she when she went to class?"

"Calm."

"I don't know what to tell you, Helen . . . Maybe, we could wait to tell her about the card tomorrow. I suppose you got rid of the flowers."

"Yes, I made sure she wouldn't see them."

"Don't say anything to Melissa about the flowers and the card. I'm going to call Cal Jessup. Melissa suggested earlier that his advice and prayers would help; and I have a feeling she's right. This game Carrington is playing is getting dangerous."

After saying goodbye and encouraging her not to worry, which he knew was a waste of breath, he called Cal's office and left a message for him.

In less than an hour, the phone rang.

"Hi, Rich. I got your message. Is everything all right?"

"No. It's Melissa. She's being stalked."

Richard spent several minutes describing the stalker's actions.

"Cal, when the flowers with the card came, I *knew* his game had turned deadly. I knew it. He's planning something he won't be able to stop."

Cal paused a long time before answering.

Carrington lives in Verity, doesn't he?"

"Yes, near the university. I looked up his address in the phone book."

"Do you know Lynn Evers at the church?"

"Not really. We exchanged names once in a Bible study class. Why do you ask?"

"I'm thinking he might be able to help you. He retired from the FBI as a regional director after a 25-year career. In one of our conversations, he told me that, early in his career, he worked on a stalking case that ended in a murder. Consequently, he has strong feelings against stalkers—believes stalkers are treated too leniently."

"Would you talk with Mr. Evers, Cal? See if he will help us. Of course, I would pay him for his time. Feel free to give him all the facts I've given you."

"I think it would be wise for Melissa to stay home for a few days 'til Lynn can arrange something. When he has, I'm sure he'll call you."

"Thanks, Cal. You're a good friend."

"Try not to worry, Rich. We'll get through this okay, with God's help."

"I believe you."

Richard called Melissa and had her relay Cal's comments to her parents. She agreed to stay home. Had she objected, Richard was prepared to tell her about the flowers and the card.

"I'm just sorry I can't go with you to Annie's studio to hear the interview. I'll say a prayer for you, Richy. I know you'll do your usual good job."

"I'll do my best. You can tell me later, as a member of the radio audience, how I sounded."

Richard was changing the sheets on his bed. When he heard his uncle's car, he met him at the front door.

"Hi, Uncle Mac. It's my turn to greet you for a change."

"Ye probably wondered where I was when I didn't come home after lunch."

"I *was* beginning to wonder where you were. It's not like you to change your daily plans."

"Aye, ye're right. On my way to the restaurant, I started to think hard aboot Melissa's stalker, tryin' to think o' a way to stop him. After awhile, I realized I'd driven out o' town and, so, I decided to go on to Riverfield and see Dr. Olson at the hospital."

"Let's go into the kitchen. I want to see how my chili's coming along."

"When is it goin' to be ready?" Mac asked, sitting down at the dinette set.

Joining his uncle at the table, Richard replied, "It needs to simmer another 30 minutes. I don't suppose you were able to see Dr. Olson, as busy as she always is. I think the only people she sees are patients."

"Exactly what I was thinkin' when I got to the hospital. But, no, I found Karen in the cafeteria having a cup o' tea. She asked me to join her, so we talked while I ate lunch. She's a charmin' woman."

"And attractive, too. So you're on a first name basis now?"

"Aye. I've been thinkin' aboot her lately, wonderin' if she would go oot with an old Scot."

"Ask her and find out."

"I did, laddie, and she said, yes. On the way home, I bought her a box o' See's Candies and had them sent to the hospital. That's why I'm late."

"A good reason, Uncle Mac."

"I told her aboot the stalker, and she agreed that he could become very dangerous."

Richard then told his uncle about the flowers and the ominous card that accompanied them. He also related his phone conversation with Cal Jessup.

"As a former FBI agent, Evers would have a lot o' connections that the average person wouldn't have. I wonder what he'll be able to do?"

"I don't know. But Melissa and I both felt that he would be able to help us."

"Aye. God may work His will through Lynn Evers."

After 15 minutes of conversation about Garden View's tenants with Annie Anderson on her radio talk show, Richard was given the signal the interview had ended. He was getting ready to leave, when Anderson stopped him.

"I'd like to ask you one more question, Richard."

"Yes?"

"Shouldn't the needs of the majority—as protected by law—come ahead of the needs of the few?"

"I believe it's the moral responsibility of the majority to protect the interests and well-being of the few. It's one of the promises of democracy.

Thomas Jefferson, in his "First Inaugural Address" makes essentially the same point. I can paraphrase what he said, if you want me to."

"Yes, please do."

"He said, The will of the majority has to prevail, but to be right, it must be reasonable. He went on to say, the minority have equal rights, with equal laws to protect them. Any violation of their rights is oppression. In this case, Annie, the city, with its majority power, is acting unreasonably and, therefore, is wrong."

"Thanks, Richard for taking time to be on my show. By taking the side of the folks at Garden View, you've made many of us in the community realize it's a larger issue."

The next day, Richard and Mac hurried over to the Ingrams after receiving a morning call from Melissa. Don greeted them at the door.

"Melissa's with her mother in our bedroom. Helen's pretty upset. We received this card this morning in the mail."

Richard took what appeared to be a condolence card. Inside, it said: "May God's peace be with you in this time of grief."

"That mean, contemptible rat!" Richard declared, squeezing the card into a shapeless lump.

"Don't insult the rats, laddie."

"I hope Lynn Evers knows how to stop Carrington. Because, if he doesn't, I will!"

"There, there, laddie. I'm sure Evers will know what to do to catch this stalker."

"Excuse me, the phone's ringing," Don said, leaving the living room. He returned quickly. "It's for you, Richard."

"This is Lynn Evers. Cal told me I could probably reach you there. I have to be brief. I've a meeting coming up. But I wanted to let you and Mac know as soon as possible. You and Miss Ingram don't have to worry anymore about the stalker. He's left town for New York City, and won't be back. I've made sure of that."

"How did you manage it so fast, Mr. Evers?"

"Cal can fill you in, Richard, as soon as he receives a copy of my operative's report. Right now I have to go. Be sure I get an invitation to your wedding. Goodbye and best of luck to you and Miss Ingram."

"Goodbye, Mr. Evers."

"It sounded like Evers took care o' the stalker."

"He told me that Carrington has left for New York City and won't be back."

Everyone at the Ingram house was relieved. They could relax their defenses, and put aside their well-founded fears.

"Helen, what say we all go out for lunch," Donald suggested. "Our Melissa has been cooped up for days."

"Sounds good, Don. And we won't have to worry about running into you know who!"

After lunch, the Ingrams planned to return home—events had taken their toll on Helen. Before Melissa parted from Richard, she whispered in his ear, "If you're good, later I'll tell you what I thought of your interview with Annie."

That night, when Richard was about to go to bed, he received a call from Cal.

"Rich, I figured you'd want to hear the report from Lynn's operative, who convinced Carrington to return to New York City."

"Yes, definitely."

"I'll read it for you:"

I followed Parker Carrington to the university library, where he took a seat on an upper floor. I saw he was looking at a condolence card. I sat near him and told him stalking Melissa Ingram had angered a highly-placed law enforcement officer. When he denied it, I said I found the florist who sold him the flowers, and he was seen buying two condolence cards. I said, the person I represent knows your father is in debt and has borrowed heavily on his property, including your home. He could call authorities and reduce you and your father to paupers. The person I work for also knows you forged the name of your father's company treasurer on several large checks that your father has hidden from his board of directors. He begged me to keep that a secret. I made it clear, to avoid unpleasant consequences, he should leave Verity today for New York City and not come back. I assured him, since yesterday he had been watched night and day and would be watched in New York City. Before I left him, I mentioned, he would be wise to leave town immediately, so no action would be taken against him.

"Rich, the private investigator Don hired told Lynn's operative that Carrington packed his bags and left town an hour after he was told to leave. He said he looked and acted frightened. The P.I. followed him a long distance to make sure he was going."

"Thank Lynn Evers for helping us. And thank you, too, Cal. We'll all sleep better tonight, because you and Mr. Evers came to our aid and likely saved Melissa's life."

36

Good News, Bad News

"U NCLE MAC!"

"I'm on the porch, son!"

"Been standing out here, keeping an eye on the neighbors?" Richard asked, teasingly.

"Noo. I came out here to sit quietly, where reminders o' God's creation surround me. I wanted to thank the Lord for keepin' Melissa and ye safe from the stalker. I was aboot to go in when I looked across the street at my neighbor's flowers. They're dyin' from neglect."

"There are people who like to plant flowers, and people who like to care for them. Mr. Galiger is a planter," Richard remarked matter-of-factly.

"What di' ye need, my boy?"

"Your copy of *The World's Greatest Speeches*—I couldn't find it in the bookcase."

"Cal borrowed it. Wait a minute, though. I think he brought it back . . . aye. Look under the stack o' magazines on the coffee table."

"I want to take a quote out of George Washington's 'Farewell Address.' I plan to use it in a speech Mrs. Hopkins asked me to give."

"I thought ye were goin' to tell her no," Mac said, smiling.

"I did. But, Mrs. Hopkins is a very persuasive woman, as you well know. If she sold encyclopedias, I'd probably own a set now. I hope *I* can be as persuasive in behalf of the folks at Garden View. It's been a long time since I've given a speech."

"I'm sure Mrs. Hopkins has picked the right man for the job... I heard the gathering had to be moved from the community center to the large university lecture hall to take care o' the expected crowd."

"Oh? I hadn't heard that. I suppose, twice as many people should make me twice as nervous. I'm glad I took a few extra days off, but I've got to get back to ADE Monday. That gives me three days to work on my speech and appear on *City Talk* one more time. I'll rehearse the speech in Dallas and come home weekend after next."

I can't see several hundred people making my speech their Saturday night date, he thought, smiling to himself.

This desk is a mess. If, as they say, a messy desk is a sign of creativity, I must be brilliant. I think it's just a sign of messiness.

"Mr. Hawkins, Sam Dill would like to see you."

"Send him in."

"I'm sorry to disturb you, Mr. Hawkins. Cindy told me you were in the middle of a report for Mr. Grant."

"That's okay, Sam. What's up?"

"There's been a security breach. Since Grifith's replacement isn't here, I thought you'd be the one to notify."

"Sit down, Sam, and tell me about it."

"It happened two weeks ago, but Mr. Lester only told me today. A well-known scientist, whom he knew only by reputation, a Dr. Michael Gunderson, paid him a visit. He asked Mr. Lester to speak at a dinner honoring a retiring professor Mr. Lester studied under. A lab assistant needed help and Mr. Lester excused himself and left Gunderson alone in his office. When he returned, 10 minutes later, Gunderson was gone, leaving a note saying he had an appointment. This morning, Mr. Lester discovered his old professor wasn't retiring. He remembered his note-book was on his desk when he left Gunderson alone. He's worried, be-cause his notebook described his work on a secret project."

"I wouldn't think Gunderson could have learned much from Karl's notebook in 10 minutes."

"Someone bent on industrial espionage would likely have had a camera on him."

"That's true. Do you know if Karl tried to contact the real Michael Gunderson?"

"He did. Dr. Gunderson took a leave of absence and is out of the country."

"Sam, write a report on what Karl told you and send it to John Grant."

The next day, Richard met with Karl and convinced him that the thief wouldn't have had time to learn anything useful.

"I don't think you need worry about a stranger reading your notes," Richard assured him with a smile. "They're indecipherable for anyone who hasn't learned to read your writing. Just be more careful in the future."

"Yes, I will. I once saw Dr. Gunderson's picture in a science journal. I remember, he was bald and had a beard like this man. Anyway, I've learned my lesson. Is my writing really that bad?"

"Frankly, yes. I bet," Richard said, somewhat facetiously, "the phony Gunderson thought you'd written in code."

Both men laughed.

Richard returned from Dallas the day before he was scheduled to speak. He closeted himself in his bedroom to rehearse and make last minute changes. His speech on the intended demolition of Garden View revolved around the larger issue of eminent domain. It called for more community involvement in a government's decision to confiscate private property for public use. Richard included a story about Cornelia, a Garden View tenant, whose worry over losing her home of many years may have caused her recent heart attack.

"Is it right for a city government to turn 18 people into displaced persons to widen an avenue and build another bus stop? We should…"

A knock at the door interrupted Richard's rehearsal. "It's time for dinner. Would ye like me to bring ye a tray?"

"Yes, I would appreciate that, Uncle Mac. I'm finally getting somewhere."

"I'll be right back, son."

"We should see this as a *moral* question" he continued. "As George Washington, in his 'Farewell Address,' said, 'It is substantially true, that virtue or morality is a necessary spring of popular government. The rule, indeed, extends with more or less force to every species of free government.' Our leaders who propose civic improvements should take into account the morality of what they propose."

Saturday night, Richard spoke 45 minutes to an overflow audience, receiving at his conclusion a standing ovation.

Two days later, he confided to his uncle, "I was amazed at the turnout."

"Ye might not have noticed, but I counted eight times the crowd applauded, not counting the ovation at the end. Your father and mither would have been very proud o' ye."

"I hope my speech does some good. Do you know how Cornelia is doing?"

"No, nothin' new. She's in Intensive Care and her condition is stable. Let's lift her up in prayer."

"Good idea, Uncle Mac."

After the two men had prayed, they sat in the living room and chatted about recent events.

"How's ADE doin' since Grifith was forced to leave?"

"Well, when the word got out that Mr. Grant removed him from ADE, some employees blamed me. They have the crazy idea he was removed so I could take his place."

"Are there many who think that?"

"Probably not. But enough to create a morale problem. Karl Lester thinks it's mainly Grifith's bowling team stirring up hard feelings against me. John has received several unsigned letters accusing me of things I didn't do. In fact, one letter accused me of something Grifith did," Richard said, chuckling.

"Where's Grifith now?"

"He was transferred to a new Grant Corporation company in Hungary—I think Budapest. John says he likes it there. He's still a manager, but at a lower level. Mr. Grant's giving him a second chance, because he was helpful when John was kidnapped."

"I thought ye might be keepin' company with Melissa today."

"We had a long time together yesterday after church. We agreed she should work to get caught up in her classes. Her grades went down when Carrington came into the picture. So, you're stuck with me this afternoon and evening."

"That's just fine, laddie. When di' ye head back to Dallas?"

"I was planning to leave Wednesday, but I think I'd better head back tomorrow. I want to meet with certain employees and try to resolve our differences."

"Let's put aside our problems and concerns for the time being and relax the rest o' the afternoon."

Richard turned on the TV while Mac ordered pizza.

"How aboot a nice salad to go with your pizza? I have lettuce, tomatoes, cabbage, carrots, and cucumber."

"Sounds good!"

Their dinner was only a pleasant memory when they turned on the local news at 6:00 PM. To their surprise, the first segment showed film clips from Richard's speech and his recent appearance on *City Talk*.

"Richard, last time you were on the show," Matt Crouch was saying, "you were critical of the city's leadership in keeping our streets repaired. Do you still feel that way?"

The news gave Richard's reply:

"Well, Matt, I didn't mean to come across as critical. I was puzzled, and still am. The city wants to add miles of new paving to one avenue, when we have numerous busy streets in poor shape. Our citizens should say to the city: 'Don't widen avenues, fill pot holes!'"

The studio audience vigorously applauded.

"Richard, we just heard a stirring sound of agreement. I feel sure many viewers are also applauding."

Crouch's words ended the news segment.

"Ye're receiving a lot o' coverage on your public appearances. There's a nice piece on your speech in the editorial page o' the *Banner*, with a photo o' ye waving your cane."

"I just hope the coverage translates into support for saving the homes of the Garden View tenants."

"Billy Bulwer said in a speech the ither day, widenin' the avenue would modernize traffic flow, but he dinna say how."

"Do you think this attorney who's decided to run against him can win?"

"Anthony Corelli is a gude man. He doesn't have Bulwer's money, but he's more likeable. I've played golf with him. That's a sport that shows how honest ye are. He counts every stroke whether anyone's lookin' or not."

The next day, Richard was on the plane for Dallas. He read articles in a couple of electronics' magazines, and made notes on what he might say in his meeting with disgruntled employees. When he arrived in Dallas, he looked for a taxi.

On my last trip back, Joe was waiting to chauffeur me to my destination. I can see how that kind of service could grow on you.

At ADE, employees he met on the way to his office greeted him warmly.

Looks like some employees are glad to see me, even a member of our bowling team and G.H.'s former secretary.

"Hi, Cindy. Any new developments I should know about?"

"No, not really." Smiling at a phone message she'd taken, she noted, "John Grant called this morning. He said he's losing weight and needs to get out to lunch with someone who eats cinnamon rolls."

"Tell him any time after today would be fine with me."

"Okay, Mr. Hawkins. Should I mention the cinnamon rolls?"

"Better not. Like me, he's never met a pastry he didn't like."

"You just missed Ben Jackson. He stopped by to give you a letter. I put it on your desk."

"Thanks, Cindy."

I wonder what that's about? He was probably G.H.'s best bowler and best friend. Guess I'll find out.

Sitting at his desk, Richard read the letter with surprise.

> Dear Mr. Hawkins,
>
> I received a letter from G.H. Grifith. He heard that some of us at ADE thought you were responsible for his transfer. He made it clear, you weren't. As you may have learned, he's now a manager in a company in Hungary.
>
> G.H. told me he agreed to a transfer, because of a problem between himself and Mr. Bruce Grant. He accepted blame for the problem.
>
> I'm sorry I blamed you for G.H.'s transfer from ADE. I've shown his letter to other employees at ADE, so they'll know the truth. If you still think we need to meet, I'll be glad to.
>
> Sincerely,
> Ben Jackson

"Cindy, please e-mail a cancellation of today's meeting."

Nice to have that take care of itself. I'll give Uncle Mac a call and update him, so he won't worry. He should be home at this hour.

Allowing his uncle's phone to ring several times, he was about to hang up when a familiar voice answered.

"Hi, Uncle Mac. Just wanted to let you know the employee problem I told you about worked itself out."

"Perhaps, laddie, your employee problem dinna 'work itself oot.' God may have intervened in answer to prayer."

"Yes. He's always there when we need Him. Which reminds me, any news about Cornelia?"

"She seems to be makin' a full recovery. I think seein' the public interest ye've aroused in savin' Garden View has encouraged her. She now has hope she can keep her home."

"I trust that hope is well-founded. How's the Garden View Fund doing?"

"Since your university speech, donations have increased. We received a generous donation from John Grant. Tell John, laddie, his gift will finance some radio ads."

"How long before demolition of Garden View is supposed to begin?"

"Two months. So far the city has given no indication o' a change o' plans, in spite o' considerable pressure by people in the community."

"I guess I'd better get back to work. Take care of yourself, Uncle Mac."

"I will, son. Ye di' the same."

The next day, Richard sat in his office working on a budget proposal and waiting for John to pick him up for lunch.

"Mr. Hawkins, Mr. Grant's driver is waiting out front."

"Thanks, Cindy. Would you have someone go out and tell him I'll be down in a few minutes?"

As Richard anticipated, the driver was John's bodyguard, Joe.

"Hi, Joe. I see you're providing transportation again."

"Yes, Mr. H. I'll have you at BG Oil in a jiffy."

Fastening his seatbelt, Richard sat back, somewhat tense.

I believe jiffy means jet speed. I wonder how many speeding tickets Joe's accumulated.

They arrived at BG as fast as Richard expected. John greeted him on the first floor of the administrative offices building.

In the elevator, John asked, "What do you think of my driver?"

"Well, you don't have a sense of growing older when Joe's driving. You arrive before you left."

While John laughed, Richard added, "But he's very courteous and a nice guy."

Leading the way into his office, John pointed at a blueprint and an architect's drawing of a building on his desk. "Before we head for the restaurant, I wanted to show you this."

"What is it?"

"It's the future home of the Virginia Grant Foundation. It'll be located in Portland."

"Nice design—looks like the architect sees the importance of natural light. It shows a lot of glass. Good idea. Portland has many dark days in the winter months."

"Construction has already started. Dad's talked for years about setting up a foundation in Mom's memory. He intends it to be a non-profit corporation with optional expenditures."

"What do you mean by 'optional expenditures'?"

"That bit of jargon means the foundation can spend income *and* assets in awarding grants to selected projects."

"How will the foundation be initially capitalized?"

"Modestly at first—five million. Dad has the assets; he's working on the building. He needs one more thing."

"Management?"

"Correct. Dad needs a trusted director to hire staff and run the foundation. He asked for my recommendation; I gave it, and he agreed."

"Probably not anyone I know."

"Actually, Rich, you know him very well. Dad and I would like *you* to be the director of our foundation."

"You've paid me a great compliment, John. I'm sure there are more . . ."

"I thought you'd tell me there are people more qualified than you. *You* have the qualifications we want, Rich."

"What I was going to say is, there are more qualified people than I, but, even so, I'd like the job."

"That's what I wanted to hear!" John exclaimed, grabbing Richard's hand and shaking it.

"But, before I make it a definite yes, I want to see what Melissa says and Uncle Mac, and pray about it. I'll give you my answer tomorrow."

"Before I recommended you, I asked myself, whom do I know that my mother would like to have direct her foundation, and you were the first person I thought of."

Reaching into his shirt pocket, Richard took out a pen. "That reminds me, when we were trying to locate the kidnappers, Mr. Grant lent me the pen your mother gave you. I took it home and kept forgetting to bring it back."

"Thanks, Rich. I think I'll keep it on my desk. When I look at it, I'll recall the good times she and I had together. Say, how 'bout having lunch here at our cafeteria?"

"Okay, but no cinnamon rolls."

The next day, Richard was in his office, when John called.

"Can you give me an answer yet, Rich?"

"Yes. I'll take the job. I called Melissa and Uncle Mac and they were enthusiastic about it. I've been sitting here praying and I believe this is an opportunity God would have me say yes to. Please pass my thanks on to Mr. Grant. I'll work hard to deserve his trust."

"I'll tell him. We both know you'll do a great job."

"Uncle Mac asked me if this job offer had anything to do with the furor over Grifith's removal. I said I didn't know."

"Even if the employees' response to Grifith's transfer hadn't happened, I would have recommended you for the job of director. I will say, there are still employees at ADE who hold a grudge against you, and, if you stayed, *might* make trouble for you."

"I guess I was naïve to think otherwise."

"Well, that's behind you, Rich. You have a new challenge ahead. A week from now, G.H.'s replacement will be at ADE. He'll take over your HR responsibilities until he can hire someone. Be prepared to leave when he comes. I'd like you to establish a temporary office in Verity, so you can get the ball rolling on the foundation. I think it'll be about a year before the foundation has a permanent site. That'll give you time to go through the legal hoops and learn what it takes to make it a smooth operation. I'll have the architect and the contractor get in touch with you in three weeks. Feel free to bring in a consultant. And, when you're back home, Rich, give my best to Melissa and her parents and to your Uncle Mac. I leave in a couple of days for Switzerland to represent Dad in a business meeting."

"Take care, John, and thanks for everything."

"Sure thing."

37

A Political Opportunity

FOLLOWING THE ARRIVAL OF Grifith's replacement at ADE, Richard returned to Verity. The first order of business was to locate a building he could rent that would provide a suitable office space for a staff of five people and himself.

Over a period of several days, he looked at many sites, but none proved acceptable. He was hoping to find a building that wouldn't need remodeling before he and staff could move in.

At the end of a day of office hunting, he came home tired and discouraged.

"Any luck today?" Uncle Mac asked.

"No, I just gave my bad leg a good workout. The next time I talk to John, I'd like to be able to say I've rented office space for the foundation."

"Had ye thought o' askin' Don Ingram to help ye, laddie? As a realtor, he probably knows people who manage rental property."

"Why didn't I think of that? I'm too inclined to think I have to do everything myself. This evening, I'll give Donald a call and hire him to help. I feel better about it already."

"That's gude. Di' ye hear any news today?"

"No. Why? Any news worth hearing?"

"Aye. Anthony Corelli dropped oot o' the race for mayor. His wife, who divorced him two years ago to marry another man, has accused him o' physical abuse. He's denied it, but it's his word against hers. If he tried to fight it, he said, it would be hard on their children."

"Yeah, it would be hard to fight a charge like that. Even if you win, you lose. His political career is barely started and now it's over. So, Bulwer is unopposed again."

"Aye, and it's interestin' that Bulwer employs the former Mrs. Corelli's second husband. I doubt I'm the only one suspicious aboot her motives."

Twenty-four hours after he was enlisted to help in locating office space, Donald gave Richard three good possibilities. One was a building nearing completion. Richard selected this one and arranged to rent all seven offices in it.

Glad to finally have a start on his new career, he went to the university library where he'd once worked and sought to educate himself about private foundations.

After examining several articles and books, Richard reflected on what he'd read:

I should meet with someone who directs or has directed a foundation to learn how the theory gets applied in the real world. I think the notes I've taken on evaluating grant requests will prove useful. But, before I stiffen up, I'd better stretch my legs. In fact, I think I'll call it a day.

He took a taxi directly home. Getting out, he saw a BMW parked in front and assumed his uncle had a visitor. Not feeling like talking to anyone at the moment, he entered the house quietly and started upstairs.

"Laddie, come here and meet a gentleman who wants to see ye!"

Richard turned around, shook off a feeling of weariness, and went into the living room. He saw an elderly man with white hair and a kind, smiling face. Slender of build, he appeared to be in his late 60s.

"Senator Siegel, this is my nephew, Richard Hawkins. Richard, Senator Daniel Siegel. He has somethin' he wants to talk with ye aboot."

Senator Siegel got up from his chair and shook Richard's hand. "Mr. Hawkins, I've heard you on the radio and seen you on television It's nice to meet you in person."

"What can I do for you, Senator?"

"Excuse me, gentlemen. I'll leave ye to talk, while I attend to my roses."

"Certainly, Mr. MacGregor. Mr. Hawkins, I'll come right to the point. As you doubtless have heard, Anthony Corelli had to drop out of the mayoral race, leaving us without a candidate to oppose Billy Bulwer. I represent a large group of people who are politically independent, who want you as their candidate for mayor. We believe your work in behalf of Garden View has made your name recognizable and has shown you to be a service-minded person. We also did a little checking on your background and didn't find anything that could be used against you. And, unlike Bulwer, you're a graduate of our local university and a life-long resident of our city."

"I'm pleased that you and those you represent see me as someone who would make a good mayor. I'm sorry, but I must decline your gracious offer. I recently accepted a position I believe will prove enjoyable and challenging."

"Your uncle mentioned that you'd been tapped to head up the new Grant Corporation foundation. Congratulations."

"Thank you."

"Actually, Mr. Hawkins, your new position would combine well with that of mayor. Since the mayor is part-time, the current mayor works only 15 to 20 hours a week. He meets with the City Council four Mondays and three Wednesdays a month. Because the mayor receives no salary, someone in that office must have an outside source of income."

"I didn't realize that. Guess it never came up in my political science classes."

"Probably, most of our citizens are uninformed about the workings of the mayor's office. They think it's full-time, because he or she gets so much coverage in the media. And, the mayor does set the agenda for the City Council."

"Whatever I think about the man personally, Bulwer has a leadership track record in business—something I, as yet, don't have."

"Yes, Mr. Hawkins, several of us discussed that. We decided character and charisma trump experience. Accomplishment is a two-edged sword—for many people it comes at the expense of others, as in the case of Mr. Bulwer."

"Whoever campaigns against Bulwer at this point, has only nine weeks to make his or her case. On the other hand, Bulwer, in effect, has been campaigning for months."

"We know the odds are against us. But, at least we want to give our citizens a choice between two visions of the city's future."

"I'm sorry Senator Siegel. I wish I could help you—I really do," Richard said, as he and the senator walked to the front door.

"Thanks for listening to what I had to say, Mr. Hawkins. If you should change your mind, please give me a call. Your uncle knows how to get a hold of me. I'm going to meet with a retired professor in a few days. He's indicated an interest in running. But, between us, he wouldn't have a chance of winning."

After the senator left, Richard stood by the door, deep in thought.

There's something about politics I find appealing. Maybe it's Aunt Jenny's influence when she told me how she campaigned. But, she's a natural—I'm not.

Following his conversation with Senator Siegel, Richard looked for his uncle in his rose garden.

"Uncle Mac, did you know why Senator Siegel wanted to talk with me?"

"I dinna know for sure. But I figured he wanted to do more than just have a chin wag. Did he ask ye to run for mayor?"

"Yes, Uncle Mac, he did."

"And what did ye tell him?"

"I said I had a job I liked—that I was sorry I couldn't say yes. I'm going to call the Ingrams and leave a message for Melissa. I'm going to invite her over after her class this evening."

"Tell her to plan on having dessert. I'll put my baker's hat on and make a cherry pie."

"That would be great. Do we have ice cream?"

"Does it rain in Oregon?"

"Okay, Uncle."

A knock at the front door signaled Melissa's arrival that evening. Opening the door, Mac welcomed their guest with a hug. "To see ye, is a balm to these old eyes. If Robert Burns had seen someone like ye in his day, he'd have sat right doon and written a poem."

"You're sweet. But, I don't think Robert Burns would have been so easily inspired. I'm sorry I'm late. I had a research paper due."

"Don't worry aboot it, my dear. Ye're never too late or too early in this hoose. Let's go into the livin' room. I want to show ye some photographs o' Richard when he was a wee bairn that I came across the ither day. Right now, he's upstairs makin' himself handsome for ye."

Mac guided Melissa to the sofa in the living room, where he'd placed an old photograph album. The two of them were looking through the album when a freshly-shaved Richard appeared.

"Uncle Mac has been showing me your baby pictures. You were a cute little guy—and now you're a cute *big* guy."

Getting up, Mac said, "I've got a cherry pie in the oven I'd better check on. I'm assumin' I could force a slice on ye a little later."

"I'll be ready for pie when you say the word. Richard and I will look at his baby pictures."

"Oh no," Richard said, sitting down beside Melissa. "Why should I look at baby pictures when I can look at a beautiful woman sitting next to me? Besides, I want to tell you about something that happened today."

"Something serious?"

"Not really. Just surprising."

"What was it?"

"I know it sounds hard to believe," Richard said, repressing a chuckle, "but there are people in this city who want me to run for mayor."

"I don't think it's 'hard to believe' at all."

"You don't?"

"This city needs a mayor who is youthful and idealistic and who cares about people—someone like you, Richy. My father was saying just last night that it was too bad that Billy Bulwer is unopposed. As he put it, he would 'come into office under the radar,' since nobody would have called him to account."

"Does your father know much about him?"

"Well, he knows enough not to trust or like him. He told me he served with him on a city planning committee a few years ago, and discovered they were on different sides on every traditional value that came up. He made no effort to hide the fact that he's anti-Christian. On one occasion, he said that America's whole history is one of selfish imperialism."

"I didn't realize he held such radical beliefs," Richard said, thoughtfully.

Later that evening, after Melissa had gone home and Uncle Mac had gone to bed, Richard turned on the TV and saw a political ad for Billy Bulwer. It strongly suggested that he supported higher taxes and more government control. His slogan was "New values for a new century."

If Bulwer is elected mayor, his agenda could end up making it harder for people to find jobs in Verity.

Richard started toward the stairs to go to bed, and then changed his mind. *I think I'll give John a call. It's later in Dallas, but he stays up late.*

Three rings and John answered.

"Hi, John. I didn't catch you at a bad time, did I?"

"No, not at all, Rich. I'm glad you called. I was feeling lonely, so I was looking for some food to keep me company. Your call saved me from going off my diet. How's it going up there?"

"I finally found a building to rent for the foundation. It's under construction—nearly completed. I'll send you some information and photos, as soon as I move in."

"If you want to unofficially, Rich. But, you don't need my approval. You're in charge. How are Melissa and Mac?"

"They're fine. Melissa's working hard on her classes, and Uncle Mac's giving a lot of time to saving Garden View. You know, John, I had an unexpected job offer today."

"Oh? What is it? I'm sure we can compete with any offer."

"A former state senator came to the house and said he represented a group that wanted me to run for mayor. It seems I have name recognition and have shown an interest in serving the community."

"Yes, he's right. What did you tell him?"

"I told him I couldn't run because I was starting a new job, and didn't want to disappoint my employers. Funny thing, John, I felt sorry I had to turn him down. I wouldn't mind giving Bulwer a run for his money."

"As I understand it, Richard, mayor of a city the size of Verity isn't all that demanding. Your city's under a 100,000 isn't it?"

"Yeah, somewhat. Senator Siegel said it's a part-time position that, on average, requires less than 20 hours a week. The present mayor meets with the City Council four Mondays and three Wednesdays a month."

"It doesn't pay much. Right?"

"It doesn't pay anything."

"So, as mayor, you're expected to be retired or have a salaried position that allows sufficient flexibility to serve as mayor."

"Yes, I suppose so."

"That describes you, Rich! If you want to spend 20 hours a week serving Verity as its mayor, the executive director of the Virginia Grant Foundation has the authority to do it. Dad and I would be happy to see you as mayor. We know the city would be in good hands. Extra publicity for the Foundation won't hurt, either."

"You think I ought to tell Senator Siegel I'll run?"

"I don't know, Rich. I do know you have the ability and courage to handle that kind of leadership. I also know campaigning for public office opens you up to personal attacks by people who prefer flamboyant lies to boring truth. You need a thick skin, Rich. *Politic* and *polite* don't come from the same Latin word."

"You're right, of course. I saw that sort of thing when Aunt Jenny ran for office."

"What are your chances of winning? I mean how well liked is this Billy Bulwer?"

"I think people who don't know him like him well enough. His image has benefited from giving money to various causes in the community. I think even a well-known candidate with experience would have a rough time beating him. If I ran, he'd probably make my youth an issue—and perhaps should."

"Well, if you decide to have a go at it, I'll help all I can. And, as far as your youth is concerned . . . you're 27 aren't you?"

"Yeah."

"Remember, William Pitt in the 19th Century, became Prime Minister of Great Britain at 24. When will you decide about entering the race?"

"If I decide to run, I must contact Senator Siegel before he asks another man, whom, he says, can't win. I have to decide in three or four days."

"I'd like to serve as chairman of fund raising, if you run, Rich."

"That'd be a great help, John. But, how could you afford to take time away from corporate responsibilities?"

"I couldn't except for Rachel Fine, my assistant. Remember I introduced you to her at a meeting a couple of months ago."

"Yes, I remember. She jotted something down every time I made a comment in the meeting."

"Sure. That's because she found your comments worth recording. I've been giving her more and more of my responsibilities, so I can get out of the office and talk to people. I could easily arrange to fly back and forth between Dallas and Verity to volunteer."

"It would certainly strengthen my candidacy. I'll call you in a few days and tell you what I've decided."

"Okay, Rich. That's one call I'll look forward to."

38

Hat in the Ring

At 8:00 AM, Mac walked into the kitchen and found Richard, dressed in pajamas and a bathrobe, sipping coffee.

"I never expected to see ye up this early, laddie, when ye don't have to be."

"I didn't sleep very well last night. I kept wondering whether I should run for mayor or not. You haven't told me what you think, Uncle Mac."

"Well, Richard, I dinna want to influence ye one way or anither. It's a solo decision ye have to make."

"I suppose you're right. I e-mailed Aunt Jenny. I told her I thought my job as foundation director would go well with the part-time job of mayor. She said, 'Throw your hat into the ring! We need young men like you in politics, nephew.' Said she'd be praying for me."

"I'm sure, ye've been prayin', too."

"Yes, I've been asking God to help me make the right decision. Campaigning for office is one thing, Uncle, being elected is something else."

"I'm not followin' ye, laddie."

"Campaigning is a temporary commitment. If I lose, well, it'll just be an interesting experience."

"Aye, it would."

"But, if I *win*, I'll be taking on a long-term commitment. Would such a commitment be God's purpose for me? That's the question I've been seeking an answer to."

"Has the Holy Spirit given ye the leadin' ye asked for?"

"For the past few days I've prayed for guidance. This morning, I cleared my mind and waited on the Lord. Then, almost as if the Lord spoke to me, I thought, yes, I'll enter the race—all my misgivings were gone. As Aunt Jenny put it, I'll 'throw my hat into the ring.'"

"Why di' ye think it's important for ye to run?"

"The more I hear about Billy Bulwer, the more he reminds me of a professor I met in my coma. Though it may sound strange, he's as real to me as Cal Jessup or John Grant, or even you, Uncle. Barnhart or Barnacle—as his students called him—taught or preached, the same stuff as Bulwer spouts."

"Aye."

"Win or lose, I can give people in our city a choice between two very different worldviews. But if I don't win, it won't be because I haven't tried with all my strength."

"When di' ye plan to tell the senator your decision?"

"I'd better call him this morning and let him know I'm on the bandwagon and he can start the campaign wheels turning. He said you had his number."

"It's by the telephone. I thought ye might need it. We need the hoose ready to hold meetin's here. I'll lay in a supply o' refreshments, and rent some foldin' chairs."

"Can't we borrow chairs from the church?"

"I don't think that's a gude idea, laddie. Bulwer would get wind o' it and accuse ye o' not separatin' church and state. He may anyway, but why make it easy for him?"

"Yes, of course. I'm up against a shrewd opponent; I'd better start thinking like a politician."

"Shrewd's a kind word ye use to refer to Billy Bulwer. There are ither words that might suit him better."

Richard smiled and nodded.

The senator was relieved to hear Richard's decision.

"I can't tell you how pleased I am that you've decided to run, Mr. Hawkins. There are people you know and others you don't know, who are ready to support your campaign. Many are members of the opposing party, but most are simply opposed to Bulwer's views and values."

"That's my main reason for running. I don't like what he stands for. You know, I'm going to need to put together a campaign committee, and do it fast."

"In case you agreed to run, I made a list of potential committee members with a description of each. And, I want to introduce you to Jim Nicolson. In his home state, he managed two campaign committees, one for mayor and one for governor—both candidates he supported won. I have reason to believe he would serve as your campaign manager, if you asked him. Jim is a man of integrity and intelligence, and is plenty savvy when it comes to politics. He's also a good family man. Would you like me to ask him for you?"

"Please. Think he'd have time to take my campaign on?"

"He recently retired as head of a large law firm. He's in his late 60s and in good health. Not long ago, he told me he was tired of fishing and playing golf. He wants to be more active and your campaign fills the bill."

"I hope he likes a challenge."

"He's a tough competitor, as Bulwer may find out."

"Does he know about my disability, Senator?"

"I'm sure he does. How about getting on a first name basis, Richard? My friends call me Dan."

"Okay, Dan."

"I'll contact Jim right away. Even if he says no to serving as campaign manager, I know he'll join our committee as a senior advisor."

After the two men said their good byes, Richard found his uncle in the kitchen.

"Di' ye learn anythin' new from Senator Siegel?"

"I should say, Uncle. He has a campaign committee selected, and knows a chap by the name of Jim Nicolson, who might serve as campaign manager."

"Nicolson ye say—should be a good choice."

"Do you know him?"

"I know he's a Scotsman; he bears the name of a great Scottish clan."

The next morning, Richard got up early again and beat his uncle into the kitchen. He had a breakfast of oatmeal, toast, and orange juice ready before his uncle made an appearance.

"What? Two mornings in a row? And dressed and shaved. Di' ye have trouble sleeping again, son?"

"No, I slept like a log—whatever that means—I decided I had to learn new habits if I'm to handle two jobs. I got up pretty early when I worked at ADE."

"Aye. We learn to do what we have to do."

While they ate, Mac worked on a crossword puzzle and Richard worked on the day's schedule.

"Uncle Mac, didn't you used to have a copy of *The Dialogues of Plato*?"

"Aye. Why di' ye ask?"

"If it turns out I get a chance to debate Bulwer, I figured I should know more about the source of his belief system."

"Gude thinkin'. I'll go up to my room and get it. I was lookin' through it, after Bulwer mentioned Plato."

"I'll get it, Uncle Mac. It'll be good exercise for my leg."

"Alright, if ye insist. It's on the night stand, beside the lamp."

Book in hand, Richard headed for an easy chair in the living room. Skimming through the book, he occasionally made notes in a tablet.

This is a pathetic substitute for the Bible is all I've got to say. I feel sorry for the man—preferring Plato to Jesus.

After a short trip to check on the Foundation building's progress, Richard noticed Uncle Mac waiting for him on the porch.

"I'm glad to see ye home, laddie. Senator Siegel's bringin' Mr. Nicolson over to see ye."

Shortly afterward, Richard met the tall, slim man with wavy white hair, dressed in a blue sports coat, white dress shirt, and sharply pressed gray slacks.

I should have dressed up, myself. Nicholson looks like Charlton Heston in his role as President Andrew Jackson.

Senator Siegel introduced Richard and Mac and the four men sat.

"Richard, I was very glad to hear you're going to run for mayor. And, I would be happy to serve as your campaign manager."

"Thank you. That's good news. I'm sure you know, when it comes to politics, I'm a novice. I'm going to have to depend on you throughout this campaign."

"Well, Richard, that's exactly what a candidate should do, but many don't. And, as a result, their foolish mistakes often cost them an election. I think your opponent has made such a mistake."

"Oh? What was that?"

"This morning, Mr. Bulwer fired his campaign manager. As I understand it, he plans to take charge of his campaign himself."

"Di' ye think that will make much difference, Jim?"

"Yes, Mac, I do. The man he fired is a clever political tactician. As we say in my profession, a man who defends himself in court, has a fool for a lawyer. It's equally foolish to be your own campaign manager."

"Jim, how do I officially become a candidate for mayor? You see, I don't even have the most basic information. In my Poli Sci classes we didn't go into that in any detail."

"It so happens, Richard, I brought along the candidate application packet for Verity. There are several forms you have to fill out. We'll file *them* and the nonpartisan nominating petition with the City Recorder's Office."

"What's a 'nonpartisan nominating petition'?"

"The City Recorder will look over our sample petition, Richard, and then send you a letter authorizing the collection of signatures on the petition."

"How many signatures do ye need to have?"

"At least 30 signatures of registered voters who live in Verity. But, I would recommend at least 50, Mac. Just in case some of them are disqualified."

"Will there be any trouble about my living in Dallas for a time?"

"The City Code says that if a candidate has more than one residence, the principal residence must be in Verity. This means, for instance, he or she receives important mail at the Verity address, such as Oregon and federal tax forms."

"Yes, I've used this address for all my important papers. I recently used this address for a health insurance policy. And, for the time being at least, I'll be living here full time."

"The Code allows a candidate to take a temporary job outside of the city for a brief period. Did you transfer your church membership to Dallas?"

"No."

"Well, then, I don't think we'll have a problem regarding your residence. I'll stop by in a couple of days to see how you're doing on the forms. We should get them to the Recorder as soon as possible," Jim said, as he got up to leave.

Standing up also, Richard asked, "Is there anything I should do besides the forms?"

"Nothing right now. In the event the press learns of your candidacy, don't grant any interviews, not yet, anyway. Before you do any interviews, I want you to meet with somebody who will teach you how to respond to reporters' questions and comments. Reminds me, I brought you a copy of a TV interview Bulwer did recently. I thought you and Mac might like to watch. Well, I'd better be off."

"I hope I can make a good race of it, against a man who has more experience."

Daniel paused to give Richard a slow smile. "I remember something President Dwight D. Eisenhower once said, 'What counts is not necessarily the size of the dog in the fight—it's the size of the fight in the dog.' Right Mac?"

"Aye. Ye're right, Daniel."

After Daniel and Jim had gone, Mac said, "We'd better wait 'til after lunch to watch Bulwer's interview. I might lose my appetite. I'll bet this is the one I was tellin' ye aboot."

39

Ready to Run

A COUPLE OF HOURS after lunch, Richard asked, "What do you think, Uncle Mac? Should we tackle Bulwer's interview?"

"Well, my boy. I've seen it and I'm not ready for an encore performance. It's true I dinna see the first few minutes, but ye can fill me in later. I have somethin' more pleasant to do."

"What's that, Uncle?"

"I'm goin' to give Karen Olson a call."

"Tell her hello for me."

"I will."

Matt Crouch opened the interview by asking, "Mr. Bulwer, how old were you when you were a beatnik?"

"Now, let's get this straight, Matt," Bulwer replied. "I wasn't *ever* a beatnik. I was a hippie."

"Were they very different?" Crouch asked.

"Were they very *different*!" repeated Bulwer, his tone a little contemptuous. "Like night and day! My older brother was a beatnik. All he and his friends did was sit around in coffee houses, hating themselves. They were angry young men who figured the world wasn't worth saving. They knew what was wrong, but they didn't care to do anything about it."

"I take it, Mr. Bulwer, that the hippies not only knew what was wrong, they cared to do something about it. Is that right?" prompted Crouch.

"Right on, man! We shut down universities, businesses, and city governments 'til they heard us! We made them listen to us with sit-ins, protest marches, and rallies. Our leaders spoke with one common theme: freedom from rules and regulations imposed by outdated traditions."

"Mr. Bulwer, what did hippies achieve that you'd call positive?" Crouch queried.

"We freed people from society's big cookie cutter that stamped everybody with the same outlook. We taught people to question authority, whether parents, teachers, cops, or presidents. And, I'm proud to say, Matt, that the hippie movement is still influencing our society today. That, I might add, needs to continue, so that people have personal freedom to do their own thing."

"Where does the word *hippie* come from?"

"You don't *know*? Come on, Matt."

"I wanted your definition, Mr. Bulwer."

"Well, as most informed people know, we were called 'hippies,' because we were *hip*. That meant we were aware. We were tuned in. With it. You see, Matt, we knew the score, what was in and what was out."

From this point on, the interview focused on subjects that Mac had earlier reviewed with Richard.

Shaking his head, Richard was impressed by how passionately Bulwer spoke of Plato. *It's a wonder he doesn't refer to him as his mentor.*

"I understand, Mr. Bulwer, you hold Plato in high regard."

"Matt, Plato taught that the difference between virtue and vice is the 'sacred and golden cord of reason' which we need to grab hold of and never let go."

"I see," responded Crouch in a tone lacking sincerity.

After watching the interview, Richard went in search of his uncle and found him on the porch, pruning a windmill palm in a large terra cotta pot.

Turning from his task, Mac asked, "Di' ye hear anythin' interestin' from Billy Bulwer?"

"More disturbing than interesting. I was amazed at how candid he was. He let it all hang out, as they said in the 60s. I don't think he speaks for the average person in this city, though."

"Aye. He certainly doesn't speak for me or my friends. But, I've heard he does speak for many o' the people in the community."

"I'm sorry to hear it. I wonder if they really know what he believes."

"Probably not to the extent they should."

"Well, I'd better work on the forms for the City Recorder. I want to get them done right away, so I can go over them with Jim."

After several hours writing responses on the City Recorder's forms, Richard called Melissa to update her on what he had learned earlier from Jim. They planned to meet the next day for dinner and to discuss wedding arrangements.

Richard hummed a tune and washed breakfast dishes, while Mac sat at the kitchen table, reading the morning paper. "You know, Uncle Mac, you're welcome to join Melissa and me at dinner this evening."

"What di' ye say, laddie?"

"I said you're welcome to join us this evening for dinner."

"It's gude o' ye to ask me. But, ye see I have a date with Karen Olson, unless one of her patients needs her."

The telephone rang.

"If it's Melissa, tell her to hold for a couple of minutes."

After a brief absence, Mac returned. "It was Jim Nicolson on the phone. He'll be here in aboot an hour."

Upstairs, Richard carefully reviewed the forms that the City Recorder's Office required.

"Richard! Jim's here!"

Jim handed Richard several sheets of paper. "Here are the nominating signatures you need. There are more than 100, all registered voters who live within the city."

Glancing quickly through the list revealed no familiar names. "I don't seem to recognize any of these people."

"Actually, Richard, most of them don't know you either. They only know what I and others have told them. Frankly, many are voting against Bulwer by supporting you. But that's politics."

Smiling, Richard replied, "I hope I can get their support for what I am, and not just for what Bulwer isn't."

"I'm sure you will once the voters have a chance to see and hear you. I was told you majored in communications in college."

"Yes. I studied interpersonal communication, public speaking, and debate—along with other subjects."

"Debate you say. Good. Now, did you have any trouble with the forms?"

At that point, Mac entered quietly with cups and a pot of coffee, and left without saying anything.

"There is one other form you have to file."

"Oh? What's that?"

"A candidate's statement of expected expenditures. Then, during the campaign, you must submit financial reports regularly on donations and expenditures. From what you told me, your friend, John Grant, will be in charge of the financial reports."

"Yes, that's right. How much money do you think we'll have to raise to finance the campaign?"

"I don't know exactly. I would guess in the neighborhood of $80,000. I believe Bulwer has spent about $30,000. You can be sure when he finds out he's no longer unopposed, he'll spend a lot more. He'll put more ads on television, including attack ads against you. And, of course we'll run some ads of our own. Those ads will be a big part of our budget."

"You mentioned you wanted me to meet with someone who would tell me how to talk with reporters. When do you want me to do that?"

"As soon as possible. Before we take your candidate application forms to the City Recorder—and before the press learns you're going to run for mayor."

"Well then, how about tomorrow?"

"Yes, I think I can arrange it that soon. They're already hired. It's just a matter of making sure they have time available tomorrow. They need three to four hours. Rod and Kay Stevenson are a husband and wife team. And believe me, they know their business; they've helped several people get elected to state and national offices." Jim took a last sip of coffee and got up to leave.

"One last thing. Give John Grant a call and see if he can be with us early next week for a campaign committee meeting. I'll stop by the Stevenson's office and see if they can meet with you tomorrow. They'll call to let you know."

The two men shook hands at the door. Before leaving, Jim said, "Tell Mac he makes a good cup of coffee."

40

Facing the Media

RICHARD AND MAC ROSE early ready to receive their guests. Richard's media mentors, Rod and Kay Stevenson, arrived promptly at 7:00.

"Could we move a few pieces of furniture in your living room?" Kay asked.

"Aye. Can I help?"

"No, Mr. MacGregor, but thanks for offering."

Seeing Richard's puzzled expression, Rod said, "We want to simulate a TV studio set for an interview. Kay will sit down with you and ask some questions and you'll answer the way you would for a TV audience. I'll have my camcorder set up to get it on tape."

Rod and Kay then moved all the furniture away from one wall, except for two chairs that they placed facing each other.

Rod picked the wall he thought would provide the best light.

"Now, Richard," Kay said, "if you'll walk onto the set the way you would in the studio."

"I can walk better, if I use my cane."

"By all means, use your cane."

Richard walked to his chair as instructed.

"Do you have to walk with your head and shoulders bent?" Kay asked.

"No, I guess it's just a habit from looking out for anything I could trip over."

"You should walk onto the set with your head up and your shoulders back. Let your body language show that you're a confident leader with a message you believe in. That you're glad to be here."

"Okay, I'll try it again." And he walked to his chair.

"That's better, Richard. But you still need to get your head higher. Think about keeping your chin up. And look more relaxed, less serious."

Richard stood as straight as he could and started to walk.

"Yes, good posture," Kay said encouragingly. "Now, imagine you're going to see your fiancée. Yes. That's the expression I want—looking forward to something pleasant." "I was for a moment," Richard said with a smile.

"Walk onto our set one more time and sit down," Kay instructed. "Then I'll sit down and begin by introducing you briefly to the audience. I'll look at the camera and you look at me."

When they were seated, Kay began, "Mr. Hawkins, I want to thank you for coming onto the program to talk about your run for mayor. I know our viewers want to hear why you are running."

"I grew up in this city, Kay. I went to public school here. And I attended our local university, where my father, before his death, was a professor. I had jobs here that taught me about life. I owe this city a great deal. I want to contribute my leadership abilities to make it an even better city for more of our citizens. As mayor, I would work to preserve and strengthen the family values and great traditions that have made our city livable, prosperous, and safe."

"Mr. Hawkins, do you foresee any problems that might make Verity less livable in the years to come?"

"I would rather use the word *challenges* instead of 'problems,' Kay. In the last two years, Verity has seen a 10,000 person population increase. Many have come from other countries. We're a city of just under 100,000 citizens. This fast growth has put a strain on civic services and facilities. As a result, we face new challenges that threaten the welfare of people in our neighborhoods and communities."

Richard was next questioned about a proposed sales tax and, while gesturing, knocked his cane to the floor that he'd propped up against his chair. "Excuse me," he said, as he bent to pick it up.

Before the exercise was over, Richard responded to questions on the subjects of urban renewal, environmental issues, street gangs, and road maintenance. Occasionally, Kay would interrupt him to see how he would react.

At the close of the exercise, Kay said, "I must say, Mr. Hawkins, I didn't expect you to be so knowledgeable about such a wide variety of topics."

"I've grown up discussing local and national issues with Uncle Mac. When I was in college, I worked in the library and got used to reading the newspapers daily. After I went to Dallas, I had the papers sent to me, so I could keep up with the news."

After a short break, Richard and the Stevensons watched the interview.

"Notice, Richard, your body language showed irritation when Kay interrupted you. Don't react. Expect to be interrupted. The reporter is doing her job."

At a later point in the interview, Kay remarked how she paused after Richard answered a question, which caused him to say more on the subject. "That's a technique reporters use to get you to fill the silence, and perhaps say something you didn't intend to."

"Yes, and I stepped into the trap," Richard said, shaking his head.

"Well, it's a natural tendency to talk to fill a silence," Kay replied. "But, you did avoid a leading question I hit you with."

"Oh, when was that?"

"Remember toward the end of the interview, I asked you: 'Don't you agree with most people that the police need to do more to control street gangs?' And you answered: 'It's a complex issue. Street gangs haven't been a serious problem until recently.' A good answer. It leaves you free to say more later."

"You were also careful," said Rod, "not to say anything negative about your opponent, even when Kay gave you a chance to do so."

"The 'chance' you mention, Rod, would have required me to focus on him personally, rather than on his ideas. One thing that really bugs me about politics is personal attacks. Politicians use them to bolster weak arguments in my opinion."

"Personal attacks *can* be effective in discrediting an opponent. But the politician who resorts to them, may pay a price in perceived loss of integrity," asserted Rod.

"Unfortunately, Richard, you can expect Billy Bulwer to resort to personal attacks in debating you," said Kay. "What if Bulwer suggested that your disability would prevent you from performing well as mayor?"

"I'd respond that running for mayor doesn't mean just using my legs, it means using my brain to benefit our city."

"I like that response," said Rod, "it has a touch of humor. Although, I think Bulwer would be too smart to say something so politically incorrect."

"I think you'll be fine in talking with the press," Kay said and looked in Rod's direction, who nodded in agreement.

"I'm glad you think so. I'll do my best."

"I'm sure you will. Just remember to stay in control. Reporters look for anything controversial in what you say. It's okay to say you want to give an issue more thought before making a statement."

Rod, who had been packing up equipment and moving furniture back in place, said "The recording is on the table. We recommend that you play it again and critique yourself. Consider where you could put your cane, so you wouldn't risk dropping it. Give us a call if you have any questions."

Mac joined Richard in saying good-bye to the Stevensons and thanking them for their help.

"I hope I'm not too early," Jim Nicolson said, on entering the house at Mac's invitation. "I wanted to have Richard at the City Recorder's Office soon after it opened."

"Your timin' is gude, Jim. We beat the birds up this mornin'. Since Richard decided to run for mayor, there's been a lot less sleepin' in this hoose. He'll be doon in a minute."

"Have you had a chance to watch Richard's practice interview?"

"Aye, I've seen it twice. I gave Richard a couple o' suggestions."

At that point, Richard made an appearance. "I'm ready to go. I've got the forms and documents on my double residency that you said I should bring."

Mac stood at the front window and watched the two men get into Jim's car. As they drove off, he prayed, "Lord, be with my boy. Help him to clear this first hurdle, if it be your will."

Then to get his mind on other things, he went into the kitchen and cleaned away the signs of breakfast. *It shouldn't take long to drop off the forms and come back.*

But an hour and a half passed and still no Richard. To further distract himself, Mac took his weeding stool out to the backyard to work.

Two hours later, he was beginning to worry when he heard a car engine in the driveway and voices. He walked around the house in time to wave at Jim as he left. Mac joined Richard on the porch.

"I hope you weren't worried about me, Uncle Mac. But I'm learning that in politics, you never know what's going to happen."

"Can ye tell me, laddie, what *did* happen?"

"Well, we spent about an hour in the City Recorder's Office. We provided the forms and nominating signatures. And I had to answer a lot of questions, before my candidacy was approved. While we were there, someone must have tipped off the press. Because when we came out of the building, there were newspaper and TV reporters waiting for us on the lawn. So, I've had my first press conference."

"Di' ye think it went okay?"

"Jim said I did fine. Mostly they asked me questions that Rod and Kay told me to expect. So I was pretty well prepared. Though I did get one question I didn't expect."

"What was that, laddie?"

"One reporter asked me: 'Don't you think many voters won't vote for you because of your age?' And I answered: 'You're right! Some voters will think I'm too old'. Everyone laughed. I added: 'Seriously, two things age you. One is time, and the other is circumstances. I've aged because of both. Therefore, I'm older than I look.'"

"Gude for ye, Richard. I'm glad ye could keep your sense o' humor."

"You'll be able to judge how the press conference went yourself. It'll be on the 6:00 o'clock news tonight. And there'll be a story in the morning paper."

"I'll tell ye what, laddie. Let's go oot to dinner tonight to celebrate the start o' your campaign for mayor."

"Great. If we leave early, we can be back for the news. I'll call the Ingrams. Melissa will want to watch it too."

In the following weeks, Richard met with his campaign committee several times. Membership included two speech writers—both under 30 and experienced in writing speeches for politicians. They soon learned to adapt to Richard's style, humor, and his careful structure. As he gained more knowledge of the issues and confidence in speaking, he made more changes in the speeches written for him. In a speech at the university, he held his cane high above his head and said, "We need to push against the artificial ceiling of mediocrity." After that, audiences expected him to gesture with his cane whenever he emphasized a key concern.

41

The Race Is On

THREE WEEKS BEFORE THE election, Richard met with Jim to develop strategy for the last phase of the campaign.

"Remember in the early weeks of your campaign you were 30 points behind in the polls?" Jim asked. "Well, according to a poll released today, you've cut Bulwer's lead down to 10 points."

"Yes, thanks to you and the other members of my committee."

"Don't sell yourself short, Richard. You've been a persuasive candidate on the stump. And, I think you'll be persuasive as a debater."

"What do you mean? Why should he debate me when he's ahead?"

"The press has been hinting that he's afraid to debate you. I've been counting on his arrogance to lead him to agree to one. I got the news last night—he's ready to debate you on Matt Crouch's show."

"When is it?"

"That's the part I don't like. He wants it Wednesday—five days from now."

"That's okay with me. I've been prepping for a debate for weeks. Give it to the press. Tell 'em I look forward to giving the public a chance to compare two very different points of view."

Wednesday afternoon, Richard arrived early at the television studio. He knew his chance of winning the election hinged on this debate.

By contrast, Bulwer sauntered in late. He affected an arrogant, superior manner toward everyone, including the host, Matt Crouch.

Staging put Crouch in the center, seated at a small table. Richard was seated on Crouch's right, and Bulwer on his left.

After a brief introduction, Crouch turned to Bulwer first and asked why voters should prefer him to Richard Hawkins.

Obviously pleased with the question, Bulwer replied, "The voters see in me an experienced leader. I run a successful organization. I'm an able-bodied man, who can take the strain of leading a thriving city. I'm not wet behind the ears. I'm in possession of my faculties, something Mr. Hawkins can't say for certain, poor man, after three months in a coma. I've had the advantage of growing up in a home with two loving parents, whereas my opponent, sadly, was raised by a distant relative. This puts him at a disadvantage, through no fault of his own, in grasping what a normal family is up against in putting bread on the table."

Bulwer's rudeness and disregard of political correctness left Crouch speechless for a moment. Then collecting himself, he turned to Richard with an apologetic expression and asked him the same question.

With no sign of anger or hurt, Richard responded, "I seek the votes of my fellow citizens, because I believe I can make a difference as mayor. If the voters call me to service, I promise to deal with problems we face before they become crises. I'll strive to make the best use of assets, human, financial, and material. During my campaign, I've met with a series of focus groups on such topics as jobs, education, environment, energy, and crime. I believe the combination of my youth, my upbringing, my three *weeks* in a coma and my disability has made me sensitive to people's needs and given me a desire to do something positive to help."

As the program went on, Crouch asked the candidates questions on various key issues. He allowed each man a few minutes to react to the other man's statement. He asked the candidates about jobs, which provoked little disagreement. Then he asked about a sales tax that would pay for city services. Bulwer spoke in support of a sales tax. "Verity then," he said, "could provide services that would create jobs."

Richard took the exact opposite position, which caused Bulwer to go on the attack.

"Hawkins is simply tellin' voters what they want to hear. The truth is the city needs revenue for projects that would impact employment."

"What do you say to that, Mr. Hawkins?" asked Crouch.

"I don't believe a sales tax is the way to go. It would raise the cost of living, which would reduce consumer spending on goods and services. As a result, the local economy would produce fewer jobs. Plus, companies, that would bring jobs to our city, would be less likely to build here. Also, a sales tax would hit the poor the hardest."

"Speaking of taxes," said Crouch, "one of the dominant concerns of taxpayers in our city is the cost of public education. They want to know why all this money hasn't reduced the number of high school dropouts? Would you like to comment, Mr. Bulwer?"

"Yeah, Matt. You can't force somebody to learn—if they don't want to. I think it's better to wait 'til they're ready. I remember one time in high school, I was sittin' in a classroom, and some of us saw snow comin' down. And one of my friends asked if we could get out early. The teacher looked out the window and said, 'There are no more flakes outside than there are inside.'" Bulwer chuckled as he recalled the situation.

"Mr. Hawkins, how would you respond to Mr. Bulwer?"

"I agree that the students have to want to learn to stay in school. But we shouldn't give up on them. We need graduates who can fill 21st century jobs that require specific knowledge and skills. Many students, I've discovered, have been passed along before mastering the content of the previous grade. Then in high school, they reach a point where the material is so far beyond them they become frustrated and quit."

"I'd like to conclude this debate. What book has influenced you the most? Mr. Hawkins, let's start with you."

"The book that's been most helpful, especially when I've needed direction for my life, is the *Bible*."

"And, Mr. Bulwer, which book would you choose?"

"Matt, one book is real now—*The Dialogues of Plato*."

"To leave our audience with a little wisdom, would you each share two favorite quotations, from secular sources. Uh, Mr. Bulwer, do you have a couple to pass along?"

"Hmm, let me see. A friend of mine who chose living in Canada over fighting in Vietnam gave me this: 'A wise man sees as much as he ought, not as much as he can.' And then on our company calendar: 'The farther backward you can look, the farther forward you are likely to see.' The first is from Michel deMontaigne, and the second from Winston Churchill."

"Now your two quotations, Mr. Hawkins."

"Secular sources, huh?"

"Yes."

"A quote I've come to like since my accident is: 'Great thoughts reduced to practice become great acts.' That's from William Hazlitt. A second quote I like is: 'Whatever is saved and comes to good is saved by the power of God, as we may truly say.' The source . . ."

"Hawkins, didn't you hear Matt? He said *secular* sources," Bulwer rebuked sneeringly.

"That's correct, I did, Mr. Hawkins," Crouch affirmed gently.

"Yes, I understood, Matt. The source is Plato."

Mac later reported that when the camera zoomed in on Bulwer's face, it was beet red. "Hard to tell whether from anger or embarrassment."

The next afternoon, Richard had a scheduled meeting at Jim's. He arrived a little late to find Jim waiting for him at the front door.

"I've been looking forward to shaking your hand, Richard! You did a great job last night! Did you happen to catch the news on the radio this morning?"

"No, I'm afraid I overslept this morning. I got ready in 45 minutes," Richard added with a smile, "so I could get here late."

"I heard on the radio that the TV station did a poll immediately after the debate. The results found, that 63 percent of those who viewed the debate thought you'd won. Believe me, Richard, that is a big upset for Bulwer's supporters in the press."

"Were they so sure that Bulwer would win the debate?"

"Yes, I believe they were. In their editorials this morning, they devoted their talents to making excuses for him. Let's go into my study and I'll read one of them to you."

Richard followed Jim and took a seat. "I thought I'd won," he said, "but I'm surprised that the poll showed I won by that big a margin. Of course, I'm glad."

Picking up a newspaper, Jim said, "Here's how one editorial writer explained your win: 'It wasn't that Mr. Hawkins won. It was that Mr. Bulwer lost. His candid comparison between himself and his young opponent foolishly violated the rules of political courtesy. He called attention to Mr. Hawkins' disability, something in today's cultural climate, a politician simply can't do. One must admit that Mr. Hawkins showed class in the perspective he offered on his disability.' He goes on to say that by winning the debate, you now have a chance to win the election. I agree."

"After you told me that the polls had me within 10 points of Bulwer, I really began to believe I had a chance. Winning the debate has made me think that I *can* defeat Bulwer for mayor."

"Of course you can. Headquarters fielded calls from at least 50 people who watched the debate last night and now want to work as volunteers on your campaign. You'll be happy to hear that a lot of them were university students. They especially disliked Bulwer's negative remarks about your youth."

"I'll never be able to repay the many volunteers who have worked on my campaign."

"Being the person they believe you to be is repayment enough. But, there is a potential problem—one editorial hinted at it. And I've heard that Bulwer has started a whisper campaign to turn it into an issue."

"I can't think what that would be."

"Some people are saying you're running for mayor so, when elected, you can prevent the city from widening the avenue by leveling Garden View Apartments. Your opponent is saying that's the only reason you want to be mayor."

"But that's not true," said Richard with concern.

"In politics it doesn't have to be true. I'm sorry to say, truth doesn't count with some politicians. If I remember right it was the historian Henry Adams who said, 'Practical politics consists in ignoring facts.' I think you should offer a rebuttal right away."

Richard made no response for a moment. "Let me think . . . In my next speech, I'll say something like this: Some people who oppose my candidacy have said I seek to become mayor just so I might help the Garden View tenants retain their homes. That would be carrying concern beyond common-sense. If I should be elected, my commitment would be to all neighborhoods and communities in our city."

"Yes, you answer the accusation and stay on the high road doing it. I like that line, 'carrying concern beyond common-sense.'"

"What do you think I should do in the final week of campaigning?"

"I've lined up several speaking events for you. And, you should get more press coverage now after winning the debate. We'll also run a new TV ad with segments of your debate."

"Whatever you think, Jim. I think what I'll do now is call a taxi, go home, and get some rest—before you put me to work again."

For the next five days, Richard delivered speeches each day to various civic groups. Melissa adjusted her schedule so she could be with him at these events. After he would deliver a speech, he would take her arm to steady himself while he shook hands with audience members. This arrangement allowed him to introduce his fiancée to the people he met.

Following his last speech, Melissa was driving Richard home, when she asked, "Are you glad the campaigning is over?"

"Oh, I don't know. In some ways I am, I guess. But overall, it was a good experience. I've made a lot of new friends I wouldn't have made otherwise. And you know, Melissa, I hope the voters give me the chance to put the ideas I talked about in my speeches into practice. This campaign has made me realize how many things need to be done."

"I don't have to tell you that if you're elected, and you try to do the things you said in your speeches, there will be certain groups that'll fight you."

"Yeah, you're right. Before my accident, I don't think I could have taken the spins and smears as well as I can now. But since my accident, I'm tougher. Personal attacks don't bother me much. Maybe because in my coma I saw the weakness of the hippies' attacks against traditional values. We hear the same attacks today. And when we take a stand against them, we prove how weak they are."

"I guess a leader who wants to accomplish anything," said Melissa, shaking her head, "can't worry about being popular with everybody."

"That reminds me of something Jim told me. He quoted Abraham Lincoln as saying: 'Avoid popularity if you would have peace.' I wrote those words down, so I wouldn't forget them."

"Oh, there's Mac on the porch," Melissa said, as she drove up in front of the house. "Can you come in for a while?"

"No, I promised Mom I would help her get ready for a meeting at the house."

"I'll call you this evening," Richard promised.

Richard took a seat beside his uncle on the porch. "I used to take those steps two at a time," he said. "But that seems like a long time ago."

"Aye. Some experiences seem to make us older faster. By the way, ye missed a call from Jim."

"Did he leave a message?"

"Aye. He said to tell ye that two polls show the race tightenin' up. Ye're within four percentage points o' Bulwer."

"That's great! Melissa might just marry the mayor!"

"There was anither message, not so pleasant. Lynn Evers called. He wanted ye to know Parker Carrington is headin' our way. Mr. Evers' contacts in New York told him that the truth got out about Carrington passing bad checks and, apparently, he thinks ye and Melissa told. Before he left, he stole bonds from his father's company, so the highway patrol in several states is on the lookout for him and will take him into custody when they stop him. Mr. Evers said we don't have to worry—he won't get far."

"I hope and pray he's right."

42

Call for Concession

O N THE MORNING OF Election Day, Richard rose early and joined Mac in the kitchen. But neither man felt like eating a very big breakfast.

"Well, laddie, today's the day. Tonight, we'll see if God has somethin' new for ye to do."

"Yes, in a short time, I may find I have yet another new job and a big one. I never realized before how a politician must feel. After months of hard campaigning, it all comes down to one day."

After voting late in the day to avoid reporters, Richard and Mac headed for home to a simple dinner.

That night, Richard, Melissa, and Mac sat in the living room to watch the election returns come in.

"I thought Jim was goin' to be here with us," Mac said, sounding disappointed.

"No, Uncle, he decided to join the gathering of our campaign committee members and volunteer workers at the hotel. John Grant's with them, too. They have several TVs set up so they'll be getting the same election returns that we are."

"Will there be many people at the hotel, do you think?" asked Melissa.

"Jim said they were expecting more than 500. They're planning a victory celebration. It was nice of your mom and dad to help arrange the committee party. I hope they won't be too disappointed if I lose."

"Ye're not goin' to lose, laddie. The voters can see ye're a feelin'-hearted man who wouldn't bamboozle them."

"I don't know. Remember this morning's exit polls showed a majority voted for Bulwer. And look there—the latest totals put Bulwer ahead by over 1000 votes. And that's with 26 percent of the vote counted."

"Is the phone ringing?" asked Melissa.

"Aye. I'll get it," Mac said, hurriedly getting up from his chair.

When Richard saw his uncle returning, he asked, "Was it for me?"

"Aye. It was Daniel. He gave me a message for ye."

"Oh? What is it?"

"He said to tell ye not to be worryin'. He said the returns they're puttin' up now are from districts in the Northwest. That's where Bulwer has the strongest support. Daniel also said ye're doin' better in his districts than expected."

"It was good of Dan to call. I was beginning to feel a little discouraged."

"Daniel told me that after the vote count reaches 50 percent, ye'll see the numbers begin to change in your favor."

On hearing this latest information, Richard leaned back in his chair and allowed himself to relax.

I gave it my best shot. I gave the people another point of view to think about. Now, it's in God's hands. He'll let me know His purpose for me. He felt a warm peace sweep over him.

Minutes later, Mac exclaimed, "Ye see, laddie, your vote count is comin' up."

"He didn't hear you, Mac," Melissa said, lowering her voice. "Imagine being so calm at a time like this that he can go to sleep!"

Mac gestured to Melissa to follow him out of the room. He led her into the kitchen and said, "All this campaignin' has left my laddie tired out. I sometimes forget he has to work harder to walk the same distance as I do."

"Yes. And he never complains. Would you like me to make some coffee for us?"

"Aye, Melissa. I'd rather drink your coffee than my own any day. And while ye're makin' the coffee, I'll go back to the livin' room and turn doon the TV a wee bit, so it won't wake Richard up."

"Could I fix you anything else?"

"Hmm, I wouldn't turn doon a jeelly piece."

"I imagine that's a Scottish dish. How do I make it?"

"Oh, it's just a jam and butter sandwich—I like a lot o' jam."

"Alright, one jeelly piece coming up, heavy on the jam."

Mac was gone several minutes. When he returned, he wore a big smile. "With a touch more than 50 percent o' the vote counted, Richard is slightly ahead o' Billy Bulwer. He's givin' him a run for his money! I'm thinkin' aboot now, Bulwer is feelin' a bit bangie."

"I would guess, 'bangie' means in a bad mood," Melissa said, smiling.

"Aye. I'm thinkin' he figured Richard would be easy to defeat, bein' young and disabled. I see ye have my coffee and sandwich on the table. I'm glad ye fixed yourself a sandwich. What kind di' ye make for yourself?"

"I decided to go Scottish and have a jeelly piece too."

Sitting at the table, the two ate and talked. Occasionally one of them would go into the living room to see if Richard was awake and check on the vote count. Sometimes the report brought good news that Richard was leading and sometimes bad news that Bulwer had forged ahead.

"It's been two cups of coffee since one of us went to see how the vote was going," Melissa said nervously.

"Aye, nearly all the votes should be counted. I've been hesitatin' to look. There should be a winner by now. Well, Melissa, let's go see who it is."

The two walked into the living room and stared intently at the television screen. They heard a newscaster say their projected winner would be announced after the commercial break.

"Do you think we should wake Richy up for the announcement?"

"Aye."

At that moment, Richard opened his eyes. "Did I hear something about an announcement? What announcement?"

"They're going to announce who's mayor."

"Finally, the waiting is over." His tone suggested the relief he felt.

"Here it comes," Mac said solemnly.

"In the mayor's race 89 percent of the vote is counted," the newscaster stated. "The vote total includes nearly all of the absentee ballots. For most of the evening Billy Bulwer held a lead in the vote count. At times, he held a commanding lead that seemed to promise victory. But that lead began to shrink when returns came in from the city's Southeast districts. This was an area where Richard Hawkins had strong support. At this hour, Mr. Hawkins leads Mr. Bulwer by 3219 votes. Given the fact that the remaining votes yet to be counted come from districts known to favor Mr. Hawkins, we can predict he will handily win the mayoral election. It follows one of the most intensely watched political campaigns in our city's history. We understand that Mr. Bulwer will shortly concede the election at his campaign headquarters. Our cameras will be there, and at the Verity Hotel when Mr. Hawkins gives his victory speech."

"Congratulations!" said Melissa and gave Richard a kiss.

"Congratulations, my boy. I wish your mither could be here to see this day. She would be very proud o' ye."

"I wish so too, Uncle Mac . . . If she were here, would she see me doing a good job as mayor? I suddenly feel inadequate. I'm not sure I'm wise enough to lead this city."

"Richard, ye can take God at His word. Remember His promise in James, Chapter 1: 'If any o' ye lacks wisdom, he should ask God who gives generously to all without findin' fault, and it will be given to him.'"

"Thank you, Uncle Mac, I need to . . ."

The telephone interrupted.

"I'll get it. It's probably for me," Richard said, as he left his chair with the aid of his cane.

He returned to the living room almost immediately.

"That was fast. Was it a wrong number?"

"No, Uncle. It was Billy Bulwer. He conceded the election and said I should call on him if I needed his help."

"Humph!" said Mac.

The telephone rang again and this time Mac answered it. Calling from the next room, he said, "That was John Grant on the phone! He's sendin' a car to pick us up and take us to the hotel, so ye can give a speech there, Richard!"

"First, I need to call Aunt Jenny with the news and see how her own election went. I'll make it fast."

"What did Jennifer have to say to ye?" Mac asked as Richard returned.

"She was reelected to the senate. She said my father would be surprised we have a mayor and a senator in the family."

When Richard and Jim Nicolson walked onto the ballroom's decorated stage, applause and cheers filled the room. After giving the audience a few minutes to react, Jim asked for quiet so he could introduce Richard. He said, "I'm happy and proud to present the honorable Richard Hawkins, mayor elect of Verity. I have it on good authority that he'll be the youngest mayor in America in a city the size of Verity." The audience once again applauded and cheered.

The audience finally grew silent when Richard started to speak. "Thank you for your wonderful reception," he said. "This night could never have happened without your hard work and loyal support. I promise, as your mayor, to devote myself the next four years, to earning the trust you've placed in me. I'll seek good results, rather than good reviews. I'll not try so much to be popular as to be right. After tonight, I'll continue to need your help and your prayers, so that together, we can make our city as fine as we dream it can be." Then Richard gestured with his cane, as he had so many times during the campaign. He stood there, waving at people in the audience, when a sudden commotion erupted as two security guards grabbed a man in the crowd and escorted him roughly from the room. Smiling and nodding in response to cheers and applause, Richard waved his cane one last time and left the stage.

After Richard and Melissa spent an hour talking and shaking hands with many of the people at the hotel, John Grant offered to drive them to their respective homes. They gratefully accepted, and relaxed in the back seat of his car.

Concentrating on his driving, John remained silent while his friends conversed. But after a few minutes, he said, "You have to learn to pace yourself, Richard. You look tired."

"I must admit, I feel tired. But now I can take a few days to rest up. And we can plan a nice, simple wedding. Right, Melissa?"

John snickered.

"Silly, we have to have a bigger wedding now. Many of the people we spoke to tonight will expect an invitation. Mother and I will have to plan a reception for a lot of guests. After all, Richy, I'm marrying the Mayor of Verity."

"Hmm, I hadn't thought about that."

"And, we should do a lot of entertaining to help you get support for your goals."

"Say, how is Uncle Mac getting home?"

"He was having such a good time talking with someone from Scotland, I didn't have the heart to interrupt him. But don't worry, I'll see that he gets home, Rich. I mean Mayor Hawkins."

With mock seriousness, Richard responded, "Since you're such a good friend, you may dispense with protocol and simply call me 'Your Worship.'"

"You're very kind," responded John, laughing.

The three of them talked about the events of the evening until John announced, "Here we are Melissa." He parked, got out of the car and opened the door for her.

"Thanks for the ride, John." She gave Richard a good-bye kiss. The men waited until she was safely inside—her parents hadn't returned yet from the hotel celebration.

As they drove away, John said, "You know that disturbance in the crowd when you were speaking?"

"Oh, yes, the drunk who had to be removed."

"He was no drunk. Someone at the hotel told the security guards he had a gun. They called the police and handed him over. Underneath a wig and beard, they identified Parker Carrington, Jr."

"I assumed police had arrested him by now."

"He slipped through a state police dragnet. The police think he was at the hotel to shoot you, Rich. With other charges back home, he'll likely get significant prison time."

"I don't know; prosecutors would have to prove intent. He has a license to carry a gun. I'm glad the law has a hold of him, at least for now. I hate to have to tell Melissa about it. But I suppose it'll get into the papers."

"Count on it."

"When they reached Mac's house, John said, "Do you mind my asking you a none-of-my-business question?"

"No, go ahead."

"What made you decide to run for mayor? It's a tough job without much thanks."

"Yeah, probably more criticism than thanks. I don't know if it sounds Christian, but mainly, I wanted to force Bulwer to reveal the man behind the mask, so voters would know who he really is. I guess, too, I wanted to prove to myself I could put up a strong fight against his non-traditional views."

"You certainly did. And, for what it's worth, I think it's Christian to fight for what you believe."

"Looking back, John, I can see how the things that have happened to me have brought me to this point in my life, including my coma. Have I come to the place where God wants me to be? I'll work for the city and the foundation, as if I have."

"I believe you were in God's will when you went to ADE. I'm certain I wouldn't be here now if you hadn't been there to help track down the kidnappers. And because of you, our employees have grown spiritually. You remember Ben Jackson?"

"Yes, he wrote me a letter that said he didn't blame me for Grifith's transfer."

"Karl led him to Christ after he became a believer. Now, Ben's attending church and witnessing to ADE's bowling team."

"That's great! I hadn't heard."

"Seems to me, God's purpose brings a passion to serve others—I see that passion in you, Rich."

"Thank you, John. I hope to put passion into practice in how I lead in the future."

"Melissa will help you, Rich."

"Yes. She already has."

Epilogue

Richard looked around for someone he knew as he walked through the crowded terminal of the Portland airport. *I've taken a commuter flight here from Verity three times a week for four months, and yet I don't see a familiar face,* he thought, shaking his head. A cab took him to the Virginia Grant Foundation.

"Good morning, Mr. Hawkins," a security guard said, as he opened the front door for him.

"Morning, Jerry. Anything to report?"

"Nothing serious. Yesterday, I caught a kid about to decorate our new sign with graffiti. I told him our surveillance cameras could identify him."

"Good work," Richard said, heading for the elevator that would take him to his third-floor office.

"Mr. Hawkins, Mrs. Hawkins is on the phone. She's been holding for a few minutes. I was looking out the window when your taxi drove up."

"Thanks, Lori. Put her through."

"Richy, I have some bad news, though it could be worse."

"Has something happened to Uncle Mac?"

"Oh no, he's fine. I talked to him this morning—only a few minutes. He had to see a doctor, if you know what I mean."

"Looks like Dr. Olson may be exchanging her white coat for a white gown one of these days, if Uncle Mac has his way."

"That reminds me—our wedding pictures finally came. There's a nice picture of your Aunt Jennifer pouring coffee for Dan Siegel. You look real handsome in your tux."

'I was just window dressing beside the prettiest woman in the church."

"That's sweet, Richy. Since it's our third week anniversary, we should celebrate. Would you like me to make a reservation at the Hilton?"

"Sure! But what was the bad news?"

"Try not to be too disappointed. It was on the radio an hour ago. The city has delayed demolition of Garden View Apartments for the last time. Tenants have three months to find a new home."

"Well, I guess I'm not surprised. I still feel it's the wrong thing to do, but I'm glad they've been given another three-month delay."

"You did your best. The news report said so."

"I haven't done anything since becoming mayor. During the campaign I promised, if elected, I wouldn't use my office to pressure the City Council. But maybe I could have done something."

"Have you thought about creating a grant to help with relocation costs for low income people like the Garden View tenants?"

"You are both beautiful and brilliant. I'll get started on it next Tuesday."

"By the way, the extra copies of our wedding party photos came too. I have copies ready to send to John and Karl, as you wanted."

"Maybe our wedding will give John ideas about finding a wife. Personally, I think his assistant, Rachel, would be a great choice. But I'm afraid if she doesn't hit him over the head with a club and drag him off to her cave, he's not likely to notice anytime soon."

"When I met Rachel and saw her with John, I got the impression she might have a club ready to use," Melissa responded impishly.

"He told me if he ever got married, he'd want Cal to perform the ceremony in the same way he did for us, Melissa. I said his bride and her family might have other ideas."

"Do you think Dad paid Cal enough?"

"I happen to know he was very generous. I'm sure your folks paid out big bucks for the wedding and reception. I hope it didn't put a financial burden on them."

"They'll manage okay."

"I'll see you tonight, Lovely. Right now, I must decide if I should approve $23,000 for a bus to transport special ed children to the coast several times a year."

"Lori, let the staff know I won't be in tomorrow. I'll be out of town Friday and through the weekend. As usual, I'll wear my mayor's hat on Monday. Tuesday, I want to meet with Stu and Leo to discuss the

Boyalton grant. Hold my calls for about an hour, while I decide about the bus request."

"Yes, Mr. Hawkins."

On the plane for Verity, Richard pulled the *Banner* out of his briefcase where he'd stowed it that morning. One story, buried deep in the paper, grabbed his attention. He read:

"Parker Carrington, Jr. received a five-year prison term in his trial for theft yesterday. An investigation into an alleged murder plot against Verity's mayor, Richard Hawkins, failed to provide authorities with sufficient evidence to charge Carrington with the crime."

I can't say I feel sorry for Carrington. He's a dangerous man, and he won't be less so after a stretch in prison. I wonder what he'll do, or be when he gets out? Squeezing the handle of his cane, he thought, *Will he be a threat to Melissa and me? I haven't had a psychic vision to give us a warning.*

The plane began dropping to a lower altitude. The sign flashed: **Fasten seatbelts.**

Richard looked out the window as the plane dove through clouds into clear, blue sky on a direct landing pattern for Verity. *Clear sky ahead, like God's purpose for my life. The cloudiness that obscured His plan is gone; my course is set, with Melissa at my side.*

THE LIGHT OF HEAVEN

In the world of selfish dreams,
We follow the endless run.
The prize is always ahead of us,
The race is never done.
We build with gold and silver,
But sin is never new.
Seeing life in the mirror,
We live the backward view.
The growth of wisdom do not reject,
The way of Jesus we can reflect.
Looking to the light of heaven,
From childhood we will have grown.
Only then will we know ourselves,
As we are fully known.

—David Lane

Discussion Questions

Warning: Questions contain things to discover by reading the book.

1. What is the downside of growing up without parents or siblings? How would you assess Mac's efforts to provide Richard with a home and love? What stands out in Mac's actions that show this? What more could Mac have done to give Richard a normal home life?

2. Assuming you were physically capable, would you have acted as Richard did to save Melissa from being kidnapped? If not, why not?

3. When Richard spoke about prayer to the youth group, was anything said that caused you to consider prayer more deeply? Can you put it in one sentence?

4. What strengths and weaknesses do you see in Tony as a person? Why do you think Richard liked him and spent time with him?

5. What responsibility, if any, did Richard have for the accident that put him in the hospital?

6. Dr. Olson is experienced in treating patients in a coma. What misconceptions regarding coma do you think she revealed in her conversations with Mac?

7.   How would you describe what occurred in Richard's coma: (1) a dream? (2) a fantasy? (3) a miracle? How does Richard describe it?

8. Do you know any former hippies? If so, do they have anything in common with Tony?

9. Is there anything in your past experience that leads you to believe psychic ability is more than fiction? If you're a Christian, do you believe psychic ability could be a spiritual gift? Can you relate to Richard's concern about the spiritual implications of his new found psychic ability?

10. Besides his desire to help his uncle, why did Richard work so hard to prevent the city from demolishing Garden View Apartments? Did you learn anything from Mac about Richard that would help answer this question? Have you ever had to take a stand to protect one or more persons?

11. Richard doesn't believe HR management is God's plan for his life, but he hopes it may lead to something that is. Read Jeremiah 29:11. What does Jeremiah say that may encourage you as it encouraged Richard?

12. Do you think the man stalking Melissa was a serious threat as Richard, her parents, and Mac believed? Why did Lynn Evers ultimately fail to neutralize the stalker? What would you have done to stop the stalker?

13. How much did Aunt Jenny's participation in state politics influence Richard to enter the race for mayor?

14. Most politicians running for office have a connection with some religion, which voters tend to expect. Billy Bulwer didn't. Would the fact that he was an atheist cause him to lose votes? Do you think Bulwer would find a belief in Jesus more fulfilling than a belief in Plato?

15. Is it realistic to believe a person can be both an effective politician and a committed Christian? If so, why? If not, why not?

16. Will Richard's disability have any impact on his marriage to Melissa and on his performance as mayor?

17. A theme running through *The Light in the Mirror* is the need to know God's purpose for your life and Richard's desire to know what that purpose is, especially after his accident. Have you found God's purpose for your life and, if not, what's preventing you?

18. What does the author say about the importance of the family?

About the Author

David I. Lane holds an M.S. degree in Training and HR Management from Leicester University (England), which he received with Distinction. He has a TESOL (Teaching English to Speakers of Other Languages) certificate from Northwest Christian University, where he also received his B.A. degree in Communication and Music, *magna cum laude.* He was elected to *Who's Who in American Colleges and Universities.* As a teaching assistant at NCU, he worked with students to improve their English. He has worked as a volunteer with charitable organizations to help needy people in the community. David serves as a vocal soloist at his church. He collects nineteenth-century Christian literature and songs of the '60s, '70s, and '80s. He is Office Manager for Lee Lane & Associates. David makes his home in Eugene, Oregon, where his parents and older brother reside.